JUST THE WAY YOU ARE

ERIKA KELLY

Just The Way You Are
Erika Kelly

ISBN-13: 9781677310388
Copyright 2019 EK Publishing, LLC
All rights reserved

Cover design and formatting by Serendipity Formatting

Praise for The Calamity Falls series

KEEP ON LOVING YOU

"I adored this book! It is exactly what I love in a second-chance romance. The characters are so vibrant and real, I was rooting for them with every page." —*USA Today* Bestseller Devney Perry

"KEEP ON LOVING YOU is such a fun and sexy second-chance romance that I didn't want it to end. Their connection is a swoony blend of tender first love and sizzling heat, and Erika Kelly delivers a highly entertaining and sigh-worthy romance that shouldn't be missed."
—Mary Dube, USA Today

WE BELONG TOGETHER

"I loved every sweet, heart-wrenching, crazy, mixed-up minute of this book. It was an emotional journey from the first chapter to the last. This is Erika Kelly at her best, and this is a not-to-be-missed book!" —Sharon Slick Reads, Guilty Pleasures Book Reviews

"Erika Kelly damn near pulled my heart from my chest with Delilah and Will's story. It's so well-written that you feel everything. My heart got tugged so hard! I honestly cried at a few moments in the book. I fell all the way in love with "Wooby." It's hard not to, really." —Ree Cee's Books

THE VERY THOUGHT OF YOU

"Wow, THE VERY THOUGHT OF YOU was simply OUTSTANDING! This second chance, friends to lovers romance is enchanting and entertaining." —Spellbound Stories

"I just finished this story, and I want to start all over again. Or maybe at the start of series. To once again feel the events, the emotions, that brought these amazing characters together. To hear the banter and the arguments, the sorrow, the loss and the happiness that brought a family together and closer." —Nerdy, Dirty, and Flirty

JUST THE WAY YOU ARE

"An alpha cowboy and a smart, sassy princess collide in JUST THE WAY YOU ARE in Erika Kelly's latest, and it was fabulous! I was cheering for Brodie and Rosalina with every page. If you love stories with heart, steam, and plenty of swoon, don't miss this one!" —USA Today Bestselling Author J.H. Croix

"With the Calamity Falls series, Kelly doesn't shy away from charming. She captivates with delectable characters that wrap themselves around a heart. From the first hello to the final goodbye, Rosalina and Brodie are a match made out of the unpredictable, but the sweetest kind of heaven. JUST THE WAY YOU ARE is the perfect example of why I am hooked on this series. SWOONWORTHY READ!" —Hopeless Romantic Book Reviews

IT WAS ALWAYS YOU

"This book was full of every emotion you could ever feel. Gigi and Cassian proved you can conquer anything with true love." —Cat's Guilty Pleasure

"I could not put this book down! Erika Kelly always delivers a great love story and never disappoints! I recommend this book for romance lovers looking to get lost in a great love story." —Reading in Pajamas

CAN'T HELP FALLING IN LOVE

"I love everything about this emotional and sexy, second chance story. Erika Kelly writes a story that makes me feel like I'm right there with the two main characters, Beckett and Coco. It is a slow burn, passionate story with lots of underlying tension. I not only enjoyed this story, but I found it impossible to put down." —Cocktails and Books

"I loved everything about this book. I loved all the characters, from Beckett, 'I don't believe in love,' to single mom, small business-owning, closed-off Coco, to a fairy-believing five-year-old who will steal your heart! I cannot gush enough about how spectacular I thought this book was." – Bookcase and Coffee

WHOLE LOTTA LOVE

"BRILLIANT! This book was incredible, I could not put this book down, that is how good Lu and Xander's story was. I fell in love with these two characters instantly." – Harlequin Junkie

"Whole Lotta Love was absolutely perfect! You will instantly love this couple and their journey to find happiness!" – Just Love Books

YOU'RE STILL THE ONE

"Griffin and Stella really are soulmates. They bring out the best of each other, and when they're together, everything is better. Their world is better with the love they feel for each other. And I think they made my world better a bit, too." – Jersey Girl's Bookshelf

"WOW! WOW! WOW! Welcome to all the feels! I ADORED Stella and Griffin's story. I was completely lost in this book and didn't want to put it down. I FELT everything, and I can't tell you how much I loved it." – Books According to Abby

Titles by Erika Kelly

The Calamity Falls series
KEEP ON LOVING YOU
WE BELONG TOGETHER
THE VERY THOUGHT OF YOU
JUST THE WAY YOU ARE
IT WAS ALWAYS YOU
CAN'T HELP FALLING IN LOVE
COME AWAY WITH ME
WHOLE LOTTA LOVE
YOU'RE STILL THE ONE
THE DEEPER I FALL
LOVE ME LIKE YOU DO

Rock Star Romance series
YOU REALLY GOT ME
I WANT YOU TO WANT ME
TAKE ME HOME TONIGHT
MORE THAN A FEELING

Wild Love series
MINE FOR NOW
MINE FOR THE WEEK

Sign up for my newsletter to read the EXCLUSIVE novella for my readers only! You'll get two chapters a month of this super sexy, fun romance! #rockstarromance #teenidolturnedboyfriend Also, get PLANES, TRAINS, AND HEAD OVER HEELS for FREE! I hope you'll come hang out with me on Facebook, Twitter, Instagram, Goodreads, and Pinterest or in my private reader group.

This book is dedicated to Kristy deBoer….you've been there from the beginning, and you always make everything better.

Acknowledgments

To Superman, the love of my life. You make me a better person.

To Olivia: you're welcome for making you the third reader this time! Thank you for always reading my books!

To Sharon: thank you for believing in me so fiercely.

To Kristy deBoer: I appreciate your friendship so much and can't wait to watch this next part of your journey.

To Melissa: I am so grateful to you for everything you do, especially making me laugh!

To Erica: thank you for always being there for me and for being so kind with all my changes.

To the romance writing community: I couldn't do this without the bloggers and reviewers like Obsessed with Romance, Guilty Pleasures Book Reviews, About That Story, Reading in Pajamas, Zoe Forward, Shirin's Book Blog and Reviews, Reads and Reviews, and Isha Coleman—to name just a few; and my friends in writer groups like the Dreamweavers, the DND Authors, and my monthly plotstormer girls.

Chapter One

I DID IT!

With her jar in hand, Princess Rosalina Anais Isabella Villeneuve crossed the lawn, breathing in the scents of freshly mown grass and clean, crisp June air. Sunlight glinted off a sleek blue BMW, and her heart clutched with happiness. *He's here.* She couldn't wait to show her fiancé. *He's going to love it.*

Climbing the stone steps, she opened the back door of the castle to find the staff eating breakfast at the weathered table. "Something smells delicious." On the island, she found a platter of buttery eggs, sliced bread, and strawberry jam.

Everyone looked over at her and smiled. "Morning, Miss."

Chef started to get up, but Rosalina shook her head. *Don't bother.* It was her fault she'd missed breakfast. *Again.* "I'll eat later. I'd like to catch Marcel before he takes off." She grabbed a croissant from the basket and bit into it. "Mm. So good."

1

"It would've been warm and flaky if you'd had it fresh from the oven three hours ago." Chef got up anyway and filled herself a mug with coffee from the French press, dropping sugar and cream into it.

"But then I wouldn't have this." She lifted the tiny glass bottle.

"Oh, you've got it, then?" Her father's valet scraped his chair back on the stone floor and came over. Twisting off the cap, he closed his eyes and inhaled. "Ah. It's perfect." He broke out in a big grin. "Spot on."

"Here." Rosalina dipped a finger in and smeared a glob onto the back of his age-spotted hand.

The older man, in a black suit and a full head of salt and pepper hair, rubbed it in. "Rich…creamy." With two fingers, he tipped her chin, and she caught the exotic scent of her family's perfume. "It's lovely. You've got it just right."

"And it only took two and a half *years* to nail it. But, whatever, it's done, and they can't possibly say no this time."

As if jerked by a string, they all looked down at their plates.

Rosalina's stomach pinched with dread. "No, it's different this time. You'll see."

Chef patted her shoulder. "We have all the faith in you, my love. It's the tide of history you're swimming against we're worried about."

She knew the challenge she faced—after ninety years of running a successful business off one product, her family wasn't inclined to shake things up. But, this time, she'd come up with an idea that would fit seamlessly.

Chef offered a fork and a bowl of mixed fruit, but

Rosalina couldn't eat a thing. "I'll be back for a proper breakfast, but right now I have to catch Marcel before he heads to the airport." At the doorway, she turned to the staff who'd loved and protected her all her life. "And then we'll celebrate the new product line." Taking another bite of the croissant, she waved the jar at them with a mischievous grin.

A few rallied with warm smiles, but the others focused on their breakfast.

Well, obviously, if she went straight to her parents, they'd reject it outright. *That's why I'm going through Marcel first.* Her fiancé's father was the business manager for House of Villeneuve, and he oversaw the family's Nocturne perfume company. Once she convinced Marcel and his father of the value of her idea, she'd let *them* present it to her parents.

They wouldn't ignore advice from the people running their business.

Besides, she had a different angle this time. While at school, she'd created several truly lovely perfumes, and they'd rejected all of them. *They don't fit our brand.*

This time, she'd simply expanded the product line by creating bath and body products based on the same essential oil that had been in the Villeneuve family for centuries. And she'd created proprietary ingredients to make them every bit as luxurious as the perfume itself.

She was *adding* to what they already had. They couldn't say no.

As she headed down the cool hallway, her ballet flats shushed on the hundred-year-old runner. On either side, her ancestors lined up as though forming a gauntlet. *You're wasting your time*, their expressions said, noses in the air.

"You're wrong," she whispered. Anyone who bought the perfume would want the soap and body lotion to reinforce the scent.

The thick stone walls of the castle muffled sound, so she only heard the quiet conversation when she reached the grand parlor. *Shoot.* She didn't want to get pulled into one of her mother's meetings. Hanging back, she peered into the room crammed with antique furniture, the walls covered in *trompe l'oeil* murals.

Sitting demurely on the embroidered sofa, her mother spoke quietly to a woman in a pastel-colored skirt and beige flats. On the glass coffee table, tea service had been set with fine china and silver.

Having only just crested the corner of the parlor, Rosalina figured she could quietly step back before being noticed.

"Oh, darling, there you are." Her mother got up, gesturing toward the guest. "I'd like you to meet Marguerite, the wedding planner."

The shock hit her system like a car crash. *Wedding planner?* For one unbearably long moment, she heard the ticking grandfather clock as if it were inside her head.

But, of course, she snapped out of it and shifted into full princess mode. Flipping on her royal smile, she gave the woman a nod. "Good morning."

"Good morning, your Highness."

"Come." Her mother strode purposefully out of the room. "She's brought her portfolio and samples."

"Unfortunately, this isn't a good time. I'm already late for my meeting with Marcel." If only she'd brought her phone with her, but she'd left it charging in her bedroom before heading to the lab that morning. *Please don't go until I talk to you.*

"This won't take but a moment." Her mother's low heels clacked across the marble foyer. "It's just a preliminary meeting."

Rosalina stopped just under the massive crystal chandelier. "Mother."

Her mother slowly turned to her, one brow arched. No one used that tone to speak to Her Serene Highness the Princess of St. Christophe.

But, while her mother's haughty expression made her cringe—she would normally never challenge her mother publicly—she truly couldn't spare a moment. "Marguerite, I'm so sorry I don't have time to discuss my wedding plans right now, but I do look forward to working with you."

"Of course." The woman reached into her tote and pulled out a thin silver case. Plucking a white card out of it, she handed it over. "Please call me at your convenience, and we can get started. I'll leave my portfolio with you."

"Perfect." Rosalina tucked the card into the pocket of her capri pants. "Thank you."

As her mother walked the wedding planner to the door, Rosalina spun back around and headed for the stairs. As excited as she was about her formula, she didn't actually know if Marcel's father would support her idea. He was very much of the same mind as her parents. As her American roommate's father used to say, *If it ain't broke, don't fix it.*

"Rosalina," her mother called.

Crap. Her fingers itched to text Marcel and ask him to wait for her. *Why didn't you bring your phone?* He might've left by now. "Yes?"

"Come with me."

She recognized her mother's tone for what it was, and so she did as she was told. At twenty-five, it was time for the Hereditary Princess of St. Christophe to step into her mother's shoes. Get married, give birth to an heir, and devote her time to a few established charities and one of her own creation.

Yes, she knew the expectations, and she would get there. But, right now, she needed to see her project through. She had the rest of her life to be a wife and mother.

Her mother led the way into the oak-paneled library. The scents of old books, lemon furniture polish, and her father's spicy shaving cream filled the large room.

Oh, what about shaving cream for women? She'd use synthetic materials for that, though.

As they entered, her father lowered one side of his paper, a tea cup in one hand. "Oh, dear." He shot a look to the door, as if calculating his getaway.

"Exactly." For a moment there, she considered showing them the lotion, just to get the conversation away from wedding plans. As the hereditary princess, it would fall on her and Marcel to keep the company running. She'd be showing them that the family legacy was in good hands.

Ha. Good one.

Let Marcel lead the charge. Her fiancé had her back.

Her mother stood beside her husband's chair. "I don't appreciate you sending away my guest. I invited her here to launch the wedding plans, and I found it rude and disrespectful that you asked her to leave."

"I'm sorry. It did come across as rude, but I wish you'd have discussed it with me first. I wasn't prepared to meet with anyone this morning. In fact, if I don't go right now, I'll miss Marcel. He's leaving for Zurich in a few minutes."

Her father set down his paper, and his tall, lanky frame rose out of the chair. Pulling his cell phone from his pocket, he tapped out a text. "There. Marcel will wait."

Uh oh. Her dad had something to *say*. Tension pulled at her skin, and she became aware of the cool breeze sweeping through the room, riffling the pages of magazines.

Pulling an engraved handkerchief out of the pocket of his slacks, he took the croissant out of her hand and wiped the buttery remnants off her fingers. Balling it up, he dropped it on the side table that held his silver teapot. "My sweet Rosalina, I think you can agree we've been more than generous in supporting your choices. We assumed, once you graduated from university, you'd come home and marry Marcel, but you wanted to continue your education, and we love you very much, we want you to be happy, so we supported that decision. But it's time, my love. It's time for you to assume your duties here."

"Of course. I know that, and I'm absolutely going to marry Marcel. In fact, when I go upstairs, I'll talk to Fabiana, and she'll set up a time for me to meet with the wedding planner."

"This is not the first time you've put off this discussion," her mother said. "Darling, this is *your* wedding. You must take it seriously."

Impatience rumbled under her skin. Why would she bother thinking about the details, when they were already set in stone? "What's to talk about? We're marrying in the church, and the reception will be held in the grand ballroom." She shrugged. "I'm being fitted for my dress next week." A tiny flicker of interest teased her heart.

The designer lived in the United States. An old wild

west town, Calamity had cowboys and ranches, saloons and gold mining. It even had a *bison* preserve.

Imagine that—bison!

"There is much to discuss," her mother said. "And the top priority is setting a date so we can send out invitations."

"Honestly, whatever works best for your schedule. It doesn't matter to me." Because it would be a performance in front of the entire country.

"Your enthusiasm for this wedding is underwhelming," her mother said.

"Well, sorry, Mama, but it's not like I have a say in anything." Other than the dress and cake, none of the rest reflected her personality at all.

The newspaper rustled, as her father picked it up and sat back down. "Is there something you'd prefer?"

She scanned his handsome features. *Does it matter?* He gave her a deep nod.

Well, then. "Actually, I'd love to get married in the meadow." The night-blooming flower used in Nocturne only blossomed for a few weeks in June. "If we could have the service at twilight, then the lyantha would perfume the night air during my reception."

Her mother's features tightened. "That would mean waiting a *year*."

She watched the silent communication pass between her equally strong and stubborn parents.

"As long as the date is set and invitations go out before the vote," her father said. "We can wait for the actual ceremony."

"Really?" Since when did her family break from tradition? "Then I'd prefer a date in the middle of June, so that if we don't get enough precipitation and the flowers bloom later, I won't miss out."

"Then, that's what you'll have," her father said.

She could hardly believe it. "It doesn't have to be in the church?"

"I would *prefer* the church," her father said. "But I've learned to pick my battles with my oldest daughter."

The comment swiped across her heart like a claw. She knew her father wasn't referring to what happened all those years ago. Intellectually, she knew her single act of rebellion hadn't caused his heart attack, but the two would forever be tied in her mind.

"What if, instead of having the wedding in the meadow, we fill the church with the lyantha?" her mother asked.

Rosalina reared back, as if her mother had suggested burning the castle to the ground. "We're not cutting my flowers."

Her father tried to suppress a grin. "Not to worry. The ceremony itself is far more important than the location. No harm will come to your precious lyantha."

"You'll be the first in six hundred years to marry outside the church." But her mother sounded like she'd accepted Rosalina's decision.

"I know, but it's my one and only wedding, and the meadow just fits me."

Her mother broke into a luminous grin. "Then, the meadow it will be."

"This makes me so happy." Her parents were being awfully accommodating. Maybe… Her fingers curled around the glass jar. But, instead of presenting her idea to them, she found herself blurting, "I think I'll go to the States for my fitting."

They looked at her like she was the fly that had just landed in their soup bowls.

Spin it. "Marcel's in Zurich for the week, and we'll want to plan the wedding together, so the timing works out well. Besides, asking the designer to fly all the way out here seems ridiculous. I'm not her only client."

Her mother pressed a hand to her shoulder. "That is enough, Rosalina. You take your life and your position in this country for granted." She had a fierce look in her eyes. "But we face a formidable opponent with the People's Party, who are passionate in their plea for an egalitarian society. Every minute you're out of sight, still unmarried, still not pregnant with an heir, you reinforce their position that the monarchy's dying out. When they liken us to 'an ancient tree that no longer bears fruit,' they're not only referring to my inability to produce a male heir but to our oldest daughter, who shows no sign of settling into her role." She glanced at her husband—not with an apologetic look because she'd had to stop bearing children after two girls but with a look that said, *Back me up here.*

"You've traveled the world, had your experiences, and now you must come home and embrace everything that entails," her father said. "You must live here to understand the needs of the people so that you can choose a cause you feel passionate about. You need to stand with us in showing that our family may be small, but we're devoted to our country's well-being."

"I understand." With her sister at university, the eyes of the people were on Rosalina. She needed to be seen with Marcel, moving forward with wedding plans, so when the voters went to the polls, they went knowing the monarchy would continue.

And she was fine with that. She didn't need to go to

Calamity right now. She would have plenty of time to travel, once she set up her philanthropy, got married...and had a baby.

Marriage, baby...what was this resistance deep inside of her? Why couldn't she just go along with what was required of her?

It's not like you've ever had any other expectations for your life.

"It's fine. Besides, the designer's scheduled to come out here next week, so she's probably already bought her ticket. Okay, well, now that we've set a date, I really do need to go."

"Won't you at least have a look at the invitations?" her mother asked.

Oh, dear. But she appreciated her mother's efforts, so she stepped closer to the table, skimming the choices. "Any of those are fine." Honestly, they all looked the same.

Her father laughed, before shaking open his newspaper.

"I'm glad my choices please you," her mother said with an unfortunate amount of sarcasm. "But you still need to work out the wording, the font...the color of the envelopes."

"Of course. Let me talk with Fabiana, and we'll set up a time to go over all the details." She kissed her mother's cheek. "Thank you, Mama, for doing this for me."

The moment Rosalina left the library, she opened the jar and let the fragrance fill her senses. She waited just a moment for the two scents to merge—the lotion and her mother's perfume. And...*yes*. Perfect match. Given the complex mix of ingredients—the shea butter and ceramides and acids—recreating the exact scent had been difficult. But she'd gotten it. And, even better, the lotion was sumptuous, so it fit their brand.

She made her way up the stone staircase that led to the business offices. At the landing, she glanced out the rectangular window and got that familiar rush of joy.

Villeneuve Castle sat atop a ridge overlooking the capital city. Wildflowers carpeted the hills, and the snow-covered Alps created a cozy fortress for her picturesque little town. Below, the two-lane highway snaked through the valley like a black river. Heavy mid-morning traffic meant the businesses were thriving, and it made her proud to think how well her father ran this beautiful, safe country.

Hushed, urgent voices upstairs drew her attention. A woman and a man.

But the urgency wasn't anger or frustration…it was passionate. Yearning.

An office romance? Not many employees worked in the castle—only the finance department—and most of them were married and had held their positions forever. She would be devastated to learn someone was having an affair.

As she climbed the steps, she let the soles of her ballet flats slap on the stone to alert them, but their impassioned conversation didn't stop.

"But you don't love her." The hushed, fervent voice came from behind the closed door of a supply closet.

A spike of recognition hit the base of her spine. *Fabiana.* But her personal assistant and friend wasn't dating anyone.

"You don't marry someone you don't love." Fabiana sounded overwrought. "It won't work. Not when you're in love with *me*."

One single second had never held so much tension. *Who's she talking to?*

Who?

A man let out a rough exhalation. "It's a different kind of love, Fabi. It might not be wild and crazy like I feel for you, but I *do* love her. I've known her all my life."

Marcel.

Chapter Two

Rosalina went into freefall. Her mind scrabbled to grab hold of something, anything, but she plummeted.

This isn't happening.

Marcel and Fabiana?

Beads of perspiration popped out on her hairline. Her skin went cold, then hot.

"You love her like a *sister*." Her assistant had never sounded so emotional. "You can't marry your sister. It won't work. It can't."

"Fabi, I'm going to marry her. You know that. You've always known that."

This was a Marcel she didn't know. Desperate, pleading.

Her fiancé wore pressed khakis, starched button-down shirts, and leather shoes. He kept his hair short and neat, his jaw clean-shaven. He was steady, reliable.

The voice of the man hidden in a closet with his mistress wore rumpled clothing, had several days growth, and showed up late to work hungover. She'd never met this man.

Her palm pressed against the cool wall. Nothing made sense. She'd become a piece dropped into the wrong puzzle.

"Marrying her won't flip some kind of switch," Fabiana said. "You've never been so crazy for her that you took her up against the wall or…or threw her down on the bed and ripped off her clothes. All the things you talk about with me…? You're not going to suddenly want to do them with her just because you've exchanged vows."

The man she'd known her whole life, the only man she'd ever been with…

He doesn't love me?

She felt so small, so…insubstantial.

So *sick*.

"Fabi, stop. God, just stop."

"No, I won't stop. The wedding planner is here. We have to talk about it right now, before things go too far and you can't undo them."

Rosalina pressed her hot cheek against the stone wall. She felt dizzy, disoriented. How had she not seen this? She'd hired Fabiana during her first year at university, because she hadn't been able to keep up with her duties as well as her studies as a chemistry major at the Sorbonne. Over these seven years, they'd become good friends.

Or so she'd thought.

The truth hit her bloodstream like ice water. This entire time, her closest friends had been lying to her.

Her stomach lurched, twisted, and she thought her knees might give out.

"Listen to me, Fabi. I do love her. I've always loved her."

"You're a passionate man. You need more than she can give you. What will happen a year from now? Two? Ten? When she's involved in raising children and her lab work, when there's no time for you. Will you find someone else to pull into closets and send desperate text messages to?"

Every word struck her heart like a mallet, smashing it to a pulp.

He doesn't love me.

He'd never spoken to Rosalina as though the possibility of losing her felt like his soul was being ripped out of his body.

Shame spread in a rush. All of their intimate moments were a lie. He'd been making love to her, while imagining Fabiana.

"We can't discuss this here," he said. "We're at *work*. Someone will hear us."

"For God's sake, we have to tell her before they announce the wedding date."

"Would you just stop? Stop touching me. You're turning me inside out. I can't call it off. I'm marrying her. I *want* to marry her."

"Out of duty, not out of love. Just answer me this, have you ever once kissed her the way you kiss me? Are you desperate for her the way you are for me?"

Rosalina held her breath, her body suspended over a bed of needles. The wrong answer would pull the lever, releasing her, leaving her skin pierced and bleeding.

"No, okay? What you and I have…it's exciting and…I can't sleep at night for wanting you, but I *am* going to marry the princess. I mean, the passion fades in all relationships, but at least with Rosalina, I'll be left with my best friend. Please, please understand. I never meant to mislead you."

Every word slapped across her skin like a whip, leaving her raw and hurting. A pain unlike anything she'd ever known.

"She's not *capable* of passion. She'll never satisfy your needs. You don't want her sexually, so let her go. What kind of life are you going to give her, when you're lusting after me?"

Rosalina couldn't take it anymore. Climbing the last two steps, she grasped the doorknob.

"You're only marrying her so your family can become the royal bloodline. That's all you care about."

"*Of course* that matters. We want our due, but it's not the only reason. I love her, and she's my dearest friend."

Their *due*? The Allards had worked for her family for generations. They'd been like cousins, included in all the celebrations and dinners and special moments. They were paid well, given housing and all kinds of benefits.

Nobody owed them anything.

"I could never hurt her by calling it off. And I do think we'll be happy."

Enough. Rosalina flung the door open so hard it slammed against a cabinet. Both of them whipped around to face her. Fabiana—the woman who'd held her hand through a pregnancy scare, who'd shared the most important moments in her life over the last seven years —looked horrified, and Marcel—her best friend, the only man she'd ever been intimate with—rushed toward her.

"Oh, God. Rosalina." But the threatening look she gave him made him freeze.

She could only stare helplessly at her assistant. "I trusted you. In every possible way." God, she hated how weak she sounded. But she couldn't process it. She wanted them both to break out laughing. Tell her the scene had been staged. They'd pulled a prank.

Gotcha.

But their expressions told the truth. Anger, hurt, disbelief created a mix so toxic it burned her skin. "Fabi, how could you do this to me?"

Marcel reached for her. "It's not like that. Nothing's happened. We haven't—"

"Shut up." She couldn't even look at him. Her friend, wearing a plain wrap dress and beige and white heels, stood there with her shoulders slumped, the energy drained out of her.

Rosalina wished so badly she had the presence of mind to find the right words to cut them both down to size, but she was too discombobulated. Nothing made sense.

"I'm sorry." Fabiana looked down at the floor. "I never meant for this to happen."

"You never meant to fall in love with my fiancé? You never meant to kiss him in closets and *sext* him?"

"No, I didn't." Her gaze snapped up. "I resisted it for so long. You have to believe me. I didn't want to fall for him. But you've been away so long, and we spend so much time together…it just happened."

Energy started flowing in. "That's the most ridiculous thing I've ever heard. Nothing just happens. Every step you took toward each other was a choice. And don't talk like I've been out of touch all this time. I've come home from school often. You've both come to visit me plenty of times. We still have sex." She turned to Marcel. "Does she know that? Or have you been playing the role of neglected boyfriend?"

"What? No." He had the nerve to sound outraged. "It's not like that at all. Look, give me a chance to—"

"Give you a chance? Marcel, I gave you my *trust*, and you tossed it in the garbage."

"Rosalina, listen to me. It's not what it looks like. I haven't slept with her." His tone was pleading.

"Do you think *that's* what matters? Whether you stuck your penis in her? God, Marcel. What you did is so much worse. A random hookup is bad enough, but all of this emotion, this passion?" She felt gutted. She wanted to crash. Fall to her knees and hide her face in her hands.

Only, she couldn't. Not yet. She needed to finish this.

"I'm sorry." He looked miserable. "I don't know what to say. Everything got so out of hand."

"I don't know what you heard," Fabiana began.

"I heard everything I need to see who you really are." The very core of her trembled, like a palm tree in gale force winds. But she needed to stay strong, say what needed to be said. "As my friend, you should've walked away the moment you realized you had feelings for my fiancé."

"Walked away *where?*" Fabiana said. "I work for you."

"Then you should have quit."

Her assistant's eyes widened, like the suggestion was as absurd as telling her to move to Jupiter.

Rosalina couldn't take it anymore. Not one more second around these people who'd, in an instant, become strangers to her. "You're fired. Get your things and leave the building."

"Rosalina, no." Her former assistant turned teary-eyed.

Rosalina reached out to Marcel. "I need your phone."

He immediately pulled it out of his pocket and handed it over.

It struck her, the moment she touched it, that this simple piece of hardware had countless words and images of betrayal stored on it. After shooting off a text to her head of security, she literally threw it at him. She couldn't be rid of it fast enough.

"We haven't been together like that," Fabiana said. "It's nothing more than words and a few kisses. I swear it."

"It's so much more that it makes me sick to my stomach to even hear you say that. You looked me in the eye as though you were my friend, while going after my fiancé behind my back."

When Fabiana looked to Marcel for support, he cast his gaze to the floor. "*Marcel.*" But even her plea didn't get his attention. She stood there, each second stretching to the point of snapping. "I'm sorry. Rosalina, please, you have to know I never meant for this to happen."

"You were just trying to talk my fiancé out of marrying me. Your intentions are perfectly clear." Heavy boots pounded up the steps.

"You called security?" Fabiana whipped around to face the door.

"Do you think I trust you in any capacity?" she said.

Just then Harrison, six-seven, two-hundred and sixty pounds of hard muscle, stormed into the room. "What's going on?"

"I found my assistant begging my fiancé to dump me." Tears stung, and she frantically blinked them away.

Her bodyguard had been with her for most of her life, so when he went rock solid, her tension loosened just a fraction. *He's got me.* He watched her for a long, heavy moment, then shifted his attention to Fabiana. "Let's go." With a jerk of his head toward the door, he got the woman moving.

Her former assistant cut one more look to Marcel. "Are you really just going to stand there?"

Apparently, he was. He didn't even look at her.

With a disgusted look, Fabiana led Harrison out the door.

That left her alone with the boy she'd grown up with. Trusted. And loved. The boy who'd snuck out of his boarding school and boarded a train to be by her side after her dad's heart attack.

Now, he was a stranger. All the times they'd experimented with sex, all the awkward moments and kisses and orgasms, all of it rose up and engulfed her in shame.

Because he'd never been attracted to her.

I'm not attracted to him. The revelation struck like a blast of cold water. It seemed, somehow, even worse. How had she not cared about something so fundamental?

What's wrong with me?

She couldn't contemplate these questions. First, she had to deal with him. "I didn't even have a clue you were unhappy."

"I'm not unhappy. I'm not. I love you, Rosalina."

"Yes, like a sister. I heard. How long has this been going on? All seven years I've been away?"

"Of course not."

"How long?"

"I don't know." He let out a huff of breath. "It's been gradual. It started out with stupid flirting, but then it…it just got bigger."

"*How long?*"

"Maybe since last Christmas."

She felt like she was in the last room left in a burning building, flames licking underneath the door, smoke billowing, taking up all the space in her lungs. "I'm just… trying to wrap my head around this. For six months, you've led a double life? You've been lusting after her, whispering….stealing moments together…*kissing* her?" She pressed a hand to her forehead. "I'm such a fool." The pain was so big and bright, like a sun that was swallowing her whole.

"No, you're not. You're the best person I know." He seemed to have found his purpose. "I swear to you, I've never slept with her."

For some reason that stupid comment made her stronger. "Would you stop saying that? It's not your free pass. Every second with me for the past six months was a lie. Every time you had sex with me you saw *her* face. God, Marcel, why didn't you tell me something was wrong? Why didn't you ask for more?"

"Can you give more?"

The careless comment kicked her so hard in the stomach she felt nauseated.

"No." He reached for her, but she shrugged him off. "I didn't mean it like that. I meant…you've been in school, developing your products…when you come home, you have to do your duties here…there hasn't been time for us. I'm not blaming you. I swear I'm not. You've amazing. I admire you."

"I guess admiration doesn't inspire a man to rip off a woman's clothes. I'm not sure, though, after hearing you lust after another woman, that I can stand to hear how well you think of me." She drew in a shaky breath and looked him fully in the eyes for the first time. "I trusted you, Marcel. With everything in me, I trusted you, and you broke my heart."

All the anxiety, the urgency to fix the situation, seemed to crash, and he just looked defeated. "I'm sorry." He shook his head. "I'm so damn sorry."

She believed him. She did. "I don't care. While I've

been believing in *us*, you've been stealing secret moments with your lover behind my back. I don't see how we can come back from this."

"What're you saying? We're still getting married. We have to. You know—"

"Do *not* talk to me about my duty to this country. When my parents find out what you've done, they won't want me to marry you."

"They might not want it, but they'll need you to."

Now that straightened her spine. "Are you threatening me?"

He looked horrified. "Of course not. Rosalina, I messed up. I did. But can you allow me one screw up? I've never done anything like this before. We've been friends our whole lives, we *will* be happy together." He brought his hands to the sides of his head, scraping his fingers through the short strands of hair. "What have I done?"

"Do you love her?"

His attention snapped to her. "No. I mean, I know that's not what it looks like, but I don't love her the way I love you."

"Yes, I got that. Which, of course, is the whole problem." The jar had gone warm in her hand. "Look, I need you to do something for me." She handed it to him. "I've finally got it, the formula for the body lotion. I need you to convince your father that expanding our product line will—"

"You're talking to me about business? That's what you want to discuss right now?"

"Well, we could talk about what a two-faced liar you are, but that doesn't seem all that productive."

"I deserved that, but don't you think it's sad that in our worst moment you want to talk about your lotion?"

"No, what's sad is that for all these months, you didn't *do* anything. If you were unhappy, if you were developing feelings for another woman, you could've done something for *us*. Plan a getaway…surprise me at school…*take me up against the wall*." Something stirred to life inside her, a long dormant curl of desire, like steam rising from a tea cup. "Instead, you turned to another woman."

She left the room in a haze. There was too much happening inside her body to separate each individual strand of emotion. Marcel's betrayal had her reeling, but Fabiana's words *terrified* her.

Because they were true.

I'm twenty-five years old, and I've never felt passion.

She'd had crushes, of course, but she'd shut them down—simply by changing her patterns. She'd sit in a different section of the lecture hall or go to a different café or bar with her friends.

"Rosalina," he called. "We'll work through this. In the meantime, we've got to be seen as a happy couple. The vote's six weeks away."

Right then, she got a flash of her wedding gown. The famous designer lived, of all places, in a cowboy town in Wyoming. "I think you know me better than that. I wear my emotions on my sleeve. There's no way I can act like I'm in love with you."

She'd seen images of the place and had found it charming. Iron hitching posts, strapping men in dusty jeans, pickup trucks, and lassos.

And right then she made a decision.

She was going to get away. To a world that didn't resemble this one at all.

I'm going to Calamity.

Chapter Three

Leaning against the wall, Brodie Bowie watched the guests gather around the bride and groom in the atelier he and his brothers had built as a surprise wedding gift for Gray's girlfriend…sorry, Gray's *wife.*

Yeah. Gray was *married.*

Soon, his oldest brother, Will, would make it official with Delilah, and the youngest, Fin, would tie the knot with Callie….and it just felt weird.

Kind of like when Brodie was nine years old, and he and his brothers had snuck out of the house to go skiing under a super moon. Long shadows had disoriented him, and he'd soared right off a cliff. He'd landed on a hard patch of ice, shredding the ligaments in his knee and cracking his skull.

On a helicopter, in the dead of night, he'd come back to consciousness, aware only of a big hand holding his. "Hey, little guy," his dad had said. Nothing had been scarier than seeing his rough, mountain-man dad turn all sweet and soft. "Next time you're up for an adventure, invite your old man, huh?"

Head screaming with pain, vision blurry, he'd had no idea what was going on. All he'd known was that one moment he'd been laughing his ass off, caught up in rebellious fun with his brothers, and the next, he was being Life-Flighted to the University of Utah.

On that chopper, his brothers nowhere to be found, he'd felt utterly and completely lost.

That's what this feels like. Knowing his brothers were gone—well, obviously, not literally *gone*. Everyone lived on the ranch, and they all still hung out. But it wasn't the same. That all-for-one, one-for-all bond was over. His brothers had transferred the oath to their women.

And it just baffled him.

One day, they'd all been having a blast snowboarding and surfing, jumping on the jet to go wherever the hell they wanted, free as the wind—and the next three of them were giving dopey-eyed grins to girlfriends. Getting *married*.

Hard to begrudge them anything, though, considering he'd never seen them so happy. So, that was good. But he missed them. Missed knowing they were all in it together.

The door to the salon pushed open, and the hotel's manager peeked in. He seemed surprised to find Brodie standing there. "Oh, hey, we've got an issue."

Brodie didn't want to ruin his brother's wedding reception, so he followed the man out the door, closing it behind him. "What's up?"

"Princess Rosalina's here, and she's got a problem."

"Who?" He looked past the manager to see a couple of beefy men in black suits standing in the middle of the lobby.

"The princess of St. Christophe. She called yesterday to book a suite, but the one we gave her's too small."

He had no idea why the manager would ask for *his* help. "Well, I can't do anything about it right now, so I'll let you figure it out." Eighteen months ago, Brodie had turned the ghost town adjacent to his family's three-hundred-thousand-acre legacy ranch into a living museum.

He'd built it, but he'd never been involved in the day-to-day running of the individual businesses.

"Yes, but the only suite that will accommodate her entourage is the three-bedroom."

Ah. Okay. Now it made sense. "You want me to give up my room?"

"She's here for a fitting with Knox." He lifted a shoulder, like it was obvious what Brodie should do. "And she's a princess."

"Of a principality the size of my left nut."

The manager cracked a smile. "I'll be sure to tell her that."

He supposed he could crash with one of his brothers. He opened the door to see the wedding party surrounding a small, circular table. Knox, a dark-haired beauty in an extravagant wedding gown of her own design, plucked the fresh pink and white flowers out of the frosting on the tiered cake. Callie stood in the shelter of his youngest brother's arms, and Delilah canoodled with Ruby, his half-sister. Looked like the chef was singing a song to the rapt little girl.

A strange ache in his chest had him turning back to the hotel manager. He wouldn't be staying with any of them. "How about putting her detail up in some double rooms? We're in between tourist seasons." Which was why he was staying in the hotel to begin with. "I'm sure we've got some vacancies."

The man gave a proud jut of his chin. "Actually, we're completely booked."

"Has she checked out the saloon?" They'd restored the original structure, turning the downstairs into a lively tavern and converting the upper levels into a bed and breakfast.

"Brodie, come on, man." He leaned in. "You want me to tell a *princess* to find somewhere else to stay?"

"Yeah, okay, fine. I'll talk to her." Brodie headed across the wood floor, polished to a high gloss, taking in the lobby he'd designed to fit the time period. Damn, his dad would love this place. The original settlement of Calamity had been too close to the Teton Mountain Range, so they'd moved it a couple miles deeper into the valley. His dad, a history nut, had purchased the ghost town a few years before his death in an avalanche.

Last year, Brodie had hired historians and worked with preservationists to bring the town to life. He'd hired costumed actors to walk the streets and populate the restaurants, the saloon and B&B, and the stores. Scheduled shoot-outs took place throughout the summer. It was pretty cool.

As he approached the bodyguards, the larger one headed toward him with his hand out in greeting.

"Hello, I'm Harrison Vachon." He spoke with an unusual accent—sounded French, but different.

"Brodie Bowie. So, I understand you need a larger suite?" And, right then, he caught a glimpse of the princess. With her luxurious dark hair, huge black sunglasses, and bright red lipstick, the bombshell tapped furiously on her phone.

Too busy updating your social media accounts to deal with your travel plans, princess?

"When she booked, she'd only planned on bringing me." The man was the size of a linebacker. "Gustav was a last-minute addition."

"Is there a problem?" Maybe he'd underestimated her tiny principality. He didn't need security issues in Owl Hoot.

"Not at all. But she's the princess of St. Christophe, and her parents are protective of her."

Awesome. A pampered princess. "Okay. I'll take care of it." He gave the man a curt nod and made his way to the front desk. Nodding to the clerks, he slipped into the manager's office. "Go ahead and clear out my suite. Rosie and her entourage can stay there."

The manager gave an amused grin. "*Rosie?*"

"Come on, man, she licks barbecue sauce off her fingers like the rest of us." On his way out, he rapped his knuckles on the door frame. "Think you can get someone to bring my stuff over to the bunkhouse?"

"You got it." The manager got up. "Sorry for kicking you out."

"No big deal. I'm not home all that much."

As he crossed the lobby, the princess glanced up at him, and their gazes caught. Held. It was the strangest feeling, but time slowed, the chatter in the lobby dulled to white noise, and he watched her jaw slacken, red lips part, and her pale cheeks turn pink.

On any other woman he might've picked up attraction, but this one just looked flustered. And it was reinforced when she quickly dropped her gaze back to her phone.

He had no idea what that was about, and he didn't much care. Pampered women weren't his thing. He sped up to get back to Gray's reception. Throwing open the

29

door of the salon, he found his brothers gathered in serious conversation. But, by the time he'd reached them, they'd dispersed.

He caught up with Will. "Hey, what was that all about?"

"We were just talking about that email from Pierce," Will said. "Trying to figure out how we can help him. I've got Ruby, so I can't do it."

The oldest sibling had taken on the full-time job of raising their half-sister. Over the course of one summer, Will had gone from being the nine-time world freestyle ski champion to stay-at-home dad. It was humbling.

Brodie admired the hell out of his brother. "What email?" And why would the general manager of the Owl Hoot Consortium talk to his brothers? They'd had very little to do with the creation of the ghost town. "Help him how?"

"Didn't you read it?" Will asked. "He says they're underwater. Main Street's half empty because no one's going to open a business unless there's enough traffic coming through town."

"We have plenty of tourists." Even though not the intention, Brodie took it as a rebuke. "This hotel's booked solid even in the shoulder months."

"Right," Will said. "The interest's there, for sure, but the town's not getting repeat business. There's not enough going on. It's pretty expensive to come all the way out here just to see a staged shoot-out and eat in a fancy restaurant."

That stung. "Why didn't anyone tell me?" *This is my baby*.

His brother looked at him like he'd just asked him to pitch handfuls of wedding cake at him.

"You've moved on." Will said it like it was obvious. Like he hadn't given a single thought to including him. When he looked surprised, his brother said, "You've got great ideas, you get them up and running, and then you move onto the next project."

"The next project was Knox's digital platform," Brodie said.

Gray's wife had decided to sell her couture wedding gowns online. Brodie had only meant to talk to some three-D modelers about the concept but had found himself immersed in the whole project. Pretty interesting stuff.

"Don't know what to tell you." Will shrugged. "We all got the same email."

"When?"

"Couple days ago." Will grinned. "Actually, it was Tuesday. I remember because Ruby had a play date at someone else's house. My girl walked in the door, spotted their Bernese Mountain dog, and chased him all around the living room. Broke a lamp."

"Will?" The bride waved him over.

"It's cool," his brother said. "We'll figure it out."

He took off, leaving Brodie alone. He felt restless, uncomfortable in his skin—which wasn't normal for him.

Pulling out his phone, he scrolled through his emails looking for Pierce's name. How was it possible that Owl Hoot wasn't making enough money to cover its costs?

He found the email and quickly scanned it.

…only three shops in the hotel…
…constructed the artisan stalls but never filled them…
…your father's vision has gone largely unfulfilled.

A sharp pain hit his chest. After his dad died, the four of them had gone through his belongings. Brodie had found a file labeled *Ghost Town*. In it, he'd found schematics for revitalized buildings, along with cocktail napkins and scraps of paper filled with ideas for attracting tourists to the area.

For a couple of weeks, Brodie had kept the folder to himself. As he often did, he let things burble in his subconscious, until the living museum concept popped up. From there, he'd created a resort spa, a train that took people from Calamity to Owl Hoot, and an amphitheater for live music and Shakespeare in the Park plays.

He'd set up the consortium, hired a general manager to oversee the running of the town...and then he'd gotten involved in Knox's business. So, yeah, he'd stopped paying attention.

He stepped out to the lobby to take in the shopping arcade. Other than the recently completed wedding gown atelier, the hotel had a gourmet food shop and a clothing boutique. He'd covered a tourist's basic necessities—souvenirs, picnic lunches, bathing suits for swimming in Calamity's large lake, and essential toiletries.

Hardly an *arcade*.

Heading outside, he shielded his eyes from the bright June sun and took in the boardwalks on either side of the street. The costumed jailor was chatting with a cowboy who was just tying up his horse, and patrons entered the saloon for lunch.

In the opposite direction, the work had been completed on a row of connected booths. Given the volatile climate of the region, he'd covered them for inclement weather but gave them doors that opened wide to enable tourists to watch the artists at work.

His dad had envisioned blacksmiths and cobblers, but Brodie had added his own ideas to include leather toolers —handbags, belts, journals—and jewelry makers. He'd have to dig up his notes. He'd had a lot of ideas.

But, yeah, he *had* dropped the ball. That didn't sit right with him. Not when he'd done it for his dad. He pulled out his phone and shot off a text to Pierce.

What's a good time to meet about Owl Hoot?

Shoving his phone in his pocket, he headed back inside.

"Brodie?" Vanessa, his architect, strode toward him. She gestured to the bank of elevators. "I just went to your room." When she leaned in for a kiss, her sleek blonde hair spilled forward.

Without thinking, he gave her his cheek, forcing an awkward brush of her lips against his jaw. He only realized she wanted his mouth after her eyes flared, and her cheeks burned. "Hey. What's up?" Who kissed someone on the mouth? That was for girlfriends and wives, and Vanessa was neither.

She held up the drawing tube that held his blueprints. "I wanted to show you the adjustments I made. Thought we could grab lunch at the same time. Maybe order in?" She was all business, so that was good.

"Can't. I have to get back in there."

"Has she seen it yet?" Vanessa had done the drawings for the atelier.

"Yeah."

"Well? Come on, what does she think?"

"I haven't talked to her yet. She's been busy."

The door opened, and Callie stepped out. "Oh, there

you are. We need you for pictures." She smiled at Vanessa before retreating back inside, leaving the door open for him.

"Pictures for the website?" Vanessa asked. "I'd like to be in them. It'll be good for my business."

"No, wedding pictures. Gray and Knox just got married."

Her features froze, and she stared at him in confusion. "Your brother got married? Just now?"

"Twenty minutes ago, but yeah."

Stepping around him, she peered inside, scanning the room from one side to the other. "You didn't invite me."

"*I* didn't invite anyone."

She gazed up at him, those brown eyes searching, and he realized he was looking into the eyes of a woman. Not his architect.

A woman he'd hurt.

"Brodie…" So much accusation in her tone. "Why didn't you tell me about it?"

He didn't know what to say. It hadn't occurred to him to invite her. His brothers liked to joke that he was clueless about women. That he only found out he was in a relationship when they asked him to meet their parents or expected him to go to a work party.

Is that what's happening now?
Does she think I'm her boyfriend?

Not once had he asked her on a date. On the rare occasion he sent a text, it was business-related. Sure, they'd slept together, but that was when they'd both had an itch to scratch. They'd be working on house plans, ordering food in, and then they'd get naked. But, after, they always went their separate ways—either back to work or home.

They'd never spent the night at each other's places, never… held hands or whatever couples do.

So, what had he done to mislead her? He honestly wanted to know, because he didn't like seeing her hurt. "We need to talk about this, but right now I have to get back in there." He held her gaze a moment longer, long enough to see that she very much wanted to be included in the family photos. "I'll call you later."

As soon as he joined the wedding party, Callie said, "Where's your girlfriend?"

"Vanessa's my architect. Not my girlfriend."

She gave him a look that said, *Here we go again.* "Brodie, you've been dating her for months."

"I've been working with her. On my house and this atelier."

She searched his eyes, as if checking to see if he was serious. When she found he was, she gave him a pitying look. "Sometimes you need to get your head out of your ass."

Chapter Four

"You can't expect me to marry him." Rosalina leaned against the railing of her suite's terrace. Exhausted from jet lag, she knew she should be sleeping, but every time she closed her eyes, she saw Marcel and Fabiana in the closet, relived their heated exchange, and it shook her wide awake.

In the darkness, the peaks of the Tetons cut a jagged line across the star-speckled sky. Unfortunately, the betrayal felt as vivid here in Calamity as it had at home. How had she thought traveling five thousand miles away would change the scenery in her heart along with the landscape?

Well, it hadn't. The hurt burned inside her like a lit match she was frantically trying to extinguish but couldn't reach.

"It is *essential* that you marry him, darling," her mother said. "But we certainly don't blame *you* for their reckless behavior. He swears they never had a physical relationship, though I know that's small comfort."

"You talked to him?"

"Of course we did. While we won't diminish what he's done to you personally, the fall-out has dire consequences for the monarchy. You might not be ready to hear it, but he's genuinely sorry."

"I don't care what he is. I'm so angry with both of them. I can't get over the fact that Fabiana looked me in the eye every single day, while going after my fiancé. Is she a sociopath? How can she lie to my face like that?"

"I don't know, my love. I'm devastated for you. For all of us. It's such a difficult situation. We need this marriage. We need an heir."

"This is the twenty-first century. It's absurd that our line of succession falls to men. You're every bit as capable of governing as Father."

"You're preaching to the choir, but now is not the time to dwell on things we can't change."

As soon as her parents learned they couldn't bear more children, they'd petitioned Parliament to change the line of succession to include women, but the idea was soundly rejected. They'd seen no reason to change laws that had been in place since the fifteenth century. The People's Party, of course, consistently voted to maintain the status quo in the hopes the monarchy would die out on its own.

A soft breeze fluttered across the meadow surrounding the hotel. It was too dark to see the acres of wildflowers, sagebrush, and tall grasses, but the night air's perfume made her desperate to get out there and explore. *Tomorrow*. "It's sexist and misogynistic."

"Of course it is, but it's not the point. The point is that we've got to keep the People's Party from gaining seats, and the only way to do that is through your marriage to Marcel."

"We're educated, intelligent people. We can come up with another solution."

"Not in time for the vote. Now, listen, make good use of your time away. Clear your head. It's the only reason we agreed to this trip of yours. If you'd stayed here, the whole world would see just how you feel about your fiancé."

"Then I'd better stay here for the next six months." She'd meant to say it with humor, but there was no disguising her bitterness…which spoke to her mother's point.

"No, Rosalina. This is not open for discussion. You have five days to pull yourself together, then you'll come home and assume your duties. You'll need to be seen with Marcel on occasion, but you can rest assured his father will keep him extremely busy. He's no more pleased than we are." Her mother let out a frustrated breath. "I'm sorry, darling. I can't imagine how you must feel right now, and I wish the timing didn't coincide with such an important vote. But it does, so unfortunately you're going to need to hold your head high and paste a smile on that lovely face."

"Okay, Mama. I promise to be completely over the betrayal of my fiancé and assistant in five days."

"I don't know how on earth I raised such a smart-mouthed girl."

Her phone beeped, and she pulled it away from her ear to see who was calling. Adrenaline spiked through her when she saw her fiancé's name. "That's Marcel. Let me take the call."

"That's fine. We'll talk later in the afternoon. Well, in the morning for you. Try to get some sleep."

"Okay." But before she got off the phone, she needed to know. "How's Papa doing? Is he…okay?"

"Yes, of course, darling. He's quite confident in the people's desire to maintain the monarchy."

"He doesn't need the added stress of my engagement blowing up."

"Stop being so dramatic. Nothing's 'blown up.' Now go talk to your fiancé and give him a piece of your mind."

Her mother hung up, and she accepted Marcel's call. "Hello?"

"Hey." He'd never sounded so down.

Well, she wouldn't make it easier for him. The volatile brew of hurt, anger, and helplessness made her shaky.

"I'm an idiot."

Did he think she'd laugh? Sweep aside what he'd done? She remained silent.

"You know I've never been with anyone else, right?"

God, she hadn't even considered other women. "If you could make love to me after kissing Fabiana, then I don't know you at all. The man I trusted, gave my heart and body to, is a lie. He doesn't exist."

"No, no, he exists. He very much exists. But there's more to me than that man. There's the guy who wouldn't have minded going to parties and getting drunk and banging hot girls."

She sucked in a breath, which cut off his words.

"I'm sorry to be so blunt about it, but surely you've felt the same way over the years. We've grown up in the public eye, and we're so good at doing what's expected of us. And, while I like my life, there's still a part of me that wanted to backpack through America, sleep in hostels, drink cheap wine, and hook up with strangers on trains."

Every image rose clear and powerful, the alternate life they both might've lived had they been born into different circumstances. She loved her family. She truly loved the people of St. Christophe. But she'd never done any of the things Marcel had just described. She'd been so dutiful she hadn't even allowed herself to fantasize.

Lusting after things she couldn't have would lead to frustration, so she'd squashed them before they'd had a chance to bloom.

"I wish you'd told me, Marcel. Instead of turning to my assistant, why didn't you just talk to me? I don't think you understand what you've done. It's bad enough that you cheated, but the worst part is that I'm now doubting myself. It's all I can think about. Am I not sexy enough? Am I cold?" She supposed his silence was answer enough. "What is it about Fabiana? Is there a whole other side of her that comes out in the bedroom? Does she wear lingerie and have a sex toy drawer? I just don't understand. Why, Marcel? Why did you do this?" She only realized she'd been shouting when she heard the scrape of a chair on the terrace next to hers, followed by the quiet snick of the French doors shutting.

I don't care.

I don't care who heard me. I just want answers.

"I don't know what to say, other than the obvious. I got a thrill out of sneaking around. All those text messages and stolen moments? It was…exciting."

"You said you don't love her, but I heard your voices. You were both so…passionate."

"It's not love." He said it wearily. "And I know it's not, because now that it's over I don't miss her. I don't long for her. All I feel is embarrassed and ashamed of myself for acting like a fool." He let out a rough breath. "I just need you to know that I never had sex with her."

"Oh, my God, you have to stop saying that. It makes me want to burn down everything in my path. You betrayed me, okay? There's no other interpretation. You cheated on me with my *friend*."

And the part that cut so deep she didn't think she'd ever stop bleeding was that he'd never lusted after *her*.

Because I'm not sexy.

A bolt of fear lit her up inside. Truly, doubting herself had turned out to be the worst consequence of this whole, horrible situation. Up until she'd found them in the closet, Rosalina had believed she was nothing but loved and accepted. It had formed the very foundation of her sense of safety and security in the world.

Now, it had all been ripped from her, leaving her vulnerable and questioning herself. "I feel like I'm going out of my mind. I have to know. Were you faking it when you were with me? Imagining you were with Fabiana? You have to tell me the truth because it's tearing me up inside."

"Rosalina, stop. Stop doing this."

"I can't. It's all I think about. I know I'm not wildly sexy, but it never mattered before because I thought we were happy. Now, I know we were just…complacent."

"We've been together so long, and I think…I think Fabi was safe to lust after. I certainly couldn't flirt with anyone else in St. Christophe."

"So, it wasn't her specifically? Fabiana doesn't drive you wild?"

"No. She doesn't." He went quiet for a moment, and in that space, she knew she was hoping for some sparkling piece of insight that would make everything stop hurting so badly.

"When I was thirteen, my father took me camping," he said. "I was excited to spend time alone with him, but that first night, he talked to me about my duty and his expectations. And I felt sick to my stomach because, while

I'd always known I was going to marry you, it had been nothing more than a concept. But, in that moment, I understood that my crush on Angelica Brun could go nowhere. Obviously, I didn't know about Ibiza raves and hookups yet. I just knew he'd put a lid on my life."

"And you think it's any different for me? You think I like always having to be on my best behavior? God, Marcel, I feel the same pressure. But I don't have sex with you while fantasizing about another man."

"I'm sure you must feel it, too, but you asked me why, and I'm trying to explain it the best way I can. All I can tell you is that, even though I've had my entire future mapped out for me, I've never met anyone I'd rather spend my life with than you. I've never visited another country I would rather live in than here. Even though they took away my choices, I have lived enough and fantasized enough to know that I want to marry you. I don't love Fabiana. I was using her to live out a school boy fantasy. I know that sounds terrible, but I only figured it out after my life blew up."

"You never told me about your fantasies. You never asked me to take a train ride with you so we could have sex. Did you think I wouldn't do it?"

"You're Princess Rosalina, and I'm the future prince. If someone had caught us having sex on a train, we'd have created a massive scandal that would affect the monarchy. That's a lot of pressure for one man to bear."

"That's not my question." She couldn't stop herself from smoothing a hand down her stomach and around to her bottom, wondering if he was attracted to her at all. Was she not his type? Or was she just not a sexy woman? "Did I ever star in your fantasies?"

He went quiet.

"Marcel, we have to have this conversation. You can't possibly hurt me more than you've already done, so just talk to me."

"No. I didn't think about you like that."

He'd never fantasized about her. And, just as she sank into the embarrassment of that truth, she realized she'd never fantasized about him.

"I know you want my forgiveness, but I can't give it to you right now. Don't call me or text me. Give me the next five days to myself, and we'll talk when I get home."

Worn out, Rosalina powered down her phone. Her body might be exhausted, but her mind was wired. She couldn't marry Marcel, and yet she had to. What was she supposed to do with that?

You don't have to do anything about it for the next couple of days. She'd try on her wedding dress, explore Calamity, and get a handle on this soul-shaking doubt.

The wind shifted, bringing a scent that triggered the one thing she cared about more than anything. Perfume. "Oh, my God." She filled her lungs with the scented air.

It wasn't exactly the same as her flower, but there was no doubt it was the same genus. She shoved her feet into her ballet flats, grabbed the keycard to her room, and ran out the door.

As Brodie drove the bulldozer toward the site, the blade kicked out rocks and plumes of dust. He figured, once he cleared out this rough path, his crew could come in to widen and level it. In building his house, he wanted only one road in. He'd do as little damage as he could.

Depositing a pile of shrub and dirt, he paused to take

in the view. The rising sun cast a pink glow to the snow-crested mountains. Little red flowers fluttered across the vast, open meadow.

This is it. He knew without a doubt he'd chosen the right site.

It'd only ever be him living here, but he wanted a few extra bedrooms. One for his office, another in case a friend needed a place to crash. He supposed his future nieces and nephews might spend a night or two. So, yeah, four bedrooms, no more.

Okay, back at it. The moment he accelerated, the engine roared, and a woman came dashing out in front of him, waving her arms hysterically.

Oh, fuck. He jammed on the brakes. Shifted into park and killed the engine. Grabbing the bar, he swung out and landed on the soft earth. "What'd I hit?" He crouched at the front of the machine, looking for a body. A nest. Anything. "What?"

She had her hands on her head, her eyes wide, like he'd run over her dog.

"Jesus, just tell me," he shouted.

"What are you *doing*?" She had an accent—French? She had to be part of the princess's entourage.

"Did I run over something? What'd I do?"

Bending low, she snatched a handful of earth. She shook off the dirt to reveal a bulb and one of the plants with the red flowers. "This is lyantha. I'm not sure which species, because I've never seen it before." She thrust it at his face. "Smell it."

He breathed it in. *Nice.* "That's why you're pissed? Because I drove over some flowers? It's June. The county's full of them." *What a nutjob.* "It's cool."

"It's not *cool*, and I can guarantee you won't find this

flower anywhere but right here. It grows in very particular soils and climates, and it only blooms in late spring and early summer, and only for a few weeks. It's precious. It's rare. It's…" She blew out a breath. "Were you going to plow up the *whole field*?"

"'Course not. Just right there, where I'm building my house." He pointed to the site. Wooden stakes with neon orange flags delineated the area.

"You can't build anything here." Her pale features flamed red. "This is a national *park*."

Well, that explained what she was doing on the Bowie ranch. "Nope. You're standing on private property."

"You own this lot?"

Lot. He suppressed a grin. "It my family's ranch, but yeah, I've staked out this parcel for me."

She surveyed the acreage. "Just one house?"

He kind of wanted to play with her for a minute, given how worked up she was over some flowers. "Might turn it into a development. I'm thinking forty-fifty nice little ranch-style houses. Community center and a gym." He cast an assessing look on the land. "Probably have room for a tennis court. Maybe an Olympic-size pool."

Sweat beaded over her lip, and her body vibrated with tension. "Okay, look, I will buy this whole piece of land from you."

"The whole thing? Land's pretty expensive here."

"Would you please stop playing with me? I'm serious about this."

He liked this woman. She was sharp, beautiful, and passionate. He wondered what she did for the princess. "I can see that, but it's not for sale."

"I'll pay you market value. We can go into town right now and talk to an estate agent."

What the hell was she up to? "Aren't you from St. Christophe?"

"Yes, I am." Her tone said, *So?*

"So, what're you going to do with a couple hundred acres in the middle of my family's ranch in Wyoming?"

All at once she relaxed, as though she'd finally found a way to get what she wanted. "My family runs a perfume company. Nocturne?"

He actually knew that one. It was his mom's "signature scent." Out of nowhere, a childhood memory hit him. He and his brothers wrestling in his mom's New York City bedroom, crashing into her dressing table and knocking over all the fancy bottles and jars. He would never forget the scent of that perfume, since it had lingered in the apartment, and he'd had to smell it every day until his mom had shipped them back to their dad.

Still, he wasn't seeing the connection. "Okay?"

"St. Christophe's a mountain town in the Alps at the same elevation as Calamity. The soil and climates are similar. I wondered if I'd find our own lyantha here. This isn't it, but it's in the same family." She held out the bulb. "I'm a perfumer, and I've been trying to convince my family to expand our offerings for years. I've dreamed of finding another flower in the same genus, so I could convince them to try something new—but still within our brand. This is it."

"Huh. So, I've got something special here."

"Well, it's special to me. Ours is the most exotic and unique scent in the world, and I'm betting I can make an equally good perfume out of this one. I understand if you can't sell a parcel of your family's land, but would you at least consider leasing it to me? I can give you a very lucrative contract."

He was done messing around. It obviously meant a lot to her. "Not gonna happen. We're breaking ground on my house next week."

He could see her mind working, intelligence firing in her eyes.

Interest kicked up. Brodie liked a challenge. *Show me what you've got.*

"Nocturne is the world's most expensive perfume. It comes from an essential oil my family's been making for centuries. I could do the same thing with this flower. I could make you a very wealthy man."

Maybe because he wore jeans and a well-worn T-shirt, he looked like he needed cash. He didn't know. But, while his dad's estate was worth billions, he and his brothers had always lived on their own earnings. And they all did pretty well for themselves. "I don't need much."

"Well, this is about more than your bank account. This is about creating a legacy for your family, your children…generations to come. Providing the essential oil for House of Villeneuve…it's an honor. It—"

"Can't really see myself having kids."

"Oh, my God. This is not a game to me." She growled out her frustration. "Look, now that you know about this rare plant, you can see how criminal it would be to plow it up. Especially when you can build a house anywhere on this property."

"I don't know about criminal, but I do know I'm only plowing one little section of it. Besides, they're bulbs. I can always dig them up and plant them somewhere else." Okay, so he'd play with her *just* a little.

Her gaze turned steely. "I'd like to gain exclusive rights to this flower on your property. I'll pay you for the annual use of the land as we collect the petals and then assure you a dividend as long as we make and sell the product."

Christ. Time to get back to work. "Look, I don't need your money. I'm not selling or leasing the meadow. But I'm always down for a new business project, so thanks for cluing me into some value on our land I didn't know about. I'll be sure to look into the essential oil thing." He turned back to his bulldozer.

"Hang on, what does that mean?"

"It means, if it's as good as you say, I might want to use it in my hotel's spa products. What we have now's kind of bland. Something like cucumber and Earl Gray." He reached down and picked up another bulb, sniffed it. It *was* nice. "Isn't the sense of smell the strongest memory trigger? Every time a tourist uses our body lotion or wash, she'll remember her great trip to that old wild west town in Wyoming." Yeah, this was a good idea.

Her laugh held no amusement. "It's not that simple. You can't just bottle the smell. It took years to get the Nocturne formula just right, and it's got proprietary ingredients."

"I'll tell you what. I have no interest in getting into the perfume business. How about you create the essential oil and then we'll work together? I'll use it for my hotel, and you can use it for your perfume company."

"Oh, no. My parents would never go for that. We'd have to have exclusive rights."

"And since that's not going to happen, there's nothing left to talk about. Let me know if you need help finding your way back to town."

"I can't…I can't just let this go. This is too important."

"I don't know what you want me to say. I'm not giving you the rights to a plant that grows on my property. If I want to make something out of it, I'll hire a chemist or… perfume maker. Whatever I need."

"I'm a chemist *and* a perfumer. Let me just explain something to you. Almost all perfumes and certainly all body lotions are composed of synthetic ingredients. You don't need these flowers to make a good, quality product. Using an essential oil is extremely costly and, frankly, isn't worth it when you're just making toiletries for your hotel. It's only worth it if you're going to have a luxury perfume."

"Got it. Thanks for that." He gave her a look that said, *We done?*

"You really won't make a deal with me, even after I've explained that you've got no use for it?"

"Nope. I won't. And now I'm getting back to work."

"Plowing up more lyantha?"

He put his thumb and forefinger together. "Just a tiny bit more."

Her expression, as she took in the meadow, hit him right in the solar plexus. This mattered to her.

Had anything ever mattered this much to him?

He thought about the way he'd bailed on Owl Hoot… just stopped paying attention to it. The same with designing Olympic half pipes. He'd moved on without even thinking about his team or the design company.

He climbed back on the bulldozer and turned the key. It roared to life, but the woman didn't budge, her focus on the meadow.

"Hey." He shouted, but she couldn't hear him over the rumble of the engine. *Dammit.*

But then she turned to him, her face glowing with inspiration. Pink flooded her cheeks, and she gave him a smile so beautiful it made his heart pound. She waved him over.

He cut the engine and jumped off the machine. "*What*?"

"How about this? What if my family uses the flowers for House of Villeneuve, but we have an exclusive contract with you to provide the toiletries for your spa? You'd be the only hotel in the world that offered our products." Her smile widened. "And we wouldn't charge you for it."

He liked the way her mind worked. "As long as I get a percentage of the profits, I'd take a deal like that all day long."

Happiness flooded her features. "Yes."

"This means a lot to you."

"This is my heart, right here." Delicately, she caressed a red petal. "I've just recently created bath and body products for Nocturne, so the formula's already made. With everything in place, it won't take long to get this product up and running."

He pulled the key from the ignition and locked up the bulldozer. "Looks like I've got to find a new building site."

Chapter Five

He had his own Cyberpedia page. "An Olympic hopeful?" *That's impressive.* Rosalina clicked on the Images bar and couldn't believe how many photographs appeared for Brodie Bowie. Good God, she'd never seen a more handsome man. Thick, dark hair, bright blue eyes…and that smoking hot body? Broad shoulders, bulging biceps.

The door to the suite flew open, and a sting of embarrassment shot through her.

"They didn't have baking trays, but will these work?" Harrison held up aluminum roasting pans. Behind him, Gustav came in, arms loaded with grocery bags.

"They're perfect, thank you." Rosalina closed out the search engine, pushed aside her laptop, and got up from the kitchen table. She hoped they hadn't seen her screen. *What're you doing looking him up, you stalker?* "I'm so excited."

Harrison set the bags on the counter and pulled out a bottle of palm oil. "You realize you're only in town for four more days, and instead of getting out there and seeing the sights, you're working."

"Oh, come on. This is a huge discovery." And one that might not go anywhere. Her parents would never agree to let some random hotel in the middle of nowhere use the House of Villeneuve's signature scent for their bath products, and Brodie had made his position perfectly clear...*so yeah, not looking good.*

But that wouldn't stop her. If people worried about all the reasons why something wouldn't work, nothing would ever get done.

Brodie. He'd been so detached. Aloof. And yet something about him made her heart pound and her skin tingle. As the daughter of a ruling prince, she'd grown up around dignitaries, kings, and queens. She didn't intimidate easily. But Brodie Bowie scrambled her brains.

Well, until it came to his lyantha. She'd fight to the death for her flowers.

"Besides," she said. "This phase isn't time-consuming." The petals needed to steep in the oil before she could replace them with fresh ones. "I'll get out there after I set everything up."

"You know, you could've gone to the store with us," Harrison said. "No one's going to recognize you here. It's a whole different world."

"We could get you some cowboy boots and a jean skirt," Gustav said. "Then, you'll look like a local."

"I'm not going to be here long enough." Although the idea of being totally unrecognizable—reinventing herself —gave her a thrill. All those things Marcel said they couldn't do...she could do them here.

With Brodie.

Shut up. That's never going to happen.

"This place is crazy," Gustav said. "We drove past a bunch of people staring at a swamp." He tipped his head toward Harrison. "I made him stop so I could get out of the car. I asked what everyone was looking at, and someone pointed out a *moose*. Can you believe it? I looked at it through binoculars." He pulled paper towels out of a sack and set them on the counter. "At least go into town. I've never seen anything like it. They've got a store that sells stuffed, dead animals. And it smells amazing."

"The dead animals?" she asked.

"The barbecue," Harrison said.

As she set the petals in the pan, she could feel Harrison watching her. He'd been with her since childhood, so she knew him well. "I know what you're thinking, but I'm telling you, the wheel would never have been invented if everyone had said, 'Don't bother, your parents will never approve.'"

Harrison released one of his deep-throated chuckles. "You got me there."

She lifted a petal to her nose and breathed it in. "I can't believe it. This is even better than our flower."

"I'll take your word for it." Harrison stuffed all the sacks into one bag and set them on the counter.

"Of all the people in the world to work with me, I have someone with no sense of smell."

"I don't work with you, Princess," Harrison said. "I work for you."

She gazed up at him with an affectionate smile. "Says the man who shared an entire box of macarons with me at the top of the Arc de Triomphe as we watched the sunset." Pouring enough palm oil to cover the petals, she handed off one pan to Harrison and pulled the other one forward. "This won't be perfect, but at least we'll get a sense—"

Someone banged on the door. The three of them

exchanged confused glances, until Gustav went to answer it.

"Lookin' for Rosie."

Gustav's big body blocked her view, but she didn't need to see him to recognize that deep, gravelly voice. It roused an awareness deep inside her.

And *Rosie?* Why did she love the sound of that? Especially in a voice she'd only expect to hear first thing in the morning when she was snugged against his body, his erection hard against her bottom.

What?

Where did that come from?

She turned back to her pan. "It's Brodie. You can let him in."

"Sir," her bodyguard said. "What can I do for you?"

"Your boss around?" Brodie said.

Afraid of her reaction to him, she took a moment to cover the petals with oil. Then, bracing herself, she wiped her hands on a dishcloth and turned to face him.

Oh. My. God. It was one thing to see him outside, when she was all worked up over the meadow; another thing entirely to have him consuming all the space in her hotel room.

His dark brown hair looked as if he'd just scraped a hand through it, and his blue eyes zeroed in on her with such intensity she got a jolt to her chest.

"Good morning." Her voice actually *shook*.

That's embarrassing.

"Hey." He gave her a chin nod. "The Princess around?" He glanced around the large living area of the three-bedroom suite.

She and her bodyguards shared a look before they all grinned. In St. Christophe—or anywhere in the world she might be photographed or recognized—she dressed like a princess. But, in her lab, she wore plain clothes, no accessories, and very little make-up. "We haven't been properly introduced. I'm Princess Rosalina." In America, people shook hands, so she reached for his.

His big hand engulfed hers, and the rough, calloused texture came as a surprise since the men in her world had smooth palms. Everything about him threw her off-kilter. He was just so rugged, so big and charismatic. He looked her straight in the eye, his grip firm and sure, and it made her feel as giddy as meeting her celebrity crush in person.

The way he held her gaze—as if *he* didn't need a search engine to take her measure—unearthed something foreign...something so primal and raw, it made her skin go clammy.

What would those hands feel like on her skin?

Scraping over my nipples? A current of electricity ripped through her, as images filled her mind. Her hands full of all that thick, silky hair, her legs wrapped around his hips, her breast stuffed in that hot, wet, expressive mouth.

His virility shook her.

And scared the heck out of her.

He released her hand. "I thought you said you were a chemist and a perfume maker?"

Hoping to calm down, she forced a princess smile. "I'll bet you're more than a hotel owner, a bulldozer driver, and a home builder?"

"You got me there."

"What can I do for you? Please tell me you've reconsidered and are here to sign an exclusive contract for your lyantha?"

"Ah, no such luck." He did a quick sweep of her body, taking in the beige capri pants and striped boat-neck T-shirt. "Knox asked me to stop by, make sure you're okay. She was expecting you at the fitting. Apparently, you haven't returned her texts."

She clapped a hand over her mouth. "I completely forgot." The wedding gown.

The *wedding*.

And that was all it took to sink back into the bubbling vat of betrayal. For a few hours, immersed in her work, she'd forgotten all about the reason she no longer had an assistant to remind her about her appointments. "Is it too late? Can I still make it?"

"You flew all the way out here. She's available whenever you want."

"Great. Let me get changed, and I'll head over there." She looked to Harrison. "Do you have directions?"

"I do."

"You can just follow me," Brodie said. "I'm on my way there anyhow to help Knox with some technical issues with her new website."

"Give me five minutes," Rosalina said.

He seemed surprised. "It only takes you five minutes to turn into a princess?"

"You got a timer on that fancy watch? Start it now."

She headed for the bedroom but stopped when she heard him ask, "So, what's cookin'?"

"She's making an essential oil out of the flower petals," Harrison said.

"Really?" Brodie's deep, rumbly voice sounded interested. "What's the process, exactly?"

"Sorry." Harrison chuckled. "That's not my area of expertise."

"How have you not been paying attention?" Gustav asked. "Basically, the oil leeches the scent out of the petals, and then she uses ethyl alcohol to separate the fat from the smell. Something like that."

She had to smile at Gustav's simplistic description, but she liked that he paid attention. With the clock ticking, she closed the door, hurried to her suitcase, and grabbed her skinny black pants. Then, she headed into the closet where she'd hung a couple shirts and a blazer.

Grabbing the closest, a pretty black and white striped blouse, she nabbed a pair of vintage Louboutins she'd found in a little boutique in London. In the bathroom, she pulled off her T-shirt, got dressed, swiped on some red lipstick, flipped her hair upside down, spritzed a holding product, and then straightened. *Done.*

But, as she gazed in the mirror, she couldn't help wondering what Brodie saw when he looked at her. Did he see the scientist? An attractive woman?

Actually, what she really wanted to know was whether sexiness came naturally or if it took effort. Like, were some people just born sensual or was it a conscious choice in their clothing and make-up choices, in the way they moved their bodies?

It struck her that she already had her answer. She wasn't attracted to Marcel, so she didn't feel sexual around him. And she only knew that because around Brodie she felt…aware of herself. Her breasts, her hair, her smile, the sway of her hips.

It changes everything.

Of course, it wasn't about Brodie. After Monday, she'd never see him again. It was about what he'd awakened in her. On her way out the door, she yanked a black silk scarf out of her suitcase and wrapped it around her neck. *Done.*

As soon as she stepped into the living area, she grabbed her purse. "Ready."

The moment Brodie turned to her, his aloof vibe dropped, and he stood there staring, slack-jawed.

Or maybe she was the one staring at him. Because he was the most handsome, rugged, and potently masculine man she'd ever seen. He looked like a man who didn't share his secrets but knew all of yours, like a man who didn't have a care in the world but would drop what he was doing to help with yours. He looked like he played hard, expected to get dirty, and wouldn't spare a moment on people who didn't throw themselves into life the way he did.

He looked like the kind of guy who grabbed a fistful of a woman's hair and pushed her down to her knees to get exactly what he wanted.

Sensation tore through her, lighting a path down her spine, flaring across the tops of her thighs, and settling between her legs in an insistent throb.

Where did that *come from?*

Okay, you need to stop this right now. "Was I over five minutes?"

Harrison grinned. "You've got thirty seconds to spare."

"Perfect, because I left my phone charging on the nightstand."

And then she ducked into the bedroom, leaned against the wall, and closed her eyes.

Holy Mother of God, that man is hot.

"I've never seen a hotel like this." As they crossed the lobby, she felt like an extra on the set of a gold rush film. Actors dressed as gunslingers bellied up to a brass-rimmed bar, the female staff wore hoop skirts, and the men wore suitcoats with vests and woolen trousers.

A valet opened the door for her, and she stepped outside to a lively shoot-out scene taking place up the street. She breathed in the dusty air tinged with sage and wildflowers. "I love it here."

"Glad to hear it, princess."

This place was doing things to her. Like…prying open her senses and making her hungry for every little thing. "Did we have breakfast?" She actually couldn't remember the last time she'd eaten.

Brodie shot her an odd look but didn't say anything.

"I brought you up a croissant," Harrison said. "Not sure if you had it."

"I had a cowboy breakfast," Gustav said. "Bacon, sausage, eggs, biscuits. It was delicious."

Brodie gave a chin nod. "Yeah, we don't do Continental breakfasts in Owl Hoot."

"No, I suppose you wouldn't." Rosalina looked to the mountain range that had thrust violently out of the earth six million years ago. Her Alps weren't quite so dramatic, having formed sixty-five million years ago. "Not with all the adventures you must offer here. White water rafting, hiking, rappelling. I'll bet you even offer heli-skiing."

"I—" Brodie's mouth snapped shut. For the first time, raw emotion gripped his features. He looked down to his scuffed black boots, and then determination had his gaze swinging up. "Not yet, but we will."

Well, that was an odd reaction. A black town car glided under the portico, and as her bodyguards moved to open the door, she couldn't help noticing the way people stopped and watched.

Probably wondering if I'm some famous American actor.

Not only didn't she want to draw attention to herself,

she actually liked that Brodie never showed any deference towards her. It was…freeing.

And that's exactly what I'm here for.

She couldn't pull herself together while inhabiting everything that made her Marcel's fiancée and Fabiana's boss and friend. She needed a complete change.

"My bike's parked just over there," Brodie said. "Hang on."

"Whoa," Gustav said. "What kind of motorcycle is that?"

Brodie's gruff demeanor cracked, exposing the teenage boy underneath. "Triumph Rocket."

It was sleek, black, with shiny chrome features. It looked dangerous and wicked, and…

I want to ride it.

"That is *badass*." Gustav gawked. "What kind of horsepower?"

"Hundred forty-eight."

"Damn, that's sweet."

Harrison swatted the back of the younger man's head, and Gustav instantly turned serious. "Sorry." Back in security mode, he scanned the area, but he couldn't hide his awe as he took in the boardwalks and costumed actors.

Brodie waved his keys. "Back in a second." He started off, his long-legged gait powerful. He had an athletic grace and an air of fearlessness that captivated her.

He was her Pied Piper, only instead of a boy, he was a testosterone-charged man. And she wanted to follow. "Wait."

He turned around but kept walking backwards.

"I'd like to ride with you."

"Rosalina." Harrison's tone held a warning she realized she never wanted to hear again as long as she lived.

But Brodie's grin was pure challenge. "You want to ride the beast?"

"Maybe another time," Harrison said. "We've got to get her to the fitting in one piece."

"Oh, I'll get her there safely." The growl in his voice made her want to knock those mirrored aviators right off so she could see the challenge in his eyes. "She just might not look so…" He waved a hand at either side of his head. "Princessy. What do you say, Rosie? You gonna ride with me?"

His assumption that she was some frail, sheltered socialite made her want to snatch the keys out of his hand and take off by herself. But, while she'd done her share of dirt biking, she'd never ridden a motorcycle.

"Okay, sir, I know you do things differently here," Harrison said. "But she's the princess of St. Christophe—"

"No." She cut him off. "Here, I'm Rosie."

His initial surprise settled into concern, but Brodie gave her an approving smile.

She touched Harrison's arm. "It can't get out that I'm in America, apart from Marcel. If I'm Rosie, no one will care. But the driver, the bodyguards…this is just drawing attention to me." She turned to Brodie. "How many people know who I am?"

"My family knows. The manager. That's about it. We don't talk about our guests. That's basic policy in hospitality."

"Can I trust everyone to keep my identity under wraps?"

"Of course. One of the reasons we get so many celebrities out here's because of our attitude towards privacy. Nobody asks for autographs or selfies. Our state motto's Equal Rights, and that's because we were the first state to give women the vote, but it's also because, to us, people are just people."

A guy walking by clapped Brodie on the back. "I thought our motto's, Where the Men are Lonely, and the Sheep are Scared." He cracked up and kept walking.

"Fuck off, Chris." But Brodie was smiling. "So, yeah, you're safe with us."

She liked the way he unapologetically swore around her. Now, for the more difficult conversation. She addressed her bodyguards. "You may not like this, but I think it's best if you stay in the hotel until I get back."

"I can't do that, Princess," Harrison said. "You know that."

"You can."

Brodie came closer. "Is there some threat I should know about?"

"Not at all," Rosalina said. She held Harrison's gaze. *It's all right. Let me do this.*

"Some of the most famous actors, athletes, and entrepreneurs in the world live here," Brodie said. "And no one bothers them. If she's just Rosie, the chemist, she'll be left alone."

She gave Harrison a gentle push towards the lobby doors. He didn't like it, but he gave her a terse nod and stepped around the car to talk to the driver. A moment later, the car pulled away.

"You take care of her." Harrison pointed a finger at Brodie. "She's precious cargo."

"We got this." Brodie turned and strode to his motorcycle, not even waiting to see if she'd follow.

But follow she did.

Chapter Six

THE WIND LOOSENED THE SCARF ROSALINA HAD wrapped around her head to keep her hair from becoming a tangled mess. It started to break free, and she tried to grab it, but Brodie's ridiculously swift reflexes caught her hand and pressed it to his hard stomach.

Good Lord, this is too much. Tearing down the highway was exhilarating enough, but the feel of her breasts pressed to his back, her thighs straddling his hips…she'd never been this close to a man other than Marcel. It felt different, strange. Thrilling.

His muscular body, the scent of his herbal shampoo and leather jacket…it all smacked her with a heavy wallop of attraction.

The "beast" roared, the wind whipped, and the engine between her thighs made her body vibrate. Both arms wrapped tightly around him, her chin on his shoulder, she leaned into him and enjoyed the ride, hoping he couldn't tell how excited he made her.

Her scarf flapped around her ears, loosening even more, until it flew away. She twisted around to watch it billow and soar like a black kite, before landing in a crumple on the asphalt.

The town dropped away, the businesses thinned, until there was nothing on either side of the highway but wide, open meadows. Colorful wildflowers mixed with the tall grass and scrubby brush.

Her gaze snagged on something in the distance. *What the heck is that?* In the middle of the field stood a large, wooly animal—

"That's a bison." She bounced in her seat, her helmet clacking against his, as she gestured to the side of the road. "Pull over, please."

He slowed, easing onto the shoulder. Idling, he dropped both legs to the ground. "What's up?"

"I want to take a picture." She climbed off the bike.

"Of what?"

"That's a *bison*." Digging around in her purse, she pulled out her phone and hustled back the way they'd come. Her high heels wobbled, the soles crunching on gravel. After she took a few shots, she pulled up the best picture and started to send it…

When she remembered.

The two people she would've sent it to were no longer her friends.

All the freedom she'd felt on the back of that bike, the wind blowing in her hair, fizzled out like a damp fire-cracker.

She felt a wall of powerful energy at her back. "What's wrong?"

"Nothing. I'm just going to send this to…my parents. They'll get a kick out of it." She took in the scene around her, the puffy white clouds scudding across a bright blue sky, the yellow, red, and white flowers dotting the meadow.

"You okay?"

She tried to rally and give him a smile, but the loss had her firmly in its grip. It hurt that Marcel had cheated. It sickened her that Fabiana could be so two-faced.

But, in the end, she wasn't out a fiancé so much as alone in the world. There weren't many she could trust, and so she'd given it all to them. Now, she had no one. "Sure."

The skin around his eyes crinkled, and he seemed to struggle before giving her a terse nod. "We should get you to your appointment."

"Of course."

But, in that moment, she didn't know how she could do it. She'd rather swim with stinging jellyfish than try on her wedding dress.

"I'm sorry to be so difficult."

Brodie glanced up, not liking the heaviness in the princess's voice. Something had happened out there on the side of the road. She'd gone from wild and free to…sad. All from sending someone a picture of a bison.

"Trust me, you're easy compared to most brides." Knox, his brother's wife, knelt on the pedestal, a Velcro bracelet of pins strapped to her wrist. "I want you to love this dress, so we'll keep at it until we nail it. There's no rush, right?"

Rosie stared at the frothy white gown in the full-length mirror in Knox's office. "Not at all."

"Then we're good." Knox got up. "Let me grab my

sketch pad, okay? I want to remember every detail we talked about."

"Should I stay in the dress?" From her almost panicked look, Brodie had the impression she wanted to strip the gown off and fling it across the room. Maybe stomp on it, for good measure.

"Definitely. Be right back."

The moment Knox left, Brodie hit send on the email to the modeler, giving his list of adjustments. Then, he got up and leaned against the desk, arms folded across his chest. "You want me to unzip it? We can jump on the bike and head for the hills."

"It's that obvious?" She rallied with a smile. "I'm not very good at hiding my feelings."

"You don't like the dress, tell her. She'll start over if you want." The princess was certainly paying enough.

"It's fine."

"Fine? Shouldn't it be better than fine?"

"No, I mean, I love the dress." He watched her slip back into princess mode. "With a few alterations, it'll be perfect."

He pushed off the desk and took the few steps over to her. "Remember what I said about privacy? You're safe here, princess. You don't have to pretend with me."

Color crested in her cheeks. She grabbed handfuls of the fancy white material and turned to face him. She wanted to say something, he could tell.

He wasn't the kind of guy who got into people's business. Other than his brothers, he didn't ask too many questions or get too involved. But there was something so vibrant, so vital, about this woman, that he didn't like seeing her reduced in any way. "Something happened back there, when you were going to send the picture."

She gave a bitter laugh. "My two closest friends let me down. That's why I came out here, instead of letting Knox come to me. I just needed to get away from them."

He didn't think any words he had to offer would help, so he stayed quiet.

"It came as such a shock…I'm still not sure how to process it." She relaxed her hold on the fabric. "I can't stop thinking about how, all the time I was with them, completely being *myself* around them…they were working against me. I feel like a fool. I feel—"

"Like you don't matter."

Awareness dawned in her eyes. "Yes, that's it exactly. Before I caught—before I found out about the betrayal, I thought I'd mattered very much. As much as they'd mattered to me." She turned away from him, as though embarrassed by her outburst.

He got up on the platform, standing close enough to see the tiny streaks of black in her unusually pale green eyes. "When I was a kid, someone led me to believe I mattered more than anyone in the world. She lied to me for months. I ignored my gut feeling, because I was so hell-bent on getting things to go my way. When I finally figured out she'd been playing me, I got mad. The kind of mad where you flip tables and upend boulders, sending them crashing off hillsides."

He got his first genuine smile since the bison incident. "I think we process betrayal differently."

He grinned. "Maybe, but in the end it's the same. The good news is that I had a dad who talked me through it."

"What did he say?" Her eager expression made him glad he'd decided to open up to her.

"He told me that anger was the bully showing up to stand in front of my heart. And that *I* hadn't done anything wrong. It wasn't about me being a fool…or being unimportant, it was about the person who'd betrayed me. She had bad character, and there wasn't a damn thing I could do about it. He told me I needed to let go of the things I couldn't control."

"I think I'd like your dad." She turned back to the mirror. "It helps to see it that way."

"Because you've been blaming yourself?"

"No. *Doubting* myself. And I hate it."

"Ah, hell, no, Rosie." He held her gaze in the mirror, making sure she heard him. "Don't give them that kind of power over you."

"Here we go." Knox came in, waving her notebook. "Let's make this your dream dress."

He held Rosie's attention a second longer, until she rewarded him with a sweet smile.

Fuck. That did something funny inside his chest. "You're going to need more room for your project, so you're welcome to use the bunkhouse." Brodie had no idea where that idea had come from—it would mean sharing his place with her for the next few days.

Then, again, he did know. She'd just lost her two closest friends. She felt alone. Since everyone hung out at the bunkhouse, he figured she'd appreciate being surrounded by people other than staff.

"I don't know what that is," Rosie said. "But if it's not too far from the hotel, I'd love it. Thank you."

"Sure thing." He glanced between the notebook and the dress. "I'll wait for you outside."

"Run, Brodie," Knox said. "Run. You don't want to catch wedding cooties."

. . .

"I should get out of your hair," Rosie said.

He looked up from his laptop. "What?" *She's leaving?*

"Did I say it wrong? I thought that was an American expression?" She wiped her hands on a kitchen towel, surveying the rows of baking pans she'd laid out on every counter in the kitchen.

"No, it is." He'd come home a few minutes ago with a head full of ideas for the Outfitting business, and he wanted to write them down before he forgot them.

But he didn't want her to leave.

"My roommate at university was American, and her dad used to say these really corny things. He's from the Midwest, and he was absolutely the sweetest, most down-to-earth man you'll ever meet. He'd rub his hands together and say, Okay, girls, let me get out of your hair." She reached for her black leather tote bag.

It was her first day in the bunkhouse, and they hadn't considered how it would work with him living there. "You don't have to go."

"It's late, and you're home, so..."

"Well, wait." He headed into the kitchen, taking in her work. "Are you done?"

"I'll come back in the morning."

"Go ahead and finish up." He didn't know why he was pushing. *Let her go.* Except...she only had a couple more days left.

"Well, I mean, if you're sure you don't mind, I'd like to replace the petals in these last couple of pans. As many as I can do before I leave will make me happy."

He nodded, aware of an uncomfortable tension between them. But he couldn't figure out the source. It wasn't like they were at odds with each other. She understood she couldn't have an exclusive on his meadow; she seemed fine with it. So, why did he feel this strange push-pull?

The slant of light from the lowering sun hit her hair in a way that made him notice the different colors within the strands—copper, mahogany, even a hint of bronze. It accentuated the feminine slope of her shoulder and landed at just the right angle to spill into the V-neck of her dark red blouse, highlighting plump cleavage. "Stay." His voice came out funny, and he had to clear his throat.

"Wonderful. This space is a thousand times better than the suite. I can create a much larger sample."

Even her voice struck a chord in him, like hearing a song from his childhood that took him back to a particular place and time. Confused, he broke away, reaching into the refrigerator for a bottle of water. "Want one?"

"I'd love one, thank you."

"So, what's the plan? You still leaving the day after tomorrow?"

"Ah, don't remind me." She reached for a mason jar. "I'm going to transfer the petals into these jars and ship them home. They'll need to soak in oil for several weeks. After that, I'll add pure ethyl alcohol to separate the scent from the lipids. That'll take another few weeks. Once I've got the essential oil, I'll send it to you, and you can let me know if you like it."

"Assuming I do, what then?"

"Then we've got a really special perfume."

"Which I'm not handing out to hotel guests."

"No, but remember I said I can use the essential oil to make bath and body products?"

"Which means you got the okay from your parents?"

"Uh, no." She tilted her head, not looking too hopeful. "It's not the right time to bring it up. I'm actually waiting to hear back on another idea I'm proposing to them." She hunched a shoulder. "Truthfully, I'm ninety-eight percent sure they'll reject the idea of adding this perfume." She gave him a hesitant smile. "But I live in that two percent zone, so I'm comfortable there. But even if they do…well, can I tell you a secret?"

"You can." He shouldn't feel so interested, so turned on by a simple conversation. Nothing she could say would rock his world. He certainly didn't care about her essential oil the way she did. If this product didn't work out, he'd hire someone to develop a signature scent for his spa products. This one in particular didn't matter. He'd do it more cheaply, anyway, using synthetic materials.

"Between you and me, I've been trying to convince my parents to expand our product line for ages, and they're just not interested. So, even if they say no to this, I'm still going to make it for you. What do you think about opening up a store? Most spas sell their own products, right? What if you sold our perfume, along with body lotion and wash?"

"I like the store idea a lot." And, just like that, he had another one to add to the shopping arcade in the lobby.

"Oh, good. I'm so glad. Then, after I make the perfume, I'll start working on the lotions."

"And what'll you get out of it?" He knew her well enough to know she'd have given the idea some thought.

"I'd like fifty percent of the sales."

"You got big plans for all that money?"

She grinned. "Well, yeah. I'm going to start my own company, so *I* can be the decision-maker."

"Knock, knock." Vanessa let herself in.

Irritation flashed through him. He didn't want anyone interrupting his time with Rosie.

And yet you invited her here so she could be surrounded by people, instead of alone in a hotel room.

His architect headed toward him with a big smile, which faltered the moment she reached the kitchen and found him with Rosie. "Oh. Hello, I'm Vanessa."

"Rosie. Nice to meet you."

Vanessa looked to him for an explanation, so he said, "She's using one of the indigenous plants on our property to come up with a signature scent for our spa products."

"What a clever idea." Vanessa set her briefcase on the counter. "I didn't know you were working on that."

"Yep. Looking for ways to finish out Owl Hoot."

"Well, she's definitely going to need a better space to work in." Vanessa took in the crowded counters. "Actually, I might have a place for you. School's out for the summer, so we might be able to get the Home Economics kitchen."

"Oh, I'm not staying in town," Rosie said. "I'm going to bring everything back to my lab and work on it there. This is just temporary." She reached for a kitchen towel and wiped her hands. "I can finish up tomorrow. I'll leave you two to this lovely evening."

"No," he blurted.

Rosie jerked to a stop.

"Finish what you're doing," he said. "And then I'll drive you back to the hotel."

"That's a great idea." Vanessa rubbed his arm, and it made him uncomfortable. "I'll go with you, and then we can try that new restaurant in Jackson."

Rosie looked uncertain, so he took the towel out of her hands. "You've only got a few days to get your work done. Stay here and finish." He turned to Vanessa. "I can't go out tonight. I'm having dinner at the main house."

He didn't like Vanessa's disappointment, and it made

him wonder what had changed between them. When had her expectations shifted? "It's my night to hang out with Ruby." His half-sister, only three years old, was a handful, and he and his brothers took turns giving Will and Delilah a break.

Vanessa melted. "You're such a sweetheart."

Her softness hardened him. "So, what's up? You came by to see me?"

"I sure did." She tapped the tube sticking out of her briefcase. "I want to show you the changes I made." She got up on her toes, her hand sliding down to the small of his back, and whispered in his ear, "And I'm in a mood, so let's go to your room, get some privacy."

He didn't want to leave the kitchen. He wanted to go back to his conversation with Rosie. But when he looked her way, he found her focus on Vanessa's hand, where it rubbed circles on his back.

It made him step out of Vanessa's reach. Which made no sense. Why should he care about Rosie's reaction? She was leaving the day after tomorrow, and his life would go back to normal.

Except, he no longer knew what was normal. Not since he'd discovered Vanessa was hurt about the wedding. *Right.* They needed to have a conversation about that. *Not in front of Rosie.* "Yeah, let's go."

It occurred to him that he'd learned more about Rosie in the past eighteen hours than he ever had about Vanessa. In the six months they'd worked together, they'd never talked about anything other than their projects. He didn't know about her family dynamics or any of the things a man should know about the woman he was dating.

As he headed toward the hallway, Vanessa jammed her fingers in his back pocket. Brodie couldn't help glancing at

Rosie. He found her focused on the point of contact and looking oddly unhappy. When she noticed him watching, she broke out in a shy smile.

A pop of excitement rocked his nerves.

How the hell could one little smile have so much power over him? *Fuck.*

Brodie saw the world pretty much in black and white, so this riot of emotions made him uneasy. Rosie was a houseguest. He shouldn't care what she thought of anything outside her project. He certainly shouldn't be reacting to her *smile.*

At the end of the long L-shaped hallway, he turned left into his master suite. Vanessa closed the door, giving him a seductive look. She reached for the top button of her silk shirt.

"Hang on a second. We need to talk." But not in his bedroom. He led her out the French doors onto his small, private patio. A warm, sage-scented breeze rustled the tall grasses of the surrounding meadow. Twilight turned the granite mountain range purple.

The moment he turned to face her, she sidled up to him, running her palms from his stomach to his collarbone. "Mm, I've missed you."

He caught her wrist. "Wait. I want to talk about the wedding. I didn't mean to hurt you by not inviting you."

She dropped her arms to her sides. "Well, you did. I mean, did it even occur to you to bring me?"

"No." He could probably be less blunt. "We're not dating, so if I had, it would've changed our relationship." *Created expectations.* "We're not…" He couldn't say "in a relationship," because friends with benefits was one. Probably best to ask her. "Let me start over. Where do you see us?"

"Honestly? I like what we have. It was only the wedding that made me start thinking about what we're doing. We might not be *dating*, but we're in a relationship, right? Have you been seeing anybody else? In the six months we've been working together?"

"No."

"Neither have I. And we're obviously a good fit. We're both at that stage in life where we care more about our jobs than romance. And I'm not one of those women who wants you calling and texting all day long or sending me flowers. You know how hard I'm working to start my own firm, and I don't need anything more than what you're already giving me."

He didn't know that he was giving her much of anything. They'd never even gone on a date.

"But I wouldn't *mind* doing more with you, you know? We get along. The sex is good." She shrugged. "Like tonight, you're having dinner with Ruby. I'd like to tag along, get to know her a little better. Why not, right?"

"Nah, that's my time with her. She needs my full attention."

His patio had a view into the kitchen. Rosie sat on the counter, laughing at something her bodyguard said. The other, younger, guy dumped a load of supplies beside her. Which meant she didn't need Brodie to drive her back to the hotel. And he didn't like that.

He watched her for a moment, thinking about what her friends had done to her. The tug in his heart surprised him. Rosie didn't deserve that. She was a good person. Open, smart…she obviously cared deeply about her business. Who would fuck her over like that?

"You like her." Vanessa's voice tore him out of his thoughts.

A hot rush of embarrassment swept through him. "Sure. She's got great ideas for Owl Hoot, and she's doing something I'm not familiar with...something I find interesting. But she's only here a few more days, so I want to make sure she has all the materials she needs and the time to get her work done."

She reached for his fingers, grasping them loosely. "I like what we have, Brodie. Nothing needs to change, but I want you to know that if things *were* to change, I'd be open to it." She got up on her toes, lips softening for a kiss.

But he wasn't about to kiss Vanessa, not when the scent of Rosie still clung to his T-shirt.

This is bullshit. He liked what he had with Vanessa. As long as she didn't expect more, it worked just fine. And, anyway, Rosie was leaving. She had nothing to do with it.

So, just make things clear. "I'm not looking for more, so if you're not good with what we have…" He gauged her expression.

"No, I am." She stepped back. "Let's just focus on the house, okay? Forget I said anything. I want to show you some changes I made."

"Are you sure? Because I didn't like seeing you hurt about the wedding. I want us to be on the same page."

"You're sweet. I *was* hurt. Actually, I was a little embarrassed, frankly. We've been working pretty closely for six months, so...yeah. But I'm glad we talked about it. Consider us on the same page." She seemed anxious to move on.

"Okay, well, then I need to tell you I'm moving my building site."

"You're what?" For a moment, she just stared at him,

as if waiting for the punchline. "You're not building in the meadow?"

"No."

"Where, then?"

"Don't know yet."

"Of course you don't know. Because we spent months looking for just the right spot. We flew around in a helicopter, we mapped out the entire ranch. *Brodie*. You love that meadow. It's perfect."

The strength of her argument made him think she had an emotional investment in the location. "It is, but it turns out there's a special plant that grows there. It's the one I'm using for the spa products."

"So, this is *her* idea? She put this in your head?"

"She's the one who brought it to my attention, yes."

"How did she even find it? What's she doing here?"

He didn't usually lie, but to protect the princess's identity he would. "She found it by walking the property. The point is that I need to find a new site."

"Okay, we can do that."

"In the meantime, I'm going to be working on finishing out Owl Hoot. I've got a bunch of ideas."

"Tell me what you've got in mind." And just like that she slid right into business mode, just the way he liked it.

"I'm going to build an Outfitting business. It'll be a store that sells camping, survival, hunting, and fishing gear, but it'll also have an office where we'll book expeditions."

"Oh, that's good. You're amazing, Brodie. This is going to be great. I can't say I'm not disappointed about the house. We've worked so long and hard on it, but it's your show." Her expression turned heated again, and she pressed her hand to his chest. "I'm going to have to head out, but I still have time for a little fun."

He should want that. He had a good thing with her.

She was beautiful, smart, ambitious…

He glanced out the window to find Rosie laughing, head tilted back, and he felt awareness trip across his skin. "Sorry. Not tonight."

"Okay, well, another time. I've got to get going." Vanessa opened the French doors. "Let me know when you want to get started on the Outfitters." She hesitated, like she was giving him one more chance to take her up on her offer.

But he didn't want to hook up with her.

He wanted to get back to Rosie.

And that was just all kinds of fucked up.

Chapter Seven

Brodie parked his bike in front of The Boneyard. The main building was a tunnel of corrugated steel, housing dozens of red motorcycle lifts. Bright tubes of LED lights lent the place a bluish tinge, giving the repair shop a space-age feel.

When he pulled off his helmet, the sounds of soldering and hydraulics filled the air.

One of the mechanics who'd worked on his bike a couple times came out wiping his hands on a rag. "Hey, man, what's up? She giving you trouble?"

"Nope. My beauty's running just fine."

"Too bad. I'd like to get my hands on her." He gave a lascivious smile. "I'll treat her real good."

Brodie laughed. "That's what scares me."

The owner of the Boneyard, Griffin James, sauntered out and shook Brodie's hand. "What's going on, man?"

"I've got some artisan stalls in Owl Hoot I'm looking to fill. It's just a summer gig, but it'll give exposure to artists, maybe drum up some business for them."

"Nice idea." His guarded tone said, *What's this got to do with me?*

"So far, I've got a glass blower, a leather tooler, and a jewelry maker. I've been thinking about Jinx. Don't know if he'd want to work in Owl Hoot, but people might be interested in watching his custom paint jobs. I wanted to bring it up with you before I talk to him."

"I don't need him on-site, so if he's interested, it's cool by me. Not sure he's got the personality to work a crowd, though."

The mechanic chuckled. "Unless you want kids crying, women cussing, and men flipping him off."

"Yeah, that's exactly what I'm going for." Brodie smiled. "I want the artists to make it interesting for the tourists, but it's up to each person to run his business however he wants."

"Let's ask him and see what it says. At the very least, it'll be entertaining." The big, burly dude cupped the side of his mouth. "Jinx."

A man at the other end of the shop, wearing a protective mask and thick, black gloves, glanced over and waved him off.

Griffin gave a deep belly laugh. "You sure you want that asshole around your tourists?"

"I'm looking for something different, something that'll draw them in, so yeah. I want him."

"He does the best custom paint job on bikes I've ever seen. Couldn't believe he agreed to work here." Griff cupped his mouth and bellowed, "Jinx."

The man pulled off his face shield to give a menacing look, but Griffin and the mechanic just burst out laughing. Finally, the artist threw down his gloves and struck out to meet them.

He didn't say a word, just gave Griffin a look that said, *What?*

Griff smiled. "Don't look at me. He's the one who wants to talk to you." He tipped his chin toward Brodie.

"Hey, man." Brodie shook the guy's hand. "I've got some artisan stalls available in Owl Hoot, if you want to work outside this summer. You could hand out your business card. Should be good for business."

A little rough around the edges—with that long hair and ink—Jinx looked like he'd stopped giving a shit a while ago. He had a darkness about him, for sure.

Griff elbowed him.

"No. It'd be a pain in the ass to move everything out there. And I wouldn't want someone to steal my shit." Jinx started off. "Thanks, though."

A car door slammed. "Hey, guys." Griff's younger sister, Skylar, sashayed over, flashing Brodie a big smile. "Congrats on your brother's wedding."

"Thanks." He didn't miss the way Jinx lingered, his attention fully on Skylar.

"What brings you out to the shop?" she asked.

"Well, I came to see if Jinx wanted to work in Owl Hoot this summer, but now that you're here, I've just had another idea. I'd like to hire you."

"Ah, Brodie," she said. "It's about time you got a make-over. What kind of look are we going for?"

Griff and the mechanic cracked up, and Brodie smiled. "What's to improve about this?" Brodie's hand swept from his head down his T-shirt and jeans-clad body to his black motorcycle boots. "But I do need a social media manager for Owl Hoot to get the word out about the town." Good thing he hadn't paid someone to market it before—it hadn't been ready. It would be now.

"She's an image consultant, dude," the mechanic said.

Skylar pretended to take a hat off with one hand and put another one on with the other. "And look at that. I'm also a social media manager." She shrugged. "Hey, I've got a toddler. I'll do anything for a buck."

"Great," Brodie said. "Why don't you write up a proposal, and we'll talk about it?" He shook hands with everyone, and when he got to Jinx said, "If you change your mind—"

Jinx shot a look to Skylar. "You gonna be working over there?"

She nodded. "I am."

"I'm in," Jinx said. "When can I bring my equipment over?"

After a moment of stunned silence, everyone broke out laughing.

Except Skylar. She gave him the stink eye.

"You sure you don't mind?" Rosalina handed the packing tape to Harrison, who sealed up the last box. She couldn't believe she was leaving. Not when she'd barely scratched the surface on this project.

"Not at all." Brodie glanced at the boxes. "I'll get them to the post office first thing in the morning."

When he looked back at her with a reassuring smile, excitement sizzled in her chest. She couldn't explain this energy between them. This draw. She wasn't his type—she couldn't be. His girlfriend was tall, blonde…a sexy businesswoman. "I shouldn't have waited until the last minute. I'm sorry about that."

"I don't mind."

"Okay, well, that's it then." She glanced back into the kitchen. She'd tossed out the pans and stored the leftover palm oil in the pantry. Not a trace of her enfleurage process left.

Dread kept her rooted in place. "I'm sad to be leaving."

"You're welcome to stay longer."

Oh, she wanted that. So badly. She'd hardly even seen the town. Hadn't hiked, not once. "I can do the rest of the work at home. Besides, you don't want me taking up half your bunkhouse."

"I don't mind sharing it with you, princess."

She'd never heard that softness in his voice before. Not even with his girlfriend.

And it stirred up a longing in her she'd never felt before.

I want more.

Everything in her resisted walking out that door.

"You ready?" Harrison said. "We should get going."

"Of course. Sure." She watched him head out but still didn't budge. "I'm so excited about this. It'll be great for your spa. I'm already thinking about other products like soap and candles. This is going to be really amazing."

"You can always come back, have a hand in designing the store."

"I'd love that." But she knew it wouldn't happen. She'd been away from St. Christophe too long. "Well." She didn't know how to say goodbye to him. "You've been so generous, letting me work here."

"I stand to gain a lot. Be good, princess."

"I always am." Her phone vibrated, and she dug it out of her tote bag. "I have to take this. It's my mother. So, I'll just…say goodbye." She didn't know whether to shake his hand or go for the hug. Embracing him would be way too familiar, so she stuck her hand out. "I'll be in touch."

He laughed at her awkward handshake. "Take care." But she didn't miss the strange look in his eyes.

Longing. Did he feel this, too? *Of course not. He has a girlfriend.* She accepted the call as she headed out the door. "Good morning."

"Are you on your way to the airport?"

"Yes, right now."

"Excellent. The sooner you get home the better."

"Is everything all right?"

"No, it's not. But we can discuss it when you get here."

"You sound upset." She stood on the porch, the hot sun on her skin. "Just tell me now. What's going on?"

"Channel one just interviewed the head of the People's Party. Auguste not only discussed his intention to do away with the monarchy but to expropriate our wealth."

What? A hot coil of fear skewered through her. "They can't do that. Our wealth comes from our private business." House of Villeneuve had nothing to do with St. Christophe.

"It's more complicated than that, darling. Our family owns a great percentage of land, and they believe it should 'go back to the people.'"

"That's ridiculous. We didn't steal it. It wasn't pillaged. Our ancestors won it in battles."

"They can spin it however they like to suit their purposes."

"This is terrible." The driver stood waiting by the car, but she held up a finger. *Hang on.* She didn't want to have this conversation in front of Harrison and Gustav. Well, Harrison could hear anything, but Gustav hadn't worked for her nearly as long. "Can they do that?"

"Once they have power, they can change the laws. Which is why we must defeat this movement, and the best way to do that is to put your wedding in the forefront of everyone's mind. I know you're not going to like this, but the moment you get home, we're going to send out invitations."

"I'm sorry, Mama, but that doesn't feel right to me. I don't know that I'm going to marry him."

"For heaven's sake, do you understand what I'm telling you? It's become more than losing our royal seat, which is certainly bad enough. It's about taking away everything your ancestors have built and created."

"No, of course I understand. I'll do whatever you need me to." Now wasn't the time to argue with her mother. Besides, the wedding was a year away. Anything could happen between now and then. "How's Father?"

"He's doing as well as can be expected. Unfortunately, there's not much more he can do on his own. He needs your wedding to show continuity and strength of the monarchy. We must dive right into the preparations."

"Okay."

"So, you'll cooperate?"

"I will." *For now.*

"Good." The relief in her mother's voice was palpable. "Are you bringing the dress home with you? Actually, I never heard from you about the fitting. I've been so consumed by the vote that I've forgotten to ask. I'd hoped to see pictures."

"It's not exactly a joyful time. I hardly feel like celebrating. In any event, we made some adjustments. It looks different on me than it did in the sketches, so there were some things I didn't care for. Anyhow, let me go so I can get to the airport." She headed for the car.

The driver opened the door, and she set her tote on the seat.

"Wonderful. I can't wait to see you."

Just before getting in the car, she turned for one last look at the bunkhouse. Brodie stood on the porch, watching her go. Her heart twisted at the thought she'd never see him again. "The first order of business will be hiring a new assistant. I'm coming home with a new project. You won't believe this, but I've found a flower similar to our lyantha."

"Oh, that. Yes, I meant to tell you, Marcel told us about the bath and body products."

"Can you believe how gorgeous that lotion is? I'm so excited." But, of course, it was the last thing on her mother's mind. "We can talk about it later." She slid into the seat, and the driver shut the door.

"I'm afraid there's nothing to discuss. We know how hard you've worked on it, and we're so impressed with your talent. It really does smell exactly like the perfume."

Nothing to discuss? Oh, no. No, no, no. "Which is great because you didn't want to add a new perfume, so I've just expanded what we offer. Women want to layer their products. The body wash, the soap, and then the perfume."

"Perhaps…" Her mother hedged. "But we're going to pass. It's not the right time."

"We can talk about it after the vote. You've got enough to worry about." Besides, she'd be busy with her new project for a while. And they obviously weren't in the right frame of mind to discuss a whole new product.

At the end of the driveway, they waited for the security gate to open.

"It's not about the vote. We met with Marcel and his father, and we're going to go along with their judgment."

"Wait, so we *are* going to add my bath and body product line?" Because Marcel was definitely on board with her plan.

"No, darling. Marcel pointed out that sales have gone up three percent a year for the last five years, so he doesn't think now is the time to add any variables. Businesses come and go, and ours is doing exceedingly well. He suggests we put off this discussion for another year or two."

"Another year or two." Anger flew up and shadowboxed her. It grew hot and stuffy in the air-conditioned town car. "Do you mean after we're married, when the power's transferred from your generation to mine, which means *Marcel,* because women can't wear the pants in the royal family?"

"He didn't say anything like that, but it *is* fair for him to want to hold off on making any changes until he's in control. He's worked alongside his father for years and has an outstanding education…we trust his guardianship of our family's business."

"He cheated on me. He can't be trusted with anything." Out the window, she watched the landscape roll by, a world so drastically different from St. Christophe she could hardly believe it existed.

Marcel had failed her horribly, and it enraged her. He knew what this product line meant to her.

"He's not saying no," her mother said. "Just not right now."

"Right. Got it. Not for the next few years, during which I'll be marrying him, popping out a baby or two, and launching my philanthropy."

"That's the presumption, yes."

This plan they were all so keen on would neuter her. It

would take away her passion, her career, her *agency*, and it burned a blazing path of injustice right through the core of her being. She sat quietly, not wanting to take it out on her mother, who'd surely suffered the same frustrations and sense of helplessness.

But I'm not my mother.

And I'm only helpless if I give up who I am and fall in line.

She needed another solution, and she needed it now.

To get to the private airstrip, they had to cut across a wide swath of meadow bursting with wildflowers. She pressed the button to roll down the window. Eyes closed, she breathed in the sun-baked earth and wildflowers.

She loved Calamity. The warm, dry air, the valley filled with sagebrush, the violent up-thrust of snow-capped mountains. And the quirky people who loved nature and coveted privacy.

And she loved this new flower she'd discovered. She wanted—more than anything—to stay in town longer. This partnership with Brodie might be her only chance to turn her dreams into reality.

But the scariest truth of all? She wanted more time with *him*. *Brodie*. Even if nothing ever developed between them, he'd awakened these feelings. She was just so… hungry for them.

Calamity had uncorked her, and the very best bits of her had come bubbling out.

I don't want to lose that. Not yet. "Mama, I'm not coming home."

"Oh, Rosalina, you mustn't punish us for making a business decision. You've got so much talent—"

"I know that, and you're asking me to bury it." She shifted the phone away from her mouth to speak to Harrison. "Please ask the driver to take me back to the bunkhouse."

"You mean the hotel?"

Funny, how her every instinct urged her back to Brodie. She shook her head. *The bunkhouse.* She needed to see his reaction when she told him she was staying in town a little longer. He revealed so little, but if he were as excited as she, it would mean the world to her.

"Rosalina," her mother said with urgency.

"If I come home right now, how many times over the next six weeks would I be in front of the people?"

"Well, the Jubilee, certainly."

"Okay, so the rest of the time I'll be unseen, in the background." *It won't matter where I sleep at night.*

"The rest of the time you'll be attending meetings, choosing which causes you'll support, launching your philanthropy."

She understood, she really, truly did, and she hated to let her parents down. "I love you and Papa so much, and I'll do just about anything for you and my country." *Anything except give up who I am.*

Fear stomped on her nerves. *Am I being too selfish?* Or is taking the first step the only way to effect change? "Anything except marry Marcel." She hated saying the words out loud but knew she had to. "So, we won't be sending out invitations."

"You're telling me you're ending the engagement and staying in America during the time when your family needs you the most?"

Rosalina wavered. How did she give her loyalty to her family but also stay true to herself? It seemed an impossible task to meet all her responsibilities—to her family, her people, and herself. "I respect the people of St.

Christophe too much to pretend I'm marrying that cheating bastard just so we keep our seats in parliament. And I just don't believe it's the best solution to the problem. You keep saying we need to show strength and continuity." Once she pushed aside the fear, the answer became clear. "So, really, the emphasis needs to be on the value of the royal family. Not on our ability to produce a male heir, but in what we do for our country. I won't send out invitations, but I will come home in time for the Jubilee." She'd probably be able to stomach standing by Marcel at that point.

"One sighting of the princess is hardly going to be enough."

"The only other sightings they'd get is me in the backseat of the car, waving behind a tinted window or a paparazzi shot of me buying tampons. Besides, it's more than just showing up in a fancy gown. I'm going to announce my philanthropy at the Jubilee."

"You don't have one. And, in order to create one, you need to live here, see what's needed, in order to provide something meaningful."

That simple word—*meaningful*—triggered it. "I already have an idea. I'm going to start an internship program at our secondary schools."

"What does that entail, exactly?"

At least her mother sounded interested. "If I hadn't worked in the lab every summer, I would never have discovered my love of chemistry, which led to my passion for perfume. I would have taken the core requirement classes and probably chosen English Literature or business."

"You make a good point. I majored in Sociology,

having no idea whatsoever how that translated into real-world jobs."

"Exactly. Students have no idea what it means to be a lawyer or a plumber, a mechanic or a graphic artist. So, if we give them exposure, they'll have a more solid understanding of what they want to do with their lives. It will also give them references and job leads for when they graduate."

"That's an excellent idea."

"And, since you want us in the forefront of the people's minds for the next month, you can send out a press release saying that Princess Rosalina and Marcel Allard will be announcing their newly founded philanthropy at the Jubilee." Her mom's silence filled her with doubt. "Not good enough? It gives the impression we're still together and that we're building a future, but it's not a lie because I will be launching that philanthropy." *Just not with him.*

"Yes," her mother said. "It's enough."

"Then why are you so quiet?"

"Because it breaks my heart that such an intelligent, talented woman is not able to run this country. That a man, who is most certainly not her equal, has more power and will make the decisions that impact not only St. Christophe but our family business. I admire you, darling, and while I would prefer it if you came home and made things easier for your father and me, you wouldn't be the woman you are if you did."

"Thank you." But she remained uneasy. "Do you think Father will agree? I don't want to add to his stress."

"You didn't create this situation, Marcel did. And there will be no peace for either of us until after the vote."

Finally, the driver found a patch of worn dirt that served as a turn-out and maneuvered the car back towards the highway. She sat up straighter, dying to text Brodie. *I'm coming back.*

"You're a blessing, Rosalina." Her mother let out a dramatic sigh. "I can't say I'm happy about any of this. I'd much prefer to be planning your wedding right now, but in any event, please understand that we won't be announcing the end to your engagement, so it is critical for you to maintain your dignity. Even in a little cowboy town five thousand miles away, you're still the princess of St. Christophe and, as far as the world is concerned, you're happily engaged."

Up until her mother put the words out there, Rosalina had been thinking of nothing more than working on her essential oil…with Brodie. But three simple words—*maintain your dignity*—shook up a carbonated brew of emotion.

She wanted to break free of dignity and expectations and duty, almost as much as she wanted to work in her lab. *Okay, just as much.* "I'm not here to run wild, Mama. I'm here to work on something important. If I have to give up my career for several years while I marry and have children, then I'd like to get my business launched now. This matters to me. So much."

"I know that, my love. You've always been a wonderful, dutiful daughter. But I would be remiss if I didn't remind you that we can't afford to have any pictures hit the media of you behaving badly, particularly with other men."

She smiled, because she already had her workaround for that. "You have nothing to worry about. I'm not going to be Princess Rosalina here. I'm Rosie, and I wear cowboy boots and jean skirts."

Chapter Eight

"I LOVE THE IDEA OF CREATING SCENES THROUGHOUT the store," Vanessa said. "Like bears gathering at a stream or a pack of wolves coming out of a den. What do you think?"

Brodie couldn't concentrate. It was the damn lyantha, filling up the whole bunkhouse. "Something to consider."

Not five minutes after Rosalina left, Vanessa had come over with the floorplan for the new Outfitters. Held in place by beverage coasters, it stretched across the table. As she pointed out the various features, his mind kept zeroing in, then zoning out.

That smell would forever be associated with the princess. And, right now, it drove home that she was gone. He'd known her, what? Five days? So, it wasn't like he missed her.

No, it was the business. They'd started something good, and he didn't want to lose momentum. She'd probably get distracted as soon as she got home.

He thought of that awkward handshake, and he knew it wasn't the business he was worried about. No denying it, there was some weird kind of connection that pushed beyond the formality of strangers but stopped short of the easy comfort of a girlfriend.

Friend. He'd meant friend.

"What do you think?" Apparently, while his mind had drifted yet again, she'd shifted gears, because now Vanessa was tapping the left side of the drawings.

He noted five small rooms. "I don't think we need that many booking agents."

She cocked her head. "These are the corporate offices. I'm assuming you'll have a general manager, a buyer…I wasn't sure how many you'd need. I can adjust the size of each room to accommodate the number of employees you anticipate hiring. Actually, if we take out the wall, this becomes a conference room where you can plan the adventures you'll offer." Studying his features, she said, "You're not really focused on this. I jumped the gun." She smiled. "It's just I know how you work. I wanted to get this done before you switch to the next project."

The accuracy of her assumption pissed him off. "I'm not doing anything else until I finish Owl Hoot, but you're right. You jumped the gun. I can't move forward until I get approval from the board, and before I do that I need to come up with a few other ideas." He tapped the blueprint. "This is good, though. I'm glad you got started, but let's sit on the details until I come up with a full slate of businesses to present."

"Gotcha." Shoving aside the coasters, she rolled up the blueprint and slid it back into the cardboard tube. "Okay, let's do this instead. Let's sit down and brainstorm—"

Tires crunched on gravel, and sunlight glinted off black metal. Rosie's town car? Had she forgotten something? He jerked back so hard, he knocked over his water bottle.

Vanessa grabbed it before it spilled. "Who is it?"

A car door slammed, and a woman said, "Thank you so much."

Rosie. She might as well have been on fire for the way he hustled out the door. He found her on the walkway, surrounded by luggage…and no bodyguards. His heart thundered in his ears. "You miss me, princess?"

"I did. Well, it's more your kitchen and your meadow—does that hurt to hear?"

He couldn't remember when he'd last felt this…exhilarated. "I feel so used." He stepped off the porch and approached her, reaching for the largest suitcase. "What's up? Miss your flight? And where are your…" He remembered Vanessa. "Buddies?"

"They've gone home without me." She searched his expression. "I've decided to stay in town a little longer."

It was all he could do to keep from wagging his tail like a damn puppy. "Sounds good."

"Well, there's a problem. I called the hotel to get my room back…" She hesitated. "It's booked for the summer."

"What's going on?" Vanessa came out, shielding her eyes with a hand.

"She's moving into the bunkhouse so she can finish her work on the spa products."

Rosie's cheeks flamed bright red. "Oh, I didn't mean I'd stay *here*."

"How long are you in town?" Vanessa asked, surprise clear in the lift of her eyebrows.

"I don't have a specific timeframe, but no more than a month or so."

"Oh, well, that's too long for her to stay here," Vanessa said.

"She can stay as long as it takes to get the project done." He didn't like anyone telling him what to do—but driving Rosie away? *Hell, no.*

"I'm sure I can find a place in town." Rosie got all flustered.

"Summer season's just starting. Everything's booked by now." Brodie shrugged. "It's no big deal. We've got plenty of bedrooms, and I'm hardly around."

"Brodie, why don't you come live with me?" Vanessa asked. "We've got so much work to do anyway."

"Nah, I'm not moving again. I'm good here." He grabbed another bag from Rosie's hand and hauled both of them into the bunkhouse. "My bedroom's all the way at the back, so you can have any of the others."

Originally the bunkhouse for a working ranch, the place was huge. He and his brothers had torn down walls to create bedroom suites out of the dorm-style rooms.

"Okay, thank you." Rosie looked between him and Vanessa, clearly picking up on the architect's attitude. "I'll just…" She motioned towards the long hallway before heading down it.

"Are you sure you want someone living here with you?" Vanessa asked quietly.

"I wouldn't have told her she could if I didn't. Besides, it makes sense. We've got a lot of work to do in a short period of time."

"But you've got other, more important, projects."

"Vanessa, it's done. She's staying."

She opened her arms wide, then let them drop. "Fine. Now, where were we?"

He felt as jittery and wired as if he'd downed an energy drink.

All because Rosie was staying.

"Oh, right," Vanessa said. "You need to brainstorm ideas for Owl Hoot."

"Just a few more."

"Tell me what you've got and how many more you need."

He pulled out his phone and found his notes. "The Outfitters is going to bring in the tourists, so then I just need a few more stores to make it interesting for them."

"How about clothing? Logo wear?"

"We've got that in the hotel."

"True. Well, what are your tourists coming there for? The whole wild west theme, right? We could offer gold panning, chuck wagons, that kind of thing."

"Are you talking about Owl Hoot?" Rosie came back in, and as stunning as she was dressed as a princess, he liked her even more in a simple pair of pants and shirt.

"Yeah. I'm looking for the kind of businesses that'll bring people back, but I don't want it to feel like a tourist town." He didn't miss the way Vanessa's features flinched from embarrassment.

"So, you want the wild west theme without it feeling gimmicky?" Rosie asked.

Like panning for gold. "Exactly." *And chuck wagons.*

"I can tell you a few things that work in…" Her eyes cut to Vanessa. "My town. We have a reliquary museum. It's housed in this adorable, historic cottage. It's not like a museum with priceless art. More like quirky pieces of cultural history collected over the years, things that trigger memories across a century of—"

"We know what a reliquary museum is," Vanessa said. "We have one in Calamity."

"But this would be different." Brodie liked the idea. "It'd be all about the outlaws who lived in the valley, the original settlers. It's a great idea." He typed it into his phone, imagining the docent dressed in period costume, explaining the history of the artifacts. "You wouldn't believe the things that've been found during digs over the years. Spurs, jugs…it's crazy."

"Do you need a few more ideas?" Rosie asked.

She knew he did, and it pissed him off that she was holding back because of Vanessa's attitude.

"Yeah, I do."

"Well, a sweets shop is always a huge success."

"Sweets?" Vanessa smiled. "Where are you from?"

"I'm from a small town in Europe. Anyhow, in ours, one side is an old-fashioned ice cream parlor, and the other is a high-end bakery with everything from croissants and pies to tarts and wedding cakes."

Bells went off in his head. "A wedding chapel. Owl Hoot could become a wedding destination, too."

"I think you might be going overboard," Vanessa said. "Let's stay focused."

"Actually, I think it's a great idea," Rosalina said. "Because you don't have to do anything other than create a chapel and a bake shop that sells wedding cakes. Maybe have a flower shop in the hotel, but all you need is the basic infrastructure."

"Well, it sounds like you've got more than enough ideas." Vanessa checked her watch. "I need to get going. I've got a meeting in town. So, I'll do some research on churches in western towns in the late nineteen-hundreds and start working on some drawings. Are you going with the bakery, too?"

"Yes," Brodie said. "I like that a lot. Every tourist towns needs an ice cream parlor, but I also like the idea of a bakery-slash-café. We'll get an espresso machine and then have big bins of candy." In his excitement, he smiled at Rosie—and he felt his heart crash into hers—a wild, crazy explosion.

"Okay, then. I'll check back with you soon." Vanessa looked between them, obviously confused.

"I need to call my fiancé, let him know my change of plans."

Rosie wasn't a game player, so she really shouldn't try. But she thought he and Vanessa were together, so he appreciated her attempt to remind Vanessa she wasn't a threat. "He's okay with you being gone so long?"

"Oh, he's used to my schedule by now. That's why we're such a great team."

Team? Seemed strange that she hadn't said couple.

Vanessa pulled her keys out of her tote and headed for the door, heels clicking on the wood floor. "Talk later."

Once she was gone, Rosie sighed. "She's really not happy I'm staying here."

"It's none of her business." He headed into the kitchen and pulled a couple knives out of the block.

"Brodie, I don't want to cause problems in your relationship."

"We work together. That's it." He handed her one, and then pulled a box off the stack. Setting it on the table, he shoved it towards her.

She stabbed into the taped center and sliced it open. "Does she know that?"

"I've told her, so I sure as hell hope so." He hefted another one and opened it.

"Okay, but if it becomes a problem, let me know, and I'll find somewhere else to stay."

"Not necessary. With all we've got to do, you need to stay here."

"True. Especially since I can't rent a car." Once she'd pulled out the contents, she started carrying them into the kitchen.

"Felon?"

"What?" She looked horrified at the idea, until she saw he was joking. "No. If I'm going incognito, I can't rent a car under the name Rosalina Anais Isabella Villeneuve."

"No, you're right. That wouldn't fit on the rental agreement." He set an armful of mason jars on the counter.

"You love to have fun with me."

"Well, yeah."

"Because you can't get over the whole royalty thing?" she said to his back, as he walked out of the kitchen.

He stopped and turned to her. "Because you're a princess who ran in front of my bulldozer. Because instead of booking spa time, you spent your first day in town doing your chemistry project. Because you dress like royalty one minute and the girl next door the next."

"Yes, and while I seem like a complex puzzle of contradictions, I'm really just a girl, standing in front of a guy, asking him to go into business with her."

"Oh, we're doing this." He rubbed his hands together. "You talk to your family?"

"I did, and they're not interested in any of my plans." She looked so damn disappointed.

"To hell with them. We got this, princess." He headed back to the table to open the last box.

"Right, so, since I'll be using your flower petals and my proprietary ingredients—that took me years to formulate—I'd like a straight-up partnership. Your flowers, my formula, our product. You agree to only sell it through this one hotel—that's including the spa and the store, and when I go home, I'll open the same exact store in St. Christophe."

"You want it to look like an old western town in Wyoming? How's that going to go over in Europe?"

"Really well, actually. The whole cowboy thing is kitschy. I think it'll be a big hit."

"Sounds good, but what if I want to become a hotel magnate? What if Owl Hoot is so successful, I decide to open a string of them?"

"You've got big plans to turn ghost towns all over the west into living museums?"

"You take all the fun out of it." But he could see his spirited princess still hadn't recovered from whatever had made her turn the car around and come back. "Okay, so what do you need?"

"Well, I'll need to do some shopping."

He whipped keys out of his pocket. "Let's go."

"Oh, no. It's enough that I'm staying here. I'm not going to inconvenience you by having you drive me around."

"Let me be clear about something. I'm never going to offer something I don't want to give. I'm not that nice of a guy." *Except with you.*

"You just keep telling yourself that, cowboy. Underneath that gruff exterior is a very generous man."

"I'm a businessman. The more problems I eliminate, the more you can focus on our project. Let's go."

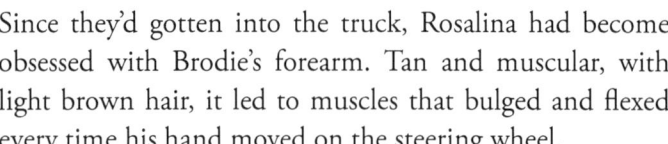

Since they'd gotten into the truck, Rosalina had become obsessed with Brodie's forearm. Tan and muscular, with light brown hair, it led to muscles that bulged and flexed every time his hand moved on the steering wheel.

As she sat primly in her seat, she fought the urge to touch him, to smooth her palm from his thick wrist to the sensitive skin on the inside of his arm, up to the swell of that incredibly powerful biceps. Of course, she didn't know him well enough to do that, but that was the problem. She *wanted* to know him that well. She wanted to put her feet up on the dashboard, roll down the windows, and touch him like he was her boyfriend.

She wanted him to throw her a private smile—no words necessary. Just a simple, *Happy to be here with you.* She wanted his big hand on her thigh giving it a squeeze. *Oh, yes.* She could imagine him caressing between her legs, his knuckles brushing her knickers.

A sizzle struck the base of her spine, shocking the hell out of her.

God, when had she become so…*aware*?

Is it because of what Fabi and Marcel said about me? But it only took a moment to reject the idea that her attraction had to do with anything other than chemistry. A healthy, normal, physical reaction to an extremely virile man. It was delicious, and she loved it.

He flicked on his signal and turned into the grocery store's parking lot.

"Is there really nothing romantic between you and Vanessa?"

Easing into a spot, he cut the engine. "Probably as romantic as you and your 'teammate.'"

The terminology lingered like a bad smell in the quiet of the truck. "My what?"

"You referred to your fiancé as a teammate."

"Did I?" She took in his strikingly handsome profile, the mirrored aviators, the strong jaw, and sensual mouth. "That's odd. I probably just—"

"What happened?" He unbuckled his seatbelt. "On the ride to the airport, what made you turn around?"

She couldn't hide a damn thing, and she was going to live with him the next several weeks so she might as well spill it. "This is a vault, right?" She wagged a finger between them.

He nodded and gave her a serious expression.

"Those friends who let me down? On the way to the airport, I found out one of them double-crossed me. He was supposed to pitch my new product line to my parents, and instead he convinced them to *not* go with it. And that's…that's such a terrible thing to do, because he knows how important this business is to me, and he's been completely on-board this whole time. So, now, to flip on me, behind my *back*—to not even give me a heads-up? He could've called me to say he was having doubts. I deserved a chance to fight for it." All this anger swirling inside her seemed to gather like pins to a magnet to form a hard, pulsating disc.

"I can keep using 'friend' as the code word for 'fiancé,' if you want, or you can just speak plainly to me and know I'll keep your secrets safe."

"Swear to God, Brodie, you can't tell a soul. There's a lot at stake in my country, and me being away, ending my engagement…the consequences are significant."

"Your secrets are safe with me. You can count on it." He opened his door. "Come on. Let's get some food."

He walked a few steps ahead of her, which gave her a chance to take in his hard, round bottom, muscular thighs, and the breadth of his strong shoulders. She couldn't miss the way people stopped what they were doing to watch him walk by.

When she caught up to him, she said, "Can you make it clear to your family and the hotel manager that I'm here as Rosie? It's really important that my identity doesn't get out."

He swung the key ring around his finger then stuffed it into his front pocket. "You got it."

The weight she'd been carrying fell off her shoulders, and she just appreciated him so much. "Honestly, it's a relief that you know the truth. I'm not sure I could hide it now that we're living under the same roof."

"Not a chance." He yanked a cart free from a long chain of them and rolled it into the store. "You wear everything on your face."

"Which is the exact opposite of you. I don't know whether you're an expert at hiding your emotions or you never get deep enough in anything to have them." She'd meant it as a joke, but his expression turned troubled. "I didn't mean that literally. I was just…"

"Nah, it's all good."

"No, it's not. I hurt your feelings, and I'm sorry."

"Rosie, relax. I'm not that sensitive. Your comment just fit with something my brothers said a few days ago. Okay, where we headed first? This is a superstore, so if you need anything for your work, we can start on that end."

"Harrison's shipping supplies from the lab, so I'll just have to wait until everything arrives and then see what I'm missing."

"What'll you do until then?" He said it with a hitch to his brow.

"I think…" She smiled. "I'll spend the next couple of days exploring the town."

"Brodie?" A young mother with a platinum pixie cut and very trendy clothes saw him and abandoned her cart to get to him. Her little boy on her hip, she reached into her big canvas tote bag and pulled out a folder. "I'm so glad I ran into you. Here's my proposal." She handed it to Brodie, as her gaze slid to Rosie. "Hello, I'm Skylar." She tipped her head toward the folder. "Hopefully, the social media manager for Owl Hoot. And this is Rocco, my little love bug."

The shy toddler dug his head into his mom's neck, watching them.

"Hello, Rocco, I'm Rosie. It's nice to meet you."

"She's a chemist and perfumer who's here to work with me on spa products," Brodie said.

"Really?" Skylar hitched her son higher on her hip. "A perfumer?"

Rosie nodded, not wanting to bore them with the details of her job.

"Will that be one of your new businesses?" Skylar asked Brodie.

"It will," he said. "This one will be in the hotel lobby."

"I love that idea," Skylar said.

"I do, too." She really did. There was just so much potential here. "At first, I was just going to make perfume, but then we started thinking about the applications for it and realized we could make it the signature scent of the hotel. Then, we figured, if we're making products to be used in the spa, we might as well sell them, too. So, now, we've got a whole business going." She looked at him, so happy to see her enthusiasm reflected in his eyes. It encouraged her to go on. "For the store, I was thinking we could make the interior reflect the ranch, with images of the meadows and mountains, the animals, and the flowers we use for the essential oils."

"We could start out with Iyantha," Brodie said. "But add different lines using plants indigenous to Calamity."

Skylar laughed. "Look at you two. I think Brodie's met his match."

"What do you mean?" Rosalina asked.

"This is what he does. He gets an idea, and he's off to the races." Skylar shook her head. "Between the two of you, I think you're going to create an empire."

Brodie just shrugged. "Let's wait until I finish Owl Hoot. Then, we'll see what's next."

She wasn't sure what Skylar had said to shut him down, but it made her realize how much he had roiling under that gruff, impassive exterior. "She's right, though. It could really grow as big as we want it to."

For the first time in days, she felt true excitement. Everything might just work out. She'd given her parents a good trade for sending out wedding invitations—a solution they both could live with—*and* she got to establish her business before becoming a wife and mother.

"All right," Skylar said. "I have to get this little guy some milk and…"

The boy's head popped up, ramming his mom's jaw. "Cookies."

Skylar rubbed the wound and smiled. "Yep. Cookies. There's a party in his preschool tomorrow, and we're supposed to make treats." She leaned in conspiratorially. "They didn't say *who* had to make them, though." She tapped the folder. "Anyhow, it's got a list of the things I'm going to do to put your town on the map. Seriously, Brodie, I can't believe you didn't think to get it on Calamity's tourism website. But I'm also going to get it in travel guides. I'm thinking we should wait until this next phase of growth is finished, though."

"Makes sense," he said.

"Okay, so take a look at my proposal and we can discuss it. Everything is negotiable except my fee."

"I don't need to look at it, you're hired," Brodie said. "When can you start?"

"You don't even know what I'm charging you."

"You're worth it."

The features Rosalina had focused on—his muscular physique, handsome face, and confidence—turned out not to be his best. *It's his kindness.*

Skylar gave him a look. "You're only saying that because I'm a single mother and need the money. Not that I'm complaining, because I'll take all the work I can get."

"Nope. I came to you because of your reputation. You're sought-after in this town."

Skylar's features softened. "How do you know that?"

"Word gets around. You made Mrs. Onato cry in the diner last year." He looked to Rosie. "Mrs. Onato was our middle school principal. She was like a mom to every kid in town. And, when she retired, she said she felt like she wasn't anyone's mom anymore. She couldn't break out of the school administrator mindset, so she made an appointment with Sky, lost thirty pounds, and changed her hairstyle and her attitude." He smiled at Skylar. "Now she does a parenting podcast and is getting married. So, yeah, I came to you because I trust you to get the job done, and I'll pay you for your work."

Skylar swallowed. Cleared her throat. "Well, thank

you. That's really nice to hear." She gave Brodie a gentle punch in the shoulder. "Way to make me cry in the grocery store." She spun dramatically and headed back to her cart. "I'm leaving now." Once she set Rocco in the top basket, she looked to Rosie. "We should do something while you're in town. Maybe get drinks."

"I'd love that." Rosie blurted it out so awkwardly that she wanted to fall through a hole in the floor. *Way to sound too eager.* But, whatever. She meant it. "How about tonight?"

"Tonight?" Skylar looked surprised.

"Or any night, really. I don't know anyone here, and I'd love to have some fun."

"Hello?" Brodie said. "Standing right here."

"Yeah," Skylar said. "But she said fun. And by fun she didn't mean learning new ways to cook sweet potatoes." Skylar gave Rosie a shrug. "I could get away for a little bit."

"Good, because I'm in a mood."

"A mood, huh? I should probably tell you right now I'm the perfect designated driver. This cutie likes to wake me up at the crack of dawn, so I don't drink much, don't stay out late, and I'm not into hookups. I'm your driver and your conscience all in one perky little package."

"I don't drink much, either, but I want to have some fun while I'm in town. I want to…I want to try everything."

"And by everything you mean ordering a wine flight from the Tavern?" Skylar asked. "All the fun, outdoorsy things to do in Calamity? Or…the more R-rated version?"

You're Rosie here. As long as you don't do anything to get on the evening news, you're free to do whatever you want. She grinned. "The R-rated version."

Chapter Nine

"We don't really have night clubs in St. Christophe." Rosalina had to shout over the loud country and western music. Maybe it was the pitcher of margaritas they'd ordered, but she hadn't had this much fun in ages.

Disco balls in all sizes hung from the ceiling. They spun out colorful streaks of light that ricocheted off shiny belt buckles and polished cowboy boots and splashed across the clothes of people line dancing. The place was alive with crazy energy.

For the first time in her life, she felt unencumbered. That lid on his life Marcel had talked about? Tonight, she'd blown hers off. She could do or say anything she wanted. She could *be* anyone she wanted.

"This is hardly a night club." Skylar rubbed the condensation on her glass with both thumbs. "It's just a loud, rowdy bar."

"Not your scene?"

Skylar perked up. "Ah, I'm sorry. Don't listen to me. It's just…I got pregnant before I had a chance to hang out in bars." She ran a hand through her short hair. "Which means I don't get out nearly enough, so this is great for me."

"I don't go out much, either. I'd almost always prefer to be home in my pajamas reading a book and drinking tea." The jolt of awareness knocked the smile right off her face.

Is that why Marcel had turned to Fabiana?

Because she was boring? She was either in her lab or reading a book or hiking or…

Wait a minute. What made *him* so damn exciting? What interests did *he* have?

No, they might not be able to party, get drunk, and hook up, but she'd never missed any of those things because she had a full life. Marcel had no interests. If he'd grown bored, he should've found a hobby.

He did. Fabiana.

Traitors.

"What just happened?" Skylar flapped her hand at Rosalina's face. "Right there. You got all butt-hurt, and then came out swinging? Literally, a whole movie just played out on your face."

"I'm sorry…butt…what?" Rosalina stuttered out a laugh.

"What were you just thinking about?"

"Well, the butt-hurt part was when I blamed myself for someone losing interest in me. The swinging part was when I realized *I'm* not to blame for someone else's choices."

"Now, that's what I'm talking about." Skylar lifted a fist, and Rosalina bumped it with hers. "Okay, so this list of *everything*, what's on it?

Now that she'd met Brodie, she understood on a visceral level what Marcel had been missing. What he'd craved. She could get it out of her system here in Calamity. "I want to have some wild adventures."

"Like?"

"Like getting drunk and…" She took in the scene around her. "Hooking up with a hot cowboy."

"Oh, boy. We've got a live one on our hands."

Rosalina laughed, but it was hollow. Because it wasn't a random hookup she wanted. It was Brodie.

Not going to happen.

You're not compromising your first—and possibly only— business opportunity with meaningless sex.

"Have you ever done that?"

"Had a one-night stand?" Skylar shook her head. "I got knocked up by my high school boyfriend. He's the only one I've been with. Have you?"

"Nope. I've only ever been with one guy, too."

"I know it's none of my business, but I'd heard you were engaged?"

Rosalina couldn't believe how much she wanted to talk to someone—other than her mother—about what happened. "We're taking a break."

Skylar's brown eyes went wide. "How close are you to the wedding?"

As much as she wanted to let it all out, get some perspective from an outsider, she had to be careful not to give too many details. "We haven't set a date."

"Because he 'lost interest in you?'"

"Bing, bing, bing."

"He's a douchenozzle. I'm sorry, but he is. So, you said you're taking a break, not that it's over. Does that mean there's hope for you guys?"

"It's hard to say it out loud. We've been together forever, and our families are so…invested in us. But, no, it's over." As much as she wanted to give her parents and her country what they expected, she had to accept the truth. She couldn't marry Marcel. Not only because of trust issues, but because she couldn't accept a life sentence of a dutiful marriage.

"Does he agree? Or do you think he'll try and fight for you?"

"He'll fight, but it doesn't matter. The issues are too big for us to overcome. In any event, I don't want to think about it—*him*—while I'm here. I'll deal with the fall-out when I get home. For now, I want to be free of it all."

"I get that."

Squeals and shouts came from the middle of the cavernous room. She turned to watch a group cheering on a woman riding the mechanical bull. The rider, who looked to be the same age as Rosalina, had unbuttoned the bottom half of her shirt and tied it over her stomach, leaving a patch of bare skin between it and tight, low-riding jeans. Her hips undulated, one arm in the air.

Rosalina couldn't stop watching her. "Have you ever done that?"

"You see that list of names?" Skylar pointed towards the DJ booth, where a tall woman in a cowboy hat and a rhinestone-studded shirt held a microphone and MC'd the bull riding. Behind her stretched an electric scoreboard. One half held this evening's highest scorers, while the other held the list of All-Time Best.

Skylar gave a wry grin. "When I was in high school, my friends and I couldn't wait to be twenty-one, so we could get our names on that board."

Do hips do that naturally, or does she practice her moves? "That woman's so sexy."

"That's Gigi Cavanaugh. She's my girl crush."

"You know her?"

"She's a few years ahead of me, and I only knew her because her dad mentored my cousin when he came to live with us in middle school. She's one of those extra cool girls who didn't care about popularity. She's just always had…flair."

"I'll bet she dated the hottest boy in school." Rosalina had only had two margaritas, but since she rarely drank alcohol, it was going straight into her bloodstream.

"The hottest boy was my cousin. They never dated because of her dad, but there was definitely something going on between them. He won't talk about it, so I'll never know the whole story. All I know is that he pretty much destroyed her. She's never been the same since. Actually, come to think of it, neither has he."

"Well, that's just sad." Just as Rosalina turned back to the bull, the ride ended.

After a snazzy dismount, the woman grinned and took in the wild applause. In a move right out of a shampoo commercial, she flipped her hair forward and then swung it back up, letting it fly and settle around her shoulders. The woman was dazzling. "You think you're born sexy, or is it something you learn?" She turned back to Skylar.

"Okay, I'm going to take a stab here, but when you said he 'lost interest,' I'm assuming you meant the douchenozzle cheated on you? Because I can't think of any other reason why a woman like you would question whether she's sexy."

"But I'm not." She saw the challenge in Skylar's eyes. "I'm not saying that like I feel sorry for myself or that I want you to tell me how sexy I am. I mean it clinically. Like, objectively speaking, I don't wear a lot of make-up. When I go shopping, I think about whether something's flattering or pretty. Not the sexy factor. I never think about how I move my body. I don't do seduction, you know?"

"Is that why that man's been eyeing you since you walked in the door?"

"Which man?" Rosalina scanned the bar. When she landed on a man grinning at her, she practically jumped out of her chair. The pearl buttons on his black western shirt glowed in the disco lights, and with his jeans and cowboy hat, he looked exactly like the cowboy she'd imagined hooking up with. "He's cute."

"I think we found your hot cowboy."

"Maybe." Except, now that she was looking at a real man, she didn't know if she could see herself going home with him. "I'm not sure I'm cut out for it." *But, then, that's exactly why you're here.* To live in a different skin.

It's not about whether Marcel's attracted to me.

Or Fabiana saying I'm not a passionate person

This is about me. Exploring, experimenting. Living.

She was done giving them all this power over her.

Then why are you watching bull riding and not doing it?

"I'm going to ride that bull."

"Seriously?"

"Why do you look so surprised?"

"You're a little prissy for that kind of thing."

"You think I'm *prissy*?" *Is that why Marcel isn't attracted to me?*

Oh, my God, shut up. You literally just said you weren't giving him any more power over you.

Besides, what's he ever done to make himself attractive to me?

"I'm so *not* prissy that I'm going to get my name on the leaderboard."

"Well, this will be interesting."

She drained her glass. "And you're coming with me."

"Nah, I don't do that kind of thing anymore."

"Have fun?"

"I have fun. It's just a different kind."

Rosalina leaned in to hear better, and the tips of her hair landed near a little cup of salsa. "What's your idea of fun now?"

"Pushing my little boy on the swings, snuggling with him before bed, and reading him books. Baking cookies and letting him lick the spoon."

And see? Rosalina wasn't ready for that yet. It sounded so sweet…but she just wasn't there. "You're a good mom."

"I hope so. I want to be."

"Can I ask where his father is?"

"He's not in the picture."

In St. Christophe, it was exceedingly impolite to ask personal questions. Which meant all conversations were shallow, brushing over the more meaningful topics.

But Rosalina hated small talk. It drove her insane. Which explained why she spent so much time alone. Well, she wasn't in St. Christophe anymore, and her friend had brought it up. "Like, at all? Does he ever visit?"

"He comes home every now and then to see his family—"

"Isn't his son his family?"

"His son is an obligation forced on him by his parents."

"What happened?" Rosalina slapped a hand over her mouth. "I'm sorry. That was rude." She pushed her drink away. "I'll stop now."

Skylar pushed it right back. "You're fine. This is what friends do. They talk."

"Most people don't talk to me."

"Because you're so beautiful?"

"What?" She snorted. Yes, she actually snorted. And she loved being able to do whatever she wanted. "Ha. No." *Because I'm a princess.* But she couldn't say that.

"Oh, come on. You're striking. All that gorgeous, shiny hair, your boobs." Skylar shook her head. "Well, I do this for a living, so if you want to make an appointment…"

"Do what?"

"Fight people's demons for them."

"I'm…I'm not…" She couldn't believe it. It had never occurred to her that what she accepted as "fact" was nothing more than a lack of self-esteem. *I'm not sexy enough. I'm not pretty enough to "wow" someone. Well… what if I am?* "Oh, you're good. You're really good."

"That's why they pay me the big bucks. Anyhow, so Rocco's dad and I were together in high school. We had big plans to move to LA, where he'd become a musician, and I'd be a stylist to the stars. But then I got pregnant and 'ruined everything.'" She rolled her eyes.

"Are you saying he just left without you?"

"Not without a lot of fighting and threats, but yes. He didn't want to be a dad, and I wasn't going to let my child feel like a mistake, not for one second of his life. Rocco's the best thing that ever happened to me."

"That makes me sad that he doesn't want to know his son."

"That's the hardest part for me. At first, I was devastated that he'd left me. It was the scariest time in my life. Twenty and pregnant? I'm lucky, though, because I've got this big, great family, so they've totally been there for me. But the thing that keeps me up at night is the fact that one day

Rocco's going to get it. That his dad doesn't care about him. And I'm so afraid of how he'll handle it. I can do everything in my power to make him feel loved and special, but I can't change the fact that his own father doesn't give a shit."

Rosalina reached across the table and clasped Skylar's hand. "There's no getting around the fact that it'll hurt him, but everyone's got wounds. None of us gets a free pass in this life. What's important is that Rocco's got a loving family to help him through it. I think he'll be all right."

"I hope so. Now, let's get-to-gettin'. I don't hang out with people who don't walk the talk."

"What does that even mean? You Americans and your weird expressions." She glanced at the bull to find a different woman riding it. This one had less finesse, but she still rode that sucker like it was her job. "I'm assuming you mean I'm all talk, and my only answer to that nonsense is to show you my back and let you see for yourself." With that, she started to get up.

But Skylar grabbed her arm. "Hold on, cowgirl." She held out Rosalina's purse.

"Oh, right." In St. Christophe, she didn't have to worry about details like that, since she had an entourage who looked out for her every need. "Thank you." She reached for the pitcher and filled her glass one more time. This one, she chugged. "Oh, God. Oh, God." She clapped a hand to her forehead, waiting for the knife in her brain to stop twisting.

"You okay there?" Skylar rubbed the middle of her back. "Brain freeze?"

Rosalina nodded like a child. The rapid infusion of tequila had her nerves jangling.

"Come on." Skylar led the way. "Let's see if we can get you on that leaderboard."

When they got to the ring, Skylar said hello to Gigi and the group of women around her, so Rosalina headed over to the MC.

"My friend and I would like to take a turn riding the bull." The woman cracked a smile, making Rosalina wonder if she'd gone about it the wrong way. "Oh, I'm sorry. There must be a sign-up sheet or something."

"Honey, you're going straight to the top of the list. You going first?" the MC asked.

Rosalina thought about the woman who'd ridden the bull like it was a sex toy.

I want to be that sexy.

I want to drive a man crazy.

"Actually, she is." Rosalina pointed to her friend. "Skylar James."

The woman gave her an amused nod. "Next up, we've got a spunky little cowgirl. Let's hear it for Skylar James."

As Rosalina headed back, Skylar parted from the group to meet her. "Thanks a lot."

"What? You've wanted to do this since you were in high school. Now's your chance." She nudged her friend. "The future belongs to those who grab their dreams by the horns."

"I don't think you should mix American expressions with tequila." Skylar handed over her purse. "Okay, girl-friend. Watch and learn." And then she strutted onto the inflatable bed, gripped one of the ropes tied around the beast's neck, and threw a leg over the saddle.

A small crowd gathered, cheering her on. The cowboy who'd been watching from the bar sidled up to Rosalina, tipping his hat. "You gonna ride?"

"I am." She hadn't flirted in... well, ever.

You're single. You're free. And, here, you're Rosie. There was no one in this entire bar who knew she was a princess. She smiled at the guy, but the tequila swirled in her brain, and she had to reach for the railing surrounding the ring.

"You okay, there? Let me get you some water."

"No, no. I'm fine. Really." A bundle of nerves just from a cute guy talking to her, Rosalina didn't pay attention to the MC calling out instructions. All she knew was that the bull jerked back, then spun sideways. Skylar raised a hand in the air, while her hips rolled fluidly with each thrust of the bull.

Her friend held on like a pro, doing that super sexy roll of her hips. She watched the bystanders, shouting and pumping their fists, clapping for her, when her gaze snagged on one man in particular.

It was the way he carried himself, his strong posture, the muscular back and arms. The thick head of dark hair, streaked with gold and bronze from all the time he spent outdoors. That zing of awareness had her fingers curling into fists.

What was it about Brodie Bowie that gave her this jolt of electric heat?

He sat at a table with three other brawny, handsome men who had to be his brothers. One of them reached for the hand of the woman next to him—a gorgeous blonde with an infectious smile—and kissed her palm. For one moment, they gazed into each other's eyes, like they were shutting out the whole world to be alone together in the chaos of the bar.

Another brother, the one with scruff and shoulder-length hair, had his arm wrapped around his brunette girl-friend—or wife, Rosalina didn't actually know—and he kept sifting his fingers through her hair. The couples were so…intimate. So sweet and loving.

The royal family didn't show affection in public.

But that wasn't really the issue, was it? She couldn't think of the last time she and Marcel had held hands. They'd never needed to touch each other like that. They were pals. Buddies. Good friends.

If she'd married him, they'd have been nothing but roommates, and she'd never know passion.

Relief seized her. *Oh, thank God.* After all the hurt he'd caused, it seemed ridiculous to say, but she could see that Marcel had done her a huge favor by playing his game with Fabiana.

It cleared the way for her to want more. Or maybe Brodie had done that. Being here had unearthed a yearning for love and sensuality. God, she craved so much more than she'd ever allowed herself to want.

As though he could feel her watching, Brodie turned and looked right at her. The laughter on his face died, and she was hit with a burst of desire so powerful, it scared her to pieces.

And, right then, she knew there was nothing wrong with her. She'd just never met Brodie before. That kind of man didn't live in St. Christophe. He lived here. He was of *this* world.

A tingling sensation zipped from the back of her neck down to the soles of her feet.

I want him.

She wanted to shove her hands in that silky hair, wanted to straddle his hard thighs, and offer her breasts to his hungry mouth. She wanted to see his eyes go crazy with lust.

For me.

And, oh, God, he was looking at her just like that. With desire, with *lust*.

"Here you go." The cowboy held a glass of ice water out to her.

"Thank you." She took a sip of the cold water and stuck her hand out. "I'm Rosie."

"Dusty." He tipped his hat to her.

"You're up." Skylar shouted, tugging on her arm.

Rosalina turned to the cowboy. "Any advice for a newbie?"

"Hold on tight." The skin around his eyes crinkled in amusement.

But she wasn't amused. She'd wanted actual tips. *Whatever. Let's do this.* Thrusting the glass back to him and the purses at Skylar, she dried her palms on her jeans and opened the gate.

Whoa.

How about next time you're going to walk across an inflatable surface, you don't drink tequila first? She practically toppled onto the bull, but she didn't care what she looked like. She just wanted to climb onto its back and stay there for the entire eight seconds.

How hard can it be? She could do anything for eight measly seconds.

"Grab hold of the rope and throw your leg over the bull," Skylar called.

"Right." She'd ride that bronco like a pole at a strip club.

I feel sexy, so that's how I'll look.

Reaching under a series of ropes, she got a good grip. Fortunately, she'd grown up riding horses, so she knew how to get in the saddle. Only, this one was much wider than hers.

"We've got a newbie in the house," the MC said into the microphone.

Whistles and calls filled the bar.

"You ready, princess?" the MC called.

What the hell? Rosalina froze, whipping around to see her. How did she know? Had Brodie told someone? But before she could find him in the crowd, the bull jolted. It jerked back and spun sideways—just as it had for Skylar. Only, it didn't move nearly as fast or as recklessly.

It actually wasn't that bad. She held on with both hands, concentrating on keeping her balance. She relaxed a little, letting her body move with the jerky movements.

She wanted to do that sexy roll of her hips, but before she could go for it, the bull snapped harder, swiveled faster. Rosalina nearly slid off the saddle. Her thighs gripped the rawhide for dear life.

Forget sexy, she just needed to stay on. Perspiration soaked her shirt and plastered her hair to her forehead. She remembered seeing Skylar hold one arm in the air, so she tentatively freed a hand and lifted it.

Shit. God. What the hell? The thing was going faster, bucking and spinning and jerking.

Her bottom slipped off the saddle, and her fingers ached from her tight grip on the rope. She wanted to find Skylar in the crowd. *Help me.* But everything was moving and shaking—

And then she was flying, the world a blur of color and faces.

Rosalina landed on her bottom on the inflatable pad. At first, she was stunned, but with the crowd laughing at her like it was the most hilarious thing they'd ever seen, what could she do but wave at them? "Thank you," she called. "And for my next act…" But she was pretty sure no one could hear her over the music and laughter.

Just as she was about to get up, Brodie leapt over the railing and knelt beside her. "You okay, princess?"

"Did you tell them about me?"

"What? No." And then he grinned. "There's no escaping who you are. You look fancy even in jeans."

She looked into those bright blue eyes filled amusement. "I don't want to look fancy. I want to look sexy."

"You were sexy in the way a very beautiful woman looks when she touches a live wire that delivers a giant jolt of electricity to her body."

She barked out a laugh. "You're a jerk." Yanking out of his grip, she rolled onto all fours on the bouncy surface and got herself up to standing. "No wonder you don't have a girlfriend."

"Come on. Let's get you out of here so someone can show you how it's done."

"I'm not going anywhere. I'm riding again. I'm going to get it right, and I'll be sexy doing it."

With a firm grip on her upper arm, he gave the MC a chin nod. *Again.* And then to the bar, he shouted, "What do you think? Should we let the city girl have another go?"

Whoops and shouts exploded around her, and after a lifetime of playing demure and elegant, she pumped her fist. "Let's do this." She leaned closer to Brodie. "Got any tips for me?"

"Lean forward. Get your upper body over your rope hand. Use your free arm for balance—don't flail it around like your hand's on fire and you're trying to put it out. Turn your toes out and dig in your heels."

"Anything else?"

"When the bull jerks left, you lean right. Keep your

upper body loose and your thighs tight." He leaned in close to her ear. "Bet you're real good at that one."

Laughing, she smacked his arm. "That's not something you'll ever find out."

"Shame. Now, go, before you lose your nerve."

She gazed up at him, and for one sizzling moment, all the noise and laughter and booming country music faded away. Her heart thundered, and blood roared in her ears, as they shared a searing connection.

She wanted to cup his strong jaw, run her fingers over his lips. She wanted to see his eyes go lazy with lust.

But he broke the spell. "Go on and show us what you've got."

Right. Turning back to the bull, she grabbed the rope and swung her leg over the saddle. Seated, she got a solid grip, then motioned for them to hit the joystick.

This time, she'd concentrate. She'd drop the fear and self-consciousness. So, when it started moving, she focused on moving her hips in time with the rocking. Her neck and back jolted, snapped, but she thought about Brodie's advice. She dug her heels into the rawhide and let her upper body flap like a flag in the wind.

I'm doing it.

I might not be sexy, but I'm fierce.

And then the speed increased, and the bull whipped first in one direction, then back in the other.

That's okay. I got this.

She pumped her arm, making an attempt at some kind of cowboy call, but even she knew it came out weird. But, whatever, she was riding the bull. Rolling her hips.

She was killing it.

And then, before she knew what happened, she was sailing—the breath caught in her lungs—and landing on her hip. She couldn't control the laughter that exploded out of her.

Brodie crouched beside her. "Now that was sexy."

"The way I'm sprawling on the floor?"

"The way you put yourself out there." He cupped her chin. "You're fearless."

Little bits of happiness pattered on her heart like warm summer rain, drenching her parched soul. She got up and bowed for the onlookers, loving it when they clapped and hooted for her.

Just as Brodie started to lead her away, she stopped, grabbed his wrist, and lifted it. "Who wants to see Brodie Bowie ride this thing?"

"Hey, now." Brodie's voice was low in her ear. "I'm not the one who's got something to prove."

She gave his rock-hard body a push. "Don't be scared now, you big bruiser. The fall's not that bad."

"It's been a long time since we had a Bowie ride," the MC called. "Come on, y'all. Help me get Brodie up here."

"Brodie, Brodie, Brodie…" The roar was deafening, and Rosalina laughed when she saw his expression. Suffice it to say he wasn't pleased.

She made her way out to the other side of the barrier and watched while Brodie sliced a hand through the air, and the bull started moving.

"Oh, this is going to be good." Skylar watched, enthralled.

But something wasn't right. The bull was out of control. "What the heck's going on?" Rosalina asked. "Why's it going so fast? It didn't go that fast for me."

"Because he's a Bowie. I swear, they make a special speed just for them."

"Because they're so fit?"

"Because they're all extreme athletes."

"All of them?" She'd read about Brodie's run for the Olympics but nothing about the brothers. She didn't need to read anything, though, to see that Brodie had more grace and athleticism than a ballet dancer, hockey player, and gymnast combined. "I heard he missed his shot at the Olympics."

"Yep, it happened when he was eighteen. He was two weeks away when he got injured. It was awful, because the whole world was watching his every move."

"Two weeks? Wow. That must've been devastating." She thought about what he'd said about not following-through with his projects, and she thought maybe it made sense. Working so hard towards a goal, pouring your whole heart and soul into it…and then having it snatched away from you. That would make anyone not want to put himself out there again.

After the full eight seconds, where Brodie's core strength had him looking like he was sitting at a tea party, he swung both legs off the bull for a swift and ridiculously elegant dismount.

While the audience shouted their approval, Rosalina went quiet inside. She was in big trouble. She wanted him in a way she'd never wanted anyone before. He awakened her sexuality, her femininity. Every single cell in her body sang for *him*.

But it didn't matter because she had a life to get back to in another country.

Besides, they were going to be business partners for a very long time.

She'd just have to work beside him and shut down all the exciting things happening in her body that she'd waited a lifetime to feel.

Chapter Ten

BRODIE DUMPED THE PRINCESS ON HER BED. EYES closed, she reeked of tequila.

He waited a minute while she settled, her long, dark hair spread all over the white pillowcase. Arching her back to yank the rumpled blanket out from under her, her tits jiggled under the silky fabric of her blouse. She moaned, and his dick hardened.

"I'll get you some water." But with her limbs splayed awkwardly like that, he figured he should straighten them out. *Probably should've pulled the covers back first.*

But then she yawned, and her sexy little body stretched and twisted. She looked hot, all loose-limbed and sleepy. Her bangs covered her eyes, and she pursed her lips to blow them away.

Get out of here. Leave her alone.

"My mouth tastes disgusting." Rolling over, she jammed her face into the pillow. "Liquid's sloshing around in my belly."

"Let me get you some Tylenol." He started for the door.

"Brodie?"

"Yeah?"

She tried to swipe the hair off her face so she could see him, but her hands didn't seem to be cooperating with the signals from her brain. "I'm sorry."

"For what?"

"You said I could stay here to work on our product. The last thing you need is to babysit me."

"How is this babysitting? We were going to the same place, so I took you home."

She scowled. "You carried me to bed."

"It was just quicker than waiting for you to get here on your own."

"You know what's funny?" Her cheek rested on her hands, and she looked so sweet he wanted to lie down beside her and—

Shit. Never mind. "What?"

"Partying seems way more fun in books and movies than it actually is."

"I've never been drunk, so I can't say, but it doesn't look all that fun."

"You've never been drunk? But you're…"

"I'm what?"

"You and your brothers…you're like party animals."

"We have a lot of fun, just not with booze. You've never been drunk before?"

"My father's not only the prince, but he's Head of State. I can't have pictures of me dancing on tables and tossing my knickers on the bar."

"Is that what they do in St. Christophe? Toss panties on the bar? That sounds pretty disgusting, actually."

"Isn't that what they do? Did I get it wrong?"

"You're thinking about Coyote Ugly, where the women dance on the bar and toss their bras on the chandelier?"

"Yes, that." Looked like she tried to lift her hand to point at him. "What's wrong with my arm?"

"It's weighed down by all that tequila."

"I don't think I'm as drunk as I am exhausted." She let out a long-suffering sigh. "I'm so tired, Brodie."

"The pitcher of margaritas didn't help."

Again, she tried to blow the hair out of her eyes. "I only had three glasses."

Dammit. He couldn't stand it a second longer. He strode back to the bed and brushed her bangs aside. When they slipped back down, he tucked them behind her ears. "You drinking to forget the two assholes who done you wrong?"

Both arms flopped on the white duvet. "*No.* I already took back my power. It's not about the douchenozzle."

"Douchenozzle? That sounds like something Skylar would say."

"I'm interesting. I'm *plenty* interesting."

"So, did you have fun tonight?"

A slow smile lit her face. "I did, but I didn't need the booze to have fun." She moaned. "I'm sorry."

"Quit apologizing. You can't work on anything until your supplies come, so in the meantime you can relax. Don't worry about anything here. If you want to get sloppy, we've got your back."

"You really do, don't you?" She tried to grip his wrist, only her fingers didn't fit all the way around. She scowled, trying to focus on it, but then let out a huff of exasperation. "I really like it here. I love my country. I do. But I have to be on my best behavior all the time. I can't dance on tables or have hookups or wear anything revealing. Even at university I couldn't."

"That would suck." He didn't like that this spirited woman had spent a lifetime on lockdown. *That's no way to live.* "You can do all that here."

An image struck him, her stumbling in drunk, late at night, with some random guy on her arm, laughing as she led him into her bedroom.

Fuck, he didn't like that at all. He had an uncomfortable feeling in his chest that almost felt like indigestion.

But then she gazed up at him, all sweet and vulnerable, and he let it go. *Rosie needs to spread her wings? She's come to the right place.*

"I know." She said it dreamily. "I like that. A lot. And I'm going to do *everything*. Except…maybe not with tequila."

"So, what I'm hearing is, I've got a Princess gone wild on my hands."

"Yes." Her smile flattened. "As long as my identity doesn't get out."

"Not to spoil the mood, but how does the fiancé fit into this plan?" He didn't want to push, but he had a feeling she'd broken up with him. She wouldn't be talking about hookups if she hadn't.

Her features tensed, and an unbearable sadness came over her. "Hello, hello, hello."

Sounded like a terrible impression of echoing. "What're you doing now?"

"Checking to see if we're in the vault."

"We are. Always." He had a feeling he wasn't going to like what she had to say.

"But, like, this is royal-jewels-in-a-safe level of secret keeping."

He drew in a breath. Did he really want to go there with her? If he listened to her unload, he'd get involved. And he was trying to keep some distance between them.

But he was drawn to this woman in a way he knew meant he couldn't deny her anything. So, yeah, he was in. Crawling across the bed, he lay down beside her. "I got you, Rosie. You're good."

She rolled towards him. "He did more than double-cross me." She stroked a finger across his cheek, moving the hair away from his ear and said, "He cheated on me," in a loud whisper.

The way his body jerked, you'd think someone had taken a cattle prod to him. "That fucker."

"With my *friend*. She's…she *was* my assistant."

"They're both pieces of shit." Jesus, no wonder the princess was a mess.

"And, to make it worse, he keeps saying he didn't sleep with her."

"Like it matters."

"Exactly. Anyhow, for a lot of really important political reasons, I *have* to marry him, but Brodie, I can't—I won't."

"You love him?"

"Before all this happened, I would have said I did. I felt…affection for him. He was my best friend. But, now that I'm away, I can see it wasn't romantic love at all."

"You're not hot for him?"

She shook her head. "But I only figured that out after I met you."

Slowly, he turned to look at her with an expression that said, *Does that mean what I think it means?*

"You do things to me I've never felt before, and it makes me see that I never got all fizzy for him. Not the way I do for you." Her hand slapped over her mouth. "I prolly shouldn't have said that."

"Nah, it's understandable. What's not to like?"

She laughed. "You make everything so easy. Which is funny, since my first impression of you was the opposite. You looked all mean and gruff."

"I am mean and gruff, but I seem to have a soft spot for you." When her eyes got all hot and her lips parted, he knew he had to shut it down. *Not going there.* "I might come off that way because I don't get too invested in shit. I don't want people telling me the stories of their lives."

"Yeah, you told me."

"Told you what?"

"That you don't follow through on things."

"That's got nothing to do with getting involved in people's troubles."

"Are you joking? It has everything to do with it. If they open up to you, you're going to get emotionally involved, and once that happens, you're invested. And then, when things don't work out, you're going to be destroyed."

"Well, that escalated pretty fast. Trust me, nothing can destroy me." Well, except his dad dying. But other than that…*oh.* Well, yeah, his mom not coming back to Calamity…that had sucked pretty hard.

"Like, I had this huge, lifelong expectation that I'd marry Marcel. I'd invested everything in that relationship, in our future together, and when it exploded in my face, it *hurt.* You expected to win a gold medal, and it was taken from you. It would make sense that you wouldn't put yourself out there anymore."

"All right, Tequila Queen. I don't know who told you about the Olympics, but it didn't scar me. It was an old injury that acted up. I missed my shot. Simple as that."

"Oh, come on. You worked your whole life for it. I'm sure it took a lot of your family's resources to get you there. And then…two weeks before you were going to see it through, it was taken from you. That would leave a deep impression. It would make you never want to care so deeply about anything again. Or anyone."

He didn't miss the look she sent him. "And now we're talking about Vanessa?"

"Well, she's trying really hard to make you love her."

"Whatever she's doing, it's not about love."

"She's trying to get you there."

He scrubbed his face with his hands. "I'm not holding back because I'm afraid of being disappointed. That's just not where we are." *Yet?*

Could he see having more with Vanessa?

"But maybe there's scar tissue that's blocking you from letting someone in, you know?"

"Maybe I'm not attracted to her the way I am to you."

"You're attracted to me?" She drew up her knees and cupped her hands under her cheek again. "Tell me more."

He smiled. She was a cute drunk.

She nudged him. "But, for real, are you? I want to know."

"Ah, come on. Don't let your ex get into your head like that. He didn't cheat because you're not sexy enough."

"He said he doesn't see me like that. That he doesn't fantasize about taking me up against the wall. Did you ever take someone up against the wall?"

"Of course."

She gave this big, dramatic sigh. "That must be exciting."

"Fucking's actually more fun in a bed. There's more room to play. Just saying."

"You know that woman who was riding the bull like it was a stripper pole?"

"Are you talking about Gigi Cavanaugh?"

"See, you even know her name."

"I know her name because I grew up with her."

"And because of her thing with Skylar's cousin?"

"She told you about that?" Sky's cousin used Calamity as a sanctuary away from the public eye, so it was an unspoken deal not to talk about him. *Sky's a loyal person.* She wouldn't have revealed his identity to someone she just met.

She nodded. "Why? Is it some secret?"

Granted, a princess from St. Christophe wouldn't recognize an American ball player's name, but Brodie wasn't going to say a damn word. *I'm not going to be the guy who outs him.*

With wide eyes and a big grin, she hiked up on an elbow. "It is. What's the secret? Are they stepsiblings? Is Gigi raising the child she never told him about? Come on, I told you mine." She nudged him. "Spill it. I won't tell a soul."

"There's no secret." At least as far as the relationship. *Nope, Gigi and Cassian played that out for everyone to see.* "He got recruited to play ball, and she went to art school."

"Star-crossed lovers." She gave a dramatic sigh.

"You're making it way more romantic than it was. Pretty sure Cassian made some shitty choices."

"He's a bad guy?"

"He's got a wild hair up his ass, that's for sure. But, honestly, for all his partying, he's still a good guy. Not many guys our age spend their free time mentoring kids. He runs a year-round football clinic—"

Her body jerked, like she'd been bit by a snake. "Wait a minute. Don't tell me Skylar's cousin is Cassian *Ellis*."

Shit. How the hell did she get *there*?

"Oh, my God. Cassian Ellis grew up here?"

"*That's* the secret, so keep that on lockdown.

"I will. I swear. I can't believe he's Skylar's cousin."

"How do you know him?"

"Uh, because he's the three-time pro bowler, four-time NFL passing leader? The player who holds the rookie record for passing touchdowns in a season? He's the best quarterback in the league. Who doesn't know him?"

"How do you know American football stats?"

"Because I watch football. My dad went to university in the States, and he's a fanatic. But even if I didn't, everyone knows Cassian Ellis. He's gorgeous and always in trouble." She rolled onto her back, staring at the ceiling. "Mind. Blown. I can't believe that's the man who broke Gigi's heart." She cut him a look. "Did you and Gigi ever hook up?"

"Nope. She only had eyes for Cassian."

"She's hot. And sexy. That's exactly the type of woman I picture you with."

"Lots of people are hot and sexy, but that doesn't have anything to do with attraction."

"What're you attracted to?"

You. "I don't know. It happens at an unconscious level, doesn't it? So, it's hard to define. I've never been attracted to any of the Cavanaugh sisters—and they're all hot."

"Really? But Gigi's so sexy, and she has *moves*. I'll bet if I had those moves, Marcel wouldn't have cheated on me."

"Bullshit. I hope you remember this in the morning, because I'm going to tell you a super high-level secret about men. Wearing tight jeans and showing your tits doesn't make you sexy. Confidence does. Princess, you could wear a tarp and still be the sexiest woman in the room, because of your intelligence, your feisty personality…your *passion*. If the douchenozzle doesn't find you sexy, it's because he doesn't appreciate a woman that challenges him. A woman that faces her fears."

Her eyes glistened, and her lips wobbled. "Those are some really nice qualities."

"I see he's never made you feel sexy…" *Bastard.* He couldn't stop himself from brushing a lock of hair off her cheek. "And beautiful…" His finger swept across her lower lip. "And desired." The man was a fool.

Tears brimmed, then spilled. He wiped them away with his thumb. "Whatever went wrong in your relationship, that's for the two of you to figure out. But the cheating part? That's all on him."

"Don't tell anybody, but I've only ever been with one man."

That didn't surprise him. "Nothing to be ashamed of."

"I'll bet you've been with dozens of women. Hundreds." Her eyes widened. "Thousands."

"Somewhere in the middle."

"You've been with more than five hundred women?"

"No. I was kidding. I don't keep count."

"I'll bet you're good in bed. You're really…manly and…I bet you just take what you want."

She said *take what I want* all throaty and exaggerated. Made him smile. "Last I checked, my online rating was a nine-point-seven." Sounded like Marcel didn't give her what she needed at all.

"What did you get marked down for?"

"Even tipsy, you're smart. I like that. And the point-three was from my first time. It took me a minute to find the joy button."

"Joy…" Her eyes flared. "Oh, you mean the clitoris."

"Sometimes I forget I'm dealing with a scientist."

"Or just a grown up." She grinned.

"But once I found it, sure, I figured out how to use it. It's not all that fun unless you're both getting something out of it."

She squirmed. "Oh, I'll bet. I'll bet." She got a determined expression. "I'm going to find a cowboy who knows how to work my love button."

And there was the hooking up thing again. He didn't like the idea of some stranger getting his hands on her. "Here's another thing I hope you'll remember in the morning. You're special, princess. And, if you hook up with someone, make sure it's a man who really turns you on. Wait for the guy who makes you feel wild and exciting."

"Someone like you?"

"Nah. I'm not the guy for you."

"But you're the one who makes me feel wild and exciting."

"Now, here's something I hope you *don't* remember in the morning. You tempt me like no other woman ever has, but we're not going there."

"I get that." She gave a sigh of sad acceptance.

"Get what?"

"You're a free spirit. You can get wild and exciting any time you want. Why bother with someone who comes with all this baggage?"

"You've got funny ideas about me. First of all, I'm not some playboy who bangs anything in a skirt. I need to have a connection with someone. I need to *like* them."

"Have you ever had amazing sex, the kind that rocked your world?"

"I've had plenty of good sex. Rocked my world? I don't know about that." He did know he'd never felt about any woman the way he felt about this one. He'd never wanted to reach out and touch someone's skin just to feel the sparks between them. Never wanted to kiss someone so badly it made his chest ache. Never paid so much damn attention to the way a woman laughed, talked…never wanted to hear every word that came out of her mouth. "No. I've never had that kind of sex." *But I bet I'd have it with you.*

She went quiet, her eyes closed. Her body went still. It looked like she'd fallen asleep.

He watched her for a moment, her pale skin, that dark hair spilling all over the pillow, and all these strange feelings invaded his body. She thought she wasn't sexy, but he knew she just hadn't been with a man who did it for her. Because she had passion, and she threw herself into things. Yeah, she'd be wild, all right. She'd just never been attracted to her fiancé.

He needed to get the hell out of her room. "Goodnight, Princess."

"I'm not asleep. Do I look like I'm sleeping?"

"You look like a corpse."

"I'm trying not to move. If I move, I might fall off the raft, into the ocean. Is this a waterbed?"

"No, sweetheart." He heaved himself up. "I'll let you get some sleep."

She reached for his arm. "Stay with me. Just for a little. Please?"

Not a good idea. Soon, she'd pass out, but he'd be wide awake with a raging hard-on. "Let me just hit the lights."

He got up and flicked off the switch, untied his boots and tugged them off, and then lay down beside her.

"This is my first time on a waterbed." On her side again, she shifted closer to him, hooking her arm under his and resting her head on his shoulder. "You smell good."

He figured if he stayed quiet, she'd fall asleep, and then he could get out of here.

"Vanessa's beautiful," she said.

"She is."

"And she's smart. And successful. Is she special, too?"

"Sure. Maybe not my kind of special, though."

"But I am?"

He smoothed the hair off her forehead. "Yeah, Princess, you are."

She peered up at him, licking her lips. "Show me, Brodie. Just once, I want to be special to someone. I want...I want to feel it."

Like hell he'd deny a request like that. Pulling out his arm, he hitched up on an elbow and took her in. Her features softened with lust, those lips the color of ripe raspberries, and those eyes—those fucking eyes that looked at him like he was already licking her love button.

He lowered his mouth to hers, felt the restless shift of her legs. Oh, yeah, she'd be wild. Not that he'd ever find out.

Just one kiss. A simple, basic kiss.

Her scent, a mix of Nocturne and whatever essence rose out of her heart and soul, connected with something deep inside him in a powerful way. In a way that had him locked into place with her. Why did *this* woman feel so right in his arms?

Fuck it. I'm going in. He brushed his lips over hers,

intending to keep it clean, light, but that sexy mouth opened for him, and he fell inside her lush, wet heat. It was tentative, a little awkward, but the moment their tongues touched, a riot of sparks burst in his chest.

She tasted like tequila and a hint of salsa, her mouth velvety soft and warm. Her hands came around the back of his neck, kissing him with wild abandon, as she sucked his tongue into her mouth. Her fingernails scraped across his scalp, and as the kiss deepened, turned carnal, she gripped a fistful of hair and pulled.

Jesus. Everything he'd held back—all the lust and desire and frustration he felt around her—crashed over him, and he lost it with the clutch of her desperate fingers. The moment he rolled over her, pushing a thigh between hers, she rocked against him, rubbing her core against his cock.

Oh, fuck. He wanted her. His whole body was bursting with want for her.

But then she cried out, and he snapped out of it, jerking away.

She looked at him in horror, like she'd done something wrong.

"You're sexy as fuck, Princess. Never doubt it." He rolled off the bed, grabbed his boots, and got the hell out of there.

Chapter Eleven

WITH COUNTRY MUSIC PLAYING ON THE SPEAKERS, Rosalina took in her reflection in the mirror. The jeans fit all right, she supposed, but the blouse stretched tight across her chest, the pearl snaps barely closing.

You know what? I hate it. She hated everything she'd tried on so far.

Unzipping them, she jerked the pants off her hips—fast, like they were covered in fleas. She eyed one final pair folded on a chair. *Why bother? It's just more of the same.*

Why am I so restless? So irritable? It's just clothes.

She remembered Brodie's words last night.

Sexy as fuck.

Yeah, that was why. Because of Brodie. That kiss. He'd told her she was sexy, and it had nothing to do with the way she dressed or wore make-up or how much skin she showed.

You're sexy as fuck, Princess. Never doubt it.

She believed him. His arousal pressing between her legs had proved it.

Same with the way he'd kissed her. *God.* It had started

with the brushing of lips, so soft and sweet. She'd thought her heart would beat right out of her chest. But—just like that—it had turned carnal. He'd been so hungry for her. And it had made her desperate and hot, swollen and wild.

It had been so good. But she'd barely gotten to touch him when he'd pulled away.

Still…

Brodie Bowie thinks I'm sexy as fuck.

The problem was, *she* needed to feel it. And she didn't in these jeans that looked like something she'd wear to muck out stalls in a barn. *God, why is it so hot in here?* She couldn't stand to wear this ill-fitting shirt one more second. Yanking it off, she hurled it onto the pile of clothes she'd discarded.

"How's it going?" Skylar asked. "Can I see?"

"No. I'm not…There's nothing to see…" She sounded as frustrated as she felt.

"Okay, open the door and let me in."

"Just a second." She had to unearth her stupid, boring beige capri pants. Shoving her leg in felt like stepping into a smelly dumpster. Her whole being resisted. *This isn't me.* But she threw on her cotton boat-neck shirt and opened the door.

"I brought you…" Sky's jaw snapped shut, as she took in the mess in the dressing room. "Okay, someone's obviously ransacked your dressing room. I'm going to get security." And then she looked at Rosalina, and her humor turned to compassion. "I brought you these, but they're more of the same, so I'm just going to put them over here." She stepped back out of the room and placed the shirts on the hanging rack. Coming back, she closed the door. "Okay, what's going on?"

"Nothing fits."

"Like, literally, out of this entire warehouse, not a single thing fits you?" Skylar eyed the mountain of clothing. "Or maybe this isn't your style?"

"I mean, I want to fit in here, but no, this isn't my style."

And, really, wasn't she just trading in the princess costume for the cowgirl one?

"That's the beauty of the wild, wild west," Skylar said. "Nobody cares what you wear. I'll bet that's why so many wealthy people own homes here, because they can totally let their hair down."

She desperately wanted to ask about Cassian, but she'd never break Brodie's confidence, so she kept her mouth shut. *But, come on, Cassian Ellis lives here.*

And he's Skylar's cousin.

"Rosie, you can be whatever you want here," Skylar continued. "You want to be your glamorous and sophisticated self, do it. You want to wear sweatpants to the grocery store, no one's going to blink an eye."

"What I want is to have a style." She took in Skylar's mix of vintage and high-end fashion. "You never look like you're wearing a costume. It looks like every piece is chosen with care. Like there's a story behind each piece."

"That's true, but it's because I'm an image consultant. No one would hire me if I showed up in jammies and flip flops. I have to look like I know my own style. For me, that takes a lot of work. But, for you, it's effortless. You've got panache, and I think it comes from your confidence."

Confidence. Brodie had used the same word last night. *It's what makes me sexy.* "You know what? I've never cared all that much about clothes. But I think…I think I just want to be more intentional, you know? I want to choose the food I put in my mouth." Instead of sitting down to a meal Chef had prepared. "And try on clothes until I find the thing that makes me excited. If you were my image consultant, where would you take me to shop?"

"It sure as hell wouldn't be Western World Warehouse. Come on. Let's clean up this mess. I've got a boutique you're going to love."

With her iced coffee in hand, Rosalina crossed under the antler arch into the town green. Loads of people were out. Children chasing each other across the lawn, families eating ice cream cones on benches, and a big group having a picnic in the gazebo.

She took a sip of the sweet drink. "You're smart, making me take a break before going into another store."

"That's because I have a three-year-old, and I understand tantrums."

She nearly choked on her coffee. "I didn't have a *tantrum*."

"Tantrum, melt-down, whatever word works better to describe someone who's sweating in an air-conditioned dressing room surrounded by an explosion of denim and pearl buttons."

Rosalina laughed. "Okay, that's fair."

"But, since it was you, it was a very lady-like melt-down."

"I was a little frustrated."

"There isn't a woman alive who hasn't felt that way in a dressing room. Especially when it comes to bathing suits and jeans."

"Yeah, but before my ex cheated on me, I felt so sure of myself. Now, I feel like I'm questioning everything."

"Well, you want to live with more intention, so that might be a good thing. It's easy to fall into a rut, you know? We fall into routines, because it's easiest that way.

Like, if you're a student you wear leggings and sweatshirts, and if you're a lawyer you have a closet full of suits and ties and white shirts. Routine makes it easier."

"I'm in a rut, for sure. And I think part of my frustration is that I'm angry with myself for never questioning it. While my ex…" *Oooh.* That was the first time she'd called him her ex out loud. She'd made it official. And it felt right. No residual doubt or guilt. "While he was trying 'new things,' I was blindly going along with the plan." *Numbly*, if she were perfectly honest with herself.

"And, so now, you're in a new environment, and you get to figure out what you like. It's a good thing. If the bolo tie doesn't work for you, scrap it and keep looking. Don't settle."

Even better, she'd gotten to kiss a man who made her toes curl.

That's what I like. Kissing Brodie.

Four men came out of the diner, laughing and talking, and it was like the entire downtown area stopped to watch them.

Taller, broader, and more muscular than anyone around them, the Bowie brothers strode across the street like rock stars. With their dark hair, vibrant blue eyes, and tan skin, they had the attention of every single person in the park.

But she only had eyes for Brodie. Even though he was clean-cut next to his two younger brothers, he still gave off a gruffly masculine vibe. Like he'd toss a woman on a mattress, jerk off her knickers, grab behind her knees, and yank her right up to his hips.

She could almost feel his erection right there, between her legs, and she about jumped out of her skin.

"You and Brodie, huh?"

"What? No." Her throat seized up at the exact moment she swallowed her mouthful of coffee.

"You okay, there?"

But she couldn't answer, because she was having a coughing fit. Which, of course drew the guys' attention. Brodie said goodbye to his brothers and came sauntering over.

"Would you stop being such a badass already?" Skylar asked him. "Look what you've done."

"It's cool." He smiled at Rosalina, whose eyes were now tearing. "I get this reaction all the time."

"Is it weird that he brags about making someone gag?" Rosalina asked, voice scratchy from the coughing fit.

"Y'all, there is way too much sexual tension going on between you two," Skylar said. "Actually, I'm glad you're here. I've got a client in twenty minutes, and Rosie needs to hit one more shop. Do you think you could give her a ride home?"

She waved her hand at him. "You don't need to wait around. I can call for a car."

"How long does it take to find a couple pairs of pants?" He glanced down at their hands. "You haven't started shopping yet? I thought you'd be done by now."

Affection warmed her. He'd dropped her off in town over two hours ago. He must've been passing time, waiting for her to finish shopping. He *wanted* to drive her home.

"It took her a solid hour and a half to figure out she's not a cowgirl. But, trust me, she'll find what she's looking for at Pretty in Pink. Do you know where that is? A block south of town on Everett?"

"I got it," Brodie said.

"You go." Rosalina hugged Skylar goodbye. "I'll be fine. Thanks for spending the morning with me."

"My pleasure." Her friend pointed a finger at Brodie. "Don't rush her. It's more than a pair of pants, and you know it." With a wave, she set off for her studio.

Leaving her alone with the man who'd kissed her senseless the night before. "I didn't know you were waiting for me." A lovely breeze skittered across the green, shaking the leaves on the trees. It lifted strands of his hair, reminding her that she'd grabbed fistfuls of it.

And pulled.

Oh. My God.

I'm sorry if I hurt your scalp, but from the way your kiss turned frantic I'm thinking it didn't bother you all that much.

"I grabbed a bite with my brothers. No big deal." He tipped his chin. "What're you smiling about?"

I liked kissing you. I want to do it again. Only this time without clothes. "I'm glad to see you."

"You miss me?"

"Actually, I want your opinion. Want to come shopping with me?"

The way he studied her made her think she had whipped cream on her mouth. Delicately swiping either side with her fingers, she tossed her drink into the garbage can. He still looked like he was trying to read a hidden message on her face.

"Never mind. I'm sure you've got a ton to do. I'll just call for a ride when I'm done. I'll see you back at the house." She turned to go, but Brodie's fingers wrapped around her wrist and tugged her back. She stumbled and had to catch herself with a hand against his hard chest.

"Yeah, I want to come shopping with you, but what's she mean, 'it's more than a pair of pants, and you know it?' Is this about the douchenozzle? You looking to buy clothes that make you feel sexy? I thought I kissed the doubt right out of you."

"And we had such a great run of not addressing my drunken behavior. Come on, let's get me some clothes." They headed across the park, both of them ducking to avoid the Frisbee coming straight at them.

"Sorry," the woman who'd thrown it called.

With jaw-dropping grace, Brodie snatched it out of the air and flung it right back at her.

"Show off," Rosalina said.

"Damn, it's not easy to impress a princess."

"You've done an okay job so far." Waiting for a car to pass, they stepped off the curb and crossed the street. "Well, at least I've checked get drunk and dance on tables off my list."

"I didn't see you dance on any tables."

"It's just an expression."

"Not in Calamity, it's not. We take that shit seriously. What else've you got on that list? We live under the same roof, so I want to be prepared."

"You're safe with me."

"Not so sure about that." He rubbed the back of his head. "Still raw where you about snatched me bald last night."

As they reached the sidewalk, she burst out laughing. "Would you stop? If I'm not getting drunk anymore, you don't need to worry about me messing up your hair ever again."

"Shame. That was kind of fun."

"Yeah, that tube of bologna sitting on my leg gave me that impression."

"Tube of bologna?" He threw his head back and laughed.

Joy bubbled through her. To make Brodie laugh… God, it felt good.

"Man, you've been hanging out with Sky way too much."

"No, that came from my college roommate. As for my list, I don't have anything specific. I'm on borrowed time, and I want to do all the things I've never been able to do because of who I am."

"Get it out of your system, because soon as you get home, you're going right back into the role of dutiful princess?"

"That's right."

"But you're not marrying the douchenozzle, are you?"

"Uh, after that kiss last night…that's a hard no." She slapped a hand over her mouth and tipped her head back. "Shut up, Rosalina."

He pulled her hand away. "Your honesty's one of the best things about you."

"Well, sure. Because it feeds that gigantic ego of yours." They stopped in front of a brick storefront. Ivy climbed the walls, arching around the plate glass windows. A pale pink and gold sign said, *Pretty in Pink*. "This is the place."

He stepped forward and held the door open for her. He stood so close that as she walked past him, her shoulder brushed his chest. She glanced at him to apologize but found she couldn't look away. He'd shaved that morning, yet already had a shadow of a beard. She loved the dimples bracketing his mouth.

That mouth. Her gaze dropped to his full, sensuous lips, and the memory of the way they'd tasted slammed her.

"You looking for trouble, princess?"

"I think I already found it." She pushed past him and went inside.

The boutique wasn't huge, but she knew immediately it was her place. In the center, a large glass case held jewelry and sunglasses. T-shirts and sweaters in a rainbow of colors were folded neatly in tall, white bookcases. Countless racks of dresses, skirts, and blouses lined the walls. She ran her fingers through the silk scarves hanging off a hat rack. "This store's amazing."

"Have at it. I'll be on that bench across the street."

"Okay, but if you need to go, just text me. Don't hang around on my account." She wanted to turn back to the clothes, but, as beautiful as they were, she found herself watching Brodie cross the street.

What would it feel like to be so comfortable in her own skin? To never doubt her place in the world? She loved the way the T-shirt stretched across his shoulders, his muscular biceps and thighs, and that ass. God, she wanted to get her hands on it.

As if he heard her dirty thoughts, he glanced over his shoulder and caught her watching him.

The thrill of it made her skin tingle.

Dammit, once again, Brodie couldn't concentrate. The hot sun beat down on his head, and the words on the screen of his phone swam. He had a lot of work to do, so he needed to focus.

Not think about the way she'd watched him cross the street, like she'd slowly stripped off each article of his clothing.

He hadn't known it was possible to look vulnerable and bold at the same time.

Sexy as fuck.

"What're you doing out here?" Vanessa strutted toward him with a big smile. As she leaned down for a hug, her perfume enveloped him. "Were you hoping to run into me?"

"Why would I do that?"

Her smile wobbled, and he felt like shit for once again hurting her feelings.

"I meant, if I wanted to see you, I'd let you know." Okay, that sounded even worse. Damn. "Vanessa." He tipped his head back. "Things are a little too complicated here."

"No, they're not. That's my office right there, across the street, dummy. I was coming out of a meeting, when I saw you." She sat beside him, crossing one leg over the other, her toned thigh outlined in the tight skirt and her shiny high heel catching the sunlight. "Well, I saw this really hot guy with broad shoulders and dark hair, and thought, *Well, hello, my type.* And then I realized it was you. So, what're you doing sitting out here? It's a gorgeous day."

"I'm getting some work done, while Rosie shops."

"Are you kidding me? That woman is *ridiculous.* Who does she think she is, asking you to wait around for her?"

"She didn't ask me anything. She had plans with Skylar, so I gave her a ride into town. I can get my work done here as well as anywhere." His phone vibrated, and when he saw Pierce's name, he held up a finger and answered. "Hey."

"Brodie. Sorry, it's taken me a few days to get back to

you. Been on vacation. I'm happy to set up a meeting, but can you tell me what it's for?"

"You bet. First, I want to apologize for dropping the ball on Owl Hoot. I got carried away with Knox's digital shop, but that's no excuse. Secondly, I've got all the artisan stalls filled now, so that should make things interesting for the tourists. I've also hired a social media manager to get us in tourism guides and travel websites. She's already created some pages for us, and she'll be posting pictures and announcing events on a daily basis."

"This is great, Brodie. I can't tell you how happy I am to hear it."

"There's more. I just had a meeting with my brothers, and we've got some business ideas to run by you. We'd like to build an Outfitters store that offers guided adventures. Fly fishing, rappelling, skiing, wildlife watches, things like that."

"That's…fantastic." He sounded emotional, and as glad as Brodie was to have resumed his responsibilities, he felt like shit for neglecting them for so long. He hadn't once considered what stepping away meant for the team he'd hired to run the place.

"We're also thinking about an ice cream parlor and a reliquary museum. Gray brought up the idea of an indoor sports complex in case of bad weather. A climbing wall, a paint gun room, stuff like that. I just need to get the board's approval, and then we're good to go."

"Damn, Brodie. When you set your mind to something, you knock it out of the park. Okay, let me get with the board and come back with a few dates for you. Thank you."

"I'm only doing what I should've done last year."

"No, you'd made it clear the work would be done in phases, and that's exactly what we're doing."

The moment he hung up, Brodie checked the text messages that had come in while he'd been on the phone. Fin needed him at the training facility. He wrote him back. **Be there soon.**

"Sounds like you've made Pierce happy."

"Yeah."

Led by a black lab on a bright red leash, an older couple walked by. Once they passed, Vanessa asked, "So, are you and Rosie seeing each other?"

"Like I told you, we're working on a project together."

"Don't get so defensive. Friends can ask questions like that."

"You never did before."

"That's because you've never looked at anyone the way you look at her."

Damn. He knew she was right. "I like her, sure." He glanced across the park to the boutique. "She's engaged."

"Right. I forgot about that."

"All right, well." He got up. "I've got to get back to the ranch."

"You want to grab a coffee or something first?"

"Can't. Fin needs my help. I'll catch up with you later." Something had changed between them. He didn't know if it was because she'd decided she wanted more, and he wasn't giving it to her...no, that's not it.

It's me. It was meeting Rosie and learning the difference between a casual interest in a woman and a volatile, crazy attraction.

He crossed the street and headed into the boutique. Over the smell of new clothes, he caught the scent of vanilla from the big jars of candles. He didn't see the princess, and the saleswoman was busy with a customer, so he wandered toward the dressing rooms. "Rosie?"

A velvet curtain parted, and she peered out. "Hey." She looked concerned. "Do you have a minute? I want to show you what I've got."

There was something about her smile, her voice, that melted his tension, and made him want to be nowhere else but right here. "Sure."

She gave him a sparkling grin, before slipping back behind the curtain. He pulled out his phone and texted Fin. *How soon do you need me?*

Can you come right now? Where are you?

In town.

Never mind. Let me see if Will's home. Need help right now.

"Okay, come on in."

Parting the curtain, he stepped into a small room stuffed with an orange upholstered chair, a gold-framed full length-mirror, and pink and purple wallpaper. Clothes hung neatly on every bar.

Facing the mirror, Rosalina stood barefoot, her toenails painted a pretty shell pink. One hand held the top of a dress to her chest, making her breasts plump. His palms ached to feel their weight. "Can you zip me, please?"

"Sure thing." He stepped behind her, and the heat of her body, the scent of her skin, made his dick go hard. In that moment, he realized he was making a big mistake. They kept flirting with each other, pretending they could control themselves. But they were wrong. Every minute with her weakened his resolve. If they kept this up, she'd be flat on her back, naked, and he'd be kissing every inch of her hot body.

Instead of zipping her, he said, "I have to get back to the ranch."

"Oh. Okay." She turned to him. "You go ahead. I can get a ride, no problem."

Good plan, terrible execution. He didn't need to strand her in town. "Forget it. I'm an asshole. I can wait till you're done here." He made a circling motion with his finger, and she went back to facing the mirror. Catching her hair in his hand, he lifted it and dropped it over her shoulder. He towered over her, so he got to watch it scatter over her cleavage. Tugging the fabric together, he pulled up the zipper, but it wouldn't budge.

She twisted away from him. "Never mind. I thought maybe it was just that I couldn't reach back there, but it doesn't fit."

The fabric tucked in at her waist and flared at her hips, but he couldn't get the zipper up over her chest. "You want it?"

"I want it so much." They looked at each other in the mirror, and he didn't miss the pretty flush that spread across her chest, up her neck, and fanned across her cheeks.

"Then get it. Knox can fix it."

"Oh, that's a great idea. I hadn't even thought about that." She glanced at another dress hanging on a rack. "Close your eyes. I want to see if you like this one."

Turning to the wall, he pulled out his phone. But, instead of reading the new texts, his brain tuned into the shushing sounds of clothes dropping to the floor, gliding over her nearly-naked body. She hummed quietly, and he had to wonder why he never felt like he was standing on solid ground around her.

"Okay, look."

Against her shiny, dark hair and pale skin, the grass-colored dress popped. It tied at the back of her neck, completely covering her breasts—and yet at the same time drawing attention to them.

"I thought you needed clothes so you could work? Like jeans and shirts."

"I do." She gestured to a stack of clothes folded on the chair. "But I love these summer dresses. They're so pretty. I'm worried this one's too bright, though."

"Nope. It's perfect. Now you just need a reason to wear it."

"I have one." She watched him carefully in the mirror. "I'm going on a date."

"A *date*? With whom?"

"The guy I met at the bar the other night."

Part of her checklist. Get freaky with a cowboy. "And he's already asked you out?" Of course he did. She was beautiful and fun. Smart and sexy. What guy wouldn't want to be with her?

She nodded. "What's that expression for?"

He wouldn't pretend with her, so he leaned in—real close. "He better be special, princess. That's all I'm saying."

"Sometimes, all it takes is a moment." She faked a dreamy expression. "Sometimes, you look into someone's eyes and you just know. He's your one and only. Your soulmate."

Okay, she was fucking with him. He straightened. "So, is Mr. Wonderful moving to St. Christophe to wear the crown or are you moving out here to work his ranch?"

"Details. We're just going to wing it, let true love run its course." She laughed. "It's just a date. It's not a big deal."

"Yeah, but he might expect things."

She covered her mouth with a hand, her eyes comically wide. "You don't mean…s-e-x, do you?"

"All right, smart ass. Get dressed. Let's pay for all this crap and get out of here."

"Wait. There's one more thing I want you to look at." She made a circling motion with her finger.

"Fine."

"And close your eyes for real this time. No looking at your phone."

"Why? You gonna get nekkid?"

"Actually, yes, and I don't want you to go crazy and start pawing at me."

"I think I can control myself."

"I don't know. All I did was ask one for one little kiss, and you were all over me."

He smiled. "Sure as fuck was. So don't be asking me for any more kisses, unless you want what I've got to give."

"Oh, okay, bad boy. You've got me running scared now. Just keep your eyes closed. I'll be ready in a minute."

Brodie wanted to watch her strip out of that dress more than he could ever remember wanting anything. He wanted to see her tits pop out as she leaned forward to let the straps fall from around her neck, her ass sway as she lowered it over her hips, and her smooth skin bared in the soft light of the dressing room.

He wanted to see that shy smile and feel those bold fingers, wanted to feel her hips rock up and grind against his hard cock. How many minutes would it have taken before she'd gotten herself off last night? If he hadn't walked out on her, she'd have come. He'd have gotten to watch her features go slack, her body seize in ecstasy.

Fuck, yeah. He wanted to see that.

Wanted to be the one to make her come.

He heard her moving around in the dressing room, the smack of elastic, and then it went quiet. "You ready?" he asked.

"Um…"

He turned around to find her in a black bikini. Two scraps of spandex covered her plump tits, and the bottom was a strip of fabric connecting two patches of fabric.

"Brodie."

"What?"

"Eyes up here."

"How can I give you my opinion if I'm looking in your eyes?"

"Can you at least wipe the drool off your chin? It's very unbecoming."

"You going to wear that for the hot cowboy?"

"Yes. I thought I'd answer the door in it and pretend I just got back from the lake, tell him I'm running late. Good strategy?"

"Are you such a smart ass in St. Christophe?"

She got a panicked look. "Shh."

"No one can hear us." He flicked his fingers at the bikini. "You sure you need that thing?"

"Okay, I'm getting from all these questions that you like the way it looks. I don't usually wear such…flimsy swimsuits. I just wanted to know if it looks all right."

"You wear that, you're going to wind up pregnant, and then what will your parents think?"

She leaned close and whispered, "Then I'll get the heir without the husband. Pure win."

Stay there. Stay right the fuck there. It took every ounce of his restraint not to touch that smooth skin and cup those bouncy tits. *Jesus.* He needed to adjust himself, but if he reached between them, the back of his hand would graze her bare belly. "It fits fine. Can we go now?"

"Why's your voice all funny?" She said it all sassy, as if she didn't know about the bulge in his jeans.

"Because you're fucking hot, princess, and I want to do filthy things to you."

She got all squirmy. "No one talks to me like that." Her eyes went all drowsy with lust. "I love it." And then she broke out in a saucy grin. "You want to kiss me so bad right now, don't you?"

"You don't want to know the places I want to kiss you."

"What if I do?"

I want to kiss those tits and then suck them into my mouth. "Shit, princess. We have to stop this." He was going out of his mind with want for her.

She sobered. "No, I know. You're right. We're going into business together."

"Exactly. So, save those damn kisses for your cowboy." Made him sick just to think about it, but what the fuck could he do? "I'll see you outside." He'd just reached for the velvet curtain, when he heard. "I don't want to kiss him. I want to kiss you."

"Dammit, Rosie." He dropped the curtain and reached for her. Grabbing her hips, he hauled her to him. He wasted no time in claiming her mouth. Her silky hair brushed over his arms, and her scent filled his senses. Everything about her fired him up. What *was* it about this woman? He skimmed his hands up her sides, thumbs caressing the stretchy fabric holding in her breasts. "I'm going to go out of my mind if I don't get my hands on these."

Pulling away, she yanked the tie at the back of her neck and let the top fall down.

And, Jesus, there they were, those round, plump tits. With reverence, he cupped them, watching her nipples pebble from the slow strokes of his thumb. "You're fucking perfect."

She wrapped her arms around his neck, licking inside his mouth, teasing his tongue into a sexy dance. She tasted like coffee and sweetness, and her hips swayed restlessly over his cock.

"Fuck, Princess. *Fuck*." He backed her against the wall, hangers rattling, and he cupped her ass cheeks and lifted her. With legs wrapped around him, she pumped her hips, moaning. He squeezed her round, firm cheeks, and she gasped, grinding against his cock. "So hot."

"Everything okay in there?" the saleswoman called. "Can I get you a different size or color?"

Eyes lazy with lust, Rosie let her head fall back against the wall. "Everything's great. Really, really good." But then, with a look of resignation, she sighed, and dropped her feet to the floor. "Actually, can I give you the things I'm going to buy, so we can start ringing everything up? My ride needs to get home."

"Sure, just hand me what you want."

With that black bikini top dangling, and her tits jiggling, Rosie squirmed out of his hold and pulled on a blouse. She gathered as many hangers full of clothes as she could carry and handed it all off to the saleswoman. "I'm getting a swimsuit, too, so let me just change, and I'll be right out."

"Great. See you in a minute."

The curtain fell shut, and Rosie turned to him. "Okay.

That is the *last* kiss you're going to get." Her lips were wet from his mouth, swollen from his kisses.

He didn't answer her. Couldn't. He was too shaken.

"I'm serious, Brodie. God, I lose my head around you, but there's nothing more important to me than our business. My family's not going to support any of my ideas, which means our company is the only shot I get for a long time. I can't risk it."

"No matter what happens between us personally, I'd never take away your half of the business. You're the one who discovered the flower, made the essential oil…you even came up with the idea for the store."

"I know, but things could get derailed."

"What's that supposed to mean?"

"It means you're juggling several different projects. If you lose interest in this one, then I'm out of luck. So, I'm not going to mess it up."

"By hooking up with me?"

"By falling for a guy who gets started with projects and doesn't follow through."

Chapter Twelve

In full princess regalia—her beaded evening gown and royal jewels—Rosalina panned the audience at the Jubilee. She hadn't looked at her notes once. She didn't need to.

"If it weren't for the summers I spent apprenticing in my family's business, I would never have uncovered my passion for chemistry and perfuming. And, so, I would like to change the world for the children of St. Christophe in the same way. The Villeneuve Apprenticeship Program will be open to all secondary school students and will enable them to choose from a comprehensive list of jobs in all fields, from agriculture to government to the arts, so that each student can experience a job before committing to careers and university majors."

Encouraged by the enthusiastic response, she continued. "In addition to the list of participating companies, the students will be able to submit wish lists of the specific types of careers they're interested in, and we'll approach the appropriate businesses to encourage their participation in our program."

Applause broke out, and when it didn't subside, she realized she'd said enough. "Thank you. Thank you so much. More details to come soon." With a dignified nod, she turned to step away from the podium and bumped into Marcel, who grasped her wrist and linked her arm through his. Together, they walked off the stage.

The moment she stepped onto the ballroom floor, the press swarmed her. Ignoring their microphones and trying not to squint from the blinding lights of their cameras, Rosalina said, "We'll hold a press conference later. Tonight, it's the Jubilee. Let's celebrate."

"Marcel." One of the reporters lunged forward. "What's the timeframe? When will this apprenticeship begin?"

"Our program will be up and running by next summer."

Our? She shouldn't care that he was taking the credit. *This appearance is about the vote, nothing more.*

"What about the students who can't afford to participate?" another one asked him. "Children from farm families work during the summer. Isn't your program skewed toward wealthy people like yourselves? Isn't a summer internship a luxury?"

"We're going to provide—" Rosalina began, but Marcel touched her hand to silence her.

Rage sparked, coloring her vision the same shade her cheeks must have been. It took everything she had not to shove him aside.

"We appreciate your concerns," Marcel said. "And to that point, the royal family will not only provide a stipend for the participants, but we'll offer scholarships, as well. We want this opportunity to be available to every student in the country."

Who the hell did he think he was speaking on behalf of the royal family? Shaking with the effort to keep her emotions in check, she said, "Participants will also have the option to choose part-time work, in case they have to—"

A reporter shoved a microphone in her face. "Princess, who made your gown?"

She looked the woman square in the eye and didn't miss a beat. "Work in their family's businesses. To a teenager, a job is nothing more than an idea. The program will give them a glimpse into the actual work, so they can determine if it's right for them. It will also provide references and potential job leads—"

"Princess, have you and Marcel set a wedding date?"

"We have—" Marcel began.

This time, she was the one to reach for *his* wrist. She gave it a hard squeeze. *Don't you dare.*

"We'll hold a press conference soon," Rosalina said. "And answer all your questions then. Tonight, we're celebrating the six-hundred-year history of our country. Let's all raise a glass of champagne together."

With a hand at the small of her back, Marcel tried to move her deeper into the ballroom, but she jerked away from him.

"Rosalina." His voice held warning.

Yes, she knew the attention was on her. And the whole point was to present the image of a happy couple. *For God's sake, I'm doing the best I can.* But it was her sister's look of alarm from a few feet away that told her she wasn't doing a convincing job. *Get me out of here*, she mouthed. Immediately, Genevieve, with her unusual gown and pink-streaked hair, handed her champagne glass to her date and pushed her way through the crowd.

"Please excuse me," her sister said. "Mama would like to speak with us."

Clutching her hand, her sister led her out the ballroom doors, where they bumped into their parents.

"Well done, Rosalina," her father said.

"That was a lovely speech." Her mother's eyes narrowed on her, obviously picking up on her agitation. She abruptly turned, forcing the three of them to follow her into the parlor. She nodded to Genevieve to close the door. "You've got the devil in your eyes, Rosalina. You must get yourself under control."

"And this is why she's in Calamity this summer," Genevieve said. "Instead of pretending to be happily engaged to that asshole."

Her mother cut her a glance, but Genevieve didn't back down.

Exasperated, Rosalina said, "They addressed all their questions to Marcel, as though he's leading this project. As if the program were his idea. And do you know what they asked me? Who designed my dress."

Her father reached out and cupped the back of her head. "That's the way of things—not just in St. Christophe, but in the world, and you know that. Now, listen to me, in my role as Head of State, I am bombarded every day by absurd issues and affronts that make me want to go running, screaming into the dead of night. But, as a leader, I don't have the time nor the energy to waste on petty issues. I must stay focused on the good work we're doing."

"We can stomach being mannequins in designer gowns, because we know the important work we're doing behind the scenes," her mother said. "And the times *are* changing. You will have more of a voice than I've had.

You'll just have to find a way to gently assert it. Give it some time, darling."

"What's important," Genevieve said. "Is that you've got a winning idea, and you're going to help so many teenagers find their path in life."

"What's *most* important," her father said. "Is that you've reminded the voters about the compassion and decency of the royal house. Once the monarchy is secure, then we will take on each issue, one at a time. Of course, you'll soon learn, change moves at a glacial pace in politics."

Nothing they said calmed her. She felt restless, agitated. And it didn't make sense, because none of what she'd experienced tonight was new. "You're right. I'll learn to handle it better." But it actually did make sense. Because, in her very short time in Calamity, *she'd* changed. Her dutiful way of life no longer seemed acceptable. "For now, if you don't mind, I'm going to my room to freshen up."

"Of course, darling." Her mother bussed her cheek.

"You want me to come with you?" her sister asked.

"No, thank you. I won't be long." She tried to smile, but all she wanted was to get out of this room. Constrained by the sheath of silk around her legs, she made her way along the hallway, but it felt like a pack of dogs chased her. Almost panicked, the hairs at the back of her neck stood on end, and she wanted to break into a run.

I am bombarded by ridiculous issues and affronts that make me want to go running, screaming into the dead of night.

Ha. Right there with you, Dad. She didn't know where

she wanted to go, only that she needed to get out of the castle. She needed to breathe. As soon as she reached the kitchen, she kicked off her heels and padded toward the back door.

Once outside, the cool grass tickled the soles of her feet, and she filled her lungs with clean, fragrant mountain air. Pulling her phone out of her clutch, she knew there was only one person she wanted to talk to.

He answered on the third ring. "Princess? Everything all right?"

In the background, she heard laughter and conversation. "I called at a bad time. We can talk later."

"Hang on. Don't go anywhere." He must've pulled the phone away from his mouth, because his shouted, "Give me five," sounded muffled. "Okay, talk to me. How's it going? You give your speech at the gala?"

"I did. What am I interrupting?"

"I'm helping out at the training center. What's going on?"

Glancing around, she realized she couldn't speak out in the open like this, so she headed for her lab. In her tight gown, she had to, basically, do a squat in order to pull the key from under a potted lemon tree. She let herself in, her whole body giving a sigh of relief at the familiar scents of Nocturne, shea butter, and chemicals. "I gave my speech, and I think they like my idea."

"That's good. Then, why do you sound like you want to put in a mouth guard and go a couple rounds in the cage?"

She smiled. "Because, instead of asking me questions about the program, they wanted to know which designer made my dress."

"And which one is it?"

"Shut up." She laughed, and he might as well have peeled three layers of winter clothing off her for all the relief he gave just by being himself. "My idiot ex answered the hard questions, and I got, Have you set a date for the wedding?"

"I'm not hearing anything new. What's got your panties in a twist, exactly?"

"It makes me sick that I have no agency here. I mean, some of those reporters are women. Can you imagine how they'd react if I interrupted their questions to ask what color lipstick they wore?" She tipped her head back, taking in the glittering array of stars through her skylight. "But you're right. It's nothing new. It's just the way it is here."

"It's the way it is a lot of places, but that doesn't stop women from kicking ass."

Pretty much what her parents had said. "I'm overreacting. I know that."

"I didn't say you're overreacting. There's no right or wrong way to react. It's a shit situation. I guess you just have to sort out what's important. Did you accomplish what you set out to do?"

"Yes. I did."

"Then maybe that'll take the sting out of the douchenozzle taking credit for your idea."

"It's not just that. I started to answer a question, and Marcel put his hand on me *in front of everyone* to shut me up."

"You keep your sights on the day after the vote, when you kick him to the curb. From that moment on, it'll be all about your philanthropy. Never about him again."

"You're right. You're absolutely right." She perched on

the edge of her stool. "I want to come back. To Calamity."

To you.

"Your room's waiting."

Do you miss me as much as I miss you?

Do you have a hard time falling asleep, because every time you close your eyes you remember that kiss in the dressing room?

Because I do.

"Hurry back, Princess."

"Where are you off to so early?" Rosalina called from the kitchen.

Damn. He'd hoped to sneak off before she woke up. "Got some things to do." Because, as much as he hadn't liked living here without her, having her back felt dangerous.

Brodie set his gear by the front door.

As soon as she'd come home yesterday afternoon, she'd gotten to work. When he'd heard her whispering calculations in the kitchen, he'd itched to trot in there, see what she was working on. Later, before dinner, he'd heard her in the shower, and he imagined the water hitting her naked body.

They'd both agreed not to act on this attraction, but how the hell was he supposed to do that when she was sleeping right down the hall, and he knew what she looked like with her hair spread all over her pillow?

What she sounded like when she kissed him?

The way it felt when she ground against his cock?

Well, he couldn't avoid her. Heading into the kitchen,

he smelled the coffee. She must've been up a while. "You still on St. Christophe time?"

"I don't sleep much." The pale green of her pajama shorts and top matched her sea glass eyes. Cupping a mug with both hands, she leaned against the counter, legs crossed at the ankle.

He'd gotten a handful of her tits, cupped her ass, but he'd yet to skim his hands over the curve of her calf, the back of her knee, and the soft skin on the inside of her thigh.

And he wanted that more than just about anything.

"It's when I close my eyes at night that the gears start cranking." Behind her, she had different colored petals in plastic bags. She set down her mug and picked one up, started kneading it. "If I add the ceramides…if I use less shea butter…and then I'm just dying to get up and try out the adjustments."

He grabbed a water bottle from the refrigerator. "And what had you up this morning?"

"While I'm waiting for my supplies, I thought I'd play around with another project."

"Something that requires you to abuse those pretty petals?"

Her smile and the mischief in her eyes were exactly what he'd wanted to avoid this morning. He'd even considered moving in with one of his brothers, just to escape the temptation.

"Bruising them releases the scent."

Except that's exactly what I want. Her temptation. It surprised the hell out of him, but he liked how she got him so worked up he couldn't think. It was bizarre, this need to be around her all the time. Made no sense.

She's just a woman. Yeah, she's pretty. She smells nice. She's smart and interesting.

But she's just a woman.

As he twisted off the cap, an uncomfortable thought stirred in his mind. His brothers thought he didn't follow through. Callie had called him a dumbass for thinking he wasn't dating Vanessa.

Even Rosalina, who barely knew him, thought he might be putting off Vanessa because he wouldn't commit. Didn't want his expectations dashed.

So, then, was Rosie a distraction? A way for him to not go too deep with the woman he'd already started a relationship with?

Vanessa's pretty, smart. She lived here, and she was just as focused on work as he was. She didn't need flowers and romantic shit. And yet here he was getting all worked up over a woman he couldn't have, instead of seeing if what he and Vanessa had could develop into something more.

I don't even want a relationship, so why am I thinking about this crap?

He tipped the bottle and drank. "What's the project?"

"You mentioned using other indigenous plants to add products for our store, so I took a long hike this morning and explored a bit of your property." She gestured to the baggies. "Found some really interesting flowers." She caught sight of his gear. "You're snowboarding today?"

"I'm going up in the heli to scout a new house location. But, also, my brothers and I were talking about ideas for Owl Hoot, and we came up with a pretty obvious one."

"And what's that?"

"A triathlon."

"Sponsored by world-class athletes? Oh, that's brilliant.

You've got the terrain, and if you make the pot big enough, you'll be successful right from the start."

"Sounds like you know your stuff."

"Philanthropy is a big part of my life, so I've spent a lot of time organizing events." She grinned. "I think it's cute that you're going up for business, but you just happened to bring along a snowboard. Like, just in case there's a slope that needs your attention."

"Might as well get in a ride."

"You're going alone?"

He'd wanted to make sure he was gone the whole damn day. "It was a spur of the moment idea, so I haven't really asked anybody."

"Would you like some company?"

It took him a minute to figure out she meant her. And then…ah, hell. He was trying to keep his distance, but he knew she wanted some experiences. "You're welcome to come for a ride on the helicopter. After he drops me off, he can just take you back with him."

Damn, the woman couldn't hide a single emotion. Her disappointment was clear.

"Okay, sure." She set the bag down. "I'll change my clothes." As she started out of the kitchen, she said, "Is it safe, though, for you to freeride alone?"

"What're you asking, princess?" He'd planned on dropping in on the glacier, but he supposed he could choose an easier slope. "You want to board with me?"

"I'd love to, but I obviously don't have any of my gear here."

"Let me make some calls. Between Callie, Delilah, and Knox, I'm sure we can find some things in your size."

Who was he kidding? It wasn't about giving her experiences. It was about spending time with her.

Because he was a sucker for this woman.

He should've given her the window seat, that way she wouldn't be leaning across him. Between his jeans and long sleeve T-shirt, he might not be able to feel all that silky hair on his skin, but he could smell her shampoo.

She pressed against his arm, but not like a woman trying to get a man's attention. Like a scientist taking in all the geologic and topographic features. Her nearness gave him a strange feeling, kind of like how he felt at the entry ramp, right before approaching the rails on the halfpipe. And it was really starting to piss him off that he couldn't get a hold of himself around this woman.

She pointed. "What're those?"

"Antelope."

"They're so graceful." She gazed up at him, probably hoping to share her delight, but all he felt was supremely uncomfortable, because the promise in her green eyes made him want to get naked with her.

Not cool. Since the whole point of the trip was to scout a new building site, he forced himself to look out the window. It was just that, every time he focused on the terrain, his mind wandered to her mouth. Those lush, pink lips that had kissed him like…like he was the one she'd been waiting for. Like, now that she'd finally found him, she had to make up for a lifetime of missed kisses.

That's it right there. He sat up a little straighter. When he hooked up with a woman, it might be good, might be fun, but it wasn't anything special.

But with his princess, it was fucking magic. No one had ever felt so right for him. They fit. He'd never had that before.

She shifted again, and he started to go a little crazy with want. He wanted to grab under her arms and drag her onto this lap. Fuse their mouths and gather those tits in his hands.

He wanted to peel her shirt off and watch her breasts bounce with the helicopter's choppy moves. And then he wanted them in his mouth, the bead of her nipple hard on his tongue.

Raw, burning hot lust tore through him. He could not *believe* her asshole ex had fucked around with another woman. Had taken Rosie for granted.

Guys could be such assholes, expecting women to be porn stars in the bedroom, but not giving them the kind of pleasure that would unleash them.

An image hit him, his face between her legs, his hands clamping down on her straining hips. Licking her into a climax that made her arch off the mattress and cry out.

"That lake's the perfect size for your triathlon."

Jerked from his dirty thoughts, he cast a glance out the window. A breeze rippled the surface of the navy blue water, the choppy waves creating white crests. He dragged a hand across the perspiration forming on his hairline.

She leaned even further, pointing to the right. "Looks like, if they ride their bikes along the highway and cut across the meadow for the run up the Bowie Pass, they'd wind up right at that lake for the swimming portion of the race."

He and his brothers knew every inch of the property, and they'd thrown out ideas for possible courses, but she'd nailed it. Sometimes it took an outsider to see the obvious. "You're right. I like your brain." So much so that he'd given up the rare chance to board the glacier just for the pleasure of her company.

"Where's the pilot dropping us off?"

Brodie leaned back, pointing to a glistening sheet of hard-packed snow on the face of the mountain. Smooth, easy. She'd do just fine.

So why did she look so disappointed? "You have something else in mind?" he asked.

A smile bloomed across her gorgeous features, and she pointed higher up the mountain.

"You think you can handle the glacier?" For a moment there, he'd forgotten she'd grown up in the Alps. He'd obviously underestimated her. "Let's do this."

The only reason he'd felt comfortable landing on top of the glacier was because of the way Rosie had staked out the mountain. She'd pointed out a few features, a copse of trees they needed to avoid. Clearly, she knew what she was doing.

Still, from the moment they'd jumped out of the chopper, Brodie had watched her carefully, wanting to keep her safe. Just his nature. He'd ridden this glacier about a hundred times.

But Rosie hadn't even hesitated. And it was hard to reconcile the woman jibbing across a boulder right then with the princess he'd first met in the lobby of the hotel. She soared off the edge, tucked her board up tight and then, to his astonishment, she pulled a backside method, before landing smoothly and continuing down the mountain.

Yeah, he'd underestimated her, all right.

Just above the tree line sat a plateau large enough for a chopper to land. Theirs waited for them, its rotors glinting in the sunlight. As they neared it, he cruised over a mogul and landed on fresh powder.

She slid to a stop beside him, spraying snow out from under her board. She grinned, cheeks red, and when she tore off her ski mask, he got the gift of seeing her eyes shine with happiness. "That was amazing."

He tugged a lock of hair. *You're amazing.* "Let's get back to town and grab something to eat."

Chapter Thirteen

"This smells so good," Rosie said.

On their way home, they'd grabbed take-out from a local barbecue joint. The scent had filled the truck, making Brodie's stomach practically crawl out of his body to get some of the succulent, spicy meat.

Now, they sat out on the back patio of the bunkhouse, twilight painting the mountains purple.

If she liked the smell so much, why was she just staring at the ribs on her plate? It was a messy meal, so maybe she needed more napkins. Snatching some off the pile on the table, he set them in front of her. "Dig in."

Spread out before him, he had a glass of water, some slaw, a rib rack, and a pile of juicy chicken. Picking up a breast, he bit into it, and all that smoky flavor hit his taste buds.

After swallowing, he downed some water. "Man, when you sailed off the boulder, I nearly lost my shit."

Picking up the plastic knife and fork, she tried to slice meat off a rib. "That's because you still see me as a princess."

"Yeah, but you ride like a pro."

She watched him tear off another bite with his teeth, then looked back at her plate.

"Come on. You can dial in a fat three with a safety grab on a *glacier*, but you can't eat ribs with your hands?"

"Well, I mean, is that an actual requirement?"

He loved the humor in her eyes. "Not at all. Have at it." He stabbed his fork into the cole slaw. "Would it go down easier if I brought out the silver? Maybe, while you're here, I should hire a butler?"

"I don't need fancy flatware. I just need to figure out how to get the damn meat into my belly." Plunging her fork in to stabilize it, she sawed away. The tines snapped off, and she grumbled, "Okay, you win." Setting down the cutlery, she looked at the greasy meat. "This is so unnatural."

"It's the most natural way to eat, princess. Do it like this."

She watched him lift his chicken breast, sink his teeth into the flesh, and tear it off the bone like a starved animal. She laughed. "You do you. I'm good doing me." With a napkin in each hand, she picked up the rib and nibbled from the center, careful not to get sauce on her face. But the paper dissolved, leaving her with a soggy mess. "Fine, I'm starving. If I have to become a savage, so be it." Picking up the rib, she clamped her teeth into it and twisted her head like a dog with a chew toy. Sauce dripped off her fingers and smeared across her chin, and she looked to Brodie with an expression that said, *What now, genius?*

Licking the sauce off his fingers, he made a popping sound when each one left his mouth.

"You're disgusting."

"Am I, though?"

She nudged him. "This is delicious. And, I have to admit, it tastes better when I eat it with my hands." She sucked sauce off her thumb. "So, I have to get something off my chest."

"Is that another American saying from your room-mate's dad?"

"Yes. Did I get it right?"

He nodded, then gestured. *Go on.*

"I was mean when I said you're the kind of guy who doesn't follow through. I'm just upset about my situation. The Jubilee really drove everything home for me, you know? I'm valued for my womb, and that scares me to death because there's so much more I want to do, and I don't know if I'll ever get to do any of it in St. Christophe." She lowered her wrists to the edge of the table, looking defeated. "Brodie, I can't do anything to jeopardize our partnership, but…"

"But you want to lick barbecue sauce off my naked chest?"

"That's too gross to even address." But she gazed down at her plate for a moment. "Is that…have you done that before? Licked barbecue sauce off someone's breasts?"

"Not barbecue sauce, no. I'm not that into mixing food with sex. Mostly, I want to taste your tits, not sauce."

A wave of desire fluttered across her features, and she tensed.

"You like that dirty talk, huh?"

"Well, apparently." She said it so primly, it made him crack up. She balled up a napkin and tossed it at him. "Anyway. I'm sorry for taking a shot at you. That wasn't nice."

"We're good, princess. You didn't say anything that wasn't true."

"But you're following through now. With Owl Hoot."

He ripped open a moist toilette and cleaned his hands. "Thing is, Owl Hoot...that was my dad's dream."

"I haven't met him yet. What does he do?"

"My dad passed away nearly four years ago. In an avalanche."

Her eyes went wide, before her features crashed in sorrow. "Oh, Brodie. I'm so sorry. That's...devastating."

"It was. Hardest thing I've ever been through. My dad was a great man, and I miss him every day." He thought about the man's big, booming laughter. The thing about Mack Bowie was that he'd held nothing back. He'd lived loud and hard and had encouraged his sons to do the same.

He'd believed in natural consequences, so he hadn't disciplined a whole hell of a lot. He'd been a fair man, and he'd loved his boys more than anything.

Even after all this time, Brodie still walked into the main house expecting to hear his dad's voice, and he always landed hard when he remembered the old man was gone.

He balled up the wet-wipe, staring at his plate. "Owl Hoot's pretty much my way of giving him what I never did while he was alive."

"You don't mean the gold medal, do you?"

"I do. He devoted his whole life to us, and we didn't make it easy for him. We were a pack of wild-assed boys growing up in the mountains, and my injury was a big wake-up call for him. By the time I came back after physical therapy, he'd hired a coach to live on the ranch and train us. He figured the only way to keep us safe was to teach us how to work with our bodies on this terrain. I think, also, he used training to give us a reason to say no when our friends were partying in high school. To me, that gold medal was a way of saying, *You did good by us, Dad.*"

A long-forgotten memory came up out of nowhere. "I remember my first year of competitions. I sucked. Couldn't make a clean run to save my life." Of course, his twelve-year-old self had been checking the crowds for his dad every couple of minutes. He'd lived to see his dad's smile of encouragement, his pride. "And then, toward the end of that first season, my dad came into the tent with me, while I waited for my next run, and he said, You know, it just occurred to me...I don't think anybody remembered to let you in on the joke."

"The joke?"

"Yeah. He said, See all those kids? They think they're here to win. But nobody told them that it doesn't matter whether you win or lose. It's about doing the tricks over and over until they become as natural to you as walking. That doesn't happen in your first year or even your second or third. So, take winning off the table. We're not here to bring home medals. We're here to get you experience. Quit thinking about winning and focus on getting the tricks right. The rest'll come naturally."

"That's a really great thing to say."

"It was perfect. From that moment on, I focused on the tricks."

"And the next season you began winning?"

"No. I didn't win right away. It was gradual. I started placing and, eventually, I took home the medals. But my dad never rewarded me for winning. He commented on my style and my technique." He went quiet, letting his feelings for his dad fill him up.

He missed having his dad around for advice. For companionship. He'd taken for granted that his dad would always be around…he wished he hadn't done that.

Wished he'd been able to hug him before he'd left that morning. To tell him how much he loved him.

He'd never get that chance, and that was tough to live with.

As hard as he tried to suppress it, sorrow spilled over, blurring his vision and making it hard to swallow. He gave it a moment to subside. "Everyone thinks I was devastated about the Olympics itself." His voice came out a little rough, so he waited for the hard knot in his throat to stop hurting.

And he fucking liked that Rosie sat there quietly, all still and peaceful, giving him the room he needed to pull himself together. "But it wasn't that. I just wanted to give him something back. I was a kid. It's not like I had anything to give him." He grabbed a napkin and swiped across his mouth. "He was there for us, came to all our competitions, took us freeriding on the sickest mountains in the world. I mean, he taught us how to be men. How to live with honor and integrity." Fuck, what was happening to him? His skin was so damn hot he wanted to tear his shirt off. "In any event, I wanted the medal so he could see it in the trophy case and know that everything he'd given up for us had paid off."

"I obviously didn't know your dad, but from the way you describe him, it sounds like the best gift you could give him is to become a good man. The medals were just to keep you focused and driven. He didn't care if you won them or not."

"That's actually a good point." Brodie never talked about this shit with anyone, but since he'd started, he might as well go on. He picked up a plastic knife and tapped it on the table. "Sometimes I think…I just wish he could see us now. A lot has changed in the four years since he's been gone. I think he'd be proud as hell of Will. To your point, my brother's won more medals in freestyle skiing than anyone in the world, but it's the way he dropped everything to raise our half-sister that would make my dad proud." He gave her a smile. "So, yeah, you're right about that."

"Is it all right if I ask about your mother?"

"Sure. There's not much to say, though. She hasn't been in our lives in years." He tapped the knife. "Which goes back to how I got injured in the first place. When I was nine, my brothers and I went night skiing. I messed up and had to get Life-Flighted to a hospital in Utah. Right after that, my mom took me to New York City for physical therapy. She never came back to Wyoming."

She looked appalled. "Why not?"

"My mom's a New Yorker. She met my dad at Stanford —a university in California. When they graduated, he hit it big in venture capital, and they lived the high life in San Francisco. But, after she kept popping out boys, my dad moved us back here, where he grew up. My mom hated it."

"Okay, but her sons lived here."

"She didn't like us much." It sounded weird to say it out loud. Parents were supposed to love their kids.

"That's…I don't even know what to say about that. She lost out on knowing some of the most amazing people I've ever met."

He sat forward. "But, see, that's my point. We're good

people because of my dad. My mom had nothing to do with it."

"Wait, so, what happened in New York? You obviously didn't stay there."

This was the part he hated thinking about. "Right after I got out of the hospital, she took me and my younger brothers there so I could get the right kind of therapy, and when she figured out she couldn't handle us any better in the city than she had in the Tetons she sent us home."

"Hang on. Will's older, right?"

He nodded.

"So…you're not saying she left him behind, are you?"

"Yeah." He gave an awkward laugh. "It's a pretty shitty story. From her perspective, Will was a hellion, and she couldn't control him. From my dad's perspective, she didn't want to be a parent. She wanted Will, the oldest, to keep us in line. And when he didn't, she got pissed."

"I can't imagine how he processed the fact that his own mother left him behind. What a terrible thing to do to a child."

"Yeah, and he heard her say it, too. He felt like shit the night I got injured, blamed himself. So, he went to see how I was doing, and he heard my parents going at it. My mom basically threatened my dad, saying if he didn't send Will to boarding school, she'd leave. My dad said there was nothing wrong with him. He was a normal boy, and that maybe she should try being a better mom. The next day, she packed up me and brothers and took off."

"How long did you live in New York?"

"We were gone a year." A year, where it was just Will and his dad. "My brother was eleven." Gazing out at his beloved mountain, the sun setting on its peaks, Brodie tapped the knife again. "I was her favorite."

"It was that obvious?"

"Oh, no. She told me." He shook his head. "All the time. She'd given up on Will, so I was next in line to control my brothers. She used my injury as a way to manipulate me."

"How did she do it…like, what would she say?"

"She'd tell me, if I stayed with my dad, I'd never walk right again. That she was the only one who cared enough to make sure I got the right care, that she loved me the most because I was the most intelligent, the most well-behaved, and that if I'd just keep my brothers from acting out, she could come home and we'd be a family."

"No offense, but she sounds horrible."

"No offense taken. Like I said, we don't really have much to do with her. It all fell to shit, though, when my brothers and I wanted to play hockey on the iced-over pond in Central Park. Crashed right through." He smiled at the recollection. They were completely fine, but paramedics had taken them to the hospital, and their mom had come stomping in, pissed as hell. "She sent us home after that." Here was the tricky part. He never talked about this time in his life, but somehow…he couldn't stop the flow of words. "I assumed we were all going home—including her—but she wasn't packing. And, every time I asked about it, she'd say she was busy, that she had a project to finish up. Which, if you know my mom, is horseshit. The only project I ever saw her work on was making sure she was on the list for the latest 'it' handbag. Finally, when it came time to get on the plane, I said I wouldn't go unless she came with us, and she swore she'd come as soon as she closed up the apartment. Of course, she didn't, so I kept pestering her."

"It's hardly pestering, Brodie. Your mom should've come home."

"You know those regrets that hit you while you're taking a shower? Slam you in the middle of the night and wake you up so hard there's no going back to sleep? That's one of mine. The way I kept after her. I got so damn worked up." He could remember it clearly, harassing her on the phone.

But you said you're coming.
When?
Are you coming for my birthday?

That one was the worst. With each month that went by, each fresh batch of excuses given, he'd grown more anxious. Each call became more aggressive, more insistent. And, then, with his birthday approaching, she'd sworn she would come. He'd believed her.

"When did you give up on her?"

"My eleventh birthday. I wore her down until she promised she'd come. My dad even showed me her airline ticket on his laptop." *She's coming, son. And she's got a big surprise for you.* "Like an asshole, I got all geared up for it. Cleaned my room, made sure Marcella had the right kind of food in the fridge. Made my dad promise not to do the things that made my mom crazy."

"Like what?" she said with a soft smile.

"Like hiding out in his office. I told him he couldn't work while she was home. She always complained that he looked like Sasquatch, so I made him shave and laid out the clothes he could wear while she was in town. And he did it. Went along with everything. I had everything set up just how she'd like it."

"And she didn't come." Her voice carried the weight of disgust. "Your mother sucks."

"From the mouths of princesses…"

She looked at him thoughtfully. "You know, I had it all wrong."

"You had what wrong?"

"You. I thought you didn't follow through because you'd had such enormous expectations for the Olympics, but it's not that."

"You still trying to figure me out?"

This time she didn't smile. She grasped his hand. "It was your mom. You put yourself out there—begged her to love you, to be the mom you guys deserved—and she let you down."

Her indignation poured like water on the dry, cracked patch of memories he'd long ago abandoned. He didn't want to fertilize the old wounds, so he tried to pull his hand away.

But she wouldn't let go. "You were a pure, innocent little boy, filled with love and kindness…and, as you Americans like to say, piss and vinegar." She smiled. "And your mom crushed your spirit."

No. No one had that much control over him. "I think I turned out okay."

"You turned out great, but that doesn't excuse her monstrous behavior towards her children. I feel like the one thing we all have in common is that none of us gets through life unscathed. No matter what circumstance we're born into, life throws stuff at us, and it puts kinks in our souls." She smoothed her hand on his forearm. "Your mother put a kink in your ability to trust people. I think she made it hard for you to put your whole heart into anything ever again, because it hurt too much to be let down."

"Yeah, my mom's a piece of work." He wanted to deny

it, wanted to punch the words right out of his brain, but Rosie was right. His mom might not have "crushed his spirit," but she had shut down a whole side of him. "We were better off without her. We had my dad, my uncle, and Marcella—she runs the house and was, basically, our stand-in mom."

"I'm glad you had her."

"You done eating?"

"Oh, of course." She got up and started gathering the take-away containers.

"Not rushing you. I want to take you somewhere."

"Right now?"

"Yep." *Timing's perfect.* "By the time we reach the cliff, it'll be dark, and you can see the valley all lit up."

"I'd like that."

Her phone rang, and he saw the name *Marcel.* "You gotta take that?"

"No." She silenced it. "I'm on vacation from reality."

Her words punched him in the gut.

For a moment there, he'd been lulled into that weird space with her, where he felt like…like they belonged together. *Whatever that means.* But she didn't live here. Would never live here. In a few weeks, she'd go back to her country and resume her life as a princess.

Which was just the reminder he needed to focus on his own work.

It was past time to be the man who follows through.

"I think this is my favorite smell in the world." She scanned the forest. "Pine and dusty earth, sage, and a hint of sweetness from the flowers."

Brodie watched her profile, as she tipped her head

back and closed her eyes. "What's it like for you, as a perfumer? You must notice every smell out there."

"I do. In perfume school, we had to memorize five hundred scents. Three hundred and fifty are synthetic, and the other hundred and fifty are natural. So, yes, I *am* trained to pick up everything."

"And what do you smell right now?"

"Well, in this mountain perfume, the first thing that hits my nose is sage. That's the top note. The heart—that's the middle note, the foundation of the scent—is the wild-flowers, whatever deliciously manly soap you use, and something that's just unique to you. I've noticed it before, and it…I don't know how to describe it, but it just *connects* with me on the deepest level. Gets me all stirred up."

"Rosie…" His tone held warning.

"What? You asked what I smell."

"I didn't ask if it turned you on."

"Sorry if you can't handle our 'chemistry.'" Grinning, she gave him a little shove.

Why did he find this woman so adorable? "You know, you're awfully fancy for a science geek." Her complexity was so much of her appeal. On the surface, she was stunningly beautiful, elegant, and refined, and yet underneath she had an insatiable curiosity, an unexpected awkwardness in social situations, and a mind that fired on all cylinders twenty-four seven.

Sometimes he felt so damn lucky that she'd stumbled into his life.

"Aw. You're such a lady's man. You always know just what to say."

At the bend in the road of the Bowie Pass, he led her to the vista that looked out over Jackson Hole. They'd timed it just right, as the sun was about to slip behind the Gros Ventres Mountains to the east. At the edge of the cliff, she stood right beside him, slipping her arm through his, as easily as if she'd done it a hundred times.

And in this private, quiet moment, just the two of them, it almost felt like she had.

"This is gorgeous." Her voice came out a whisper of awe. "Thank you, Brodie. For the best day I've had in forever."

His heart lurched and started beating too fast—like he'd just tripped on the stairs. It almost felt like a panic attack. It wasn't, of course. *Everything's fine.* And, yet, he couldn't catch his breath.

"Figured you could use a day of fun. Soon as your stuff gets here, you're going to be busy. We've got a lot to get done in a short amount of time."

When she pulled her arm away, he regretted sounding so cold and…gruff.

Fuck that. He wasn't sorry at all. This chumminess was just another way to avoid focusing on what mattered. Like Owl Hoot. Instead of putting together his proposal for the board members, he'd spent the day with Rosie.

"Besides, I'm going away this weekend." The words came out fast and hard, like he was hacking them up. But he didn't have a choice. They couldn't keep doing this, acting like they were dating.

"You are? Where are you going?"

"Vanessa and I are going away." She'd called him last night to let him know about a house she'd heard about, made entirely from renewable materials. Said she was glad he'd postponed the build because she wanted to take a look at it this weekend. He'd told her he couldn't go, but that was because Rosie had just gotten back from St. Christophe, and he'd wanted to be with her.

But it has to stop. "To Bozeman. There's a house she wants to show me." But instead of feeling right about his decision, he felt uneasy. Ever since the princess had come into his life, he hadn't felt right in his own skin.

All the more reason to go away with Vanessa. He felt like himself around her.

"That sounds wonderful." She sounded sad, and that made him feel like shit. Wandering away from him, she reached down to pick up a pine cone.

He wished he hadn't hurt her, but...*come on.* They had to stop this game, the push-pull of attraction they'd both agreed they wouldn't act on.

So, no, he'd done the right thing. For both of them. She'd figure that out.

Lifting the pine cone to her nose, she inhaled. "It actually works out great for me." She shot him a look. "Since I've got a date with a hot cowboy tomorrow night."

Chapter Fourteen

THIS IS MY HAPPY PLACE.

For the base note, Rosalina added vanilla extract. *Hm, what else?* She reached for the ylang ylang oil and poured some in. Closing her eyes, she breathed in the combination…it wasn't quite right, not full enough. Maybe she'd add lavender. She found the jar of essential oil and poured in the heart note, loving its soothing scent. Now, for the top note—

An image flew up in her mind, like a sudden rainstorm, splattering the windshield, blurring her view. Brodie and Vanessa. Laughing as they drove down the highway. The vision cut deep into her heart, the sting so painful she had to set down the jar.

Stop it.

He's not yours.

He can never be yours.

She couldn't live in Calamity, and no one as wild and rugged and free-spirited as Brodie could survive in St. Christophe as part of the royal family.

The reminder eased the pain. *Focus on what you're here*

for. Your business. Your joy. Okay, the top note. Neroli oil? But she pressed her hand to her heart, because words had no real power over her heart.

Is that what Marcel felt for Fabiana?

Which made her wonder…what if she'd met Brodie in St. Christophe? If they'd worked together on a business at home, would she have felt this same wild attraction? Would she have snuck into closets for make-out sessions?

She'd never know. But one thing she knew for sure, Brodie would never sext with an engaged woman. He'd never let it get that far.

"Hello? Rosie?" Knox Holliday strode into the bunkhouse with her long, wavy hair and bright smile. Everything about the designer screamed flash, style, and confidence. "Am I too late?" She held out the dress from Pretty in Pink.

"Not at all." *Wait—what time is it?* The smile fell away, as she glanced at the rooster clock over the sink. "I can't believe I lost track of time."

"Oooh, it smells so good in here," another woman said. The vivacious blonde had been making goo-goo eyes in the bar at the oldest brother, Will. "What'cha got cooking?"

"Can we come in?" A third woman came in, the brunette who'd been cuddled up with the youngest brother.

"Please do." She headed toward them with her hand out. "I'm Rosie. It's so nice to meet you."

"We've been dying to meet the woman who's got Brodie's attention," the brunette said. "I'm Callie, and this is Delilah."

She shook both their hands. "It's lovely to meet you

both, but I'm sorry to say, Brodie and I are just business partners."

"Trust me when I say, you're way more than that," Delilah said.

"He's letting you live here," Callie said.

"He doesn't let anyone into his lair," Knox said.

"Well, he's off on a romantic three-day weekend with his girlfriend, so maybe he's changed."

"If you mean Vanessa," Callie said. "She's his architect. And, as much as she'd like to be more, she's not his girlfriend."

That little tickle of hope? She crushed it under her heel. Because it didn't matter what they felt for each other. She was on borrowed time here.

Would you listen to yourself? On borrowed time? God, her parents were fighting the battle of their lives, and she was wringing her hands over some guy.

You're here to work, period.

"I'll tell you how I know exactly what he thinks of her," Callie said. "He didn't invite her to Knox and Gray's wedding."

"I didn't even know they were a thing," Knox said.

"Uh, you've been a little preoccupied," Delilah said. "She just launched her online wedding gown atelier. It's a big deal."

"I'll bet. She made me the most gorgeous wedding gown I've ever seen." *And I won't be wearing it.* For the first time, she could honestly say she was over the shock of Marcel's betrayal.

Which is pretty sad. But it did drive home how wrong the marriage would have been.

She took the pretty sundress from Knox. "Thank you for fixing this. I love it so much."

"You want to try it on right now?" Knox asked. "What time's your date getting here?"

"Oh, I'm meeting him in town. At Sweet Baby Jane's Tavern."

"That's smart," Delilah said. "You don't want to be alone with him in the middle of nowhere."

"Says the New Yorker," Callie said. "Calamity's super safe, but you're right, it's pretty isolated out here."

"Also," Rosalina said. "I don't really know him. We didn't talk much at the bar the other night."

"Does Brodie know you're going on a date tonight?" Callie asked.

"He does. And he doesn't care because he's driving to Bozeman, where he'll check into his hotel room and get naked with his *girlfriend*." The hanger perched on one finger, she headed off to her bedroom to try on the dress.

"Not his girlfriend," Callie said in a sing-song voice.

Rosalina liked the sound of that.

Except, it didn't really matter what he and Vanessa were to each other, did it? They'd still be having sex.

Probably having it right now. She'd seen the way Vanessa had her hands all over him, rubbing his back, digging into the pocket of his jeans. Her seduction game might've been a little forced, but it was strong.

Jealousy got a firm grip on her stomach and twisted.

Because no matter what box Brodie wanted to put Vanessa in, the woman was getting him all to herself for the whole weekend.

And Rosalina wanted that.

Too much.

"This is going to be so much fun." Vanessa reached for his hand on the console. "I'm so happy to be away from work and all the distractions. Oh, did I tell about the Hanson project? I got it. I can't believe it. Between the work for Owl Hoot, your house, and the Hanson's place, I'm going to be able to go out on my own by my target date."

Even though the boulevard was pretty empty at this hour, he pulled out his hand to grasp the wheel. "That's great."

"Dinner was fun. I haven't been in Bozeman in ages, so I had to look up some restaurants. I think I picked a good one, don't you?"

He didn't take his eyes off the road, but he felt her watching him. Wanting something from him. And it was tearing him up. "You picked well. Thank you for putting in the effort."

Because he wasn't thinking about Vanessa. He was thinking about Rosie. Not all of her supplies had come, so she'd continued working on other scents. He'd like to be there for that, see her process.

"Did you like your leg of lamb? You didn't eat much. Which is totally not like you. You usually scarf down your meat, whatever I leave over, and then eye the plates on all the tables around us."

No, I don't. But whatever. She was trying to make conversation, keep things fun. It wasn't her fault her forced cheer was wearing on him. "I've got a lot on my mind."

"I know you do. You usually only work on one thing at a time, but you've got so many balls in the air. Why don't we put off the house? Get Owl Hoot squared away. Between the Outfitters and the triathlon, you're not going to be able to think about anything else."

Except Rosie. He couldn't stop thinking about her.

Was she on her date right now? It was only six. As soon as they'd gotten into town, they'd checked into the hotel. Since he hadn't wanted to be alone with Vanessa in a room that didn't have much more than a king-size bed, they'd gone for an early dinner.

What would Rosie wear for her date? He thought about her hair, all mahogany and sleek. She was so regal… and yet she'd shredded on that glacier. He smiled at the memory.

"Look at that. I got an actual smile." Vanessa nudged him. "So, that's what we'll do. We'll put off the house while you focus on Owl Hoot. It won't take you long to get things going, and then you can hand it off to someone else, and we can get back to the house. It'll give me time to look into eco-friendly materials."

He didn't like the way she took ownership of his plans. "You can do the research if you want, but I'm not committing to anything. The house isn't a priority right now."

"I know. That's what I just said." She tapped her fingers on her thigh in rhythm with the song playing softly on the radio. "You know, I love how intuitive you are. Where other people have to-do lists out the wazoo, you keep it all organized in your head. It's like you've got the perfect executive assistant in your subconscious who delivers ideas at exactly the right moments."

He cracked a grin. "That pretty much nails it."

"See? I know you." She rubbed his biceps. "So, what's the top priority?"

"Getting this project launched with Rosie before she leaves." *Rosie. Fuck.* His chest got tight, thinking of her getting ready for her date.

"Right, but that one's mostly on her. I can set her up with a graphic artist to handle the packaging. One less thing for you to think about." As he turned into the hotel parking lot, she leaned across the console and sifted her fingers through his hair. "I'm so glad we're doing this, Brodie. Just the two of us. If we'd stayed in town, we wouldn't be able to get away from work."

But we haven't gotten away from work. That's all we talk about.

With Rosie, he talked about everything. Including the topics he'd always had on lock-down.

She removed her hand to unbuckle her seatbelt. "I'm glad we're in early. We can just relax...get to the good stuff."

"I'm using Jinx for the packaging, but thanks for the offer." He'd said it to make a point—she was his architect., not his business or life partner. But, now that he'd said it out loud, he realized it was a good idea.

"Doesn't Jinx do custom paint work for motorcycles?"

"He's an artist. Before his dad died and he dropped out of school, he was studying at Parson's in New York. Not sure how he got into bikes, but I know from Skylar that he still does art."

"There's something going on between those two, which I didn't see coming from a mile away. I wouldn't think she's his type at all." She looked at him like an idea had just popped into her head. "Hey, what exactly is your type?"

Funny, Brodie hadn't really thought about it. "I don't think I have one." He'd been with all kinds of women. For him, it wasn't about beauty or a certain body shape. He wasn't specifically a legs or an ass man. He was drawn to... personality. A smile. That rare and inexplicable spark.

With Rosie...damn. It was like the Fourth of July. He thought about the mechanical bull. How, after she'd fallen, he'd expected her to go back to her table and pour another drink. Instead she'd insisted on trying it again. He liked her determination, her passion. Her grit blended with her innate elegance was such a fucking turn-on.

Another thing he really liked was that, even though she felt tremendous loyalty to her family, she stuck to her guns. She wouldn't compromise herself for some archaic belief system.

He admired the hell out of that.

Emotions swirled in him, thick and hot.

Vanessa had a hand on the door, legs turned, ready to get out, when she cut him a look. "How come you're not turning off the engine?" She swiveled back into her seat. "What're you thinking about?"

Rosie.

His pulse kicked up hard and fast. He didn't have much time left with her, so what was he doing in Bozeman with another woman? Vanessa was beautiful. She was smart and ambitious.

But she didn't excite him. She didn't move the needle.

There were no sparks, and there never would be.

He wasn't the kind of man who settled. He'd rather be alone than with a woman who didn't get him fired up.

Through the windshield, he took in the hotel. And, suddenly, he knew spending a night with Vanessa was wrong. It wasn't where he needed to be. "Vanessa…"

"Don't say it." She closed her eyes and let out a breath. "God, Brodie, I'm trying so hard."

That's the problem. "It shouldn't be this much work."

"No, it shouldn't." When she opened her eyes, she gave him a sad smile. "I like you so much…well, I think I like the idea of you. I would love to be part of your family. I see you guys at the Tavern or the diner, your brothers with their girlfriends, and you guys just do everything so hard. You play hard, and you love hard. And…I really want you to love me like that."

"I don't know about the love hard part for me. I don't think I'm like my brothers that way." Except for Rosie, but she didn't count because he couldn't have her.

"I think you are. One day, you're going to turn all that intensity on a woman, and she's going to be the luckiest girl in the world." She gazed out the windshield. "But it's not going to be me."

Brodie drove fast, the forest a blur of green and brown on either side of him. He made it back to Calamity in three and a half hours and dropped Vanessa at her condo. Only as he drove through town did he slow down. Was Rosie somewhere here on her date?

He thought about parking, storming into every bar, the Tavern, the diner, the ice cream parlor. He wanted to see her, knock the cowboy on his ass. He wanted to bring her home, so it was just the two of them. Just how he liked it best.

But he wasn't an asshole. She was loving her freedom here, and she wanted to date.

Besides, what exactly did he want from her? He might be racing home to be with her, but nothing had changed. Unless *he* wanted to be her hot cowboy hookup.

He wanted more than that, but there wasn't much more he could have. Maybe just to be with her until she left. Would she go for that? If he promised her it wouldn't compromise their long-term working relationship?

Images assaulted him—his lips on her soft, sweet-scented skin, her hands grabbing his ass and squeezing. Excitement tore across him. Fuck, he wanted that woman.

Maybe he could bring it up. Come up with a contract that made sure both parties got what they wanted, and no one got hurt.

It was pretty much impossible to get hurt, since they both knew ahead of time there was an end-date.

He turned onto the ranch driveway, and as he waited for the gate to open, he nabbed his phone out of the cup holder. Scrolled through a bunch of messages that could wait till tomorrow. Nothing from Rosie. *Damn.*

He passed through and watched his speed as he veered left at the fork toward the bunkhouse. Had she kissed the cowboy yet? It was only ten-thirty. They were probably dancing, drinking.

Would she get drunk around the guy? Would the asshole try and fuck her if she was?

Yellow lights pierced the darkness. *She's home.* Maybe she'd bailed on her date early.

Fuck, yes. He accelerated. Once at the bunkhouse he parked, grabbed his overnight bag, and jogged toward the door.

He'd known that guy wasn't right for her. Brodie could tell just by his smirk that he was too superficial. He didn't go deep. Rosie did, though.

You don't need deep for a hookup.

Brodie threw open the door. "Rosie?"

Her head popped up from the couch, hair all tousled, eyes wide in surprise. One hand clamped her blouse shut where it gaped at her bra.

Adrenaline assaulted him. *What the fuck?*

She pushed a dude in a blue and white-checkered shirt off her. "*Brodie.*" She scrambled to her feet. "What're you doing here? I thought you were gone for the weekend? I mean, it's your house. Of course, you're welcome here. I just...I thought you weren't coming home until Monday."

Her date lifted off the couch, tucked his shirt back into his jeans, and then reached out a hand. "Hey, man. Dusty."

Brodie gave him a chin nod, his gaze slicing over to Rosie. Her cheeks were pink, and her mouth looked puffy from some other man's kisses.

She tried to button her shirt, but she kept fumbling, so he cut around the couch and batted her hands away to finish the job. His fingers were too big, and he wound up skipping a hole and popping off a button. She gazed up at him, and the connection struck the center of his heart like a fist, the jolt reverberating throughout his body.

"I made it worse." He shook his head, fighting a smile and abandoning the project. "I'll leave you to it." He grabbed his bag. "I'll stay at the main house tonight. Which is good. I can have breakfast with Ruby. Maybe I'll take her on an early hike. Have our breakfast on the ridge. She loves that. So, you go on and…" *Shut up and get out of here*.

"Oh, my goodness, no." Her clap of laughter was completely out of character. "You don't have to go anywhere. This is your house, and besides Dusty and I—" She giggled, waving her hand in front of her mouth. "I'm sorry. I'm…" Then, she doubled over, and Brodie couldn't keep the grin off his face. "Give me a second. I just…I'm only laughing, because I'm so embarrassed. I've never been caught making out before." She fanned her face, now shiny with perspiration. "Oh, God. I feel like I'm fifteen, and my dad just came home. Not that you're my dad. I just—" Another set of giggles had her reaching for the arm of the couch. "Okay, okay. I'll stop. Dusty, I'm so sorry. I think our date's over. Let me walk you out."

Giving them time alone to say goodbye, Brodie tossed his bag against the wall by the hallway and went into the kitchen to grab a water. He could hear Rosie and her date murmuring.

Were they making plans for tomorrow night? He didn't want her seeing Dusty again. He wanted her for himself. But he couldn't have that. The only contract she wanted to sign was for their partnership.

He had to face it. *This business might be the only one she ever gets to run—and if that means she doesn't want to sleep with me, then…*

Fuck. Then, he'd still spend time with her. Because he wanted to be with her more than he wanted to be with anyone else. So, if they could only be business partners— friends—he'd take it. He'd take whatever she wanted to give.

The door shut, and a moment later she came into the kitchen, the blouse still askew from the way he'd buttoned it. "I am *so* sorry you came home to that."

"Not your fault. I told you I'd be gone." He poured himself some water. "Should've texted you." *Before flying like a bat out of hell to get home to you.* "Looked like the date was going well."

"Actually, I was about two minutes from ending it. It, uh, escalated pretty quickly."

His glass froze in front of his chin. "What's that mean?" He took in her messy hair, the red lips.

"No, nothing bad. Just that…I pictured the evening going very differently. I was supposed to meet him in town, but he said he'd rather come over, that he had a little picnic for us. Well, he didn't say *picnic*. I don't remember his exact words, but I took them to mean picnic. I figured he'd come over, we'd open a bottle of wine, chat for a while. Instead, he brought a six-pack, cracked open a beer, slapped his knee, and said, "Come on, girl. Let's get this party started." Her exaggerated southern accent made him smile.

"No wonder you were laughing so hard."

"Exactly. It was the ridiculousness of the whole night, not just that you walked in on us."

"If it was so ridiculous, what were you doing rolling around on the couch with him?" Oh, damn, he shouldn't have said that. *It's none of your business what she does.*

"I'll tell you exactly why. Because no guy in St. Christophe would ever come over, set me on his knee, and start making out with me, and I liked that. It was thrilling…for about five seconds. But, then…" She crinkled her nose.

"What?"

"He didn't smell right."

"Body odor?"

She shook her head. "Oh, no. Nothing like that."

"Wet dog?"

"What? *No.*"

Her grin, the sparkle in her eyes, made his chest tight. "What then?"

"Like clothes that've been worn a couple times in a row."

"Isn't that body odor?"

"No, it's kind of an oily…well, not oil exactly. It's just a particular smell. And he must've had steak for dinner because there was a hint of roasted meat in his shirt. And he just tasted nasty."

"Bitter? Like tobacco?"

"I don't know what tobacco tastes like. It was weird because it was mint, which you'd think would be fresh, but it was also bitter."

"Chew. He tucks a pinch of tobacco between his gums and his mouth." Brodie would bet the guy had spit it out right when he got out of his truck.

"It was gross. But, also, I didn't like the way he kissed."

He kept his mouth shut, because anything he might say would come out wrong. *Possessive.* She didn't need that from him. From anyone.

"Fortunately, we'd only just started."

"He almost got your shirt off." Which pissed him off. Unless they were swept away by passion, the guy should've taken his time with someone as special as Rosie. Made sure she was feeling it.

"I know, but I thought I'd give it another minute to see if it would…you know, ignite or whatever." She leaned against the counter. "But, now that he's gone, and I feel so relieved, I realize I was doing it for the wrong reason."

"And what reason's that?"

"Marcel wanted excitement. He got off on sneaking around." And there was that sadness again, dragging on her pretty features. "Whenever I'm alone, I keep playing their conversation in my head."

"What conversation?" He set the glass down. "You caught them in bed?"

"I caught them in a closet. My assistant was begging him to break it off with me so they could be together, and he said he was still going to marry me, that he loved me… But it wasn't their words that got to me. It was the drama. My assistant, who's the most calm and rational woman you'll ever meet, was tortured and emotional and…"

"Passionate."

"Yes." The word shot out of her mouth like a dart. "Exactly. And even Marcel, who's only ever been polite with me, sounded like he was all torn up."

Those fuckers had done a number on her. "So, tonight you were looking for payback? With the cowboy?"

She shook her head. "It's not about that. I wanted to know if I'm capable of igniting." She faced the counter, moving around a few baggies and shifting some beakers. "What if I'm just flat? Unemotional?" She glanced at him over her shoulder. "What if I'm not a passionate person?"

"Fuck that. I've never met anyone so passionate." He picked up one of the beakers. "You light up when you talk about this stuff."

"Yeah, but that's work. It's not...*sex*. It's not bodies and hearts and minds. I love my work, but I want to be wild in bed. I want..." She shrugged, tightening the cap on a small bottle. "Never mind. It's stupid. Do you want to see what I was working on?"

She reached for a dark blue glass jar, when he caught her arm. "What do you want, Rosie?"

The way she looked at him made him feel like she was searching to see if she could trust him with her deepest secrets. *You can*, his eyes told her. *I want to be that man for you.*

He saw the moment she relaxed. "It's not so much that I want to be wild in bed. I want to *feel* wild. I want sex to yank me under." She let out a rough exhalation. "That desperation, that yearning I heard in my friend's voice? I want to feel that. But I realized, after about five minutes with Dusty, that it's not something that just happens. I can't close my eyes and feel some guy's hands on me and suddenly ignite because I want to. Honestly, I don't know how people do it—have fun, crazy hookups—because I didn't feel anything except annoyance. And he didn't do anything wrong. He's good-looking. He's got a nice body. But there just weren't any…"

"Sparks." He got it. "He's not right for you."

"You say that like I should just wait for the right guy, but it's not going to work like that. When I go home, I'm going to become marriage-minded. It won't be Marcel, but it'll be someone I meet in the not-too-distant future. And I'm so afraid of settling again. Maybe it's just the pressure I feel to get everything in before I leave here, but I'm terrified of going home, getting numb again, and settling for another guy I don't have any sparks with, and God, Brodie, I just want to feel it once, you know? Just once, I want to have headboard-banging, electrifying sex."

The way she looked at him, soft mouth and lazy eyes, made him think her thoughts matched his. *Bet I'd feel it with you.* But, then, with a wave of her hand, she broke the mood. "So, what happened? Aren't you supposed to be off on a romantic weekend?"

"Romantic? No, I told you. Vanessa wanted to show me a house in Bozeman."

Rosie gave him a look that said, *Really? You're that clueless?*

"Yeah, I mean, obviously she hoped for more. But we addressed it, and we agreed we're going to stick to a business relationship."

"Is she devastated?"

"Devastated? Nah. She doesn't want me. She just likes the idea of marrying a Bowie."

"Well, I can see why." He caught her wistful tone, and he hated what her life must be like in St. Christophe, the constant scrutiny, the limitations. The weight of a future that didn't fit her.

She would come alive in Calamity. She'd become her best self here.

"Have you ever been in love?" She unscrewed the cap on the blue bottle and sniffed it, her facial muscles relaxing.

"And we have a winner."

She smiled. "We do."

He could read her so well now. Awareness flashed like sunlight glinting off a mirror. That's what he liked about her. The way his mom had played him, he'd bought her lies. *That* was why he didn't trust. But Rosie was transparent—and it made him feel safe with her.

"So, have you?" she asked. "Ever been in love?"

"Nope."

"You don't want what your brothers have?"

He remembered what Vanessa had said. *You play hard, and you love hard.* The strangest sensation crept over him, like a wand sweeping over his body and activating each cell, until his whole body vibrated.

I could love Rosie that hard.

What a fucking revelation.

The reason he hadn't understood his brothers' choices was because he hadn't met Rosie. "A week ago, I would've said no. But now I think I get what they have. It's not about settling down. It's about meeting one particular woman. The right one." *You.* "And somehow I don't think that happens all that often."

"I don't think so, either. And that's what scares me." She screwed the cap back on and set the bottle down. "You know what? Don't even listen to me. I'm all messed up because you walked in on me while a cowboy was feeling me up." She headed out of the kitchen. "Well, I'll leave you be."

"You don't have to go on my account."

"You certainly didn't come home to hear me whine about my life."

He had to hold his arm to his side, close his hand into a fist. He had to let her walk away because...why would he ask her to stay?

But, then, at the last minute, right before she turned to go down the hall, he said. "You sleepy?"

"Not at all. Why?"

He checked the rooster clock. They'd make it in time for the second showing. "Come on. Let's have some fun."

Chapter Fifteen

Rosalina read the menu on the wall behind the counter. Hot dogs, cheeseburgers, nachos, sodas, candy. "The nobility could learn a thing or two from you about date nights."

He'd taken her to the Ponderosa Drive-in movie theater, and she hadn't had this much fun in ages.

Wrapping an arm around her waist, he pulled her against his chest. "For the record, I don't date. But, for you, I'd make an exception." His voice, right in her ear, came out gravelly and one-hundred percent grade A sex.

Mm, he smelled good. She pressed her nose into his shirt and inhaled.

"How you doin' down there?"

She laid her palm on his chest. "Bergamot with pear, sunflower seed oil, aloe...pine." When he chuckled, she felt the rumble against her hand.

"Damn, if you were my girl, I'd probably have to shower three times a day just to make sure I don't stink."

"It's pretty fascinating, isn't it? We each have our own biochemical bouquet, and there's something about yours that excites me." The moment she realized she was talking to him about pheromones, she pulled away. "Oh, my God, I can't believe I just said that."

"I dig your bouquet, too, princess."

She gazed up at him, swimming in a pool of delicious feelings.

"What can I get you?" The young woman behind the counter killed the moment.

Probably for the best. Rosalina straightened. "Um. What should I get?"

"Depends on what you're in the mood for." He pointed to the hot dogs. "You want pork trimmings and mechanically separated chicken with some organ meats thrown in? Or soybean oil tossed with salt and chemicals?"

"Are the pork trimmings stuffed in a sheep's intestine?"

"Yup."

"Tempting. But I'll go for a tub of oil and salt-slathered popped corn instead. And…" She glanced into the candy case. "Let's get one of each." She pointed to the colorful bags of candy made into bite-size pieces.

"One of *each*?" the young woman asked.

Rosie nodded. "I can't remember the last time I had candy."

"Any carbonated water with a shit-ton of sugar and preservatives?" Brodie asked.

Rosalina rolled her eyes. "It's no fun to eat junk food with an athlete. If I came over for dinner at the main house, what would I get?"

"Let's just say we could write our own cookbook for all the ways to use a sweet potato."

After paying, they carried their goodies back to the truck. On the huge movie screen, images from advertisements flashed and flickered, and as they passed cars, she could hear muffled laughter and conversation.

As soon as they climbed inside, Brodie fiddled with the radio dial until he found the right station to hear the movie.

She plucked a few greasy kernels off the top of the bag. "I didn't even ask what we're watching." Popping them in her mouth, she chewed. *Yum.*

"Some James Bond movie."

"Oh, cool." She settled into her seat and reached for the seatbelt.

"You get that we're parked, right? Unless Yellowstone's volcano blows and sends us flying, we'll be stationery the whole time."

She burst out laughing. "I'm dutiful."

He leaned over and released the belt. "And now you're free."

Caught in his gaze, she took in the curve of his sexy lips, the strong lines of his jaw, and the most vividly blue eyes she'd ever seen. She did feel free—freer than any other time in her life. She didn't want the ticking clock of the vote, of her inevitable return to her country.

God, he was *right there.* She lifted a hand to cup his strong jaw. "How come you and Will are clean-cut, and your younger brothers are all long-haired and scruffy?"

"I don't know. Personal preference, I guess."

"I'll bet there's more to it. Like, I'm the dutiful sister. I look the part, whereas my younger sister, she gets to be whatever she wants. And the funniest thing? If my country ever changed the law to a female line of succession, my sister, with her pink-streaked hair and patent leather combat boots, would be the best ruler our country's ever had. Not me."

"You don't want to rule?"

"I think you know the answer to that. I want to make perfume. Literally, that's all I want to do. I love the whole process. I love discovering a flower and turning it into an essential oil. I love mixing ingredients together to come up with a magical scent. I love the way things smell." She scrunched her nose. "Except for the mechanically separated chicken. I didn't love that one." She tore open a bag of candy. "Can I live off popcorn and candy?"

"You can do anything you want."

With the rush of desire flooding her body, making her hot and restless, she knew she had a problem. *My heart only desires one thing.* She was here for such a short time, and she'd never felt this way around anyone before. "Do you mean that literally?"

He swallowed, glancing toward the screen. For a moment, he seemed lost in an epic struggle, and during that battle she held her breath, each second ticking by with excruciating tension. But then he turned back to her and said, "Yes."

She didn't even hesitate, just set the popcorn and candy on the floor of the truck, wiped her hands on her jeans, and cupped his cheeks. And then she kissed him. At first it was awkward—*who just lunges at a guy like this?*— but then her tongue licked his bottom lip, and something in him snapped. His mouth opened, and he took charge.

Vaguely, she was aware of headlights flashing, engines rumbling, and cars pulling in beside them. She loved the tangle of their tongues, the twist of raw need in her belly. Loved the smell of him, the taste, and the heat of his body.

She gripped the back of his neck like she was afraid he'd pull away, his mouth so sensual and hungry it made her burn.

His hand pushed between their bodies, reaching for her breast. *Yes. God.* The way he squeezed her, with so much lust, made her squirm. *More.* She needed more of his hard body pressed against her, so she leaned over the console, desperate to get closer. When she gave a frustrated growl, he flipped it up and slid closer to her. "Yes."

"You didn't want to do this, remember?" He murmured against her mouth, grabbing a fistful of hair to pull her back far enough to see her expression. "You didn't want to mess up our working relationship."

"I know, but I've never felt this before. Didn't even know I could. God, Brodie, *you* make me ignite."

"Fuck, yeah, Rosie." He released her. "Climb into the back."

Grabbing both headrests, she climbed over the console and toppled onto the wide leather seat.

He followed, and the moment he dropped beside her, he got his hands on her hips and dragged her toward him, unbuttoning her jeans and sucking her bottom lip into his mouth.

"Bet you're glad I didn't eat the pork trimmings."

"Gonna feed you my cock in a minute, so it doesn't matter what you ate."

Oh. Oh, God. He made her so crazy. "You could be arrested for talking to the princess like that." She arched her back, desperate to get closer, squirming beneath him.

"Worth it…" He unbuttoned her shirt, spreading it wide, and palmed her breast. "If I get to suck on the prettiest tits I've ever seen."

Tits. Desire beat a wild tattoo through her. She slid her hands under the waistband of his jeans, gripping his ass, and squeezing. He sucked in a breath, his mouth lowering to her breasts. The moment his tongue hit her nipple, her body jerked.

"So fucking sexy." Pulling her into the wet, heat of his mouth, his tongue flicked and swirled.

Sensation spiraled through her, flooding her body with a pleasure she'd never experienced before. Her hips pressed up hard into him, and she ground herself against his hot, thick erection.

"Like that a lot, princess."

His deep voice pulled her out of the haze, making her keenly aware of herself. She was humping him. In the backseat of a car. In a crowded parking lot of a drive-in movie theater in Jackson Hole, Wyoming.

The windows had steamed over, and the scents of leather and Brodie and sex drove her out of her mind.

She brought her hand around to the front of his jeans, desperate to touch him. When she gripped his hard length, he groaned.

"Harder, princess. Don't go easy on me."

She rubbed her palm on him, and God, she needed so much more. "I can't…" Frustration had her on edge. "I need…"

"I know what you need." Batting her hand away, he unzipped her jeans and reached under the elastic of her knickers. His finger parted her curls and tenderly traced her slick folds. "So wet."

"For you, Brodie." She'd never felt like this, like her blood had turned molten, like she was nothing more than a churning pool of desire and need. "Only for you."

And then he brushed over her sensitive nub, and electricity arced through her, making her cry out. His hand went between her legs, caressing, gliding in her slick heat, and she couldn't stand it. The unbearable anticipation, her body's inexorable need to burst. "*Brodie.*"

"You keep saying my name like that, and I'm gonna have to fuck you right here."

"No. Not yet. First, I want you in my mouth." She felt greedy for him. All of him.

He went rigid, his hand faltering. And then his mouth came over hers, and he was kissing her again, like the world was on fire, and he had to take what he could get before they went up in flames. He jerked her jeans down over her hips, spread her thighs, and then his mouth went between her legs.

Bliss burst inside her. Her bottom rose off the seat, as her fingers gripped his hair, pulling hard. "God, Brodie."

He licked her nub, one big hand under her bottom, lifting her to his mouth. He made sounds of hunger, approval, and deep, dark desire. And then a sensation took hold of her—so big and powerful it catapulted her right out of her body—and her hand reached out to the seat-back to brace herself before she burst into a hundred million shards of light. Her hips writhed, her breath caught in her throat, and the orgasm just kept going, fueled by his wicked, unrelenting tongue.

Her knees slammed together, boxing in his head, as she jerked and twisted. She rode the tide of lust as it slowly receded, and she came back into her body. When her bottom dropped back down onto the seat, she let out a whoosh of breath.

Sitting up, Brodie swiped the back of his hand over his mouth. With his jeans undone, his thick erection poked out the waistband of his black boxer briefs.

"Come here." Was that her voice? All hot and sexy and commanding? "I want you in my mouth."

"So the hell do I." He got up on his knees, and she shifted closer, her knees bent, one foot pressed against the door. With a hand on the headrest, Brodie yanked down his briefs. His cock sprang out.

Her mouth literally watered, and she reached for him. "You're the sexiest man I've ever seen."

As she grasped him, he gave a pained expression, and she ran her thumb along the vein under the mushroom-shaped head. His broad shoulders blocked out the dim light from the foggy windows, and his bulging biceps flexed as his fingers dug into the cushion.

She could see he needed release, so she took him into her mouth, licking him from head to root to get him nice and wet.

"Ah, Jesus."

She loved the way he trembled, so she sucked him deep into her mouth, letting her tongue slide all over him. He was gasping, his powerful hips making short thrusts. She could tell he was holding back, letting her choose the rhythm.

She didn't want that, so she pulled him out of her mouth. "I've had a lifetime of boring sex, where all I did was get the guy off. I want more, Brodie. Pretend like you feel totally comfortable with me, and just be yourself."

"Don't have to pretend." He grabbed his cock and prodded her mouth open with it. "Now, suck me."

A sharp wave of desire crashed over her, and she took him in, as far as she could.

Brodie started pumping, his thighs shaking, as he watched his cock slide into her mouth. He let out a shuddery breath, before cupping the back of her head and pushing in deeper. "Can you handle that?"

Forcing her throat to relax, she nodded, letting her

tongue flick along his hard length. His eyes rolled back into his head, and he rocked his hips, stuffing his cock as far in her mouth as it could go. She thrilled at the sight of this big, strong, powerful man coming apart at her touch.

"Can I come in your mouth?" That voice. He was on edge. About to lose it.

All she could do was nod, because the way he talked to her turned her reckless. His features pulled in tightly, his hand gripped the back of her head, and then he thrust in hard and stayed in her mouth as he pumped his release down her throat. His head tipped back, and he let out a deep groan.

"Ah, fuck." Exhaling roughly, he eased out. He swatted at her knees, and she sat up, giving him room to crash on the seat beside her. "Damn, princess."

But she didn't have words. The sides of her mouth stung a little where he'd stretched it, and she still tasted him. She was a little stunned, because she'd just had the most amazing sex of her life.

And that sucked so badly.

Because, now that she'd had a taste, she didn't know how she could go back to the bland life she'd had before she met him.

Crashing into the bunkhouse, Brodie kicked the door shut. Not bothering with the lights, he gripped her sexy ass and lifted her, carrying her towards the hallway with their mouths fused.

He might've come less an hour ago, but his body raged with need. He tripped on the edge of the rug.

She laughed, tucking her face into his neck. "Put me down."

"On my bed."

She cupped the back of his neck, drawing him to her, and she whispered, "Let's do it on the couch."

"Fuck, yeah." He'd wanted to take his time with her, kiss every inch of her gorgeous body, make it last as long as possible, but he'd have to do that next time. Because, now, he just needed to get inside her, relieve this pounding, driving need.

The moment he set her down, she pulled the blouse over her head, exposing all that creamy skin, the sexy curve of her waist, and the flare of her hips. She unzipped her jeans, hips swaying with each yank until she stepped out of them. That flash of pink on her toenails made his blood hot.

She glanced up at him, a hint of vulnerability that made him realize he was just standing there, watching her.

Heat rushed up his neck, spreading across his cheeks. *Caught.*

Caught liking her. Liking everything about her.

Shit. Fuck.

He *liked* her.

The way Will liked Delilah.

And Gray liked Knox.

And Fin liked Callie.

He understood liking a woman enough to want to hang out with her exclusively—his future sisters-in-law were awesome—but now he understood what his brothers had given up just to put a ring on it.

Because there wasn't anything he wanted more than to watch Rosie take her clothes off. There wasn't anyone he wanted to be with more than her.

He wanted to watch her bruise petals. Snowboard with her and figure out the logistics of a triathlon.

He wanted to kiss her, and he needed to fuck her into next week.

He wanted everything with Princess Rosalina Anais Isabella Villeneuve.

He reached for her, gentler, his feelings more tender, but when he leaned in for a kiss, she playfully dashed away, heading around the back of the couch. "Take me from behind." Excitement shone in her eyes.

Reality hit him, as jolting as landing on hard-packed snow. This was fun for her. She was getting it out of her system, before she had to head back home and marry out of duty.

And using him to do it.

Of course. He'd known that. She'd just told him a few hours ago.

Even though he'd said he'd take what he could get, he'd gotten carried away. Reaching behind his neck, he pulled his shirt over his head, but his arms felt stiff, heavy. Uncooperative.

This is what she wants. So, give it to her.

Right. He popped the button on his jeans, shoved them down along with his boxers, and stepped out of them. Weird how his bones felt like jelly. *Come on. Give it to her from behind.*

He could give her a few weeks of fun.

Better me than some random guy she meets in a bar.

He headed over to her, but his legs resisted, like trying to fight his way across a river.

She turned around, resting her pink lace-clad ass on the back of the couch. Her hands cupped his jaw. "You okay? Still with me?"

"You bet." Except his voice sounded like he'd dragged it across asphalt. He loved the scent rising off her skin, the strangely pale green eyes that *saw* him. That soft, expressive mouth that had taken his cock with so much enthusiasm.

He had such great discipline, why couldn't he marshal it right now? Give her what she wanted?

"Come here." Standing up, she reached behind his neck. Her fingers sifted through his hair, as she got up on her toes and kissed him. And, oh, fuck, did she kiss him. Sexy, sweet, a slow tangle of tongues.

When her fingers curled into his hair, she moaned into his mouth, and he knew he needed to tell her.

What she meant to him.

What he wanted.

He wanted more kisses that transported him, that made his knees buckle, his heart pound, and his skin burn.

Pulling down her panties and kicking them aside, she moved in close, so their bodies could do a slow, sexy grind.

Tell her. But his words had turned to dust.

He caressed her smooth, warm back, gliding down to the round swells of her ass, and he lifted her, holding her tightly to his painfully hard cock. Her arms and legs wrapped around him, and her silky hair brushed over his arms and chest.

Goosebumps skittered across his skin, and desire thrummed through his body, igniting a fire in his belly. Christ, she smelled so good, felt so right in his arms.

He should give her what she wanted, fuck her from behind while she lifted her ass to him and held onto the back of the couch. That would be hot. But he was drowning in her kisses, this need for her drenching him, making him all soft and loose inside.

Tell her.

In place of words, he carried her down the dark hallway, swallowing her moans, squeezing her ass, and rubbing her wetness all over his cock. Kicking his door open, he carried her to his bed and dropped her onto it.

Grabbing a condom out of the top drawer of his nightstand, he tore it open and started to sheath himself, when she said, "Can I do it? I've never put one on before."

He hated the reminder that she was using him, but...*this is about her.* He wanted her to do it all here. Wanted her to associate all her best times with him.

He handed it to her, and she sat up, scooting to the edge of the bed. With her forehead tense in concentration, she started to stretch it over his dick, but it got stuck and the latex squeezed around his sensitive head.

"Here." He showed her how to pinch the tip. "Unroll it on me."

"But you're so big. Will it fit?"

Her mouth so near his dick made him ache, but he just chuckled. "Yeah, princess. It's the right size. Hurry up and get it on, before I stuff your mouth a second time."

She flicked her gaze up to him, and damn if he didn't love the way she got so worked up over his words. "Okay." She said it all breathy. With her trembling fingers, she still struggled to get the tight opening over his head, so he helped her along, until he had himself fully sheathed.

With a chin nod, he got her to lay down. Eyes heavy with lust, she did as he asked, and he crawled over her. She was so damn pretty.

"Never gonna forget how your hair looks spread over my pillow like that."

"I'm never going to forget how wild you make me feel." She grasped his wrists.

He loved when her words came out like that, all whispery and shaky, like she had too much emotion rumbling under the surface. He nudged her knee, and she spread wider for him. "You ready for me, sweetheart?"

Her eyelids fluttered, and she nodded.

He wondered at the shimmer in her eyes—tears? Hands bracketing her shoulders, he lowered himself, needing to see her face as he entered her. Slowly, he pushed into her hot, slick channel.

Her lips parted, her neck arched, and she was so damn wet, he thrust all the way in. She clutched his back, and those drowsy eyes made him lose it. He pulled back, snapped his hips, and slammed back in.

Jesus.

No one had ever felt so good. The sound of skin slapping, the sight of her breasts bouncing. *Christ.* He wanted it to last forever. He needed more, deeper, harder. *So fucking good.*

He wanted her so damn much…but he couldn't bear showing her everything he was feeling, so he tucked his face into her neck, closing his eyes, and breathing her in. He powered into her, felt the gush of arousal when he tilted his hips and hit her in just the right place.

He needed to come, so he reached between them and stroked her clit, barely able to keep a rhythm. "Gotta come, Rosie. Swear to God, I'm gonna come so fucking hard."

"*Yes.*" Fingernails digging into his back, she lifted her ass off the mattress and met his rough, reckless thrusts. Her body writhed and twisted, and she cried out.

Need to see her. He pushed up on his hands so he could watch the climax seize her pretty features, and when she came back down, when she went limp and contentedly sated, he sat up on his heels, grabbed her hips, and dragged her onto his lap. Watching the head of his cock push back inside her slick heat turned him into an animal.

Letting loose, he gave into the urgency of his need. Got yanked under by those tits shaking, her sexy mouth gaping open, her hands gripping his thighs. He'd never seen anything hotter than Rosie taking his cock and loving it.

Desire peaked so hard and fast it hurt, and he pulled her tightly against him, holding her *right there*, as his climax hit with a ferocity that blinded him. With each hard, short thrust, he emptied more of himself, until he was completely spent.

Collapsing at her side, he covered his face with his hand. He'd never felt so raw, so exposed. And a little sick to his stomach that he'd fallen this hard for a woman he couldn't have.

"Gotta deal with the rubber." He rolled out of bed and went into his bathroom. Staring at himself in the mirror, he realized he was an asshole. Telling her how he felt was selfish and not what she wanted from him. So, he'd shut his mouth and take what she had to give.

He'd trained for the Olympics, for Christ's sake. He knew all about discipline. He could keep his feelings in check and just enjoying fucking her.

He cleaned up, brushed his teeth, and when he came back to bed, he found Rosie lying there awkwardly, sheet pulled up to her collarbone. "Hey." She looked completely freaked out, but he checked the impulse to curl up next to her and reassure her. "You good?"

"I don't know if I'm supposed to stay or go back to my room. I don't want to make this uncomfortable, but I figured I should ask instead of being gone when you got back out here."

He loved her honesty. The way she put herself out there, opening her heart and laying it all on the line. "You do whatever you want. I'm up at five to go running with my brothers, so wherever you'll sleep best."

"Oh, okay. Sure. That makes it easy." Sitting up, she gave a little laugh. "Wish I'd taken off my clothes in here so I wouldn't have to make the quarter-mile walk of shame."

It was a long hallway, and he didn't want her to be self-conscious, so he pulled a clean T-shirt out of his dresser. "No shame. I had a great night."

She relaxed then, throwing off the covers and unfolding the shirt. She slid it over her head. "It was so good. I've never…well, you know."

Yeah, she was still uncomfortable. "I know. Glad you could let loose with me." All he needed to do was walk over there, wrap his arms around her and say, "Now, get back into bed," and she'd curl up against him and…he could take a full breath again. He knew he'd have the best sleep of his life.

She stood, and the shirt fell to the middle of her thighs. "I just hope I haven't ruined our working relationship."

It shouldn't have pinched, but it did. "Hell, if anything you've improved it."

Her smile faltered, dimmed, then went out completely. "Okay, well. Goodnight."

"'Night." He watched her go, felt the tug like a cord wrapped around his heart, squeezing tighter with each step.

Stay with me.

At the door, she turned, smiling shyly at him. "I like you Brodie. And I really like having sex with you."

He chuckled, even though his heart cracked and splintered. He'd never met anyone like her, and he knew down to his bones he never would again.

So, it fucking killed him to watch her walk out his bedroom door.

Chapter Sixteen

THE SLAM OF A DOOR STARTLED ROSALINA AWAKE.
Her eyelids popped open to a shock of sunlight streaming
through a part in the curtains. She jolted, but a heavy
weight held her down.

Squinting against the brightness, she found a thick,
hairy arm curving around her, holding her tight against a
hot, hard body.

Brodie.

So that explained the steel bar lodged between her
legs. She grinned.

And then she remembered last night—the backseat of
his truck, his tongue...*God*. Then, in his bed, the way he'd
yanked her up on his thighs...the way he'd watched
himself slide into her body, it was like he'd never seen
anything sexier in his life.

Without even thinking, she pressed her bottom back
and squirmed a little, enjoying the hot flare of desire that
ripped through her.

Wait a minute.

What's he doing in my bed?

Laughter came from the living area, deep male voices. "Where the hell is he?"

The voices came closer, and she rocked against him to wake him up.

"Which bedroom's he using?" a guy said.

"Must be this one. Door's closed."

The door flung open, and three brawny, gorgeous men piled into the room. All of them stared at her in bed with their brother.

"Hi. Morning." She shook Brodie's completely limp arm. "I mean, is he dead?"

"He's not normally such a deep sleeper," Will said.

"I got this." Fin, the baddest of them all, strode into the bathroom and came back out with a cup of water, tossing it into his brother's face.

Brodie sat bolt upright, water dripping down his cheeks and plastering his hair to his scalp. "What the hell?" He looked around. "Where am I?"

"Ooh, that's not gonna go over well," Gray said.

"You're in my room," Rosalina said. "You must've wandered in here last night."

The brothers snickered.

"No, I'm serious. When I left him—*after we had sex…*" She gave them a look that said she didn't have a problem owning up to it. "He was in his own room."

Brodie squeezed her thigh. "None of their business."

"Well, we're naked in bed together. We can address the obvious."

"You found me." Brodie gestured to the door. "Now, can you guys get the hell out of Rosie's bedroom?"

"Yeah, sure," Will said. "It's just, you didn't show up to run with us, so we figured we'd check in on you."

"Want to grab some breakfast?" Fin looked to Rosalina.

"I'd love that." She nudged her bedmate. God, he looked adorable with rumpled hair and the crease on his cheek. "You hungry?"

"I'm tired." He glared at his brothers. "But, yeah, sure. We'll meet you at the diner."

"Come to the main house," Will said. "Delilah's cooking."

The three of them stared at Brodie like they were wondering if she'd drugged and tied him to her bed.

"What?" Brodie snapped.

"Nothing." Fin gave the others a push. "Let's go."

Will lingered, his gaze shifting from Brodie to her and then back to his brother. She was probably reading into it, but she could've sworn the message in his eyes said, *You know what you're doing here?*

She definitely didn't miss Brodie's answering look. *None of your business. Get out.*

Once they were alone, Brodie jammed his hands through his hair. "Sorry about that."

"It's fine. I was as surprised as they were to find you in my bed."

Color rushed to his cheeks. "I missed you."

"You did?" Three simple words poured salve into the open wound he'd carved last night. "You were so cold after…when you came back from the bathroom. I guess now I know for sure I'm not the hookup type. I tried really hard to keep it fun, to not let myself get emotionally involved, but I can't. It's just not for me."

"Rosie?" He looked down at his hands, obviously conflicted. "I just want you to be happy. And if you want to have some fun with me, then I'll do it. But I…" He swallowed, his Adam's apple jumping. He turned toward her, grabbing her hand. "I want to be with you."

His gruffly whispered words made her heart soar. With that permission, she threw herself into his arms, swinging a leg over his thighs and straddling his lap. "We're in big trouble, aren't we?"

"Yeah, princess, looks like we are."

The Bowies lived in a massive stone, wood, and glass masterpiece of a home that blended in with the surrounding meadow and sat against the dramatic back-drop of the Teton Mountain Range.

"You grew up here?" Rosalina asked.

Expressionless behind the mirrored sunglasses, he said, "Sure did."

"It's magnificent." As they pulled into the circular driveway, she smoothed the skirt of her sundress. Dropping the sun visor, she did a quick check of her lipstick and hair.

The moment Brodie came to a stop, he shifted into park and placed his hand on her knee.

"Hey. You're Rosie here, okay? You can just be your-self, and they're going to love you."

She relaxed into his touch. "You read me so well."

"It's in your posture." He tilted his chin and affected the regal air of a queen.

She swatted him. "I do not look like that."

"Yeah, you do. You definitely have two modes. Princess and Rosie. Personally, I like Rosie, because she puts out."

She laughed. It seemed impossible and unfair that

she'd meet a man like Brodie but only get to have him for a few weeks.

He cut the engine, and they both got out. Meeting her in front of the truck, he reached for her hand. She liked the feel of it—the protective, possessive grip. "Every second of my life, even when I'm away from home, I'm in control. I watch what I say, what I eat, how I walk. I make sure my lipstick's perfect and my bra straps aren't showing."

He gave her hand a squeeze. "You're paparazzi ready."

"Exactly. So, here, where I don't have to do any of that, I'm just…totally out of my element."

"But in a good way?"

"In the best way imaginable."

Surrounded by birds chirping and a warm breeze rustling the leaves, they headed up the slate walkway. Once inside, she stopped to take it all in. A huge stone fireplace with a dark wood mantelpiece took up the far wall. Leather couches and club chairs made up small gathering areas, giving the vast, high-ceiling room a cozy feel. The fittings were wrought iron and dark-stained wood, and the place was spotless and well-cared for.

She followed Brodie toward the bursts of laughter and conversation in a massive, white kitchen. Everyone was gathered at the island in the center of the room, except for a little girl and an older man with a white pompadour, mustache, and beard. They were talking quietly at the table.

"Oh, hey, Brodie." Callie pulled him into a hug, then reached out to her. "Come on in. I'm so glad you could come."

"Thank you so much for having me over," she said.

Brodie squeezed her hand. "What's cookin'?"

She smiled up at him. *I'm doing it again.* It was just that… while the kitchen smelled just like hers at home, with the baking bread, buttery eggs, and something sweet and cinnamony, the dynamic here was totally different. The castle was quiet and subdued, everyone extremely polite; this family was rambunctious and loud, constantly ribbing each other.

Delilah came up to her with a big, colorful plate. "Hey, hon." She wrapped her up in her arms. "Food's ready, grab what you want and come on outside. It's gorgeous this morning, so we're eating on the patio."

"Thank you." Rosalina took in the offerings. Her mouth watered at the sight of big, fat cinnamon rolls oozing with gooey filling, white frosting dripping down the sides. Always a careful eater, she skimmed across the platters piled with bacon and sausage and settled on the fresh fruit in a pretty ceramic bowl.

But that just seemed so…blah. *It's such a go-to choice.* She wasn't sure where to start, so she reached for the pitcher of hand-squeezed orange juice—which she knew was fresh because of the halved oranges sitting in a bowl beside the juicer.

"You look overwhelmed," Knox said.

"I am." She gave an uncomfortable laugh. "My home is much quieter than this."

"I get it. It was just me and my mom growing up, but the thing is, here, you can be quiet and eat your breakfast, or you can jump on the table and belt out a Celine Dion power ballad. It doesn't matter. They're just really easygoing. So, eat what you want, do what you want, and give yourself time to get used to the Bowie clan."

"That's great advice."

"Good." Knox put a chocolate croissant on her plate and headed outside.

And suddenly Rosalina was hungry. Starving, in fact. She hadn't really eaten dinner last night, and then, of course, she'd had sex *twice.*

The memory of Brodie's cock in her mouth, his desperate expression right before he'd shoved his face in her neck, sent a blast of awareness through her. *Oh, my.* She turned to find him talking to his brothers, laughing. He was so ruggedly handsome, so powerful...he was just everything she'd never known she'd wanted in a man.

He glanced at her with a warm, sweet smile. His brother must've said something about them, because he elbowed him and said, "Fuck off."

Turning back to the island, she piled scrambled eggs onto her plate. A slice of bacon, a sausage patty...even a cinnamon roll. God, she never indulged like this.

And then, just as she was heading outside, a voice called, "Rosalina?"

The room went quiet, and she whipped around to find—

"*Marcel?*"

"Hello." He looked around the room with his superior air.

How had she never noticed that before? Her family took its role as monarchs seriously, but they viewed themselves as caretakers, guardians of the people and the country. They never viewed themselves as *better.* They were just stewards of the land their forefathers had claimed in battles.

Maybe it was the contrast of the Bowie family—all

four extremely accomplished and wealthy men were humble, generous, and viewed themselves as no different than anyone else— but in this setting, Marcel came off as pompous.

Flustered, she set her plate down and crossed the room. "This is Marcel, a friend from St. Christophe." Just as the family started to migrate towards them to say hello, Rosalina grabbed his arm and said, "Can you please excuse us?" *Crap.* Back in princess mode. Well, what the hell was Marcel doing in *Calamity*? She didn't want St. Christophe crashing in on her freedom. She led Marcel across the living room and out the front door. Once in the shade of the porch, she turned to him. "What're you doing here?"

In his khakis and white dress shirt, sandy hair held in place with pomade, he looked refined and totally out of place on the Bowie ranch. "You're not talking to me, Rosalina. You've ignored my calls and my texts. What did you expect me to do?"

"I expect you to give me the space I asked for." Each word cracked like a whip. She never spoke with such high emotion, but she was so angry that he'd intrude on her time here.

"I can't do that. We can't fix our relationship if you're pretending I don't exist."

"There's nothing to fix, you jackass. You *cheated* on me."

"Oh, that's nice. That's…" He twisted away from her with a look of distaste. "I see this place has done wonders for you."

"It has."

"Look, I never slept—"

"Shut your stupid, lying, stuck-up mouth. The fact

that you're still saying it means you don't get it at all. You don't listen to me." She paced away from him on the wide-planked porch. "It's over, Marcel. There's no coming back from who I've become."

The truth shot out, taking her by surprise. She shook her head. "I meant from what you've done."

"That's not how relationships work. Do you think our parents didn't go through rough patches? No marriage can survive decades without struggle."

"I don't care about other couples. I don't care how people suffered in loveless marriages. We're not right for each other, and I won't do it. And, no matter what my family's going through, I know in my heart they wouldn't want me to."

"It won't be loveless. You're angry right now—rightfully so—but it will pass."

"The anger *has* passed, but the doubts won't. If I stayed with you, I'd wonder every day for the rest of my life if you're cheating on me, hiding things from me, or working behind my back to sink my business plans. You've shown your true character, and I thank God every day you did it before we got married."

His features burned red. "I didn't go into that meeting with a plan to block your idea. We gave it tremendous consideration, but in the end…" He drew in a breath. "In the end, my father thought it made the most sense to hold off on any changes. Growing the business isn't the priority right now."

"It is to me. This isn't some vanity project of mine. You and I both agreed it's time to move House of Villeneuve forward, and to do that we have to grow. It's absurd to have one, single product."

"If you'd seen your father during the meeting, you'd understand why we decided to table the discussion."

Fear stuck a pin in her heart. "What does that mean?" Her mother would have told her if something were wrong. "Is he all right?"

"No, Rosalina, he's not all right. The vote's in a matter of weeks. He's waiting to find out whether the People's Party is going to gain more traction in parliament. If they do, not only will they push their agenda to kill the monarchy, but they'll try to take back your family's land. Just because you're hiding from our problems in another country doesn't mean they've gone away. Your sister's at school, you're in America, so it's just your parents. You need to come home and be seen with me. We need to send out wedding invitations."

She knew that. God, it ate through her like acid. Every night she lay awake fighting her conscience. It seemed so simple to send out the invitations. It would make things easier for her parents and give the country something joyful to focus on.

It would secure the vote for the Royalists.

But she would never marry Marcel. "I won't lie to the people of St. Christophe. I just won't play them like that."

"You're not lying. Rosalina." She'd never heard him shout. Not once. "I know that I've hurt you deeply, and I hate myself for it." He took a breath that seemed to restore his composure. "But you *are* going to marry me. You have to."

"Get over your embarrassment and pay attention to the deeper issues your behavior uncovered. We don't love each other." After the way Brodie made love to her, she fully understood that now. "And I certainly don't trust you, so get it through your head once and for all. I'm not going to marry you. Period. End of discussion."

"Even if the consequence is the People's Party winning enough seats to end the monarchy? To take the land that's been in your family for six hundred years?"

"First of all, I don't believe for one second there's only one solution. But, also, I don't have to marry *you*."

He reeled back, reaching out for the bannister. "You can't mean that."

She softened. "But I do."

He looked anguished and scared. "Rosalina, this is my *life*. This is what we're *supposed* to do. Every decision I've ever made has been driven by our future together."

"Including the decision to sneak around with my assistant. That was the part of you that knew we shouldn't marry, that didn't have the courage to stand up to your father and tell him we don't make each other happy. That, if we marry, we'll be lonely. I hope, if you're truly honest with him, you'll find out your father doesn't want that kind of future for you. I know my parents don't want it for me."

"But they need—"

"They needed me to make a gesture, and I've done that. I came home for the Jubilee and announced my philanthropy. The whole country got to see us together. But right now…Marcel, I don't want you here. I asked for this time away, and I need it. Please go back home and work on yourself. Figure out who you are and what you want. I promise, it isn't me."

And, oh God, it struck with such perfect clarity.

Brodie's right for me.

She knew it down to her bones. Knew without a

doubt she'd never meet anyone again who was so right for her.

He's mine.

I'm his.

And yet…*we live worlds apart.*

Chapter Seventeen

BRODIE SAT ON A ROCKER, RUBY ON HIS LAP AS SHE shared her croissant with her stuffed chicken. One bite for her—as those little chicklet teeth chomped into the flaky dough—and one for Squawk.

"Faster, Bwodie."

"You got it, peaches." He rocked a little harder.

While everyone around him talked and laughed, he was filled with restless energy, waiting to find out what was going on.

Had Marcel come to bring her home? Or just to win her back?

At heart, Rosalina was dutiful. He didn't think she'd marry the douchenozzle, but she *would* go home if her family needed her to play some role in advance of the vote. Because she could finish her work from there. They didn't need to be in the same country to be business partners.

His heart thundered, and his body heated up so fast his skin prickled.

What worried him most was that she'd already checked off the main items on her list: getting drunk and having wild sex. She'd also had a hell of a lot of fun riding a mechanical bull and boarding a glacier.

So, was she done here?

No. He knew her. The taste she'd gotten would only make her crave more.

His oldest brother came over, and Ruby lifted her arms for him. Will scooped her off Brodie's lap and set her on his hip.

"I hongry, Wheel."

"You've got that croissant."

She thrust it at him, one end soggy from her nibbles. "Scock don't like it."

"He doesn't? Well, forget it then." He turned and pitched the pastry off the porch and into the goat pen across the lawn.

A little hand cupping her mouth, Ruby giggled, her eyes glittering.

"Let's get you something else to eat." But Will didn't go. Towering over him, his forehead creased in concern, he said, "You have any idea what's going on?"

Brodie shook his head.

"You don't want to go check on her?"

"It's none of my business."

"It sure looked like your business when I walked into your room this morning. I don't know her issues, but I'd bet she could use a friend right now."

"I think you know if I could help her, I would. But, trust me, I'm nothing more than a little break from her reality."

Will held his gaze, intractable. After a moment, he said, "You know, Mom did a number on all of us, but she hit you and me the hardest. Me, she left behind. She took my brothers and moved across the country. Hard to get over something like that." He smoothed Ruby's hair away from her cheek and kissed the top of her head. "But what she did to you was even worse."

Brodie's gaze snapped up. *Worse?*

"Those twisted little mind games she played with you?"

Oh, that. "I'm an adult now. I'm over her manipulations."

"Not so sure about that. She played dirty."

"Yeah, not cool telling your kid he's your favorite. But it was a long time ago. I don't care about that stuff anymore."

"Maybe, but we never talk about what went on back then, and we probably should, since I'm pretty sure my perspective of the past's different from yours. Like, you probably remember asking her to come home, but I remember her telling you she wasn't sure if she should since she couldn't handle us. That I was too wild, and everyone followed my lead. That Dad didn't care enough about us to bother keeping us in line. Or to get you the right care for your knee."

"I do. I remember that."

"And I remember her saying that if you, the only good kid, couldn't keep your brothers and your dad in line, then she didn't think she should come back home."

The memory appeared, sharp, and in perfect focus.

Oh, honey, I just don't think I can do it. Your brothers don't listen *to me.*

I think you're the only one that wants me there.

I want to come home for you—*you're the best.* He remembered her laughter—but only now could he recognize how forced it had been. *But your dad doesn't want me there. He's in his office the whole time. That should tell you right there he doesn't want me around.*

Trust me, no man who wants a woman around looks like Sasquatch.

They might listen to you, though. If you can just get them to behave, just while I'm in town, it'd make it easier. You know what it's like for me.

Something teased the edge of his consciousness, but he couldn't grasp hold of it. "I forgot about that." He'd known she'd manipulated him—obviously—but where was Will going with this?

"Yeah, so essentially, she made it *your* job to create the kind of family she could live with, and if you couldn't do it, then she'd have to stay away." Will's gaze narrowed on him. "You understand what I'm saying? She had an idea in her head of what a family looked like, but instead of disciplining us, distracting us, doing any of the things a parent does, she looked to everyone else to make it happen for her. Her husband, me…and then you. You were her last attempt." Will watched him carefully. "And when that didn't work—because you were eleven years old—she had to divorce Dad."

"Are you saying I blame myself for the family breaking up?"

Will gave a terse nod. "I remember hearing Dad and Uncle Lachlan talking about how you carried the breakup of the family on your 'little shoulders.' Dad wondered if Coach should be pushing you so hard, because he thought you might only be training and competing to make peace in what was left of the family. To keep the five of us intact, since you felt responsible for Mom leaving."

Shit. Fuck. All those hazy memories he'd carried of his mother's role in his life clarified. The truth locked into place. And it made him sick. Because he had, absolutely, felt responsible for the destruction of his family. It was just something he'd accepted.

Will shifted Ruby to his other hip, adjusting the chicken between them. "We were all too young to understand that Mom never wanted to move to Calamity in the first place. She wanted to be a socialite in a big city. She wanted to shop and go out to lunch. There wasn't anything we could have done to keep her here. Even if she'd shipped us all off to boarding school, and Dad had become the perfect husband, she still wouldn't have stayed in Calamity."

Brodie was too unsettled to respond.

"So, I guess where I'm going with all this, is everybody thinks the worst thing that ever happened to you was getting injured two weeks before the Olympics. But I think it's that Mom made you feel responsible for the family blowing up. And I worry that you carry the burden of that failure in here." He tapped his heart.

"Dat your heart, Wheel." Ruby pressed her ear against Will's chest. "It goes da-dum, da-dum, da-dum. Scock gone listen now." She shoved her chicken against him.

He smiled adoringly at their half-sister, before turning his attention back to Brodie. "All I know is I've never seen you like someone as much as Rosie, and it would be a shame if you let her go because of Mom's mind games."

And, just like that, the world as he knew it snapped back into place. "It's got nothing to do with that. Rosie's got a lot going on back home."

"I'm not talking about her end of things. All relationships have issues. Couples only survive because they're invested in making it work. And, I'm telling you, when you find the right woman, you do whatever it takes. You don't look at the obstacles, you look at the ways around them. Callie had an internship in New York, and Delilah needed to run her family restaurant, but Fin and I didn't let that stop us from holding onto the women we're going to marry, have kids and grow old with. And I'm worried you'll never get to the good stuff until you see that Mom pulled a number on you. She made it hard for you to trust, for you to go all-in with anybody or anything. Look, all I know is that you can't trust Mom with your heart. That's a given. But is Rosie like Mom?"

"She's nothing like her." Rosie was real and deep and honorable. And it was her dedication to her family that would cost him a relationship with her. "But the situation's completely different. She has to go home." *I just hope it's not today*.

"You're not hearing me. I'm telling you that fighting for Mom was a dead-end, because she's a narcissist. Rosie's not. That means there's hope for you. There's always hope. Don't let Mom screw it up for you. She's done enough damage, don't you think?"

"Yeah. I do." He didn't think Will understood the whole picture. There were no weapons for Brodie to win the battle against Rosie's parents, her country, the fucking *monarchy*.

Will might not know the situation, but he'd just given Brodie a hit of hope. If there was a chance in hell to make it work with Rosie, he'd grab it. Getting up, he clapped his brother's shoulder, smacked a kiss on Ruby's cheek, and took off into the kitchen.

From the cool of the living room, he heard Rosie talking. Peering through the window, he found her on the porch. Ass perched on the banister, phone to her ear, she gazed across the meadow with a troubled expression.

When he opened the door and stepped outside, she looked relieved to see him.

"I don't know." She sounded exasperated. "I don't even know where he's staying. All I can tell you is that he looked shell-shocked. I guess I never saw that he's nothing more than his father's puppet. I'd be sad for him if I weren't so angry." She paused to listen. "Well, if he thinks he can guilt me into a loveless marriage, he's out of his mind."

Brodie came closer, reaching for her hand. She grasped it, pulling it onto her lap.

She heard something she didn't like, because she landed on both feet. "No, Mom, I won't change my mind."

Brodie could hear her mom's voice grow louder and more insistent.

"You know what? Challenge accepted. I *will* come up with a solution we can all live with." She paused. "Yes, before the vote. I'll talk to you later." She ended the call and tossed her phone onto a cushioned chair.

"All right, warrior princess, what's going on?"

"It's an impossible situation." She spread her arms wide. "I can't please my family, my country, and myself at the same time."

"They're still insisting you marry him?"

"You have to understand, the People's Party is fighting hard and dirty, so the closer the vote gets, the more stressed my parents become."

"So, it all rests on you and your marriage to the douchenozzle?"

"Yes, but only because that's been the expectation all along. I finish school, come home, marry Marcel, and get pregnant. So long as we stayed with the program, the

People's Party wasn't a real threat. Now, though, they're convinced nothing short of a wedding invitation will solve their problems."

"I could be wrong, but it sounds like your parents are holding onto the old way of things, while the other party's pushing the ball forward."

"Believe me, we've fought to change the law of succession. My father's been soundly rejected."

"When was the last time he brought it up for a vote?"

"Oh, it was…Genevieve's twenty, so I'm thinking ten years ago."

"Seems to me, if the People's Party poses an actual threat, then the citizens of your country aren't as conservative as they used to be. They're open to new ideas. So, maybe, instead of giving them a wedding, you could give them something genuinely meaningful. *You* be the one to change their view of your worth. Because, Rosie, you're worth so much more than being a vessel for the next prince."

She walked right into his arms. "I needed to hear that. I feel so guilty, so selfish. I know how much peace of mind it will give my parents if I just go home and pretend to be engaged. It's only for two more weeks." She pulled back. "But there's this other feeling in me. It's in my bones, and it says to hold my ground. Only, I couldn't figure out a way to do that and still help my family and benefit the people. Thank you for reminding me that I'm worth more than marrying the douchenozzle."

"I think, when your parents dismiss your ideas, they make what you do seem inconsequential."

"In the scheme of things right now, it's ridiculous that I'm working so hard to create a product for your spa. That's not where my time or energy should be spent."

"You're working. You're creating. You're living your life, as you should. This work is what makes you *you*. You've studied for seven years, and now you're forming a business. This is exactly what you should be doing. It would be a waste of your talents and abilities to just get married and pregnant. We can come up with a better idea."

"That's what I told my mother. Unfortunately, that might've been more bravado than actual confidence. There's not much I can do in two weeks."

"We can come up with an *idea* in five minutes. We don't need to execute."

She eyed him sharply. "You're right."

"What can you do to improve the lives of your people?"

"We have the finest roads, schools, and medical care in all of Europe." She sounded like he'd insulted St. Christophe. "We're known for the beauty and cleanliness of our country."

"You're being defensive. We can't brainstorm when you're fighting me."

She let out a laugh. "I'm sorry. I'm rattled. Marcel knows exactly how to push my buttons, and, boy, did he ever scare me."

He tipped her chin and pressed his mouth to hers. Her immediate softening hit him with a wallop of pure relief. Which made him realize how certain he'd been that he'd lost her—that Marcel had come to take her home.

"You've mentioned the People's Party wants to reclaim royal land."

"Yes. They want to 'take it back,' so the people can profit from it."

"What's it used for now?"

"There are several ancestral homes, but we've donated vast amounts of it for public parks and a botanical garden."

"I can't compare your situation to mine, but I will say that everybody loved my dad. He had a big personality but also a big heart. That bison preserve? That was part of our land once. He donated it to the state. There's a small liberal arts college in Jackson Hole, and my dad founded the business school. He figured, since so many wealthy people have homes out here, he could take advantage of their expertise. They're all successful business leaders, right? So, he set up an annual symposium, created a guest teacher program, and now it's become one of the most highly ranked business schools in the country."

"We don't have a university in St. Christophe."

Their gazes locked, and the idea struck them both at the same moment. Excitement sparkled in her eyes. "Oh, my God. Instead of sending out wedding invitations, we can make an announcement that the House of Villeneuve is establishing a university."

"No, that *you* are. It's your idea. Your family's going to oversee it and donate the land."

"My great grandmother's estate sits on five hundred acres. It was once a horse farm, so it's got several outbuildings."

"Will your parents go for it?"

"Oh, wholeheartedly. This is exactly what they love to do. Letting the People's Party steal our land would kill them, but turning my grandmother's property into a university?" She threw herself into Brodie's arms. "And the best thing is that it takes the focus away from marriage and babies and puts it on the real value of our family as stewards of St. Christophe. It's brilliant."

He wrapped his arms around her, the strangest feeling coming over him. "We make a good team." It was warm and bright, alive and throbbing.

"We do." She pulled away and started tapping on her phone. "I need to tell them right now. The sooner they make the announcement, the better." She looked at him like he was the best thing that had ever happened to her. "Thank you for talking it through with me. I love the way you're always coming up with ideas."

It filled him with a pulsating energy, and made his heart grow so big and thick it felt like it would punch right out of his chest.

And, right then, he knew exactly what it was.

It's love.

As impossible as it was, Brodie Bowie had fallen in love.

And he knew, without a doubt, there was no turning back.

"Your ex is still in town." Brodie came back from his meeting with Pierce and the board to find the kitchen table loaded with boxes. Rosie was tearing them open and pulling out bottles and glass jars, silver vats, and clear rubber hoses. "I saw him having breakfast in the hotel."

"I know. He says he's not giving up. That it's 'much bigger than the two of us.'" She stabbed scissors into the center of the next box and sliced it open.

Setting his laptop on the coffee table, he headed into the kitchen and pulled a knife from the block. He joined her at the table, watching her pull items out like she was on a game show. "Are we timing ourselves?"

She cut him a look. "What does that mean?"

"You've either just downed an energy drink or you're trying to beat a world record."

She dove back in, not a hint of a smile. "I need to get going. I can't believe my supplies sat in customs this long."

"Well, hang on. You've already created the essential oil and the formula for the lotion. You've got the supplies you ordered locally, and I know you made some calls about a production facility. We're good." No question, she'd stayed on top of everything.

"Yeah, but I still have so much to do." She tossed the empty box aside, pulled another one closer, and stabbed it.

"That fucker got your clock ticking."

"He…what?"

"Marcel. He set a timer." He reached for her hands and brought them to his mouth for a kiss. "Sweetheart, nothing's changed. We're right where we need to be with our business, the vote's still happening the Tuesday after next…just because that dickwad flew out here and rattled your cage, it doesn't change the timetable."

"I guess you're right."

"What *has* changed is that you've come up with a smarter way to win the voters' loyalty." He let her go and started pulling bubble-wrapped packages out of the box.

"It's not the timetable I'm worried about." Her shoulders relaxed. "I guess I just resent that I can't stay here longer. Now that…"

"Now that what?"

Distress pinched her features. "Now that I've found all this goodness."

It hurt to look into those pale green eyes so filled with longing, knowing he couldn't change anything. "But you're here now, so let's just live in the moment." What else could he do? Unless…had she gotten some new information? "You're not going home yet, are you? I mean, you haven't scheduled a flight?" *Oh, Jesus.* Had they run out of time already?

"No. I'm not going home yet." She reached for a glass jar and waved it at him with a mischievous smile. "Not when I have this."

She'd finished the perfume last night, and they'd celebrated in bed. Well, on the back of the couch, the shower, and *then* the bed. Grabbing it from her, he twisted the top off. Immediately, the scent hit his nostrils. Rich, exotic, elegant.

"It's really good, isn't it?"

"From now on, I think it's the only thing you should wear." No clothes, no shoes, no jewelry. Just this scent.

"Oh, I'll definitely…" She caught his expression. "You mean that literally." He didn't even have to answer. She just smiled and shook her head. "Well, I give you credit for not having me wear my Louboutins in that fantasy. My feet thank you. Oh, I think I've got a name for it. Belle Starr."

"That's a long way from Nocturne."

"I know, but it should be, right? Nocturne comes from a meadow in the Alps. Belle Starr comes from an outlaw town. I looked up the history of this place, how this valley, surrounded by huge, impassable mountains, made it the perfect haven for outlaws. When I looked them up, I found some really badass women. Belle Starr was the leader of a gang, a smart businesswoman, and she owned her sexuality." She cupped the side of her mouth and said, "She slept with a *lot* of guys."

"But maybe we won't advertise that last part?"

"We're not hiding Belle's light under a bushel."

Brodie laughed. "Not sure that's the right expression for the context, but, yeah, Belle Starr it is."

"Good. So, that's done. And now I can't wait to get my lab set up so I can get the body lotion going."

He pulled some pouches of unrefined shea butter out of an open box. "So, how does this work, exactly?"

"At home, I'd send the formula to our lab and production facility, but of course we don't have one yet. And it's not easy to find a place that'll work with us—not when we're such a small operation. A new product requires its own equipment, maybe even a separate building. It's more than most companies want to take on, but I think I've found a place in Idaho that'll handle it for us. I might've stretched the projections a little."

Given the beauty of this scent, he doubted that. "I can't believe you've already found a place." From the next box, he pulled out some bags of plant-based emulsifying wax. "Pastilles? What is this stuff?"

"So, I've got two different formulas. One's a body butter. It's super rich, and for that I don't need water. It's great for winter, when the air's dry and cold. It's also great for older women. The other's a lighter formula. For that…" She hefted a jug of distilled water. "I use water. But, of course, water and oil don't mix, so you need an emulsifier, which basically has two ends. One is a water-loving molecule, and the other likes oil, so it enables the two to mix. That way it won't separate like salad oil."

"Is it weird that I'm really turned on right now?"

"Well, we are talking about oil."

"Nah, it's your intelligence. Your passion's sexy."

He loved watching her turn from embarrassed to… awed. "I let someone strip me of my confidence. But around you? I feel like the sexiest woman in the world."

He kissed the corner of her mouth. "That's because you are." But he could tell she was still distracted, and he needed to figure out why. "You talk to your parents about the university idea?"

"They *love* it. They're seriously off and running with the idea. This is the best thing ever for my father. Good stress he can handle. Bad stress…" Her gaze went unfocused. "I just worry about him."

Bingo. "Did Marcel say something?"

For the first time since he'd entered the room, she stopped moving. "Yesterday he said, if I'd seen my father in that meeting, I'd understand why he killed my lotion idea. I hate that I'm stressing my father out. He's got enough to worry about, and I'm only making it worse."

"That fucker." Marcel really did know how to push her buttons. "Does he have health issues?"

"He had a heart attack, but that was years ago. He's changed his diet since then, cut back on his hours…actually, that's when he promoted Marcel's father to take over the finance side of the business."

"But you're still worried about him."

"I am, but it's a long story." She brought a silver vat into the kitchen, set it on the counter, and plugged it in.

Given how much she didn't want to talk about it, he figured it was important. "We can talk while you work."

"Well…" She gazed out the window, as if gathering her thoughts. "So, up until I was fourteen, I went to boarding school in Switzerland."

"Okay."

"I was a very good girl, but the price of that was closing my eyes and pretending to sleep while the bad girls snuck out at night. It meant walking past them and ignoring my curiosity to find out about their latest scheme."

"Uh oh."

"Yes, it doesn't end well. The bad girls wore eyeliner and rolled up the waistbands of their skirts, they smoked cigarettes and had sex in the boat house with the boys from the school across the lake. I just really wanted to know what it felt like to be bad. So, over spring break, instead of going home like I always did, this time I stayed in town. For a whole week, I was deliciously bad. I smoked pot and drank. We'd take the train into Zurich and hit the clubs with our fake IDs. It was crazy and awful."

"Awful?"

"It didn't wind up being nearly as fun as I'd hoped. I didn't like drinking. Hated pot. The first night in the club was fun, the second night was…less fun, but by the fifth night? I was bored out of my mind."

"So, what happened?"

"The night everyone came back, we snuck out and met the boys in the boat house. It was cold, so they built a fire."

"There was a fireplace in the boathouse?"

"No, they made a bonfire."

"Oh, shit."

"Yeah. Hang on. We drank, got wasted, and then everybody started hooking up. I'd had enough at that point, so I left. Went back to my room and went to sleep. Well, a couple hours later, the lights were on, and people were screaming and crying. The boat house was in flames. One of the girls had third degree burns all over her body. We found out a few days later that one of the boys died."

"Jesus. That's terrible."

"It was terrifying and heartbreaking." She drew in a breath. "Anyhow, they tested us all for drugs, and of course I didn't come out clean. My parents were called, and I was expelled. But...my parents didn't come get me. *Marcel's* parents did. I don't think I've ever been more scared in my life. I've never once doubted my parents love...until that night. When they didn't show up, when it was Monsieur Allard? I was sick about it."

"Maybe they were trying to keep you out of the press. If they came, it'd be all over the news."

She shook her head, the experience still alive in her eyes. "They didn't come because my father had a heart attack." She held a hand as if to stop him from speaking. "Totally unrelated, I know, but my emotions from those couple of weeks are so tied together I blamed myself. I was so ashamed, so guilt-ridden, I couldn't eat. Couldn't sleep."

"Ah, princess. I'm sorry."

Tears spilled down her cheeks, and she swiped them away. He pulled her in for a hug.

"You have to know my father. He's the sweetest, kindest man you'll ever meet. He loves his wife and his daughters, he loves the people of St. Christophe, and even though he's the prince of a small country, he lives a very pure and simple life. He wants to read the paper in peace every morning and eat dinner with his family at night. He's in bed by ten o'clock and out on the trails every morning by six." She exhaled. "I think I could've handled his anger, but he was *disappointed* in me."

"And, so, you've been dutiful ever since so you don't disappoint him again."

"Or give him a heart attack."

"Yeah, that makes sense. But, no matter how stressful this situation is, I'd bet the ranch he wouldn't want you taking responsibility for what's going on politically. I would guess, if you asked him, he'd tell you this kind of pressure comes with the territory. It's just part of the job of running a nation."

She tilted her head. "That's so funny. That's such an obvious thing, so totally true, and yet it never once occurred to me. I think, because I've never been able to talk to anyone other than Marcel and my assistant about any of this stuff, it's really just been about recycling the same ideas. Talking to an outsider gives me a whole new perspective." She placed a hand on his chest. "I like you, Brodie."

"Yeah, I like you, too."

Bracing both hands on the edge of the counter, she jumped up and wiggled back a little, opening her legs so he could step between them. Never once looking away, she scraped the hair back from his temples, then ran a finger over his lips.

A crackling energy flowed between them, shocking his heart and making his nerves vibrate.

"This…" She waved a hand between them. "Isn't usual, right?"

"If by *this* you mean the way you make me want to keep you, then, no, princess. It's anything but usual for me."

"I wish…"

He shook his head. "Wishes don't mean shit. Whatever we want, we have to make it happen."

"In this situation, I'm not sure that's possible." She jumped off the counter and went back to work. "And I don't know what to do about that."

Chapter Eighteen

"WHO'S GOT RUBY TONIGHT?" BRODIE HAD TO SHOUT for his brother to hear him over the loud music in the bar.

"She's got a sleepover with Uncle Lachlan." Will never took his eyes off the dance floor, where Rosie, Delilah, Knox, and Callie danced together. They were wild, funking it up.

Rosie looked happy, and as much as he wanted to get out there and grind all over her ass, he liked seeing her just like this. Part of his family, being her best damn self.

Brodie gave his brother a shove. "Then what're you doing out with us tonight?"

"Delilah works her ass off, and she wanted a night out."

"When are you going to put a ring on it?"

Will downed the rest of his water. "She's got a big family, and a wedding's going to be a real production. We want to do it when things settle down. When Ruby's stable, and Delilah's got a handle on her restaurant."

"You don't give a shit about a piece of paper."

"Not really. I've got everything I need." Will's thumb

rubbed the condensation on his glass. "Is it weird for you? Having the three of us locked up in relationships?"

"Yeah." He wanted to change the subject, but—for the first time in his life—there was nothing more pressing on his mind than Rosie. "I never got it, you know? The appeal. I like my life too much to have to compromise with someone, to worry about her feelings or what she wants to do."

He watched Rosie on the dance floor, her dark hair seemed to absorb all the lights in the room, making it glow and glimmer. Her tall, statuesque frame stood out among the others—even dancing, she was elegant and absolutely stunning.

Seeing her laugh so hard her limbs flopped like a human windsock made his heart hurt.

Because she was so vibrant and beautiful and passionate, and he knew he'd never meet someone like her again. He didn't want her to leave.

Ever.

"But I get it now."

Will grinned. "Because with her, nothing's more important than what she wants."

"Exactly. There's no sacrifice, because I just want to see her happy."

"Oh, hell, man. You found her."

"Well, I…" *That's not true, because I can't have her.*

But, for the first time, he didn't entirely believe that. *This is the shift Will was talking about. When you stop seeing obstacles and start seeing pathways around them.* "Yeah, I think I did."

I'm going to marry that woman.

The sudden realization had him jumping out of his chair. "I'm heading to the bar. You want anything?"

"Nah," Will said. "We're not staying much longer."

Brodie pushed his way through the crowd.

Marry her.

Where the hell did that come from?

What would that even look like? The bartender was slammed, so Brodie waited to catch his attention.

She was part of the royal family. She needed to live in St. Christophe.

Their obstacles seemed insurmountable, but nothing was impossible. Not when you wanted something badly enough. He twisted around, seeking her out in the mass of bodies dancing to the country rock song. When you needed something. *Someone.*

Her.

"She's something, right?"

Brodie jerked away from the voice in his ear. Fucking Marcel stood there, but where he'd expected to see a smug expression, instead he found sincerity. He ignored the douchenozzle and raised a finger to the bartender. The guy gave him a chin nod in acknowledgement.

"Looks like she's having a nice time out here," Marcel said.

"It'd be even better for her if you left."

"She's my fiancée. Where else would I be?"

"You can cut the shit. I know the story. And, before you get all pissy, she only talked to me because she knows I've got her back."

"Do you, though?"

Brodie stepped closer to the guy. "Not an easy concept for you to grasp, but some of us can be trusted."

The man looked almost as offended as embarrassed. "Don't presume to understand our situation. I never stopped caring about her. I just got...restless. When we were at university at the same time, I didn't notice it as much. But, then, she was away another three years in perfume school, and I was back home and…" He let out a rough exhalation. "I don't know. Something changed for her in perfume school."

"Yeah, she found her passion." Brodie's tone held contempt for the man she'd known all her life but who didn't get her at all.

"Up until then, she was my constant companion. We did everything together, texted all the time. But for those three years…"

"She didn't pay enough attention to you. Got it." Brodie caught the guy's surprise at being cut off so abruptly. "Look, man, whatever result you're hoping for, you're going about it the wrong way. If you've got a hope in hell of winning her back, you have to give her the space she asked for." *But, just to say, you don't. Not a single chance in hell.*

"I can't go until I talk to her."

Is that what your daddy told you to do? "You mean convince her. But I'm telling you, you're just pushing her away by being here. If you push her too far…"

Marcel's eyes widened. "I don't know what she's told you, but we will marry. Her parents are just giving her time to come to terms with what happened."

The bartender appeared just then to take his order. "Hey, can I get a club soda and lime?" Brodie said. Then, he looked to Marcel, who raised a hand and shook his head. *No, thanks.*

Done talking to the douchenozzle, Brodie turned away to wait for his drink. He wanted to pull off nonchalant, but inside he wasn't doing so well. Maybe it was the fact that Marcel wasn't acting high and mighty. Wasn't trying to play him.

He was stating a fact. Rosalina and Marcel would, eventually, marry. Her time in Calamity was an aberration.

He'd thought they'd come up with the perfect solution, but a royal wedding? The pomp and circumstance surrounding it, the barrage of photographs and articles, the joy pumping through society at the anticipation of the big day? As far as optics, founding a university didn't come close.

So, then, were her parents humoring her?

Jesus, they couldn't *make* her marry this guy, could they?

He didn't know them, but he did know the lengths people would go to get what they wanted. His mother was a great example. She'd used her own children. When it hadn't worked, she'd discarded them.

The bartender set his drink down and brought a glass of ice water for Marcel.

Distracted, Marcel barely spared him a glance. He leaned closer to Brodie. "I understand what she's doing. I deserve it. And I actually think it's good she's getting this out of her system. I don't think she realized before what it meant to be with one person for her entire life."

Brodie had heard enough. "I don't usually give advice, mostly because I don't give a fuck what other people do. You make your bed, you lay in it. But this involves Rosalina, so listen to me good. You care about her at all, you let her go. She's so much better than you, she's not even in the same universe. So, no matter what you think needs to happen, it's not going to. You did her a favor. You set her free. Now back the fuck off." He dropped a twenty on the damp counter, grabbed his drink, and headed back to the table.

He believed everything he'd said, but…*we're talking about the prince and princess of St. Christophe hanging onto the monarchy.*

Which meant, no matter what they felt about each other, Brodie might never be anything more than a vacation hookup.

He had a problem. A big one. But if he was the "visionary" his family thought he was, he'd come up with a solution.

Because he wasn't going to lose her.

He'd found someone worth fighting for.

While the two women talked, Brodie pulled the jars and bottles out of the boxes and set them on the outdoor table.

I could get used to this. Before, the daily routine of living with someone had seemed like a nightmare, but with Rosie…he liked the constant sense of anticipation.

He found himself waiting to eat so they could share a meal together, looked forward to the end of the day when they took a long walk and caught up with each other. He thought of last night, brushing their teeth in the bathroom and talking. Seemed they never ran out of things to say.

He'd always just done his thing, jumping from one project to the next, hanging out with whoever was in his sphere at the moment. Rosie was like the missing cord that connected him to the rest of the world.

A few weeks ago, he hadn't been able to imagine being tied to one person. Now, he got a hit of anxiety every time he thought of living here without her.

Jinx stepped out onto the patio, shutting the French

door behind him. He took in Sky and Rosie at a table cluttered with beers, guacamole, and chips. "Hope it's okay if I let myself in."

"Of course." Rosie's chair scraped on the slate, as she stood to greet him. "Thanks so much for meeting with us."

Jinx went to the chair right next to Skylar. "Hey." It was like he didn't know how to greet her. His arms hung at his sides, filled with tension. "Sky." Like he didn't know whether to pat her, hug her, or shake her hand.

Brodie suspected the guy wanted to plant a hot one on her mouth.

"Jinx." Skylar barely spared him a glance, but where she'd been relaxed a moment ago, now her shoulders hitched with tension.

"How's that stall working out for you?" Brodie asked, if only to break through the awkwardness.

"It's good. Got more business than I can handle." The moment he dropped into a chair, Jinx reached for a chip and dragged it through the guacamole. "I don't get why they want to stand there and watch me work, though. It's not like I'm talking to them."

"I'm over there every day to take pictures," Skylar said. "And I can tell you, he's by far the biggest attraction."

The stark longing on Jinx's expression made Brodie uncomfortable. "Well, you start with a blank slate, and while they stand there an image comes to life. It's pretty fascinating, especially for someone like me who doesn't have an artistic bone in his body." The attention was making Jinx uncomfortable, so he turned the conversation to Rosie. "Hey, I got a message from our glass blower today. Her mom had a stroke, so she's got to bail. Instead of leaving her stall empty, I thought we could use it to test our product."

"That's such a great idea," Rosie said. "And that's not something we need labels for, so we can do it right away. I can't wait to see what people think." She clapped her hands together. "Okay, you guys have no idea what we're talking about. We've got this new product." She held up some mason jars. "One's a body butter, and the other's a lotion." She twisted off the lids and handed them to their guests.

Sky spread some on the back of her hand. "Oh, that's nice."

Jinx took a quick sniff and handed it back.

"We're making a luxury perfume and bath and body products to complement it," Rosie said. "It's going to be the signature scent of the hotel, so we'll be using them for guest toiletries and the spa products. We're hoping the guests like it enough to buy some in the store before they leave."

"I love it," Sky said. "Brilliant."

"What's my role in all this?" Jinx bit into another chip loaded with guacamole.

"We're testing these containers." Brodie showed them some perfume bottles and plastic jars. "But once we settle on packaging, we're going to need labels." He pointed to Jinx. "We need your art."

"I put together this photo album to give you a feel for what we're going for." Rosie pushed the book toward them. "Just some concepts and colors I like."

Jinx flipped through pages filled with photographs of the ranch's historic outbuildings and meadows, along with images of the original ghost town. She even had paint chips to give an idea of color scheme. "I'm not a graphic designer."

"No, I know," Rosie said. "But, the thing is, I'm leaving soon, and I'm trying to get everything set up before I go, and Sky says you're an amazing artist, so we figured it couldn't hurt to ask. We'll pay you for it, of course."

"You like my art?" Jinx asked Sky.

"I do."

"Custom work on motorcycles isn't—" Jinx began

"I'm not talking about motorcycles." Sky shifted to face him. "Your mom tags you on social media. I've seen your real art."

"Oh." Color tinted his cheeks. "Cool. Still…I'm not a graphic artist."

"You don't need to be." Sky rolled her eyes. "Okay, I know you're hiring me to help with the marketing aspect of this, but how about if Jinx and I work on this together?"

"I'll do it," Jinx said.

Sky took the book from him, completely oblivious to the way he looked at her like she was gilded. "Let's see what you've got." She flipped through the pages.

"What do you want exactly?" Jinx asked. "Just a design for a label?"

"We're going to need a label for the jars and another for the boxes," Rosie said. "But you only have to come up with the drawing. The company that makes the labels will handle scale for each piece."

"We'll need shopping bags, too," Brodie said.

"Yep." Rosie looked to Jinx and Sky. "So, you're both in?"

"Absolutely," Sky said. "Sounds fun."

"Oh, great. Thank you so much." Rosie pushed back in her chair. "I love the idea of old barn wood for the interior walls, to give it a rustic feel. Maybe antique photographs. I can see dried sagebrush and wildflowers in clusters tied with ribbon. That kind of thing."

"I can totally picture that store." Sky grinned. "I love it."

Rosie had some great ideas, and it killed Brodie to think she wouldn't be here to put the place together herself. How could her parents snuff out this side of her?

He understood from an intellectual standpoint what they needed from her, but as a man of the west, a descendent of outlaws and mountain men, he just naturally thought outside the box. The idea of stifling someone, cutting them off at the knees…it just didn't compute.

How could forcing this woman to get married be more powerful than establishing a university on Villeneuve land?

And, really, who did the people want leading the next generation? A dynamic businesswoman or a brood mare?

"Eventually, we'll have soap, perfume, lip balm, and candles, too," Rosie said. "But I can do everything else from home. I just want to get the basics set up here before I leave."

"We can get on this right away." Jinx got up. "Come on. I'll buy you a burger and we can get started."

"I have to get home to Rocco." Sky's tone said, *You know that.*

What was this weird tension between them? Jinx was obviously into her, so why did she keep throwing up roadblocks?

"Bring him," Jinx said. "We'll go to Shirley's."

Interest flared in her eyes. What kid didn't want to eat dinner in a classic car from the Fifties, while watching a movie? The place was set up like a drive-in movie theatre, only indoors.

"That place sounds so fun," Rosie said. "I haven't been there yet. I'll bet Rocco loves it."

"He does." Skylar gave Jinx a look that said, *As you obviously know.* "Sure. Let's go. But I have to pick him up from my mom's, so I'll meet you there." She snapped the photo album closed. "Can I take this with me?"

"Yep. I made it for you guys."

"I'll get us a table." Jinx took off.

As Skylar fished her keys out of her tote, Rosie said, "Why are you so hard on him? He obviously likes you."

"Because he wants to *date* me." She said it like he'd asked if he could tie her up and stuff her in his trunk.

"What's so bad about that?" Rosie laughed. "He seems like a great guy."

"I have a three-year-old. I work full-time, while trying to be there for my son when he's awake. I have no time—or interest—in a relationship right now."

"Yeah, but wouldn't it be nice to have a partner?" Rosie asked. "Someone to share your life with?"

There was no missing the longing in Sky's eyes. Brodie had never seen that side of her. "Right now, I'm sharing my life with Rocco. But, if I ever do decide to date, it sure as hell won't be a drifter."

"I thought you said he's been here a year." Rosie looked to Brodie for confirmation.

Brodie nodded.

"And before that, he was flying around the country doing private custom jobs. He's probably got itchy feet, dying to move on to the next job."

"Or maybe he's decided to put down roots," Rosie said.

Skylar headed toward the French doors. "I'll let some other woman be the test project. Jinx Costello is literally the last person I would ever date."

"I don't want to leave." Having just come out of the bathroom, Rosie stood there in a sexy robe that ended at the tops of her thighs. Her hair dripped onto the silky fabric.

Brodie couldn't take his eyes off her. *I don't want you to leave.*

Behind every smile, every kiss, and every touch, lived the beating pulse of truth: *this might be the last one.* With the vote ten days away and the critical work done on their business, time was running out. "What if you went home for a while, put in some face time in your country, and then came back?"

"It doesn't work like that. I've been away for seven years already. My parents can't force me to marry a douchenozzle, but they *will* insist I take on my responsibilities. I have to start my philanthropy and get involved in others."

"What about the marriage part? Isn't the priority producing an heir?"

"Well, I'm not a genie." In her agitation, the robe slipped off one shoulder. "I can't snap my fingers and produce a future husband. So, the best thing I can do is jump into my life there. I'll launch my project...create a life firmly rooted in St. Christophe. That's all I can do at this point." She dragged a comb through her hair, working through the tangles. Droplets splattered onto her bare shoulder, and he wanted to lick them off. "But first— before I do any of that—I'm going to open up my bath and body shop in the capital city of Villeneuve. I want to get it up and running."

Otherwise, she'd never have a business. "And what if we're so wildly successful we want to expand?"

Excitement shone in her eyes. Not a moment later, it died out. "Hold your horses, cowboy. One thing at a time. First, let me test our product today. See if they even like it."

"They'll like it." But what he really meant was, *they'll like you*. Everyone liked her. She was open and honest, elegant, and yet down to party.

She watched him a moment, all of her certainty fading. "I know what I have to do—I've always known, and I've been fine with it. But that was before I came to Calamity. Something happened to me here. Well, *you* happened to me, and I feel like…I don't know, like I'm twenty-five, and I've never met anyone like you, and I'm pretty sure I never will again, and how am I supposed to just get on a plane and leave you and have our only communication be about sales reports and ordering new pumps, when you're the one I most want to talk to? You're the one I want to brainstorm with. Your hands are the only ones I want on my body, your face the only one I want to see next to mine on my pillow." She reached for him, clasping her hands behind his neck and sifting her fingers through his hair. "I'm not ready to leave *you*."

Then don't. He kissed her, and he lost himself in the wet heat of her mouth, the urgency of her grip. And, suddenly, it grew too much, the emotion too big, and he bent his knees, grabbed her ass, and lifted her, pressing her against the wall. "Don't leave." He kissed her earlobe. "I want us." Licking down to her neck, he sucked the tender curve. "Rosie, you're the one for me." He knew it in his bones. Pressing kisses along her collarbone, he breathed in her fresh, sweet scent. "Give us a chance."

Fingers tangled in his hair, she arched against him. "I can't, Brodie. You know that. My life isn't here."

"It could be both places. We can do this however we want, whatever way it'll work. Don't leave *me*."

"Oh, God. I don't want to."

He squeezed her ass with one hand, while the other shoved the robe aside to expose her breast. Cupping it, his tongue flicked over the nipple. "You think, now that I've found you, I'm going to just let you go? Not a fucking chance. You're in me, sweetheart. It feels like you've always been there, like we just needed to get to this place, right here and now, for our paths to cross so we could find each other. But now that we have?" He tilted her chin, forcing her to look in his eyes. "I will never stop wanting to be with you. You're mine, and I'm yours. Don't you feel it?"

"God, of course I feel it, Brodie. There's nothing else I want to feel for the rest of my life than this. *Us*."

Her legs tightened around him, and he needed her mouth. She opened to him, their tongues colliding in a shower of sparks. Everything he felt for her crashed over him, and he poured it all into this kiss. He had to make sure she knew he meant every word he'd said. He ground against her, and she gasped. "Need you. Right the fuck now."

Setting her down, he locked the door, then grabbed the neck of his T-shirt and tugged it over his head. The robe pooled around her ankles, and she stood there in nothing but pink lace panties. Dropping to a crouch, he kissed his way up her calf, behind her knee, and inside her toned and sexy thigh.

She started to pull off her underwear, when he said,

"Leave them on." She wore the sexiest lingerie he'd ever seen. "You buy these for the douchenozzle?"

"Nope." Her fingers tangled in his hair, and her hips twisted. "There's a little shop in Paris, in the Marais. Some people deal with stress by eating or working out, but me… I like pretty lingerie."

"And you thought you weren't sexy." He pushed aside the elastic and licked inside her wet, hot slit.

Her whole body shuddered, and she lifted her leg, propping her foot on his shoulder. Goddamn, he wanted this woman. He explored her slick folds, ignoring the places that didn't get a hiss out of her and doubling down on the spots that did. When he flicked her clit, she got up on her toes. "*There.* Oh, right there."

Grasping her ass cheeks, he brought her right up to his face and licked her to an orgasm that had her body writhing and spasming, her fingers pulling his hair so hard his scalp stung.

When she settled, he stood up and kissed her right on the mouth. "My fierce princess. I'll do whatever it takes." Because, as improbable as it was, the princess was his. "Okay?"

"Okay." Wariness creeped into her eyes, and she covered her breasts with an arm.

He didn't want her closing up on him, but he understood. *This is fucking scary, wanting someone—no, not wanting.* It was so much bigger than that. *Knowing you've found the one person who makes your life whole and complete—and not knowing how the hell to keep her in it.* So, he pressed kisses to the mounds of her luscious cleavage. The smell of her clean, damp skin, her shuddery sigh, the sight of those plump, jiggly tits…Jesus, he was hard as a pole. "I want to see my dick in there."

She gasped, and he liked how hot she went for him. Her arm fell away, and she cupped her breasts together. "Do it."

That was all he needed to hear. Lifting her, he carried her to the bed and set her down. She crawled back to rest her head on a pillow. He'd never seen so much excitement in her eyes.

Grabbing lotion from his nightstand drawer, he tipped some onto his palm, but she grabbed his wrist. "I want to do it." She trembled, as she squeezed the white lotion into her hands. Rubbing them together, she grasped his cock, and he about jumped out of his skin. Her touch, so warm and feminine, so unlike the feel of his own, kicked up a riot of sensation.

She slicked up his length, using both hands to tug and swirl, her thumb flicking over the head with each pass.

"Fuck, princess. That feels good."

"Give me more."

Straddling her, he didn't know how much more he could take, but he squirted more lotion into her hand. Instead of touching him, though, she rubbed it all over her breasts. *Holy fuck.* The nipples rosy and hard, the mounds so plump and bouncy, made his mouth water and his cock go impossibly harder. He wasn't going to last.

He batted her hand away. Had to have her right now.

She pressed her big tits together, eyes glittering with lust, and he slid his cock into the tight channel. Jesus, it looked so fucking hot. "Push 'em tighter."

"God, Brodie." Her hips twisted, and her back arched.

He thrust his dick in until it popped out just beneath her chin. He was going to come way too soon like this, so he grabbed the lotion, squeezed some into his hands and rubbed her tits, pinching the nipples and slathering his cock. The head was so sensitive he nearly jumped out of his skin. He couldn't take it anymore and started pumping fast. So fast, he had to grip the headboard. Jesus, the sight of her plump tits, those hard, rosy nipples, his dick thrusting between them, made his spine tingle and his balls pull in tight. Just when he didn't think he could take one more second, she tipped her chin down and licked the head of his dick. With each frantic thrust, she swiped at the sensitive head.

"Fuck, Rosie, fuck." And then he was coming, harder than he'd ever come in his life. Thick spurts creaming all over her neck, chin, and mouth.

She let go of her tits, grabbed the base of his cock, and sucked him into her greedy little mouth. She clutched his ass, holding him to her, and he groaned deep and long.

Spent, he collapsed beside her.

Emotions clashed inside him, leaving him with a chaotic jangle of nervous energy. Wired, exhausted, thrilled, and scared shitless, he was a mess.

He'd always been in control. Always had a firm grip on his life.

And now? Everything had turned upside down.

But he remembered what she'd said. *There's nothing else I want to feel for the rest of my life than this. Us.*

She was in it with him.

Which meant they'd make it work.

Chapter Nineteen

"This place is amazing." Rosalina took in Fin's Antigravity Training Center, spread over hundreds of acres and utilizing as much outdoor space as indoor.

A series of steel and glass buildings housed athletes, gyms, and physical therapy rooms. Outside, a massive, deep pool had a slide built for snowboarders and skiers to practice their runs without getting hurt.

"Yeah, it's pretty cool." Brodie released her hand to check his phone. "Vanessa's here. She'll meet us in the tramp gym." He cut her a concerned look. "You sure you're okay with me still working with her?"

"Not to be mean, but I don't see a single reason to be jealous of her."

"Nothing mean about the truth." He grabbed her hand again.

She liked that he was always touching her. He did it with an urgency—like if he stopped, gravity would send them spiraling in separate directions. "The few times I saw you with her, there just wasn't anything there."

"No, there wasn't. But she did want something more,

so if you're uncomfortable with me working with her, I can find a new architect."

"It's not like I think she can seduce you into bed."

"There's not a chance of that."

"And, after I'm gone, are you going back to sleeping with her?"

"No."

Not a trace of indecision in his tone. "I love how decisive you are. The world's very clear-cut for you. Makes me feel safe."

They reached the door to a huge gym. She opened it and took in the sea of black trampolines, all of them cradled with bright blue foam pads. A bunch of athletes gathered on one side of the room, while Fin bounced on one of the jumping mats. The other two brothers stood on a cushioned pad, watching him.

"What's going on?" she asked.

"At the start of a session, Fin likes to bring in pros to show them how it's done. Give them a visual of what they're working towards. To make it fun, he has the athletes rank us. Seems to inspire them."

"So, that's what you meant by helping Fin out? You're going to bounce around on a trampoline?"

He nodded with a mischievous grin. "But, since you're here, I'm probably gonna jump a little higher than my brothers."

"What about your injury?"

"I can't *compete* at that level anymore, but I can play around."

"Boarding a glacier was playing around?"

"Sure."

She rolled her eyes. "You will *not* be tamed, will you?"

"You wouldn't want me tamed."

"No." She turned to face him, gazing up into his star-tling blue eyes. "I wouldn't." She thought about last night. Seeing his cock between her breasts, his expression of pure lust, watching him crest that wave between ecstasy and agony...it had been the hottest, most erotic experience of her life.

It wasn't just the dirty sex, him releasing all over her chest—it had been the intimacy. Trusting him.

This might be the wrong place for this conversation, but she needed to tell him before they joined the others. Clutching his T-shirt, she drew him towards the wall. "I like who I am with you. That I can be anything I want around you."

His eyes warmed, and his thumb swept across her bottom lip.

Her tongue darted out to lick it. "It just...it means so much that, with you, nothing's off limits, shocking, or impolite. Brodie, I'm totally free here. It's not just me trusting you, it's you trusting me. It's like we're in our own world, and we make our own rules."

"There are no rules, sweetheart. As long as we're in this together, we get to invent shit as we go along." He slid an arm around her back and yanked her toward him. The moment she hit his chest, he tipped her chin and gave her a savage kiss.

And she went up in flames. She loved the way he wanted her, the way he *took* her.

He held her possessively, kissed her with so much hunger...she just knew what she had with him was richer, deeper, than anything she'd ever have again. What they had was rare, special, and she needed to hold onto him, to make it work no matter what.

His hands slid down to her ass, and he squeezed,

hauling her up against him. God, she wanted to strip off his clothes, climb him—

Applause shattered their intimacy, forcing them to pull apart. The spectators clapped and pumped their fists. "Go, Fin," someone called.

They watched as Fin twisted and turned at odd angles, came down and bounced even higher. After landing on a pad, he did a barrel roll backflip and landed on his feet.

"That was insane," Rosalina said.

Not even out of breath, Fin waved his oldest brother over. "I'm not into awards, and technical precision bores me, but this guy…" Will joined him on the trampoline. "He's a nine-time world champion. Of course, he crapped out before the Olympics, but if you'd met Delilah you'd understand why."

A mix of boos and laughter came from the rowdy crowd.

"Okay, so Will's going to show you how someone with a stick up his ass does it."

"And by 'stick up the ass,' my baby brother means discipline." Will shot off the mat, bouncing so high and landing so hard, Fin nearly lost his footing. Instead of falling though, he leapt with surprising control onto a blue pad.

The oldest brother jumped in place a few times. He had this casual air about him, like he was just hanging out. She started to wonder if he'd been away from training too long—she'd heard he'd retired about nine months ago. But then, out of nowhere, he flipped. Not once. Not twice. But three times.

And, then, it was on. He executed the most perfect acrobatic moves she'd ever seen. The bystanders were shouting and clapping in awe.

When he came to a stop, he hadn't even broken a sweat. Rosalina joined in the enthusiastic applause. "Your brothers are amazing."

Brodie watched her for a moment. "Hold my beer." Striding past her, he toed off his running shoes and jumped onto a trampoline.

"And this one's Brodie," Fin said. "Even though he retired ten years ago, he's still got more trophies and medals than all of us combined."

"But he doesn't have the one that counts," someone called from the crowd.

"Oh, low blow, man," someone else shouted.

Over the smell of sweat and rubber came a strong blast of perfume. Rosalina picked up bergamot and vanilla, with soft undertones of citrus. The scent she'd come to associate with Vanessa.

She turned to see the woman standing next to her, staring at Brodie with a look of regret…and hunger.

"Oh, hey, Vanessa," Rosalina said. "I can't believe they're so mean to him."

"He doesn't care." Vanessa never took her eyes off Brodie. "Trust me, he's used to it by now."

"How long have you known him?"

"I only moved to town six years ago. This was my first job out of college. For about five years, I watched these guys." She looked to the brothers. "Our paths didn't cross much, but every time I saw them around town, I had to literally pick my jaw up off the ground. They're just… so…charismatic."

After bouncing several times, Brodie suddenly flipped. Only—unlike the other brothers—he didn't limit himself to one trampoline. With a stunning display of core strength and athletic grace, he soared from one mat to the other, taking a crazy spin around the entire gym, his body twisting and turning, flipping forward and back—never once taking a break.

"He's a thing of beauty, isn't he?" Rosalina said. "How does he not get dizzy?"

Vanessa didn't answer, just stared, mesmerized, looking like she wanted to drag him out by his hair and have her way with him.

"Now, that's how it's done," someone shouted.

Rosalina had never seen anyone with the strength and agility of Brodie Bowie.

"He's so hot." Vanessa sounded wistful. "He says he's not the relationship type, but he makes it really confusing."

"What do you mean?"

"Well, he's just so passionate, you know? And when he focuses it on you, you get swept up in it. It's like...you *think* it's about you. But it's not. He's just intense."

"Passionate about the projects you're working on, you mean?" Because Brodie had made it clear he'd never been into Vanessa.

"Well, sure, that, too, I guess. But, I mean, as someone he's dating, you think he's so into you, because he's wild in bed."

Rosalina shot her a look. Was she trying to make her jealous? But, no, Vanessa's tone was one of pure wistfulness.

She thinks I'm engaged. She doesn't even know I'm sleeping with him.

"I thought it meant he was into me, but it's just who he is. I see that now."

A chill fell cross her body, like leaving the bright, sunny sidewalk to walk down an alleyway. She didn't understand. Brodie had told Rosalina he'd never felt for anybody the way he did for her. But if Vanessa had experienced his passion in bed…*what does that mean for me?*

She didn't doubt his feelings for her…right now. But maybe he threw himself into all the projects he cared about. At the moment, Rosalina was one of them.

It hurt. So badly. But it was just the reminder she needed. She was getting too involved, too excited about the idea of something developing between them, when the only thing she should be focused on was launching her business.

Did she actually think a man who'd never had a romantic relationship would suddenly change his spots for *her*? Sure, he was into her now. She lived with him, worked with him, slept with him. But the moment she left town, he'd move on.

I'm a project. Like boarding or launching a digital platform or a bath and beauty products company.

Snap out of it already.

Of course they didn't have a future together.

You knew that.

Can you imagine Brodie in St. Christophe? Wearing slacks and button downs, visiting hospitals, attending royal ceremonies? That regimented life would kill him.

As much as it hurt, one day soon, she'd have to consign Rosie to a memory.

And then get on with her real life as Princess Rosalina.

In the bunkhouse, Rosalina stood at the long kitchen table watching this wonderful group of people who'd gathered to package her lotions for tomorrow's market testing.

At home, she worked alone in her lab. Neither her

family nor the Allards got involved. Marcel might listen to her go on about her formulas or ideas, but his interest was limited to the business side.

It hadn't really bothered her before. She'd just carried on, convinced that one day they'd see the obvious wisdom in her plan to expand their product line.

But, here, people jumped right in. Brodie had put out the call, and a couple hours later his entire family had shown up and gotten to work. They were all entrepreneurs, so they embraced each other's ideas readily.

Fin had opened a training center, and even though his brothers were busy with their own projects, they helped out all the time. Gray's wife wanted a digital store for her wedding gowns, and Brodie had immediately set out to find a three-D modeler.

This family supported each other's dreams. They were real and honest and loyal.

And it ripped open a tear in the Villeneuve family portrait. As much as she loved her parents, the duty, obligation...the loyalty ran in one direction. They expected her to fall in line: get married, produce an heir, and step into the shoes of every princess before her.

She understood that. Of course she did. It was the way it had been done for six hundred years. But what about supporting *her*? They'd turned down every idea she'd had. They viewed her work in the lab as a hobby.

The world had changed, and her parents hadn't adapted.

If she went home and assumed the role expected of her, she would lose herself. She would bruise and wither like a petal.

And it wasn't until this exact moment that she understood the hard line of resistance she'd felt from the moment her mother had expected her to meet with the wedding planner. If she wanted their respect, then she needed to respect *herself* enough to live her truth. No guilt, no doubts. *And that's why Brodie's so good for me.* He encouraged her to brainstorm solutions that married her parents' objectives with her own dreams.

"Hey." Brodie came up behind her, wrapping his arms around her waist. "What's going on in that sexy mind of yours?"

"I'm not going to marry Marcel."

He stepped in front of her, concern lining his forehead. "Is this news?"

"It is. All this time, no matter how sure I've sounded, I've had this fear that I'd go home and ultimately wind up doing what's in the best interests of my family and my country. But I think I finally get it—deep down—that it's not in anyone's best interests. Not only don't I want to get married and have a baby—I'm not ready for that—but it's not the way to lead my country forward. You know that expression, *Be the change you want to see in the world*?"

He nodded. Hope looked almost painful in his eyes.

"The thing is, I've been waiting for my parents to allow me to add another product to our business. And, when Marcel argued against my bath and body line, they went along with him, because he's expected to take over the business when our fathers retire. Well, guess what? I'm an intelligent, educated woman who grew up in the royal house, privy to all the decisions and inner workings. I don't need Marcel—or any man—to approve my business decisions."

He cracked a smile.

"I've been so worried about upsetting my father, about me being the reason we lose our seats in parliament, and I haven't been able to reconcile who I am with what they need me to be."

"Until now?"

"Until this very moment. As painful as it might be for my parents, I'm going to have to stay true to myself. Hold my ground. And that means I can't marry and get pregnant just so we can hang onto the monarchy, because I don't believe that's what's best for our people in the twenty-first century. And, I guess, if it doesn't work for them, then my sister can step into my shoes. Because the kind of life they expect me to live…it's just not possible."

"Hey, Rosie?" Callie called. "We're out of jars. Do you have any more?"

She glanced at the wall where she'd stacked the boxes. "No. I guess that's it. Wow, you guys are fast."

"Do you need us to load the truck?" Gray asked.

"No, thank you. I'd rather leave them in the air-conditioning." Rosalina turned back to the table. "Brodie and I can do it in the morning before we head into town."

"Are you going to decorate your stall?" Callie asked. "Or just give the samples away?"

"I thought the stalls were about demonstrating your craft," Delilah said. "Maybe you could make something. What would be easy to do?"

"We're setting up in the morning," Brodie said. "Not enough time to pull something together."

"True," Delilah said. "You know what might be fun? What if I did some cooking demonstrations?"

"If you're down to do it, I'd like that a lot," Brodie said. "It'll drive business to the restaurant."

"I want my atelier to smell just like this," Knox said. "Can you make a home fragrance mist?"

"Sure," Brodie said.

Rosalina elbowed him. "Don't say that. I have no idea how to make a mist."

"Then we'll find someone who does."

She gazed up at him, her heart so full. "There are no limits with you, are there?" She admired this man so much.

"No, princess. No limits."

"Done." Fin sealed his last jar and added it to the pile. "Now, whose ass am I kicking in air hockey?"

Brodie stepped away from her. "You sure your ego can take another beating, little brother? I was worried yesterday might've broken you."

Will's chair scraped back. He got up, smoothing Delilah's long, blonde hair. "You should've seen Brodie on the trampoline."

"Show off." Gray didn't look up from the lotion he was spooning into a funnel.

"Hey," Brodie said. "Don't give me shade just because you couldn't get any air."

"Oh, I got air," Gray said. "Believe me. I was told to use *one* trampoline. If I'd known I could use the whole damn place, I'd have shown you what it looks like when a gold medalist gets it done."

Knox kissed his cheek. "You'll show them next time, sweetie."

"Okay, now I get why you finished up here so fast." Rosalina grinned. "Everything's a competition to you guys."

Brodie and Fin took opposite sides of the air hockey machine, and Will and Gray picked up ping pong paddles.

"It really is." Callie watched Fin with adoration.

This.

This is the life I want. The certainty of it gripped her with a fierceness that took her breath away.

But did Brodie want it, too?

Or was he so passionate because he knew she was leaving?

They'd just loaded the bed of the truck, when Brodie shut the tailgate and hauled her into his arms. She loved this— the way she got to touch him whenever she wanted, sleep beside him at night. She got to talk to him about every little thing that popped into her mind and listen to all the ideas going through his.

He kissed her, his hands sweeping down her back and resting on the rise of her bottom. Her body flooded with heat, and desire made her heart go fluttery. "You ready to see how much people love your perfume?"

"So ready."

"You got your notebook?"

In her mind, she retraced her steps, remembering when she'd put it in her black leather tote bag. "Yep."

"Phone?"

"Ah…no. Still charging. Hang on one second." She darted into the bunkhouse and hurried into her bedroom. Even from the doorway, she could see the screen flashing. Once she reached her nightstand, she yanked out the plug and saw that her phone had blown up with messages.

A quick scan showed her mother, Harrison, Marcel… even her father. The sting of adrenaline had her punching her father's number first.

He never called. Something was wrong.

He answered on the second ring. "Rosalina?" Her normally warm, loving father sounded terse, clipped.

"Hi, Papa. What's going on?"

"The fact that you're asking means you haven't checked your text messages. I'll hold while you do."

"Can you just tell me? I'm kind of freaking out here." But, really, thank God her father was okay. Anything other than a health scare, she could handle.

"Henri showed us a photograph of you with a young man."

Dread slammed her back against the wall. "The paparazzi's here?"

"No. Marcel sent it to him."

"Are you serious? Marcel sent his father a picture of me and Brodie?"

"*Brodie*? So, it's true? You're in a relationship with someone?"

She wouldn't lie to her father. "Yes, I am."

He blew out a breath into the receiver. "Rosalina, what on earth are you doing? The vote is next week. Can you imagine if this photograph got into the hands of the paparazzi? Do you understand what it would do to our family? This country? How do I impress upon you that the monarchy hinges on our ability to prove its continuity? And, right now, that means you and Marcel presenting a united front."

"I thought you liked the idea of establishing a university."

"I do, but you seem to think a university will win you points with the voters, when it's nothing more than our obligation as guardians to give our citizens the very best opportunities and amenities possible."

She *had* done that, hadn't she? While it was undoubtedly a great idea, she'd come up with it as a way to make up for her broken engagement.

"If Auguste replaces me as Head of State, everything the people take for granted as their right will disappear. His plans will irrevocably change not just the economy but the very essence of St. Christophe. This is not about wanting to live in a castle and wear crown jewels, Rosalina. This is our responsibility, handed down by our forefathers. I do not take it lightly, nor will I let you take for granted the lifestyle it has afforded you. For goodness' sake, you've had seven years to 'sow your oats,' as the Americans say. It's time to embrace the responsibilities that come with the luxuries."

She couldn't argue with a single point he'd made. "Papa…" After that powerful speech, she didn't know if she could keep fighting for what seemed like a selfish, entitled platform. But, for some reason, she felt the need to try.

She stepped around the bed to look out the window, where she saw Brodie leaning against his truck, checking out his phone. She held up a finger, and he gave her a warm smile and a chin nod, which somehow gave her the strength to carry on the fight. "From the moment I found out about Marcel and Fabiana, my life's turned upside down."

"I understand how much that upset you, and I've given you several weeks away to get a handle on your emotions, but—"

"Father, stop. Do you hear yourself? I'm a twenty-five year old woman. You don't get to give me a time limit. This is my life. I love you and Mama so much. I love St. Christophe. But I'm so much more than your dutiful daughter. I'm more than my royal title. I have hopes and dreams and ambitions. I have a heart, and I can't ignore it. You shouldn't want me to."

"You haven't even been away six weeks. You couldn't have gotten so far along with this young man that you've given him your heart. And, if you're going to give it away, do it here."

"It's too late. And I didn't so much as give it away as open it up to find a space carved just for him. Believe me when I tell you, I've got a very strong grip on my emotions. What Marcel did, it was a gift. Had he not strayed, I would've been consigned to a lifetime of a love-less, passionless marriage. You can't want that for me."

"I want you home, assuming your duties. The royal life is not easy, not for anyone. Along with the benefits comes a lack of privacy and freedom. But, sweetheart, it is your birthright. It is your responsibility to rule this country."

"But I won't be ruling it, will I? My husband will. I'll be every bit as unfulfilled as Mother. Do you want that for me?"

In the absolute silence on the other end of the line, she wondered if she'd taken it too far. It wasn't her place to bring up her mother. And it wasn't like her mother had ever complained.

"No, I don't want that for you. You've always had such a strong spirit. I want you to be happy, but you're going to have to find a way to blend your role in this family and in this country with your passions, just as your mother has done. I think we both know she would make an even better ruler than I, but she's found a way to enact her vision through other means. You'll do the same. You must come home, Rosalina, and take on your role here."

She understood his point, but she also knew her own heart. "Brodie's special, Papa. What I feel for him…it's so much more than what I had with Marcel. I didn't come here for this. I certainly don't want to let you down or add to your stress, but I feel like my whole, true self here."

"Rosalina, that is *enough*. You've always had this streak of rebelliousness in you. We'd thought getting expelled from school might've been enough to get it under control, but I see it hasn't. There will be no forbidden romance with a cowboy. Not when the vote's next *week*."

"I can't believe Marcel took a picture of me and sent it to his father."

"I'm not sure you understand the pressure Marcel is under. He was instructed to bring you home, and when he couldn't, he showed his father the reason why. Henri is not a patient man, and this situation has pushed him to his limit. First, his son acts out, and now you."

"I'm not acting out. That's an insulting way to look at this. I love him." *Oh, dear God.* She did, didn't she?

She glanced out the window to find Brodie watching her. Her heart swelled so big it hurt. "I'm not getting back at Marcel, and I'm not rebelling against my role. I've simply fallen in love with a man who makes me happier than I've ever been."

Her father let out a slow, tired breath. "Listen to me. I would never force you to marry Marcel, and after the vote we can talk about your business plan. I won't hold you back from realizing your dreams, but you must take on your role here. You've been in that town a matter of weeks. You can't have fallen so hopelessly in love with this man that there's no turning back. The sooner you end it with him, the easier it will be on both of you."

His concessions surprised her—and warmed her. But she couldn't believe the way her body reacted to the idea that she hadn't fallen so hopelessly in love that there was no turning back.

Because that's exactly what I've done. She pressed her hand to the cool glass, her heart so full of love she wanted to drop the phone and run right into Brodie's arms. She never wanted to leave those arms again.

"After the vote, things will be different. Between the two of us—and this goes no further—I will be firing Henri. And that means his son will go, as well."

"You're firing them? *Papa.*"

"There can be no other interpretation to him showing us the picture than to either manipulate or blackmail us into controlling our daughter. He's never disguised his ambitions, but anyone who works for the Villeneuve family must place honor and country above his own ambitions."

"But he holds all our secrets."

"And that's why we conduct ourselves the way we do, sweetheart. So that we have no skeletons in our closets."

Her father was a good, honorable man, and all she'd done was pile on the stress during the hardest period in his life. "All right, Papa. I'll come home."

When Brodie straightened, eyes narrowing on her, she knew what her expression revealed.

The clock had just about run out. "Give me one week to finish up here. I'll be home before the vote."

Chapter Twenty

"CAN'T SLEEP?"

In six days, Rosalina would never get to hear that deep, rumbly voice again. She'd never have this intimacy with him, their naked bodies under the covers, the heat of him stretched alongside her. The clutch of his hands in the middle of the night, and the sexy murmurs in her ear.

"Not really."

Brodie rolled onto his side, slung his arm across her, and nuzzled her neck. "Still buzzed?"

After giving away every sample, Rosalina had been wired. It wasn't just the fantastic response they'd gotten to the lotion, but the idea it had prompted. Brodie would open an online store for the hotel to sell not only their spa products but other gifts specific to Owl Hoot.

The spirit of Calamity and the Bowie family...she'd never felt more inspired. The freedom to create had opened the floodgates. It was exhilarating.

"No."

"What's on your mind?"

"I was thinking about the way you laugh. Usually, you're all serious and badass—even when someone teases you or says something funny—but every now and then you let loose a smile or a laugh that just slays me. You're so incredibly handsome, but your intensity can be intimidating. So, when you smile? It's like…it's like on an overcast day, when the sunshine breaks through the clouds?" She rolled to look at him. "It's like that."

He nudged her. "Come on. What're you really thinking about?"

"I'm thinking about the way you look at me. Like… like…" She had to close her eyes to conjure up his expression, so she could get it just right. "Like I delight you. Like the wavelength of my voice is meant for you alone. Like…there's no one else you'd rather be with."

The awkward silence reminded her of what Vanessa had told her in the trampoline gym. "Relax. Don't get all worked up about it. I'm not saying any of that's true. I know when you find something you like you go all in. I'm just saying how it makes me feel."

The next stretch of silence made her wish she could rewind and delete everything she'd said. Sometimes she needed to shut her mouth. She hadn't meant to make him uncomfortable. "Never mind. Seriously, just forget it."

But, then, his voice, cracked the quiet. "I didn't respond right away…because I was embarrassed."

Embarrassed? "About what?"

"That you see all that."

Because it's not what you feel? Or because it is? "Oh, well, don't be. Apparently, a lot of women see it. You just have a way about you." She instantly regretted saying that. She'd tried to sound teasing, but it was passive aggressive, and that wasn't cool.

"What the hell are you talking about?"

Best to just say it. "It's something Vanessa said. It's been bugging me for a few days. She said the reason she thought there was more to your relationship is because you're so wild in bed. She said she confused your passion for actual feelings for her."

"Fucking Vanessa." He threw off the covers and stalked to the window. Giving her a fantastic view of his hard, round ass, the breadth of his shoulders, and taper of his waist. Even in the dark, she could see the power in his muscular thighs. "She's messing with you."

"I don't think so. I didn't have any sense that she was trying to make me jealous. But I get what she means, because if you give her half of what you give me, I can see how she'd be confused."

"I didn't give her anything. And, trust me, there wasn't any passion between us. We worked together. Sometimes we'd grab a bite to eat, and it ended with a quick fuck."

She hated the image of him with Vanessa. With any other woman.

"Sorry, but it's true. That's all it ever was." Finally, he turned to face her. "The other day my brother told me about some conversations he'd overheard around the time my mom left the family, and it made me realize how different I was before that happened. I was a pretty wild kid. But, after all that went down—me demanding she come home, reaming her ass when she kept putting me off and giving me bullshit excuses—after I figured out she wasn't ever coming back, I just shut down."

He stalked back to the bed, towering over her with his imposing physique. "You're leaving in six days, Rosie. I've known it from the beginning, but I feel like that kid all over again. It's killing me, because I want you to stay. I want to *beg* you to stay. And it feels exactly the same as it did with my mom." Putting a knee on the bed, he crawled over her. "What I feel for you? I've never felt this for anyone. *You* make me smile. *You* make me happy. I never understood why my brothers would settle down with one woman, because until I met you, I had more fun with them than anybody else. But I get it now. I get why they put a ring on it. Because, when I look at you, I see my heart, my home, I see my *future.* Do you understand what I'm telling you?"

She thought she might, and it sent a thrill through her.

"So, don't listen to anyone's bullshit. Listen to *me.* You're the only one that makes me wild, Rosie. The only woman I've ever wanted to be with."

"I want to stay here. More than anything, I want to stay. But I just don't see a way to do that."

"I know." He lowered his hips over hers. "Dammit, I *know.*" His mouth closed over hers, and he kissed with an urgency and passion that melted all the worry and anxiety out of her bones.

He kissed her so deeply and fiercely that she lost her sense of time and place, until she could feel her spirit merging with his. It was the most powerful, soul-shaking moment in her life.

"Need you. All of you." She pushed him off to kick aside the blanket, so there was nothing between their bodies.

His mouth wandered to her neck, forming a neckless of kisses along her collarbone. "You've got all of me, sweetheart. Couldn't hold back if I tried."

She clutched his hard ass, sealing their bodies together.

His cock, trapped between them, rubbed her clit, and an electric, searing sensation swept through her. "Inside. Now."

"Fuck, princess." His hips lifted, and he fisted his cock before lining himself up and thrusting hard.

Her whole body went incandescent, her bones buttery soft. Desire, so rich and pure, had her in its thrall. He slid a hand under her ass, lifting her, and the angle hit just right, making her arch off the mattress and cry out.

She'd never felt more alive, more sexual, and she needed more, deeper, harder.

Brodie nudged her, and it took a moment to break through the fog of lust to understand he wanted her to roll over. Another wave of desire crashed over her at the idea of him taking her from behind, and she flipped over, getting up on her elbows, and hiking her bottom up high for him.

"Oh, yeah, princess. So fucking hot." Both hands gripped her ass, spreading her, and he slammed back inside.

Nothing had ever felt so good, her breasts bouncing, her hips slamming back against him. He drove into her, and she stretched her arms out in front of her, pressing her hands against the headboard.

The burn started in her core, a twisting, gathering, rising sensation of bliss, until it flashed out of control. He reached between her legs, found her clit, and the delicious shock of it had her arching like a cat. Pleasure rushed through her, making her body tingle and shudder. It was all so intense, she threw her head back and cried out his name.

And, then, she burst right out of her body, spiraling through a freefall that seemed to never end. A flurry of froth and bubbles exploded behind her eyelids, and she rode the wave until it crashed. Floating towards shore, she collapsed, spent, her body vibrating with satisfaction.

This man…he was everything she'd never known she wanted.

She had to make it work. Somehow, she had to find a way.

She couldn't let him go.

Brodie stabbed a wooden stake into the ground.

Fucking Vanessa. Putting that crap in Rosie's head. Well, words meant shit. He knew that from experience. He'd show his princess how much he wanted to be with her.

He'd make it *possible.*

Will took in the meadow. "This might even be better than the last one."

"I think so, too." Brodie had liked the first building site because it wasn't too far from the highway. This one was set further back, but it had shade trees and a river crossing it, so that'd be cool. He could raise a family here.

Well, damn. He'd never imagined having kids before.

"You sure you want to do this?" Will examined the blueprint before driving a stake into the earth.

"What do you mean? You just said you like this site."

"No, I do. It's perfect. I meant adding a lab. You don't think you're jumping the gun?"

"Wherever she lives, she'll need one." Rosalina had shown him pictures of her laboratory back home, so he had some idea of the proportions.

"I was under the impression she can't live here. Her life's in St. Christophe."

"It is, but that doesn't mean she can't spend time out here." He reached for another stake. "All I know is that it can't happen unless she *can* do her work here."

"I don't get it." Even so, Will counted off the steps before jamming another stake into the ground. "This isn't fucking Field of Dreams. If you build it, she will stay. Why not figure things out with her first before you build a *lab*?"

"What am I going to do? Just let her go home? Someone has to make a move. So, that's what I'm doing. I'm showing her that, no matter what, we're going to be together. Even if we have to have homes in both countries."

"You'd move to Europe?"

The mid-morning sun slanted at just the right angle to make the snow at the top of the mountains sparkle. A hawk soared over head, and the wind carried the scent of pine and sage. He'd traveled the world, and he couldn't imagine living anywhere but here. Not just for the natural beauty or the family he loved with all his heart, but for the spirit of the place. The freedom. "Sure." *I'll go wherever she is.*

"Really?" Will sounded shocked. "Don't get me wrong. I can see what she means to you. And Rosie's awesome, but she's a *princess*."

"They're not like the British royal family. Not even close."

"Still, her life's a whole lot different from ours."

He'd lose his freedom and his privacy. "I know that." He'd miss out on the nieces and nephews sure to come in the next few years. *Fuck.* Agitated, he shot his brother a look. "I can't just let her go."

"Not saying otherwise. My point is that you should

maybe hold off on building the lab until you see what happens."

"And *my* point is that the only way it's going to work is if we *make* it work. Would you have built Delilah a restaurant to make it possible for her to stay?"

Understanding settled on Will's features. Smiling, he wrapped an arm around his shoulder and gave him a shake. "Let's build a fuckin' lab."

Immersed in luscious scents, Rosalina counted out another ten drops of essential oil into the melted soy wax. Thirty hadn't created a strong enough effect, so she hoped forty would do the trick. They wouldn't sell candles yet, but while waiting for her first shipment to come in from the production facility...why not get started on the other products?

When her phone trilled from the bedroom, she considered letting it go to voicemail but guilt got the better of her. *It's bad enough you asked for another week. At least be available to your family if they call.*

Setting the jar down, she wiped her hands on a towel and hurried out of the kitchen and into her bedroom. Sure enough, her mother's name lit up the screen. "Morning, Mama."

In the full second of silence, Rosie caught the faint shudder of breath. Fear punched the air out of her lungs. "Mother?"

"Darling..." Another shuddery breath. "Your father's in surgery. He's had a heart attack. I'm going to need you to come home."

Heart attack? "Oh, my God." *Papa.* A flurry of memories shuffled through her mind in quick succession. At dinner with her family, telling them about her embarrassing audition for the school play, and her father reaching under the table to grasp her hand and hold it firmly in his. College graduation, when her father had pulled her aside to give her a special gift—a thick envelope filled with twenty-one notes he'd secretly written to her every year on her birthday.

Twenty-one beautiful, heart-wrenching, funny notes that she'd treasure forever.

And the day she'd gotten into perfume school—one of only four students they took each year—her father had hugged her and whispered in her ear, "You're the light of my life. I'm happy for you."

Tears burned, and her body went hot. "Is he all right?" *Please don't let him die.*

Oh, my God, please.

"He'll pull through by the force of my will alone." Her mother paused. "But you must come home right away."

"I will." Right before she disconnected, she said, "I love you, Mama." She had so many questions, but she knew her mother was in no frame of mind to answer them. Her mind fractured, a dozen thoughts zinging out and colliding.

Pack.

Wait, no, get a flight first.

Brodie. With shaking hands, she called him, but it went straight to voicemail. "I...I need you. Can you call me, please?" He'd gone to the building site. *No reception.* He wouldn't be gone long.

What if he dies? What if he never wakes up after surgery? His heart could give out this time. She hated herself for pushing him so far. She could've come home when he'd asked her. She should have.

Why didn't you?

Why had she insisted on prolonging her time in Calamity? No matter what, it had to end.

Pack. She'd taken one step toward the closet before she remembered she needed a plane.

She typed out a text to Brodie. **My father's had a heart attack. I need to get home. Can I use your jet? It's the fastest way.**

She waited—*come on, Brodie. Answer me.* She didn't know how to reach his brothers. And she'd never hired a new assistant, so she'd have to get on her laptop and book a flight.

Give him a few minutes. He can't be far.

In the closet, she wheeled out one of her suitcases, kicked it over, and unzipped it. She'd only take one. Leave the rest of her stuff behind. *Who cares?*

She loved her father so much. *He can't die. He just can't.*

In the distance, a sound registered. Tires crunching over gravel. "Brodie." She raced out of the closet.

"Rosalina?"

No. Not him. She met Marcel in the hallway. "What're you doing here?"

He walked right past her. "I've hired a jet. It's on its way to the local airstrip." He pointed towards her room. *This one?*

She nodded, following him in. As she stuffed her suitcase with shoes and everything that hung on the racks, he pulled more luggage out of the closet.

Glancing over, she saw him emptying her dresser drawers. "Forget that stuff. I don't need it."

"You're not coming back, so we might as well take everything."

Not coming back. It hit her like a fist to the throat.

I'm leaving, and I'm not coming back.

It's over.

Zipping her suitcase, she came out of the closet.

Marcel scanned her room. "Charger?"

"Nightstand."

He bent over and pulled it from the wall. "Got it. Passport?"

"Oh, right." She'd have left without it. Digging under the mattress, her fingers touched the cool folder. "Okay."

"Ready?" Marcel heaved her suitcase off the bed.

She nodded, and they hurried out of the room. Grabbing her purse off the kitchen table, she took a quick look around the living area. Her black flip flops sat by the French doors, where she'd left them after a trip to the lake the night before. Jars and labels and pumps littered the table and kitchen counters.

"Let's go." Marcel led the way outside.

The driver waited at the trunk of his black sedan, taking the luggage from them.

Rosalina slid into the back seat, the cold air instantly drying her damp skin. Marcel got in beside her, reaching for her. "He's going to be okay."

Her hand jerked away as if a cockroach had crawled across it. "Don't touch me."

The driver got into his seat and shut the door. Within moments, they were heading down the driveway.

Marcel leaned forward and closed the partition, but he didn't try to touch her again. "We'll be home in just over ten hours."

Her heart raced, and her stomach knotted. She

couldn't stand it. "Have you gotten an update? My mother didn't say much."

"There's no information at this point."

"Where was he? How did it happen?"

"From what I understand, he wasn't feeling well during dinner, but they didn't think anything of it. It got worse while he was reading in bed. Your mother found him in the bathroom."

"What does that mean? Found him how?" She hated to think of her strong, sturdy father crumpled on the cold marble floor.

"All I know is that she called security, and they got him downstairs just in time to meet the paramedics. He's in the private wing of the hospital. No one knows, and it obviously can't get out."

She tipped her chin down and went still. What had she done?

Why are you so selfish?

As her father had pointed out, she'd had seven—*seven*—years to find herself. That was more than enough. But, no, she had to push it, had to take more, more, more.

What if she'd gone home when he'd asked? Would he be okay right now?

"Stop blaming yourself." Marcel's voice snapped her out of her suffocating thoughts.

"I blame *you*. I would never have left home if you hadn't cheated on me."

Is that true, though? Even before you found out, you'd considered going to Calamity for the fitting.

But…had she been selfish? Or starting a business?

Did it matter?

"Don't go there," Marcel said. "We didn't cause this.

Your father has heart issues. And there's tremendous stress in his life."

"That *you* caused. I will never forgive you for this. If I could push you out of this car right now, I would." Instead, she was stuck with him for the next ten hours. "I'm serious, Marcel. Don't talk to me, or I'll lose my shit all over you."

He let out a huff, as if to say, *See what you've become? Damn right, this is who I've become.*

And she fucking liked it.

With just four days until Rosie left, Brodie had asked his new architect to rush the blueprints for the lab. On his way to the bunkhouse, the drawings in a tube on the passenger seat, he wanted to floor it. Slap them down on the table and say, *This is how serious I am.*

But he didn't want her to think he was pressuring her into staying here, so he needed to figure out the right words. Let her know he understood her duties and obligations, and he'd never ask her to give up her life in St. Christophe.

He just didn't want her to leave without seeing the possibilities. To understand that he'd do whatever it took to keep them together. He had to get it right—pitch it in a way that assured her he wasn't trying to lock her down. She didn't want marriage and kids. She wanted to work, play, live, and he wanted to do all of it with her.

Parking, he grabbed the tube from the passenger seat and jogged up the steps to the porch.

He couldn't wait to show her the new location—

upwind from the lyantha meadow, so she'd have that scent in the house every June. *She'll love that.*

And she'll go home knowing what our life will look like together.

Nerves on fire, he threw open the door. "Rosie?" He imagined her expression, the excitement, when he showed her the lab. She could design it however she wanted. State of the art everything.

Heading into the kitchen, he breathed in the scent that would forever be associated with his woman. "Rosie?"

It looked like she was right in the middle of a project…making candles? She was always working on something. She tinkered, that was her style. She'd take a break, then go back to work. Eat some dinner, go back to work. Her mind worked like his, her subconscious always working through problems. The moment it delivered solutions, she'd cruise back to her lab.

He tapped the tube on the counter. "Rosie?" Damn, but he couldn't wait another second to show her the plans.

He tried to think what she had going on today. She was waiting for another shipment of jars and labels. She'd already sent the formula to the production facility in Idaho, so everything was good there. He couldn't recall her mentioning anything specific for this morning.

Maybe she'd gone into town with Sky? Heading for her bedroom, he pushed the door open. "Rosie?"

Her nightstand, once crammed with books, hand lotion, lip balm, and water glasses, was empty.

What the actual fuck?

He strode into the room, throwing open the door to her walk-in closet. *Empty*. Except for a black cashmere sweater crumpled on the floor.

Blood roared in his ears, and he pulled out his phone. Immediately, he found a bunch of texts from her.

My father's had a heart attack. I'm on my way home.

Oh, Jesus. Adrenaline flooded him, making him sick to his stomach. Her dad meant the world to her. But, before he called her, he skimmed the rest of the messages.

I'm so scared. It's going to take me ten and a half hours to get home. What if I don't make it in time? What if he dies before I get there? I'll never forgive myself.

A smothering sense of helplessness yanked him under. He hadn't been there for her when she'd needed him most.

He should be with her. She shouldn't be alone right now. *Fuck.*

He knew the guilt she had to be feeling. Her dad had asked her to come home, and she'd put it off another week. Brodie called her. Thank Christ, she answered right away.

"Brodie?"

"Yeah, sweetheart. I'm here."

"I can't lose my father. I…"

And then she was sobbing so hard she couldn't speak. For a few moments, he let her unleash. Didn't distract her with meaningless words.

Fuck, he wanted to be there with her. Wanted to wrap her up in his arms and let her tears soak his shirt.

"Brodie."

"Sweetheart, tell me where you are. I can have the jet ready to go in an hour." Grabbing his keys from his pocket, he hurried out the door, flew off the porch steps, and raced to his truck.

"No, that's all right. We've already hired a jet. We're at the airstrip now."

He heard a muffled conversation. Assuming, she was

checking in for her flight, he said, "Give me twenty minutes. I'm heading over right now." He jammed the key into the ignition.

But then she came back on the line. "No, please don't do that."

Oh, fuck. That voice…that was Rosalina. *Shit.*

"Don't do what? I'm coming with you." He jerked the gearshift and headed towards the road.

Murmuring turned to shouting. "Don't tell me what to do, you giant asshole."

Okay, she wouldn't talk to her driver that way. "Rosie, who're you with?"

"I'm with Marcel. He's arranged for us to get home. Brodie, listen to me."

He would, but he could already feel his heart shriveling.

"You know what you mean to me, but it's…I have to go home now. Do you understand what I'm telling you?"

"I hear you, princess, loud and clear."

"Good. We can talk more in a few days, after things settle down. Thank you for being so understanding. I just can't handle—"

"I said I hear you, not that I accept what you're telling me. I'm the one who should be with you right now, not the douchenozzle. Now, listen to me, I know you're upset, but I can be at the airport in fifteen minutes. Just wait for me. I got you, sweetheart."

"Brodie." Her tone turned sharper, as if to shut him up. "You must understand that you can't come home with me. Please, just…I can't do this. I can't…it's my father. There's a very real chance he won't make it through this surgery. Even if he does, he's going to be in recovery for months."

She lowered her voice. "It's over, Brodie. It has to be. When I get off the plane, I'm going to become the hereditary princess, and everything that entails. I'm going to do whatever I need to do for my family, the monarchy, and my country. Do you understand what I'm telling you?"

"I do." He wanted to yell at her. Tell her to knock it off, let him come get her. But he knew it wasn't what she needed. Not even close. *Fuck.*

He kicked a chair, but it was tucked in tightly against the table, so it didn't go anywhere. That sense of helplessness turned into rage, and he grabbed it by a spindle and hurled it. The satisfying splinter of wood didn't erase the image of her in that car with Marcel. A man who might one day be her husband. He wanted to tear it out of his brain and rip it to shreds.

She needed to hear about the lab. "After the vote, I'll fly out there," Brodie said. "We can—"

"No. We can't. Please Brodie, *please*, don't make this harder than it already is. Just...let me go."

She didn't need his shit right now. She needed to get home and see her dad. "Yeah, okay. But if you need me, I'm here." *Always.*

"Thank you. Goodbye, Brodie."

She disconnected, and like an asshole, he kept the phone to his ear, as if he could somehow hang onto her.

He paced to the French doors, thoughts swarming like bats. He got it—the implications of this news could be devastating. With her dad's health in jeopardy just days away from the vote, they had to pull out all the stops for a show of continuity and strength.

They had no choice. Her mother couldn't be Head of State, nor could Rosie or her sister.

They'd make her marry the douchenozzle. He knew it in his gut.

They were panicking, and in their anxiety, they were relying on the old playbook.

She's going to marry Marcel.
She'll have no choice.
Jesus Christ.
It's over.

Chapter Twenty-One

HURRYING DOWN THE HALLWAY OF THE HOSPITAL'S private wing, Rosalina's heels clicked on the polished floor. The smells assaulted her—disinfectant, medicine, *sickness*.

Two of her father's bodyguards stood vigil outside his room, and a cluster of royal insiders gathered in the waiting area.

Keeping pace with her, Marcel looked up from his phone. "Your mother's in a private conference room."

"I know that. I've been in contact with her this whole time." But instead of finding her mother, she went to the nurse's station. It would be better to get details from them. When Marcel followed, she said, "Stay away from me. When it's time to put on a show, I will. But right now, in this hospital, it's about me and my family."

Reluctantly, he let her go.

At the desk, she said, "Excuse me?"

One of the nurses looked up. "Good morning, Princess."

"Can you please fill me in on my father?"

The woman stood up. "Yes, of course. They repaired his mitral valve."

"I don't know what that means. Is he all right?"

"He's in recovery right now."

"Is that…did they have to…" Pain gripped her—the idea of cracking her father's breastbone to get at his heart —it just hurt so badly to think of him that vulnerable. Tears burned, blurring her vision.

The nurse swung around the desk to stand beside her. "If you're asking whether they had to open his chest, no. Fortunately, the mitral valve is the most common repair, and he only needed a chordal transfer. It's far less invasive, and there won't be any risk of blood clots."

"Okay. So, that's good?"

"It's as good as it gets, and of course they've flown in the best cardiovascular team in the world, so he's getting the very best care possible."

"Thank you so much."

"It's my pleasure, Princess."

When she turned, she found Harrison waiting for her. She ran right into his arms. The big man held her tightly. "He's stable, Rosalina. He's going to recover."

"It's my fault," she whispered. "Why can't I just be happy with what I have?"

"Because you're so much more than what they need you to be." He released her and led her to a small conference room. Before pushing open the door, he said, "Brace yourself."

Inside, her mother stood with the staff, issuing orders.

"Why isn't she with my father?" she asked him quietly.

"The doctors are with him right now. Trust me, she's been by his side every moment. But, now, she's doing damage control. They're keeping his condition on lock-down. It can't get out."

Her heart seized at what her father's heart attack could mean for Tuesday's vote. "Mama." She pushed through the crowd to get to her.

"There you are." Her mother held her tightly, her slender body trembling.

"I'm sorry I wasn't here. I'm sorry I've made it so difficult on you."

"This isn't your fault, sweet girl."

"The nurse told me they did it the least invasive way and with the fewest complications."

"That's right, darling." Her mother looked ravaged with worry.

"Can I see him?"

"Not yet. But as soon as they give me the word, we'll all go in together." Her mother glanced across the room to where Genevieve sat alone on a plastic chair.

"Vivi." As Rosalina dashed across the room, her sister jumped up and into her arms. They held each other tightly, rocking slowly in place.

Her sister pulled back first. "Is he going to die?" Frustration warred with fear in her eyes. Streaks of mascara marred her pale, smooth skin.

"No. He's not."

"I can't ask Mother, and everyone's just giving me the, *He's going to be fine* bullshit. I'm not a child. I can handle the truth. I just want to know."

"I talked to the nurse on my way in. She said they flew in the best surgeons, and that he had the least invasive surgery. So, I choose to believe he's going to be all right. Okay?"

"Yes. I'm going to choose that, too." Her lower lip trembled.

"You can cry. It's okay. We can cry together."

With that permission, her sister crumpled against her, releasing big, heaving sobs against Rosalina's shoulder. "It's all my fault. I've been so self-absorbed."

"What?" Rosalina stroked her sister's hair. "No, you're at university. You're doing exactly what you should be doing."

"I'm not even taking summer classes. It's just that it's such a stressful time, and there's nothing I can do. I have no control over anything, so I just…stayed away. The vote's coming, Mother and Father are a mess, you're supposed to marry a cheating asshole…and I'm off having the time of my life in London."

"Hey. Listen to me. It's ridiculous for any of us to take the blame for Father's heart problems. It's a difficult time, for sure, but there really isn't anything one person can do to fix the situation." Saying the words to her sister—believing them—actually helped relieve some of her own guilt.

Harrison approached them. "Your mother's going in. She says you can come in for a minute."

"Oh, thank God." She reached for her sister's hand and, together, they followed him out of the room.

As they passed the nurse's station, she flashed a grateful smile to the woman who'd answered her questions, before entering their father's room.

Curtains drawn, monitors beeping, her father lay helplessly on the bed. A tube filtered fluid into the back of his hand. Her mother brushed the hair off his forehead and pressed kisses to his cheek.

Rosalina and her sister moved to the other side of the bed. She kissed his cheek. "Hi, Papa. I love you so much."

"Love you, too." His lips were dry, his skin gray. "Don't look at me like that. I'm going to be just fine."

"Of course you are." But he didn't seem fine at all. He looked older than she'd ever seen him. It was the first time she understood the impact of their laws of succession. Her father was truly alone in carrying the weight of the monarchy on his shoulders.

"Papa." Tears glittered in Genevieve's eyes.

It seemed to take a monumental effort for her father to lift his hand, but her sister grasped it. "Love you." Her voice came out shaky and thin.

A doctor entered the room, picking up the clipboard at the end of the bed. "I know you're worried about him, but he's just come out of surgery and needs time to recover. Might I ask you to let him rest?"

"Of course." The last thing Rosalina wanted was to leave her father, and her mother's expression revealed the same reluctance.

But they each kissed his cheek, and she heard their mother whisper in his ear, *I love you so very much.*

The vehemence in her mother's tone, the fierceness in her eyes, cracked Rosalina's heart wide open. Unwelcome tears streamed down her face. She grew hot, restless. She wanted to crawl out of her skin. Instead, she led the way out of the room.

Harrison caught her expression, and immediately went into action. Instead of taking the three of them back to the staff, he ushered them into a private room and shut the door, his big shoulders blocking the window.

The moment they were alone, they fell onto each other.

"I'm so scared," her sister said. "I don't want him to die. Please don't let him die."

"He's not going to die, Vivi." Rosalina swiped the tears from her cheeks, her sister's weakness forcing her to be stronger.

"It's his second heart attack," Genevieve said. "A heart only has so many beats."

Rosalina pressed her hand hard on her sister's back, reminding her that their mother didn't need to hear this.

Genevieve immediately pulled away. "I'm sorry, Mama. I'm just so scared."

"I know you are." Her mother patted their backs. "But let me tell you something, we are not going to talk about my husband dying. We have to be strong for him. More than ever before, he needs us to be strong."

"I didn't call him back." Tears streamed down Genevieve's cheeks. "He left messages all week, and I didn't call him back."

"Darling, he knows you love him." Her mother's voice tried to be soothing, but Rosalina heard the thread of fear.

"No, I should've called him back. He's my father, and I love him."

"Of course you do. You're also only twenty years old, and we've expected so much from both of you." Her mother stroked Rosalina's hair. "I know you're blaming yourself, darling, but that's not going to help."

Rosalina noticed her mother didn't say it wasn't her fault. "He has too much stress, and Marcel and I only made it worse."

"As Head of State, your father deals with unrelenting stress and pressure," her mother said. "This latest power play by Auguste is nothing new. The new variable is that we've discovered your father's heart had an abnormal valve, and it's now been repaired."

Though she'd never say it out loud, no one could promise them he'd recover. It was his *heart*.

"All we can do is move forward," her mother said.

A knock on the door jerked them apart, but it was only her mother's press secretary. "Pardon me, Madam, but we're ready to go."

"Excellent. Thank you." Her mother cupped Rosalina and her sister's elbows and practically hustled them back into the conference room. "We have a plan," she said in a low voice. "And I'm going to need you both to follow along with no resistance. Do you understand?"

The image struck of her father, the monitors, his gray pallor…his utter exhaustion. "Of course."

When they reached the staff, the press secretary turned to her mother. "He's here. Are we ready?"

Dread kicked in. *Ready for what?*

"Yes," her mother said.

And then everyone turned to watch Marcel walk into the room. His gaze immediately found Rosalina's, and he gave her a look that said, *I know you don't like this, but…it's happening.*

"What's going on?" In the back of her mind, the truth blinked like a neon bar sign, but Rosalina blocked it, refusing to acknowledge it.

Because…Brodie.

Calamity.

Marcel…*this isn't the life I want.*

In her mind, she screamed so loudly, she couldn't believe no one covered their ears. Around her, everyone moved with purpose. Some talking on phones, others exchanging documents.

She was going to have to marry him. The douchenozzle. She had no choice.

Her mother's press secretary stepped forward, ushering her ex over. "The camera crew's setting up at the castle right now. I need both of you to change…" She took in Rosalina from head to toe. "I'll find a stylist who can meet you there right away. We'll need to take care of hair and make-up before we go live."

"What are we announcing?" she asked.

"Our engagement party," Marcel said. "It'll be held on the castle grounds."

"This Saturday." Her mother gave her a firm look. *Don't argue.* "And we're moving up the wedding to December twenty-seventh."

All it took was that flash of her father lying in a hospital bed to shut down any protests.

She couldn't even contemplate marrying Marcel, but she'd resisted enough. She would go along with anything they asked of her, just to keep her father healthy.

"Please go to the castle right away and prepare for the press conference," her mother said.

But Rosalina's legs felt sluggish, and her brain wasn't connecting with her limbs.

Her mother and Marcel exchanged a look. He nodded and set a hand on her lower back, leading her out of the room. "Let's go." Harrison and Gustav followed.

For the sake of appearances, Rosalina let her ex touch her as they walked down the hallway and boarded the private elevator, but the moment they stepped out into the parking garage, she jerked away from him. "Harrison, can you get me home?"

"Of course."

"Rosalina." Marcel sounded exasperated. "We're going to the same place."

But she ignored him and followed her bodyguard to a different car.

Through tinted windows, Rosalina looked out on the capital city. The businesses looked right out of a fairytale with their wood and stone features, the window boxes bursting with colorful flowers and window panes of glass so old they looked to be melting.

Villeneuve was charming, beautiful, and it looked nothing like the wild west town of Calamity. Her heart ached for Brodie, couldn't bear how he would feel when he heard the news of her engagement party.

She thought about what he'd said, about working out of the old playbook. *When crisis hits, that's exactly what my family does. They rely on the archaic way of thinking.*

But it doesn't have to be like this.

Building a university on royal grounds was a move into the future.

Marrying Marcel was not.

Since boarding the plane, she'd lost all sense of time, so she picked up her phone. Friday at three PM. Parliament must surely be in session. She tapped out a text to her Uncle Girard.

I know this is highly unusual, but I would like to speak in front of parliament.

Girard Caron wasn't really her uncle, but she'd grown up with him, and he and her father were close as brothers. He was also Prime Minister of St. Christophe.

He responded right away. *And when would you like to*

do this? After the vote on Tuesday, we're in recess until September first.

Her pulse quickened with purpose. *I can't wait that long. It needs to be done before the vote.*

I'm in the middle of a session so I can't call to find out what you'd like to speak about, but I suspect it has to do with your father's condition?

We're not releasing any information on that, but yes it has to do with this situation. Please trust me?

All right. When would you like me to put you on the docket?

In fifteen minutes. Twenty if there's traffic.

Child. You are such a trial. And I love you dearly. I'll see you in twenty minutes.

She leaned forward. "Harrison? There's a change in plans. Can you please take me to the State House?"

He eyed her in the rearview mirror with a look that said, *What're you up to now?* "Is your father going to like this?"

"If it goes my way, then yes. He'll like it very much."

"And if it doesn't?"

"Then I'll…" She swallowed. "Do whatever I have to do."

Including marry the douchenozzle.

Rosalina stood at the podium in the wood-paneled room. As a little girl, she'd watched her father speak. He'd seemed so different in this context, tall, commanding…and yet he'd had an affability and sense of humor that put everyone at ease. They trusted him.

In this moment, she didn't quite have her footing, not when she felt a strange mix between Rosalina and Rosie.

Especially when all twenty men and five women watched her with grave expressions, and she knew without a doubt they didn't appreciate her hijacking their session.

Before speaking she glanced down at her phone, at the referendum she'd posted on her personal website, surprised to see she already had twenty-five hundred virtual signatures.

Proof, indeed, that it was time to throw out the old playbook. Time to join the modern age.

"Mr. Speaker, members of Parliament, ladies and gentlemen, thank you for your time this afternoon. When our principality was formed six hundred years ago, it was unquestionably a man's world, where women were treated like chattel, and where property ownership and legal power resided exclusively with men."

She wanted to drag her sweaty palms on her pants, but they'd take the gesture as a sign of weakness. *And, right now, I'm not weak. My message is strong, powerful, and vital.*

"Today." She made sure to pan the room, looking each individual in the eye. "Women have substantially achieved equality throughout Europe, where many have become heads of state and of royal households. The one exception is our beloved country, where the royal house is still defined by the masculine bloodline."

She glanced at her uncle to see whether he approved of her message. Brow furrowed, his attention seemed divided between her speech and the audience's reaction. Glancing down at her phone, she noted she now had twenty-nine hundred signatures in the thirty minutes since posting the words that had become her speech.

"This archaic remnant of our past should be eliminated. Our women should bear the responsibilities and rights of men in all matters, including those of state."

The air-conditioned room chilled the perspiration on her skin. As she continued to scan the faces, she noted that stoicism had cracked. She'd grabbed their interest. That didn't mean they'd stand with her, but in St. Christophe one only needed a thousand signatures to initiate a referendum on any law. "I stand before you as an educated, strong, industrious woman who is expected to marry a man so that I can produce an heir who will one day lead this nation. I think you can see how patently absurd it is, in the twenty-first century, to use my body as a vessel for the next male heir instead of using my mind and character to carry on the legacy of my father and grandfather and all the men who came before that carry my genetic code and who taught me how to be the kind of woman who can lead this country."

She cut a look to her phone. Thirty-three hundred votes. "With a thousand signatures I can call a referendum to any law. I've gathered thirty-three hundred in half an hour. Therefore, I wish to call for an immediate parliamentary vote to change the royal charter to allow succession to flow through the female Villeneuve family bloodline, as well as male, so that neither I, nor my sister, nor any future generation, has to marry in order to retain the royal house and bloodline or award our *husbands* the leadership of our noble house and country."

Empowered and energized, she decided to use her platform for one more topic. "And, while I have your attention, I ask that you please stand with me against the People's Party's repudiation of the royal house and its agenda to strip my family of its property, wiping out our nationhood and history, the very culture that makes us unique and powerful. I stand against this movement, not because I'm the hereditary princess, but because I love this country with all my heart. For our economic strength, our standard of living that soars above all others on this continent, for our schools and healthcare, and for our very identity, I urge you to reject it in favor of six hundred years of progressively better lives for our people." She turned to her uncle. "Your honor, will you please bring this matter to a vote?"

Slowly, he got to his feet. He reached for her hand—a gesture that made her nearly weep with the respect implied, and said, "I will."

And the room broke into thunderous applause.

Chapter Twenty-Two

As they tore across the meadow, Brodie's dirt bike sailed off a lift and landed with a bone-jarring thud.

He couldn't get Rosie's last voice message out of his head. *I hate this, Brodie. I hate it so much.*

Approaching a pile of logs, he shifted into second gear, smashed the first trunk with his front wheel, double blipped his throttle, and sailed over it.

I don't regret a single minute that I spent with you, but my time's run out, and now I have to take on the role I was born into.

The finality of it. *Jesus.* Frustration turned him wild. Heading for the next feature twenty feet away, Brodie swerved off course at the last moment, gunning it for the river.

If word gets out about his heart attack, it could destroy us in Tuesday's vote, but I just wanted to thank you. Thank you so much for... Her voice had thickened. *For everything. I will always cherish my time with you. It was the best...* She'd hitched a breath. *Goodbye, Brodie.*

Channeling all his focus into his jump, Brodie bore

down on the accelerator. Over the terrible buzz saw-sound of his engine, he heard his brothers calling him, but he didn't care.

Standing up on the foot pegs, knees bent, he took off, only vaguely aware of the brown, churning water beneath him. He leaned back slightly to gain more air. The gyroscopic spin of the back wheel brought the front end up, and he pumped the brake to pull it down. With the ground in sight, he stood up, preparing for the impact. Adrenaline pumping, he throttled up and absorbed the landing with his legs.

Pumping his fist, he unbuckled his helmet and turned back to find his brothers had landed beside him. All three of them looked pissed off.

"What the hell's the matter with you?" Fin said. "You trying to send us to the hospital?"

"What?" Crazy energy spun through him. "We're riding."

"On the track," Will said quietly.

"Since when do we stay on a fucking course?" Foot perched on a peg, his knee jackhammered.

"Since I have a three-year-old at home." Will yanked off his helmet. "You said one more ride before you build your house here. That's why we came."

"Don't deal with your problems this way, man," Gray said.

"Deal with…what're you talking about?" He hated the way his brothers looked at him, like he was losing his shit. "We're having fun." Because he *was* losing his shit. "She's getting married, for fuck's sake."

Fin cringed, Gray gave him a look that said, *You sure about that?* And Will held his gaze, strong and steady.

"She has no choice." He hurled his helmet, watched it

bounce on the hard earth and spin. "They're going to take this smart, creative, fucking amazing person, and turn her into a robot. She's going to get married, pop out kids till she has a boy, and she's never going to make perfume again. Do you have any idea how wrong that is for her?"

Worse, I fucking love her.

And every second that goes by without her feels like a living hell.

"Have you talked to her?" Gray said.

"Of course I have. But, with her dad's heart attack, it's a done deal. Besides, I saw the announcement for the engagement party. It's over."

"But she's not married, right?" Will asked.

"Not yet."

"And the douchenozzle's the wrong man for her?" Will asked.

"Of course he's wrong for her. He *cheated* on her." Brodie tipped his head back, glancing up at the dark gray sky but only seeing Rosie's smile. Thunder rumbled over the mountain, but he only heard her laughter. Her excitement when she talked about her essential oil. "The day I met her, she ran in front of my bulldozer. She was all worked up because I was going to mow down, like, fifty square feet of her flowers."

His heart—it felt like a giant fist was squeezing it like a sponge. "She wanted to buy the land from me, lease it, anything to keep me from tearing up her lyantha." The pain of his loss spread through his body, making his limbs heavy with it. "It's over for her. The thing that lights her up, that makes her who she is, they're going to strip her of it. They're going to shut her down."

"Are we talking about *Rosie?*" Fin looked to his brothers.

"Exactly," Gray said.

"I was thinking the same thing," Will said.

"What? What're you talking about?" He wanted to pull his hair out, wanted to tear up the meadow with his bare hands.

"I don't know her as well as you, but the Rosie I met wouldn't just go along with some plan," Fin said.

"Hell, no," Gray said. "She's like us. She's a fighter."

"But, mostly, she's like you," Will tipped his head to Brodie. "She's a visionary."

Which means she won't just accept her fate.

As soon as she knows her dad's all right, she'll calm down.

And come up with a plan.

"Okay, but even if she does figure out a way to avoid marrying that prick, she still has to live in St. Christophe. Still has to marry someone and get pregnant."

Pregnant. He could picture her belly rounded, her cheeks ruddy. Her smile soft, her fingers sifting through his hair, as he pressed his ear close to hear their baby's heartbeat.

Our baby. Mine.

His was the only baby she'd carry. He knew it in his gut and in every fiber of his being.

Want, need, hunger, all of it lived under his skin. Just like when he was a kid and wanted his mom to come home.

"What's really going on?" Will asked.

"As much as I want to beg her to come back, I can't. I can't stir shit up for her...it's not right. *I'm* not right for her. I'm just another complication, and she's got enough guilt over her dad's heart attack." *Fuck.* His brain was too wired to think clearly. "The reality is that she has to be in St. Christophe. She has to be the hereditary princess, marry some guy, and pop out kids. It's just how their laws work. It's fucking over, and I need to find a way to let it go. Let her go." Pushing her would only create more stress. Stress she didn't need.

Right?

"In snowboarding, we make changes all the time to make the sport better, safer," Fin said.

"They've tried changing the laws," Brodie said. "It hasn't worked."

"Jesus, Brodie," Gray said. "You want her or not?"

"Of course I do." He'd chosen this plot of land for its location, so Rosie could smell her flowers every June.

"Then quit fucking around and go get her," Fin said.

"This isn't the kind of thing you can work out alone," Will said. "It's something the two of you have to figure out together."

"Besides, it doesn't have to be Marcel she marries, does it?" Fin asked.

"No." Energy roared through him.

"Then, what're you still doing here?" Will said.

The fact that neither Rosie nor her bodyguard had responded to his text messages only became problematic when he'd arrived in Villeneuve and had no idea how to get to her.

At a stoplight, he texted Harrison again. **Just got into Villeneuve. You think I could see Rosalina?**

He'd storm the castle if he had to. His brother was right—this was a problem they could only solve together.

And Rosie wouldn't just blindly go along with anything. That was one of the reasons he loved her.

Cruising down the main street of the capital city, he

found himself still trying to get a handle on driving on the left side of road. The businesses all looked like fairytale cottages, with flower beds hanging off the windows and dark brown wooden shutters. Wrought iron streetlamps lined the pretty, clean street.

His phone chimed, and he pulled it out of the cup holder at the next stop sign. *Harrison.*

"Hell, yeah."

Yes. You can't miss signs for the castle. Follow them up the road and park in the visitors parking lot, but then come around back. I'll meet you in the garden.

A second one followed. **Took you long enough.**

Brodie smiled. It hadn't even been a week. He'd seen signs for the castle everywhere, so he pulled a U-turn at the intersection and headed up the long and winding road. Halfway up the mountain, he followed the signs to a driveway that took him through a copse of woods.

When he emerged back into the sunlight, he got a spectacular perspective of St. Christophe. Villeneuve sat in a valley created by snow-capped mountain ranges. It was green, lush, and vibrant. As he pulled into a spot, he noted how out of place the asphalt parking lot seemed beside the ancient stone castle and English garden-landscaping. Cutting the engine, he got out, surprised at the number of tourists milling about.

No wonder she had to be on her best behavior all the time. Even her private life was public.

He shot a text to Rosie's bodyguard. **Here.** Then, he headed around to the back of the castle. Harrison, a fucking behemoth of a man, couldn't be missed, striding across the lawn towards him.

"Hey." Brodie hurried over and shook his hand. "Thanks for helping me out. Does she know I'm here?"

"No, sir. It's been a hectic couple of days. Follow me." He led Brodie into an expansive, low-ceilinged kitchen. Copper pots and pans hung from wire racks, and an enormous forest green stove took up the length of one wall.

"Is she all right?" Brodie asked. "I haven't heard back from her."

"On a good day, the princess doesn't remember to take her phone with her."

"How's her dad?" Last he'd heard, the prince had pulled through but would have a six-week recovery. But maybe he'd taken a turn for the worse? Brodie nodded to the chef, who came up the cellar stairs with a huge crate of eggs.

Harrison led them out of the kitchen and down a long, windowless hallway. "On the mend."

He let out a huff of breath. "Glad to hear it. I thought maybe she wasn't getting back to me because…"

Harrison cut a sharp glance over his shoulder.

Got it. We don't talk about the prince dying. Damn, this place looked like Versaille. Family portraits hung on the walls, side tables held vases and all kinds of knick-knacks, and the rugs were well-worn.

The bodyguard crossed a marble-tiled foyer, lit by an ornate and massive crystal chandelier that hung from a two-story ceiling. They heard voices, some exercised. "They're in the library." He paused outside the large, oak-paneled room lined with floor-to-ceiling bookcases. "Hang on. Give them a moment, and then I'll announce you."

It was crowded with people. When he saw Rosie in a white dress and Marcel in a suit, Brodie's blood pressure spiked. A wedding ceremony. *Fuck.* Pushing past Harrison, he raced into the room. "Don't do it, Rosie. Don't marry him."

The tension in the room pulled tight, and everyone turned to him with stunned expressions.

Rosie's eyes went wide, her hands covering her mouth. "Brodie?"

He stalked toward her. "Marry me. You don't love this weasel." He scanned the room for her parents and couldn't miss the regal posture of a man in dark gray slacks and a white button down. "Mr.—"

Wait. Shit. He's not a mister. "Prince…sir, I love your daughter. I'd like to ask for her hand in marriage. I'm a hardworking man with the means to take care of her. I come from a good family, and…" Well, hell, he didn't know what this family looked for in a husband for their oldest daughter. It wasn't like Marcel had any outstanding qualities. "I'm a businessman. I run successful businesses."

Maybe shut the fuck up? Jesus, he felt like a sumo wrestler invading a ballet recital. *Just get to the point.* "You can't make someone with the brains and talent and…and *spirit* of your daughter marry some weak-willed *cheater*."

"Brodie—" Rosalina began.

"Hang on." He reached for her hand, brought it to his mouth and kissed her palm. "I understand your duty. I do. I understand what you need to do for your family and your country, so I'll move here. I'll marry you right now."

Her father rose out of his chair, all imperious. "Do you have royal blood?"

Brodie had to think fast, back to conversations they'd had with their dad and uncle over campfires and long hikes. "I think around the time of Mary, Queen of Scots…it's possible we—"

"Brodie." Rosalina's voice gentled. "My dad's teasing you."

Oh. Heat rushed up his neck, burning his earlobes.

She laid a hand on his arm. "I'm not marrying Marcel."

"But you're wearing…" As he paid more attention, he realized she wore a simple white sundress. "You don't have to marry him?"

"No. We're making changes, and the Allard family is part of that." She reached for his hand. "Come with me."

He turned back to her father, who grinned at him. His wife stood by his side, a stunning dark-haired beauty. "I'm sorry for bursting in here." He let out an awkward chuckle. "I thought…" *Shut up. They know what you thought.*

They nodded, but no one said a word as Rosie led him across the room. At the doorway, he turned back. "But I meant every word I said." He pointed at Marcel. "You had your shot, and you blew it. Sucks for you, because you're going to miss out on one wild ride."

Rosie tugged on his hand, dragging him down the hallway and into a parlor. "What are you doing here? How'd you even get in?" She closed the door behind him.

He reached for her, pulling her close. "*I* get to, though, right?" What if coming home had changed her mind about them?

She looked confused. "Get to what?"

"Go on the wild ride with you?"

She fought a smile. "I don't even know how to answer that. Would you please tell me how you got in?"

"I texted Harrison and asked if I could come talk to you." She smelled so good—sweet, feminine. He brushed his lips over hers, but the need was too powerful, and he swept her up into his arms. He kissed her with all the pent-up worry and heartache that'd built over the past several days. He kissed her with relief and a rush of pure love. She felt so perfectly right in his arms, and everything just felt *better* with her.

There's no one else I want to go through life with than this woman.

But he still didn't know what was going on, so he got a hold of himself. "Spell it out for me, sweetheart, before I have a heart attack—oh, damn. I'm sorry. That was a shit thing to say."

"It's all right." She smiled with affection. "My father's going to be fine. In fact, he's going to be better than before."

"Glad to hear it." His heart beat so thick and hard he could hear the drumbeat in his ears. "So, what'd I walk in on?"

"That was my father firing Marcel and his father."

"Whoa. That's…big news."

"It actually happened a few days ago, but they've been fighting it. Fortunately, as my father pointed out, the Allards don't have any dirt on us, so there's nothing they can do. They believe they've given their whole lives to the royal family, and they haven't gotten their due."

"What's that even mean? What's their due? They have jobs like anyone else. Their employer decided to fire them."

"It's a historical thing. The Allard family has worked as agents for the Villeneuves for generations."

"Doesn't mean you owe them anything."

"Exactly."

She looked so pretty, her dark hair glossy in the afternoon sunlight streaming through the windows, her lips red and wet from his mouth. His fingers flexed, because he wanted to kiss her again so damn bad. "So, what's next? If you still have to get married, I want it to be me. Like I

331

said, I'll move here. Whatever you need me to do, I'll do it."

"Thank you." That was her royal voice. She stiffened and pulled away from him. "That's kind of you, but when I marry, it's going to be for love. Not duty, and definitely not as a favor."

"Favor? Rosie, I…" *Would you slow the hell down? She's in the middle of a shitstorm.* It wasn't the time to declare his feelings. "How did the vote go? It was on Tuesday, right?"

"It went better than anyone could have dreamed. I was on my way to the castle for a press conference to announce my engagement, but I knew it was wrong on every level. It made no sense, so I put up a petition on my website. Within ten minutes, I had enough signatures to put a referendum before parliament. I pointed out how ridiculous it was for the nation to view me as nothing more than a vessel for the next heir. I also reminded them what our family has done for this country and how removing the monarchy would make us just like any other European nation."

"You spoke in front of parliament?"

"I did. Not only did they vote for the line of succession to include women, but the People's Party lost some seats in Tuesday's vote. So, it's all good."

"Does that mean you can come home? Shit. Sorry. I meant come back to Calamity. Just to finish our project?"

Another of those elegant but empty smiles. "Well, I fought for the right to lead my country, so unfortunately, it means I have to take over for my father while he recuperates. After that, I'll be working with him, so I can learn everything and be ready to take over when he steps down."

"Does that mean…"

She nodded, resolute. "No more chemistry for me."

"But that's your heart."

"It's a lot better than marrying Marcel."

He didn't like seeing her slip back into princess mode. "Sounds like you've got it all worked out. Where do I fit into this new world?"

"I'm not sure you do." Gaze cast down, voice quiet and subdued, Rosalina was back in full force.

"Bullshit." And that was it. He'd had enough. In one step, he was in front of her. Bending his knees, he gripped her ass, lifted her, and walked her to the nearest couch. Setting her on the arm, he nudged her knees apart and stepped between them, tipping her chin. "Listen to me, Rosie, I love you. I love you so fucking much there's not a chance I'm going to live without you. And if you live here, then I'll live here."

"You don't know what this life is like. It's nothing like Calamity."

"But it has you." He paused. "You love me?"

"I do." She nodded, tears glistening. "I love you so much."

He started to kiss her, but the worry in her eyes stopped him. "But?"

"But I'm scared. You're not going to like it here."

"You know that house I'm building? I designed a lab for you. We can live here, and we can spend time in Calamity. But, just so you know, if I never see Calamity again, I'm still gonna die a happy man, because I'm going to get to spend my life with you."

"*Brodie.*"

But he didn't hear anything more, because his mouth sealed over hers. Relief crashed over him. *She loves me.* Their tongues tangled, her fingers fisting in his button-down shirt.

He kissed a path to her neck and breathed her in. Yanking on the tie behind her neck, he lowered the straps of her sundress. "I fucking missed you. You ever been at the summit, so high there's not enough oxygen?"

She nodded, as she tugged the tail of his shirt out of his khakis.

"That's what it felt like after you left. All week, I couldn't take a full breath. I felt sick. Nothing felt right."

"I know. I felt the same way."

"But you were really going to move on without me?"

"My father…"

"Yeah, I know. I'm sure it scared the crap out of you. But I want you to hear me when I say that next time, you wait for me. Because everything from this minute on, we do together. You get a call like that again, know that I'll drop everything if you need me to be with you."

"I always need you to be with me." She stood up, wrapping her arms around his neck and kissed him. "Always, Brodie."

Chapter Twenty-Three

IN THE FORMAL DINING ROOM, THIRTY-SIX dignitaries enjoyed a ten-course meal hosted by His Serene Highness the Prince of St. Christophe and his wife. Their good friends, the Prince and Princess of Monaco, sat to her father's left.

After spending the summer in jeans and sundresses, Rosalina felt constricted in her form-fitting designer gown, so she couldn't imagine how Brodie, seated across the table and a few chairs down, felt in his tuxedo. Though, he did look strikingly handsome.

She doubted he was aware of the number of times he'd tugged on the collar of his shirt. Beside him sat Jean Luc, his royal protocol coach—not that anyone but the royal family knew the man's identity as anything other than Lord Fortier.

The moment Brodie leaned toward the person next to him—the Prince of Andorra—to enter into a conversation, Jean Luc discreetly tapped his thigh. Brodie immediately pulled back. She didn't have to hear them to know that Jean Luc was quietly explaining that Brodie, a commoner, could only speak when the Prince initiated conversation.

Brodie looked like he wanted to push back his chair, rip off his tie, and get the hell out of this stuffy room. And he'd only been in St. Christophe a little over a month.

Imagine him a year from now. Ten years.

This is no life for him.

She knew down to her bones he'd be miserable here.

But it's the only life for me.

A rush of affection for her parents rolled through her, and she reached for her father's hand. He cut away from his conversation—and she loved him for that, for always being there for her. "I love you, Papa."

"I love you, my sweet girl."

"I'm so glad you're all right."

"Me, too. I want to live to see my girls become the women they're meant to be. Whatever that means." He tipped his head toward Brodie. "We're about to retire to the parlor for after dinner drinks, so it's a good time to whisk your mountain man out of here."

"Thank you. I'll do that." She gave Brodie a look that said, *Ready to go?*

He didn't even hesitate. Just popped up, balled his napkin, and tossed it on his chair. With a hand on his suitcoat, he gave a short bow to the people around him and excused himself.

She met him in the hallway. "You looked like you were dying in there."

"Nah. I've suffered through plenty of fundraisers and galas in my time."

Reaching for his hand, she led him toward the staircase. "I doubt they had so many rules."

"You'd be right about that. Where we going?"

"As gorgeous as you look in that suit, I want to strip you out of it and see what's left of that six-pack you used to have before Chef got you fat on her croissants. Follow me."

He barked out a laugh, and she couldn't help glancing at the portraits lining the hallway. She'd pushed through revolutionary changes in her country, and she didn't know what her ancestors would think of them. But it didn't matter. Her generation would lead the nation into the future, and she wasn't the least bit apologetic.

"Anywhere, Princess."

"What do you say tomorrow we blow off everything and go hiking? We can bring a picnic."

"You've got your first board meeting for the apprenticeship program."

"Right." She wouldn't bail on the committee. "It's at eleven, so we can leave right after. We'll have a picnic dinner."

He shook his head. "It's your father's first day back on the job. I think he'd like you to be around to fill him in on things."

"You're right." She stopped at the bottom of the staircase and placed a hand on his chest. "Okay, then, let's go right now." She needed him to be happy here. He couldn't live the way she once had—off duty alone. Lord knows she hadn't been able to do it, and he was an outdoorsman who needed to be active. "We can hike up to the cirque lake. It's an amazing view at night."

"Sounds good."

"Great." *See, we can find a balance.* "Let me get it set up."

"What do you mean? What's to set up? We're just hiking."

"Nothing's ever that simple around here. Come on." Instead of heading up the stairs, she continued down the hallway to the kitchen, where she found Harrison playing cards with some of the other staff. "Hey, can I talk to you a second?"

"Of course." Her bodyguard's chair scraped on the stone floor. "What's up?"

She slipped her arm through Brodie's. "We'd like to hike up to the cirque lake."

"Right now?"

"Yes, if that's all right."

"Absolutely. Give me an hour to take care of it."

"Great, thank you. We'll go change." Excited, she led Brodie up the back stairs. Once in her bedroom, she shut the door and turned her back to him. "Can you please unzip me?"

"Sure." His voice sounded normal, but he didn't know she could see his face in the mirror across the room. His strained expression worried her. "What does he mean by 'take care of it?' We're just hiking up the mountain."

"I know, but he has to send a team out ahead of us to clear the trail."

"Clear the trail? You mean everyone has to leave the area?"

She nodded. "I know it sounds awful, but it's the way our security works. And, at this hour, there probably won't be many people out there."

He shook his head. "Forget it. We can hike another day. I'm not making people leave just so I can take a walk."

Of course, she understood. She quickly shot off a text to Harrison. ***Change of plans. Thanks anyhow***. "What would you like to do instead?"

He yanked off his bow tie. "I'm going to hit the gym." He reached for the buttons on his starched, white shirt.

Pulling his arm towards her, she unfastened the cuff link. "I'm sorry."

"Don't be." He sounded a little curt, and he definitely avoided looking her in the eye.

Finished with the other sleeve, she dropped the cuff links into a small porcelain bowl on her dresser. Watching him step out of his pants and into a pair of gym shorts made her unbearably sad. She handed him a clean T-shirt. "I know you hate working out in a gym."

"It's fine." He jammed his feet into running shoes and headed for the door. "Won't be long."

"Brodie?"

His muscles spasmed, and it looked like he'd used up all his restraint to stop and wait for her to continue.

"I hate this. I hate how unhappy you are here, and I don't know what to do about it."

And just like that, concern replaced his annoyance. "I'm fine, princess." He must've seen the doubt in her eyes, because he came back to her. "You don't have to apologize for your life. You just need to give me a little time to find my way here. I promise you, before long, I'll have a couple projects going and everything will be good." He kissed her mouth and walked out the door.

But he was wrong. It wouldn't be good. They were *both* dying here.

Something had to change.

She knocked on her parents' bedroom door. "Mama?"

"Yes, dear. Come in."

She found the prince and princess of St. Christophe

tucked into their big bed under a deep blue comforter. Wearing silk pajamas and reading glasses, they both had piles of paperbacks on their nightstands, and each was engrossed in a book. Her father, a science geek like her, was reading about mineral deposits in the Alps, while her mother read something for her book club.

Her father lowered his reading glasses. "Everything all right?"

"I seem to have gotten myself into a bit of a pickle."

"Americans have the strangest expressions." Her father sounded amused.

"They do. So, you know I meant every word I said to parliament, and I'm honored and so pleased the vote came out on the right side of justice."

"Yes, and we're just so very excited for you to become Head of State," her mother said. "So excited, that your father's decided to retire early."

"Tomorrow, in fact," her father said. "I've enjoyed this six-week hiatus so much, and you've done such a bang-up job handling everything in my absence…you might as well carry on."

"This isn't funny." They were joking, right? He couldn't just retire and leave her to run a nation.

"Quite the opposite," her father said. "It's invigorating, really." He tipped his chin, peering at her over his glasses. "Do you mind if I take over the lab? I'd like to turn it into my man cave."

Her mom elbowed him. "Get a big screen TV so we can watch the rest of that BBC series we started."

"Already ordered. I'd like a Barcalounger myself, with cup holders." He nudged his wife right back. "You?"

"Do they have ones with coolers? I do hate when my wine spritzers grow warm."

Rosalina grinned. "You two are nuts."

Her mother set down her book. "Darling, this life is not for you."

She perked up. "Is that terrible?"

"Do you think we know you so little?" Her father set his book down. "Come."

She crawled onto the mattress, the way she'd done so many times as a child. Settling between her parents, she breathed in the most familiar scents in the world. Her mom's hand lotion had hints of lavender and vanilla, and her father's spicy, rich, masculine soap scent infused his pajamas.

Her dad lifted an arm, and Rosalina nestled under it. "When you were a little girl, you used to sit outside with Anne-Marie while she tended the garden. You had little plastic bowls and spoons, and you'd make these concoctions out of mud and berries and leaves and grass."

"I remember that."

"You're a chemist," her mother said. "And a perfumer. And you are not complete unless you are concocting."

"And now you've fallen in love," her father said. "With a cowboy who's as comfortable in a tuxedo as I would be in assless chaps."

"*Papa.*"

Grinning, her mother bopped him over the head with her book. Wow, she hadn't seen them this playful with each other in ages. She was so glad the vote had gone their way.

"So, about that cowboy…" Rosalina watched their expressions carefully. "He says it's an adjustment."

"One that's not necessary to make at this time," her mother said.

"What're you saying?"

"I'm back now, sweetheart." Her father closed his book. "I'm going to resume my duties."

"But I need to learn so I can take over when you're ready to step down."

"While your head is in the lab," her father said. "Your sister's is in the board room. When she graduates the London School of Economics, she'll likely head to business school, and then she can come home and work with me. In the meantime…"

"I'm going to take a more visible role." Her mother sounded proud and fierce.

"It's about time." The rightness of this moment flowed through her, making her feel light and airy.

"It certainly is," her mother said. "And it wouldn't be happening had it not been for you. So, you're free, Rosalina. We give you our blessing to go wherever your heart takes you."

She was going home.

To Calamity.

With the lights out and heavy drapes blocking the moonlight, Brodie couldn't see a damn thing. Silently, he closed the door. She had a full day tomorrow so he wouldn't wake her, but he needed to talk to her, set some things straight.

He shouldn't have taken so long in the gym. Should've come back and reassured her they'd be all right. But he'd had some things to work out, and now he could be less of a dick about living here.

Cutting across the room, he headed for the bathroom.

After a quick shower, he'd get in bed. Talk to her in the morning.

She's not getting out of this bed until she knows how much I love her. And that he'd figured out a way to be happy here.

Golden light spilled out from under the closed door, and his pulse kicked up a notch with anticipation. He knocked lightly. "Princess?"

"You can come in."

He flung off his sweaty T-shirt and opened the door to find the room humid and lit up with the flickering light from dozens of candles. The tinkle of water drew his gaze to the clawfoot tub.

With her hair in a bun at the top of her head, damp tendrils stuck to her cheek and forehead, Rosie lounged in a bath. Bubbles covered her body up to her chest, and the mischievous grin she gave him had him toeing off his running shoes and dropping his gym shorts.

"Got room for me?"

"Always." She pushed up, so her nipples, all rosy and wet, popped out of the water.

"Damn, princess." He stepped into the warm water behind her and stretched out his legs, so they bracketed her thighs. An arm around her waist, he pulled her back against him. *This is all I need. Right here. My princess in my arms.* "I'm sorry for running out the way I did."

"Don't be. I understand."

"Nah. I made you feel bad, and that's the last thing I want to do. It's just I've got—"

"A million things on your mind, and it's when you're distracted that you come up with solutions."

He kissed her cheek. "That's right. And I did. I got it all worked out. What's been bugging me is that I bailed—

again—on Owl Hoot. I got all these great ideas, got everyone on board, and then I walked away. But there's no reason I can't finish everything I started. I'm going to hire my buddy Chris to run things in my absence. A couple of years ago, I hired him as executive chef of the spa restaurant, but he didn't feel qualified, so he wound up running the contest that brought us Delilah. He did a great job, so, I think he'd—"

"I think you should go home and finish the job yourself."

He sat up so abruptly, water splashed over the sides of the tub. "What? No." He shouldn't have run out on her after the dinner. She'd gotten the wrong impression. "That's what I'm saying. The board approved the list of businesses and the triathlon. I'll still be overseeing it, but I'll have Chris on the ground."

"You don't want to work with your brothers on the triathlon?"

A pinch to his heart told him he did. "Technology's made the world a smaller place. I can work with them from here."

"And the reliquary museum? You don't want to scout out the treasures?"

He'd planned on putting an ad in all the newspapers in Jackson Hole and surrounding counties, asking people to donate or loan any curiosities or artifacts they had. Yeah, he'd like to be the one to source the inventory. "I'll create an online folder, and Chris can drop in anything he thinks I might find interesting."

"Sounds good. Not as good as you being there to actually see the stuff yourself. Touch it."

Shit. Yeah, he'd like that. "You know what I really want?"

He kissed her cheek, then the corner of her mouth. "I want to wake up with you every morning for the rest of my life. I want to sit with you in the garden in the afternoon, with one of Chef's fresh squeezed lemonades, and talk about your day."

"That's nice and all, but it sounds a little boring. No offense."

He chuckled. She was playing with him. "Maybe a little, but I had an idea while I was on the treadmill. I looked it up, and you know what St. Christophe doesn't have? An excursion company."

"Kind of like the one you're starting in Owl Hoot?"

"Exactly. I could start one here."

She broke out of his hold, turning around to face him. Water sloshed over the sides, but she didn't seem to care about anything but wrapping her arms around his neck and getting his attention. "Don't. Don't start an excursion company or create an online folder or hire Chris. Go home, Brodie. That's where you belong."

Energy surged through him. He'd done a shit job of taking care of her, if this is what she was thinking. "Let me make something clear. I might not follow a lot of rules, but here are some absolutes. I live where you live. I sleep where you sleep. We're going to be together, none of this long-distance crap."

"I couldn't agree more."

"Then quit talking about me going home. I'm already there." He tapped her chest. "This is where I live—your heart."

Tears glistened in her eyes. "I don't know how I got so lucky. One minute I found my two best friends in a closet, and the next I saw you in the lobby of your hotel, and everything in me just blossomed. I love you, Brodie

Bowie. I love you with everything I am. And we're going to be so happy together…in Calamity."

Like hitting his elbow's funny bone, his body got an odd mix of tingling and numbness. "You can't leave here. You have to run the country."

"I'm not really Head of State material, you know?"

"But you fought for it."

"I fought for change in my country, and I won. Not because I'm a brilliant politician, but because it was the right moment in the world. But the right thing for me, as a woman, a chemist, a perfumer, and a girlfriend, is to move to Calamity with you."

"My girlfriend?" He grimaced. "That doesn't sound right."

"Lover?"

He shook his head. "You can only say that when you're wearing red lipstick and a thong and holding a cigarette in one hand and two fingers of scotch in the other."

"That's true." She tapped her chin. "Hm, then what am I to you…?"

He grabbed her hand and pressed a kiss to her palm. "You're the missing piece that makes me whole." He didn't think the English language had a word for what she meant to him. "You're the love of my life." Cupping her ass, he hauled her onto his lap and kissed her. He took his time, just feeling her smooth skin, breathing in her feminine scent, and tasting the minty toothpaste and heat of her mouth.

She pulled back, resting her forehead on his. "I talked to my parents tonight. My father's going back to work tomorrow with my mother by his side. My sister will spend her summers apprenticing with them, and when she finishes school, she'll run for a seat in parliament." She grabbed a fistful of hair from the back of his neck and tipped his head so she could look into his eyes. "We're going home, Brodie. My parents gave us their blessing to move back to Calamity."

"You, princess, you're my blessing. And I'm happy wherever you are."

"Then we'll be happy ever after in Calamity."

Epilogue

ROSALINA BREATHED IN THE FRESH-CUT WOOD OF the recently-framed house. She'd poured over floor plans, read home design magazines, and scoured the Internet for functionality and layouts, but this was her first time crossing the threshold into the home where she'd spend the rest of her life.

Of course, Brodie had just stormed right in, his boots pounding across the floor. "Take a look at the kitchen. I told them your suggestion, and they gave us a panoramic view of the meadow."

She didn't want to rush it, though. She wanted to savor this moment, when everything was just beginning. After one blissful year together, they were now on the cusp of the kinds of changes that would alter the landscape of their lives completely.

In this living room, they'd watch family movies. Their children would chase each other with squirt guns. These empty rooms would be filled with laughter, bickering, and love. So much love.

Her heart...*oh, my*. She'd never imagined it could

grow so big and full—and then keep stretching to accommodate even more.

Heading into the kitchen, a new image formed. Her tossing a salad, while Brodie came up from behind and wrapped his arms around her, nuzzling her neck. She could picture a little girl or boy sitting at the table, talking quietly with Uncle Lachlan about the treasures he'd pulled from his rucksack.

But her happiness hit a snag. Would Brodie want children? From the start, he'd told her he couldn't imagine having any. That he was better suited to be an uncle.

In the kitchen, she got a strong whiff of lyantha. She closed her eyes to breathe it in. "I can't believe it." When she opened them, Brodie was grinning. "I get to smell this every June. It'll fill the whole house."

"Exactly why I chose this spot."

"It's perfect. I love everything about it." She still couldn't believe she got to have this life, this man. They were building a high-tech lab right in their backyard, their store would open tomorrow in the hotel lobby, and she was surrounded by this big, loving family that accepted her for exactly who she was.

"Let's look at the bedrooms. I want to swing an idea by you." Taking her hand, he led her across the wide-open living area. When they turned down a hallway, he gestured to the first room on the right. "I'm thinking about changing the dimensions of this one, making it bigger. Figured, if we give one of the rooms to Ruby, we're going to need to share an office."

"I can use my lab for that." Once he heard her news, he might want to hang onto that privacy after all.

"We got twenty-seven inches of snow in January. I want to make sure you have office space in the house."

She got up on her toes and pressed a kiss to his cheek, loving the way he cared about her. "I can use my laptop anywhere."

"What're you saying? Why don't you want to share an office with me?"

"I just think you're going to need a space of your own."

"I don't want my own space." He studied her expression, and his petulant tone made her smile. "I want to share everything with you."

She believed him, and she loved the way this serious, intense man had opened himself to her so completely. "We do. And that's my point. We're going to be sharing so much, we're going to need our own private spaces."

"Hmph." He led her to the end of the hall. On the left, was a large master suite with a huge patio and Jacuzzi. On the right was a smaller room with a view to the mountains. "I was thinking we could give this one to Ruby. Let her decorate it however she wants. That way, when she visits, we can hear her if she needs us at night."

Rosalina stepped into the room, and the strangest sensation washed over her, making her skin pebble. *This is the nursery.* It was cozy, the corner wall curved with a window seat. She could picture dark gray walls painted with slender white Aspen trees, colorful birds on the limbs to give the room a pop of color. "No, this one's not Ruby's."

He watched her curiously. "I just mean for now, since she's only four, but I guess we could give her the one in between this one and the office. Actually, that's something else I wanted to talk to you about. I know I said I only wanted four bedrooms, but now I'm thinking we could add a long room to the back of the house, fill it with bunkbeds, dormitory-style, for when the nieces and nephews come over."

See? Having kids of his own was the furthest thing from his mind. And they'd only been together a year. *Is it too soon?*

But a joyful warmth flooded her, and she knew—just knew—*this is right*. It was exactly as it should be. Her parents would flip out, though. *I'm not even married.*

Some dutiful princess you turned out to be.

She smiled. "I don't know. To me, this feels more like Prince Archibald Fitzwilliam Charles's room than Ruby's."

"What? Who's that?"

She reached for his hand and brought it to her belly. "But we'll keep the colors neutral just in case it turns out to be Princess Sophia Gabriella Inez's room." She smiled softly. *Please be okay with this.* "We won't know the gender for a few more weeks."

His features went slack. He looked like he was two seconds away from parachuting out of an airplane at thirty-thousand feet. "What are you telling me?"

"I'm pregnant. We're going to have a baby."

"We...you and me...what?"

"You're going to be a daddy."

"Holy fuck." He turned away from her. It looked like he'd stopped breathing. A moment later, he swung back around. "A baby?"

"I know it's unexpected. I was shocked, too. I mean, really shocked. I only found out right before I came over here. It's hard to take in, isn't it?"

It happened so gradually she could actually watch as reality sank in. The slow transformation from shock to awe flipped any concern she had over to excitement.

"You and me...we made a baby?" He dropped to his

knees, his big palms splaying across her stomach. The big, powerful athlete kissed her belly button, before wrapping his arms around her waist and pressing his ear, as if listening for signs of their baby.

She cupped the back of his head, holding him there. "I think it happened that first night in the tent." Spring had hit early—mid-May—and they'd gone camping. She'd forgotten to take her birth control pills with her. It hadn't even occurred to her that she'd *forgotten* to take them. So, they'd had plenty of unprotected sex. "I mean, I'm the dummy who forgot to take my pills."

"I knew. You think I didn't notice? I didn't care. You never have to take a pill again. We can just keep popping babies out. And, since the house isn't finished yet, we can make it twice this size. We can make ten bedrooms."

She laughed. "Maybe slow down a little? First, let's get our heads on right for Archibald. But I'm so happy you want this baby as much as I do."

He gazed up at her. "Of course I want him."

"I see that, but you've always talked about not being able to see yourself as a father."

"Well, until you came along I couldn't. After…I didn't say anything because I thought you weren't ready to be a mom." He searched her gaze. *Are you?*

"I wasn't ready to produce an heir. But I want your baby. I want everything with you."

His eyes warmed, before turning concerned. "You sure about that?"

"Yes. I love you, Brodie. I love you so much, and you're going to be the best daddy in the world. Now, get up here and kiss me."

"Can't. Not yet."

"Fine." She got to her knees, wrapped her arms around

his neck, and kissed him. God, every single time they touched sparks flashed in the air around them. Only, this kiss felt softer, sweeter, more reverent. Knowing he wanted this baby as much as she did, embracing in the room where they'd one day soon change diapers and rock their baby to sleep and cuddle on the window seat reading picture books…made everything deeper, richer, fuller.

Grabbing her ass, he drew her hard up against him, and he moaned deep in his throat. His hands pushed under the waistline of her jeans and squeezed her bare ass. The kiss turned carnal.

Abruptly, he pulled away. "Damn, you get me so worked up. I, uh, I've got something to say to you, too."

His strong shoulders stretched the cotton of his T-shirt, and his dark hair curled at the back of his neck. The intensity in his blue eyes stirred a hunger deep inside her. "Can we make-out a little more first?"

He grinned. "We can make out whenever you want." But then he grew serious. "But, first, let me ask you something."

"Can we do it standing up?"

"Yeah, good idea. You stand up."

Her knees hurt on the hard wood floor, so she got up.

Brodie stayed kneeling. "A year ago, I stood in a meadow not too far from here. I had my life all planned out. I was going to build a house with four bedrooms, jump from one business project to the next, and have a hell of a time as a bachelor." His earnest expression made her pulse flutter. "Then, you came along and got knocked up and ruined everything."

She burst out laughing. "You're such a dick."

He reached for her hand. "I didn't think I had it in me to love someone this way. But, Princess, I fell so hard for you. I love you. I love you in that scary way, the one where I'm going to be chasing you throughout eternity. Because you're mine. I knew it when I met you. It just felt different, right. And, every day, it gets deeper."

Oh, God. He was proposing. They were going to get married. Her heart grew even bigger.

"I want to wake up to your smile and talk about our days at the dinner table. I want to hike with you and watch you throw-down with my brothers. I want to listen to you talk about your flowers and laugh with you under the covers. Rosie, I want to grow old with you and devote every minute of my life to making you happy." He reached into his pocket and pulled out a blue velvet ring box. Flipping it open, he said, "Rosalina Isabelle Anais Villeneuve, will you finally shorten that damn name to Rosie Bowie and marry me?"

"There's nothing I want more in the world."

He popped up, wrapped her in his arms, and said, "*Now* we can make-out."

"Can you put the ring on first, please?"

Tugging the spectacular diamond and ruby ring out of its nest, he slid it on her finger.

She had to blink away the tears to make sure what she was seeing. "It's a flower. It's lyantha."

"Yeah, I brought some to the jeweler and asked if she could design something that would look like the flower that brought us together. You like it?"

"I love it so much. I can't even believe you made this for me. It's perfect."

"You're perfect." And then his mouth was on hers, and all his love flowed right into her. Grabbing a fistful of hair at the back of her neck, he tilted her head and deepened the kiss. God, she loved the way he was always so hungry for her.

No matter who he was with or how distracted he might be, he always had a hand on her, always looked to her in a room full of people, seeking out a private moment.

"Gonna fuck you on the kitchen counter, so get those jeans and panties off. You've got five seconds."

"Really. Is that any way to talk to a princess?" But she was already running out of the room and down the hallway. Tossing off her blouse, she dashed into the kitchen.

By the time she had her pants around her ankles, he was unbuttoning his jeans and stalking towards her. "Get up there."

Instead, she turned around, hiking up her bottom and throwing him a mischievous glance over her shoulder. "I've got a better idea."

He smoothed a hand over her ass. "You always have the best ideas."

"Don't I?'

"I think I see them," someone said.

"Hello? Brodie? Rosie?" a deep male voice called.

"Shit." Brodie knelt, yanking up her pants.

She swatted his hand away. "I got it." She tipped her chin to his jeans. "Button up. No need to scare your future sisters-in-law."

"In the kitchen," Brodie called.

"Oh, my God, I love it here." Callie entered the structure first.

"Good location," Fin said. "I like it."

All three brothers and their loves came and spread out, commenting on the various features of the house.

"Who's that?" Delilah stood at the bay window at the

front of the house. "Um, guys I think some tourists wandered onto your property."

Callie came up beside her. "No, that's Skylar. You guys, are you expecting anyone? Sky's bringing people here."

Before he took off to see, Brodie cupped her chin, pressed a soft kiss to her mouth, and said, "Let's keep the news to ourselves for a bit."

"What news?" Fin asked.

"Fin." Brodie didn't even turn to him.

"What?" Fin said. "You know what he's talking about?"

"No idea," Gray said.

"What's going on?" Knox said.

Reaching for her hand, Brodie led her to the front of the house, where three people dressed in western wear came up the path. Each wore Stetsons—the man's black, the womens' red—jeans, and cowboy boots.

But there was something about the regal air… "Papa?" She dropped Brodie's hand and ran outside to greet her family. Opening her arms, she raced toward them, gathering all three of them into a group hug. "What are you doing here?"

"We wanted to be here for the opening of your store tomorrow," her mother said.

"I can see why you like it out here so much," her sister said. "I saw an actual moose."

"Why didn't you tell me you were coming?" She pulled back.

"We wanted to surprise you." Her mother cupped her chin. "And we want to be part of this journey with you, darling."

A knot formed in her throat. "Thank you, Mama."

Her father stroked her hair. "You look radiant. I can see how well this place suits you."

Rosalina turned to the rest of the family. "This is my family. Prince Albert, Princess Sophia, and my sister Genevieve."

Handshakes and names were exchanged, before Fin said, "So, what's the news?"

Brodie elbowed him in the gut. "Later."

"You have news?" her mother asked.

Brodie was about to say something, when Delilah noticed the ring. She lifted Rosalina's hand. "Are you kidding me right now?"

"What is it?" Knox saw the ring. "They're *engaged*."

"You're getting married?" Callie said.

Everyone moved in closer, touching, reaching for hugs, and she got completely swept away in their excitement.

Her father reached for her, pulling her into his arms. "I'm so proud of you."

"I love you, Papa."

He released her to shake Brodie's hand. Around them, everyone spoke over each other, celebrating the news. Brodie had an arm around her, and her mother didn't miss the location of his hand on her belly. She glanced up, a question in her eyes.

Rosalina nodded. "And I guess it's the right time to add one more bit of news…we're also having a baby."

"You're what?" Her sister practically jumped into her arms. "I'm going to be an Auntie."

"I'm going to be a grandmother?" Her mother looked stunned.

"Well, look at that," Callie said. "The brother the least likely to settle down is the first one to have a baby."

Brodie snugged Rosalina against him, kissing her

cheek, and whispering, "I'm the luckiest damn man in the world. I've got everything I could ever want right here."

Thank you for reading JUST THE WAY YOU ARE! If you love second chance romance, you're going to love IT WAS ALWAYS YOU about a bad boy quarterback who was forced to make a terrible decision years ago that cut him off from the love of his life. Now, he's got his shot at winning her back…and he's pulling out all the stops!

Do you subscribe to my newsletter? Get on that right now because I've got an EXCLUSIVE novella for my readers in 2022! You'll get 2 chapters a month of this super sexy, fun romance! #rockstarromance #whenyourcelebritycrushbe-comesyourboyfriend #teenidol

Need more Calamity Falls, where the people are wild at heart?

KEEP ON LOVING YOU
WE BELONG TOGETHER
THE VERY THOUGHT OF YOU
JUST THE WAY YOU ARE
IT WAS ALWAYS YOU
CAN'T HELP FALLING IN LOVE
COME AWAY WITH ME
WHOLE LOTTA LOVE
YOU'RE STILL THE ONE

THE DEEPER I FALL
LOVE ME LIKE YOU DO

Have you read the Rock Star Romance series? Come meet the sexy rockers of Blue Fire:

YOU REALLY GOT ME
I WANT YOU TO WANT ME
TAKE ME HOME TONIGHT
MORE THAN A FEELING

Look for LOVE ME LIKE YOU DO in September 2022! Grab a FREE copy of PLANES, TRAINS, AND HEAD OVER HEELS. And come hang out with me on Facebook, Twitter, Instagram, Goodreads, and Pinterest or in my private reader group.

Excerpt of Can't Help Falling in Love

PROLOGUE

Six Years Ago, Las Vegas

Coco Cavanaugh had never minded being unexceptional.

It came in handy during times like this, when she was surrounded by her sister's friends in a loud, frenzied club in Las Vegas. She could pretend to be having the time of her life, and none of these bright, shiny people would notice.

If she thought it wouldn't ruin her sister's night, she'd be back in their suite, heels kicked off, stripped of her too-tight dress, and butt-naked. She could almost feel the hot water saturating her scalp, as it washed away the make-up, perspiration, and bad choices.

Except, she was pretty sure she wouldn't make it to the shower. She'd walk in the door, collapse on the bed, heels dangling off her blistered feet, and bawl her eyes out. Wake up in the morning with mascara streaks on the white pillowcase.

Nope, we're not doing that. It's Gigi's night. It had taken her older sister a long time to come back from a devastating high school heartbreak, but two years ago she'd grabbed hold of an opportunity that turned her into an international pop star. She was finally healed and kicking ass. Coco wouldn't do anything to bring her down.

At that exact moment, her sister, fresh from her sold-out concert, hiked herself up on a chair and lifted her lemon drop martini. "To *Colette*,"—Gigi used her real name as if to emphasize how mature Coco had become— "happy graduation and, more importantly, happy birthday. Finally, you're old enough to drink, old enough to—"

"Gamble," one of the women shouted over the insanely loud club music.

"Become a pilot," someone else shouted.

"Play with the big boys," a deep voice called.

All of them whipped around to find a group of men sauntering over. Where everyone else in the club dressed in suits and cocktail dresses, these guys wore T-shirts and jeans. With their overgrown hair, tan skin, and laidback attitudes, they could easily have been surfers.

Her sister's entourage broke out laughing, an invitation for the guys to join them.

Gigi, still on the chair, shouted, "She's already got a boyfriend, so there'll be none of that."

The words splashed cold water on her heart, giving her a shock, but her sister didn't need to know that. She'd catch Gigi up tomorrow. For now, Coco held her drink high and said a cheery, "Thanks, guys!" She sipped her martini, fighting back the roar of anxiety that threatened to pull her under.

I don't have a boyfriend.
I don't have a job.
She didn't have *anything*.

A moment later, Pitbull's "Timber" came on, and the whole group jumped up and dashed onto the dance floor, waving their arms and shaking their booties, leaving Coco blissfully alone. *Thank God.* She could finally relax her straining facial muscles.

When her sister motioned her over, Coco pulled off her stiletto and winced, using her aching feet as an excuse to stay put. Gigi blew her a kiss and lost herself in the wild crowd.

Coco could probably go now. No one would notice if she slipped out. She'd just text her sister, let her know.

A prick of awareness had her looking over to find one of the guys still sitting at the table. Watching her, he cocked his head. *You all right?*

She nodded. *Sure.* With his honey-blond chin-length hair and muscular build, he was undeniably hot, but Coco hadn't even been single twenty-four hours. *Too soon.* It really was time to leave. The flashing lights and pounding bass held her brain in a vise.

She finished off her drink, just for the snap of lemon and rush of sugar in her mouth, and then punched in the code to open her phone. She couldn't stop the leap of hope that she'd find something from her boyfriend—

Ex-boyfriend.

Face it. He ghosted you.

She could stop waiting for him. He wasn't going to magically appear, apologize for blowing off their appointment with the realtor, and tell her he was ready to build the future they'd planned.

Nope, she was on her own.

Fear knocked the air out of her lungs.

What am I going to do now? She'd banked everything on him.

A heavy body dropped onto the couch. Long, athletic legs spread out, as the surfer dude slouched beside her. "House music sucks."

Not expecting him to say that, she actually smiled. "Then, what're you doing here?"

"Jimmy…" He leaned in so their shoulders touched and pointed to a red-haired guy on the dance floor. "He's never been to Vegas. We promised him a survey tour."

"Gotcha. So…" She ticked off one finger. "Casinos."

"He already lost two grand."

"Yikes. That's not good." She touched the tip of the second finger. "David Copperfield or Celine Dion?"

"Worse. Everything was sold out. The only tickets we could get were for the fuckin' Lollipops, which is proof just how much I love that guy, since I'm willing to lose a piece of my soul for him."

Her grin grew wider. Her sister was the lead singer of that band, but she didn't see a reason to tell him. She didn't want to embarrass him as much as she didn't want to draw out the conversation.

"Now, that's a smile." He leaned forward, drawing his legs in. Elbows on his knees, he cut her a look. "And I'll bet that one doesn't hurt."

Heat rushed up her neck and fanned across her cheeks. "Please tell me it's not that obvious?"

He watched her for a moment—studying her expression, as if he actually cared.

And it just cracked the dam she'd worked so hard to build. All of it—the fear, the hurt, the *humiliation*—started slowly trickling in.

Oh, hell, no. I'm not breaking down in front of this guy.

She needed to go to her room and have a good, long

cry. She needed to wallow. Just for a few hours, and then she'd be good as new. She'd make new plans.

A muscle in his jaw ticked. "Anyone gonna miss you if we take off?"

She glanced to the dance floor, so crowded she couldn't even see her sister. "I don't think so. I was about to head back to my room anyhow." With a jolt, she realized how that sounded. "By myself. That wasn't an invitation."

"Yeah, no worries. I'm not looking to get laid." He stood up and reached for her hand. "Come on."

As they chugged to the top of the incline, gravity nailed Coco to her seat and the cool night air washed over her skin. She thrilled in anticipation of the imminent fall.

She'd never been on a roller coaster at night, and certainly not in a city lit up in flashing neon lights. The wheels clacked, and she clutched the padded bar. "Oh, my God. I hate roller coasters. You have no idea."

Becks—that's what his friends had called him when he'd let them know they were taking off—covered her hand and gave it a squeeze. "I got you."

At the pinnacle, they paused, giving her a moment to take in the brilliant lights of Las Vegas, and then…it was on. The car plummeted, the dramatic descent whooshing the hair off her face.

Her stomach lurched, and her body smashed against the restraining bar. She laughed so hard tears streamed down her cheeks.

The moment the ride evened out, it twisted, flinging her sideways and speeding along the track. The passengers behind them shrieked. Between the G-forces and her crazy laughter, Coco had to look like something in a fun house mirror.

When they rotated upside down, the blood rushed to her face.

Finally, the ride slowed, and they passed through a dark tunnel. Easing her grip, she released a breath she hadn't even known she'd been holding. The car jerked to a stop, the safety bar released, and Becks stepped out onto the platform, reaching back for her hand.

She clasped it and got out. "That was insane." She took a step, but her knee buckled.

He tugged her up against his hot, hard body, holding her gaze for a long, intense moment. One arm around her waist, the other lifted so he could smooth a lock of hair behind her ear. "Look at you, all wild and sexy."

"I feel wild." Did she feel sexy? Normally, no. But under his hot gaze, looking at her like he wanted to know what she tasted like…everywhere? *Hell, yeah.* "Thank you. That got me out of my head."

He nodded, releasing her slowly, as if he didn't want to let go. Reaching for her hand, he led her off the platform, his scent lingering—clean cotton and spicy shaving cream. Desire hummed, making her feel more alive than she had in ages.

Once out on the sidewalk, he said, "You want to go back to your hotel or do something else?"

She chanced a look into his icy blue eyes. It wasn't just his startling good looks that affected her; it was his kindness and concern. But what was the point in pursuing this attraction to a stranger? She had a future to figure out.

Then, again, she hadn't thought about her ex in a whole hour. "What else have you got in mind?"

· · ·

As the spacious pod of the High Roller Observation Wheel ascended, Coco gaped at the view. Beyond the cluster of massive hotels and the glitter and sparkle of the Strip sat the vast blackness of the valley floor. "It's crazy to think they built all of this in the middle of a desert."

Though they were alone, Becks stood right beside her. Each time their arms brushed, it sent a flurry of sensation through her. She hadn't felt this butterflies-in-the-stomach, oh-my-God-he's-talking-to-me crush stuff since high school.

And she loved it.

"That's the club." He tipped his chin.

"Where?"

He came around behind her, boxing her in against the window. Extending his arm, he pointed. "That hotel right there." His warm breath at her ear sent a shiver down her spine. "The one with the weirdly shaped O spanning across the windows."

The moment felt dangerous. She could imagine turning in his arms, looping her hands around his neck, and pressing her body up against his. She could picture his hands grabbing her ass and lifting her against the window.

And she really, really wanted to feel his fingers push aside her panties and—

"You okay?" He perched his chin on her shoulder.

"Yes. Fine." But she didn't move—not a single twitch of a muscle or shuffle of a foot—because she wanted him to stay right where he was. She didn't want to lose these delicious sensations flowing through her. "You think they're still there?"

"Oh, yeah. My friends'll close it down."

"So will mine." Licking her bottom lip, she turned to look into his eyes. The connection sent a blast of excitement through her. "Why don't you want to be with them?" Was that her voice? All low and raspy, with the promise of a great blow job?

She should probably knock it off. She didn't want to give him the wrong impression. She wouldn't be going back to his room.

But…he hadn't shaved in several days, so he had a good amount of scruff. It accentuated the sexiest mouth she'd ever seen.

He's gorgeous.

And that hard, muscular body.

"I'm more of an outdoors guy. Clubs, loud music, shouting to have a conversation…it's not my thing." As the ride continued its descent, he stepped away. Reaching into his back pocket, he pulled out a small plastic bag. "Here."

Happiness danced on her heart. "You bought something for me?"

"Happy birthday and congratulations on graduating college." The contrast between his laidback attitude and gruff tone ignited something in her.

Sparked a hunger she'd never felt before. "I can't believe you got me a gift." Opening the bag, she pulled out a plastic Las Vegas sign jutting out of a black base. When she flicked the red switch, it lit up. She laughed. "I love this so much." In an impulsive move, she leaned in and kissed his cheek. His scruff tickled her lips, and she filled her lungs with his clean, masculine scent, as if she could bottle it and keep it forever. "Thank you."

"You're welcome."

Something about the intensity of his gaze had her staying right where she was, a whisper away from him. "This whole night…it's been perfect."

The pod landed. In a moment, the doors would open, and they'd get off.

But neither of them budged.

His big hand grasped the back of her neck, and the thrill of his possessive hold rocketed through her. "Know why I got it for you?"

She barely shook her head.

"Next time you have to fake a smile, I want you to look at this and remember to get out there and do something different. Shake things up."

"You got any other ideas for shaking things up?"

He gave her a devastating grin. "You know I do."

The waiter set a huge stack of buttermilk pancakes in front of her. A melting ball of butter sat on top. "What else can I get you?" he asked.

The table was loaded with syrup, a plate of bacon, a bowl of mixed fruit, two mugs of hot coffee, and two icy water glasses. "This is perfect." Coco smiled. "Thank you."

"You got it. Enjoy." He took off.

With the edge of her fork, Coco cut into a pancake and took a bite. Drenched in butter and maple syrup, it was the most amazing thing she'd ever tasted. She closed her eyes and savored it. "Oh, my God, this is unbelievable." She noticed him watching her instead of eating and grew self-conscious. "What? We can't all be mean, lean, fighting machines." She pointed to his vegetable-stuffed omelet. "No booze, no carbs…that hunky body. Professional surfer?"

He chuckled. "Not professional, no. But we did just fly in from Portugal. Ever hear of Ericeira?"

"No, but from the look in your eyes, I'm going to

guess it was pretty awesome."

"It was insane."

"You travel a lot?"

"Used to, but not the good kind. The grind ended a couple months ago, though. From now on, I'm free as a bird and plan on staying that way the rest of my life." He drank some coffee.

"Good for you. I know all about the grind…and what does it get you? I mean, I've done everything I'm supposed to do. Studied hard, never skipped classes. Since I don't have a…you know, passion for anything in particular, I chose a business major. Can't go wrong with that, right?" Hearing herself get all ramped up, she set her fork down and washed the taste of syrup away with some milky coffee. Just thinking about all this made her stomach squeeze.

"You going to tell me how it all went sideways?"

Why not, right? It's better than bawling my eyes out alone in my hotel room. "I had a plan. A very good one. My boyfriend—" *You have to stop saying that.* "The guy I dated in college…okay, let me go back a little bit. Keith and I decided to take a class together, and we partnered on an assignment where we had to put together a business plan. We chose my hometown, because it has two really big tourist seasons. We did a bunch of research and figured out the one thing it needed was daycare. You know, you're on a family vacation, and Mom and Dad want to go out to dinner without the kids, or maybe they want take a harder hike, go skydiving, whatever."

He nodded like, *Makes sense.*

She drank some more coffee to melt the knot of fear in her throat. "It was such a good idea that our professor asked if she could use it as an example in future classes.

That got us thinking...why not really do this? So, while everyone else was applying for grad school and jobs and freaking out about their futures, we were busy starting a viable business."

His brow furrowed.

"Correct. This story has a bad ending. So, for the past two years, I've been taking jobs to save money, getting licenses and permits, lining up contractors and real estate agents." Now, the smell of food was making her sick. She pushed her plate away. "My boyfriend—" *Dammit.* "My *ex* went home after graduation. The plan was to work and live at home until we saved up enough money to launch our business. That was five months ago. Well, the perfect location became available, so I made an appointment with a realtor, and..." She hunched her shoulders in a gesture of helplessness.

Eyebrows raised, he sat back in his seat. "And?"

"And he didn't show." She still couldn't believe it. "I haven't heard a word from him since. Granted, he's been pulling away for a while, but I figured he was just partying with his friends, celebrating being done with school, whatever. But this? Not a single word of explanation? I mean, what kind of person just blows you off like that?"

"A fuckstick"

"That's exactly right. He's a fucking fuckstick." Anxiety rising, she swiveled around to check out the diner. "Does this place serve booze? I could go for another lemon drop. That was really good."

"They don't. But we can walk out that door and find all the booze we want." He held up his hand, gesturing for the bill. "You have any idea what he's doing? Maybe he got in an accident...?"

She let out a bitter laugh. "Unless he accidentally

caught a flight to Hawaii with his high school girlfriend, then I don't think so. For three days, I've been reaching out to his friends, his parents, everyone I could think of. And then, out of total desperation, I checked out her social media pages. Get this, they're going to teach surfing. And the thing is, I can't even be angry about the fact that he's with her, because I'm too worried about my own future. I counted on opening this business, so I have no backup plan. Why would I? He was seriously in it all the way up until a few weeks ago. I have no idea what I'm going to do."

He reached across the table, turning his hand over. She set her palm on top of his, and his fingers closed around her in a warm, solid grasp. "You're going to shake things up."

The waiter appeared, scanning their full plates. "Everything all right?"

"Yep. Everything's great. We've just got somewhere to be." Becks handed over his credit card, and the waiter took off. He shifted out of the booth and slid in next to her, slinging an arm around her shoulders. "It's not over, you know." He picked up her hand, pressing his thumb over her finger. The simple gesture made her realize she'd been mutilating her cuticle. "You can still open this business. Find another partner, get some investors. You don't want a chickenshit for a business partner anyway."

She could do that. She'd thought about it. It was just…

"You don't want to do it?" he asked.

Warmth spread through her. She loved how easily he read her. "How do you do that? Read me so well?"

He brought the back of her hand to his mouth and kissed it. "It's all right there. You can't hide anything."

"Maybe, but I have a feeling it's your superpower."

He shifted. "I don't know about that."

Hm, she'd obviously tapped into something. "Oh, I do. All night, you've nailed me." She laughed. "Oh, my God, what is coming out of my mouth tonight? I swear I don't normally have such a dirty mind. Is there a portal? A wrinkle in the time-space continuum I could drop into?"

"Even if I knew of one, I wouldn't tell you about it." He made a face that said, *Forget about it.* "You're too much fun."

"And you're awesome at deflecting. You don't think you're good at reading people?" Had past girlfriends said he didn't pay enough attention to them?

He settled back in his seat, tapping his fingers on the table. "I know I'm good at it."

"But you don't want to tell me why?"

He glanced away. "I thought we were getting alcohol?"

"Do you even drink?"

"Not much, no."

"So…" She made a circular motion with her hand. *Go on and tell me.*

"Fine. Well, I lost my sister when I was twelve. She was six."

Oh, God. She rested her hand on his thigh.

He went quiet, emotions flickering across his features, like shadows beneath a frozen lake. "Worst thing that ever happened to me." He stared at the syrup bottle.

"I'm sorry."

"I was there. Saw the whole thing." He plucked a sugar packet out of the plastic caddy. "Anyhow, it wrecked my family. And I guess I learned to watch my parents' expressions, so I could…I don't know…" He shrugged. "Fix things. I could tell when my mom was sinking into a depression, so I'd get upbeat, try to cheer her up. Or she'd be gunning for a fight, and I'd distract her."

"That's a tremendous amount of responsibility for a twelve-year-old to take on."

"People show up the first couple of months after a tragedy. After that, they go back to their lives. Maybe they think bad luck is contagious, or they just don't want to be pulled into the sadness. In any event, it was just me and my parents, and they didn't much like each other." He tapped the sugar packet on the table. "So, yeah, I'm pretty much expert level at reading expressions."

"That must get exhausting."

"Oh, I don't do it with everyone. In fact, I hardly ever do it."

"Really? Why me?"

"Here you go." The waiter dropped off the check. "Have a nice night."

"Thank you." Becks signed it and put his credit card back in his leather wallet. "Let's get out of here." He slid out of the booth and, once again, reached for her hand. Like before, he didn't back up to give her room, so when she stood, she was right up against him. He brushed the bangs off her forehead. "Because there's just something about you." His breath gusted over her, warm and scented with coffee. "I *like* you." He grabbed her hand and led her out of the diner.

Out on the street, the nightlife was electric.

"Want to walk?" he asked. "See what we find along the way?"

She loved the idea, mostly because it prolonged their time together. With each passing minute, she was aware of the clock running out. "Sure."

Even at one in the morning, cars jammed the boulevard, bass thumping. A limo went by with a woman poking out of the sunroof, her arms waving, the wind in her hair.

"You were trying so damn hard," Becks said quietly. "That's why I paid attention. You did a good job—I'm not sure anyone else noticed—but I did. You're different, Coco. Elegant, quiet, and yet you've got this funky look." He tipped his chin toward her deep purple satin bustier-style dress, the skin-tight skirt covered in a flare of dark lavender tulle. "You think no one notices you, but they do. You stand out. You're confident, strong, kind…"

"And funky?"

"Yeah, funky."

"My mom's a retired model, so I grew up with…let's just say an emphasis on hair, make-up, and fashion. My sisters rebelled in other ways—boys, booze, sneaking out…the usual—but I didn't care about any of that. I don't know why, but I just didn't."

"That's the confidence I was talking about."

She hadn't thought of it that way before. "The thing I did care about was my mom telling me how to dress. When we were little, she used to set our outfits on the bed the night before school, but I didn't like what she wanted me to wear. It wasn't that I was into fashion. I just had a preference. Things that I liked. I don't know about funky, but I knew my own taste." Self-consciously, she touched her hair. "I'm the only one with shorter hair."

"And, again, that's the confidence I'm talking about."

"I hated the ritual of blowing it out, adding product to make it all sleek. Just hated it. And when I looked in the mirror, I felt…I don't know. It just wasn't me. So, I cut if off." She didn't style it, either, so she always looked like she'd just come home after a day at the beach.

"I like it. I like your style. I like everything about you. And I really liked the way you held yourself together for the sake of your friends. No matter the shitty place you're in, you genuinely wanted to be present for them. I like that."

"You're a really nice guy, Becks." Affection…desire… just so much emotion crashed over her, and she tugged on his hand, making him stop. Standing up on her toes, she pressed a kiss on his cheek.

Only, he shifted at just the right moment for their mouths to meet. The brush of lips made him inhale sharply.

He smelled so delicious—a hint of salty ocean air, the remnants of a coconut sunscreen. She wanted her hands all over him. "Becks?"

"Yeah?"

"Do you have a minibar in your hotel room?"

A noise…a hum…no, a vibration. Coco fought to awaken.

My phone.

Too sluggish to move, she willed herself to rise through the levels of consciousness.

Where am I? Her dorm? No, her mattress didn't feel like this one. Her sheets didn't smell like these.

Wait, school's over.

I'm home.

Keith.

Yes. Finally. The dick. She was going to rip him a new one.

When her eyelids popped open, two things happened. One, a shaft of artificial light blinked from the gap between the curtains and, two, someone shanked her skull with a blade.

Her phone was still vibrating, though, so she reached for it. But it wasn't where she usually kept it.

To find it, she'd have to lift her head. *God, no. No, no, no.*

For a moment, she let herself wallow in the absolute torture of the worst hangover she'd ever experienced. Gazing at the ceiling, she blinked the sleep from her eyes.

Hang on a sec. This is a hotel.

Reality seeped in. Keith had ghosted her. She'd flown to Vegas for Gigi's concert.

Something bristled against her bare leg, and she jerked it away. *What the hell?* Slowly, so her brains wouldn't slosh around, she turned to find a man sprawled out beside her.

On top of the sheets.

Buck naked.

Tan skin, broad shoulders tapering to a trim waist, and round ass cheeks with matching, deep indents.

Holy shit!

She'd had sex.

With Becks.

Her eyelids fluttered shut. *Oh, for the love of God. What are you doing with your life?*

She'd never had a hookup in her life. Always the serious one, her dad liked to say.

But then…images started to roll in. Laughing so hard on the roller coaster tears had streamed down her cheeks. Making faces at the sharks in the glass tunnel of the aquarium.

Making out like high school kids in the elevator.

And, then, the dash down the long hallway to his hotel room. Him pushing her up against the wall. She could still feel the caress of his hand on her breast, the lusty squeeze. The way he'd groaned, like he couldn't stand one more minute of being separated by clothing.

Desire streamed through her body, making her hot.

Actually…she'd had the best sex of her life.

Oh, yes. That had literally been the best night ever.

Becks had held *nothing* back. Comfortable in his skin, he'd had zero inhibitions.

Had they done it *three* times?

She grinned. They sure had.

The throbbing in her head only got worse, and she knew she needed to hydrate, like, immediately.

She reached for her phone and saw Gigi's name. *Oh, shit.* When was the last time she'd checked in? Carefully, she peeled back the sheet, shifted her legs off the bed, and eased them onto the floor. In the bathroom, she answered the phone. "Hey," she whispered.

"Hey?" Her sister sounded outraged. "*Hey?* Where *are* you? The only text I have from you said you were leaving the club to go back to our suite. You're not here. It's *five in the morning.*"

"I'm sorry. I'm so sorry."

"Why are you whispering? Are you in the trunk of a car?"

"I'm—*what?* No. I'm totally fine. But I need to find my clothes right now and get out of here before this guy wakes up."

"This *guy?* My head just exploded. There are bits of brain matter all over the floor. Coco, my level-headed, smart sister went to a strange guy's hotel room?"

"Yes. And I loved it."

"I am seriously about one martini away from snatching you bald."

"Sorry not sorry? Let me get dressed so I can get out of here." She disconnected and crept back into the room.

Clothes. Where were they? She crossed the plush carpet to find her dress by the door, her heels kicked against the wall, and her bra on a table.

Where are my panties? She didn't see them. Maybe the bathroom?

Becks shifted, his head turning toward her. She froze. Held her breath.

She had no interest in small talk. Zero. Frankly, she might've had the best time ever, but it was time to get on with her life.

Because one thing had come out of her wild night— she was going to have an adventure. She'd followed the rules for her entire life, and what had it gotten her? It was time to go wild, have some fun.

She'd take some of the money she'd saved for the business and go somewhere amazing.

By myself.

Yes.

When Becks showed no signs of waking, she quickly dressed and grabbed her purse, the light-up Vegas sign sticking out of it.

Do something different. Shake things up.

She smiled. *That's exactly what I'm going to do.* She'd take this baby home, keep it front and center, so that every time she got too mired down in work, routine, the grind, she'd remember to take an adventure.

She took one more look around the room to make sure she hadn't left anything.

A bright spot of red peeked out of his jeans pocket.

My thong.

She smiled. *And that's his souvenir.*

About the Author

Award-winning author Erika Kelly writes sexy and emotional small town romance. Married to the love of her life and raising four children, she lives in the southwest, drinks a lot of tea, and is always waiting for her cats to get off her keyboard.

https://www.erikakellybooks.com/

facebook.com/erikakellybooks

twitter.com/ErikaKellyBooks

instagram.com/erikakellyauthor

goodreads.com/Erika_Kelly

pinterest.com/erikakellybooks

amazon.com/Erika-Kelly/e/B00L0MLWUY

bookbub.com/authors/erika-kelly

Printed in Great Britain
by Amazon